He grabbed his b

Walking backward, ⸻ ⸻ ⸻ The Harrington Natur⸻

Everything was ridi⸻ ⸻ork. Everything. He'd been ⸻ to prove himself.

An image of the young intern with dark hair flashed before his eyes, replacing that of the museum. He turned toward the Jeep and heard the telltale chirp of the lock's disengagement. She was a striking beauty, really. Good thing he wasn't one to easily fall for beautiful women.

The last thing he needed was an ever-present reminder of his past failures, lingering around the museum every day.

ELIZABETH GODDARD is a 7th generation Texan who recently spent five years in beautiful Southern Oregon, which serves as a setting for some of her novels. She is now back in East Texas, living near her family. When she's not writing, she's busy homeschooling her four children. Beth is the author of several novels and novellas. She's actively involved in several writing organizations including American Christian Fiction Writers (ACFW) and loves to mentor new writers.

Books by Elizabeth Goddard

HEARTSONG PRESENTS
HP777—Seasons of Love
HP893—Disarming Andi

Exposing Amber

Elizabeth Goddard

Heartsong Presents

This novel is dedicated to my loving family. Thank you for your tireless encouragement and support. My deep appreciation goes to critique partners, Deborah Vogts, Lynette Sowell, Ronie Kendig, Lisa Harris, and Shannon McNear for your commitment. Thanks to the staff of Douglass County Museum of Natural and Cultural History who shared invaluable information, giving me a behind-the-scenes tour and answering my questions. Special thanks go to paleontologist Walter Stein of PaleoAdventures for providing details of the fossil dig experience that I needed to write this story. The views expressed in this novel are not necessarily his, and any mistakes are mine alone.

A note from the Author:
I love to hear from my readers! You may correspond with me by writing:

> **Elizabeth Goddard**
> **Author Relations**
> **PO Box 721**
> **Uhrichsville, OH 44683**

ISBN 978-1-60260-912-9

EXPOSING AMBER

Scripture is taken from the HOLY BIBLE, NEW INTERNATIONAL VERSION®. NIV®. Copyright © 1973, 1978, 1984 by International Bible Society. Used by permission of Zondervan. All rights reserved.

All of the characters and events in this book are fictitious. Any resemblance to actual persons, living or dead, or to actual events is purely coincidental.

Our mission is to publish and distribute inspirational products offering exceptional value and biblical encouragement to the masses.

PRINTED IN THE U.S.A.

one

This was supposed to be a rare opportunity, or so Amber McKinsey had been assured.

After the man in front of her finished his purchase, Amber stepped up to the counter. "Where can I find the museum director, Brandon Selman?"

The museum store cashier, an older woman who could easily have been Amber's grandmother, smiled and adjusted her glasses to study Amber. "I'm not sure if *Dr.* Selman is available. May I ask your business?"

Amber didn't miss the woman's emphasis on the title *Dr.* and felt like an idiot. Noting her name badge, she said, "Gladys, Dr. Selman accepted me as a volunteer. You see, I'm an undergraduate student. . . ." She trailed off when she noticed Gladys organizing her work center.

Uncertain if Gladys was still listening or simply multi-tasking, Amber pushed the coffee-stained acceptance letter forward on the counter. That would explain everything.

Gladys lifted it and read through the bottom half of her bifocals. "Amber McKinsey. Why didn't you say so?"

Amber nearly sagged under the weight of relief. "I'm sorry. I should have told you my name." And she would have except she hadn't thought a store clerk would be the one reviewing her internship acceptance letter.

"That's all right. I should have realized who you were. I've been expecting you." Gladys came from behind the register. "I'm desperate for some help in the museum store. We've wanted someone who has an interest in the past, rather than someone who doesn't know and doesn't care."

Amber frowned. "What. . .what did you say? The museum *store*? I think there's been a mistake." The letter accepting her as a volunteer to intern at the Harrington Natural and Cultural Museum was from the museum director. She grabbed the paper from the counter where Gladys had put it and handed it back to her.

Gladys read the letter again. "It says you've been accepted for a volunteer position at the museum." Gladys held out the letter and shrugged. "I was told you would be helping me in the store."

Gently, Amber tugged it from the older woman's fingers and stared at it again. "I. . .I don't understand."

Gladys placed a hand on Amber's shoulder. "Didn't you request a volunteer position at the museum?"

Amber nodded.

"The museum store is a part of the museum, don't you know?"

Amber pulled her stunned thoughts away from the acceptance letter to look at Gladys who scrunched her face. Slowly, her expression softened.

"I suppose so," Amber said. Gladys hadn't made a great first impression, but Amber could see she meant well.

"Let's get you settled, then. You can explore the grounds today, then tomorrow see me back here at eight o'clock sharp." Gladys handed her a map then opened a small cabinet on the wall. "You're in cabin B-3. Here's the key."

Amber took the key from her and smiled, attempting to mask her frustration. Though Amber wanted to further discuss what she believed was a mix-up, a line of people waiting to make their purchases had formed behind her. Not the best time.

Adjusting her glasses again, Gladys winked. "Don't worry. It'll work out. You'll see."

Only able to offer the smallest of smiles, Amber left Gladys to attend to her customers.

Ignoring the offerings of replicas, toys, and games, Amber pushed past a family with rambunctious children who waited in line behind her to purchase robotic dinosaurs and imitation Native American pottery. Exiting the store, Amber entered the museum lobby and drew in a ragged breath.

She always loved the peculiar smell in museums—a blend of fresh paint, commercial-grade carpet, and musty oldness. But. . .what had just happened in there? She was to present the letter when she arrived, validating her acceptance to work under museum director and notable paleontologist, Brandon Selman. Dr. Young, her professor at the University of North Dakota, had advised her that by working under a professional with a broad field of expertise, Amber could better evaluate her goals. And they had her working in the museum store?

Amber pushed through the double glass-paned doors of the main entrance. When the door swooshed closed behind her, a gust quickly whipped strands of hair into her face. The reflective glass confirmed her long, black tresses were in a mess. Another blast of air ripped the letter from her fingers, sending her chasing it across the grass and sidewalk.

Red hair whipping around her face, Cams leaned against her silver Prius, laughing. "You'd better catch that before it escapes into the North Dakota Badlands."

Finally snatching the errant slip of paper, Amber made her way to Cams, her roommate at UND for the last two years. Somehow, over that course of time, Amber had given Carmen Milewski the nickname. But Cams didn't seem to mind.

Amber held up the key to the cabin. "You ready?"

Cams smiled and nodded as she made her way around to the driver's side. She would take Amber and all her junk over to the cabin. Amber's car simply wasn't long-haul worthy, so she'd left it parked at a friend's house in Grand Forks. Cams had brought her across the state, loaded down with her bicycle and enough personal belongings to last for the summer.

Thankfully, Amber had gotten permission to bring Josh, her ruby-eyed white Netherland dwarf rabbit, as long as he was in an appropriate cage.

"Okay, so where is this cabin?" Cams asked as she drove to the nearest parking lot exit.

Amber pulled the map out and directed Cams. The museum offered cabins free of charge to college volunteers and interns on a first-come-first-serve basis. As the Prius bumped slowly down the one-lane gravel road, Amber spotted a trail. Perfect. She could take a jog later.

"That building didn't look big enough, on the outside at least, to be a museum," Cams said.

"You should have come in with me so you could see for yourself."

"I didn't want to cramp your style or anything."

Amber chuckled. If Cams only knew—her "style" had been cramped anyway. At the moment, Amber felt like the size of a tiny unimportant fossil. "There's a few thousand feet of floor space, though even that is considered small for a museum. And though I didn't get a chance to browse, I've heard the exhibits feature fossils and dinosaur replicas, period displays, and dioramas of local history themes, including Western and American Indians."

"Sounds. . .uh. . .interesting."

Amber laughed again, knowing full well Cams had no interest in history.

"Here we are." Cams stopped the car in front of a genuine log cabin, nestled behind a copse of trees.

Amber carried her luggage to the door and unlocked it. Unsure if her cabin mate had arrived yet or not, she strolled in cautiously.

"Hello?" Other than furniture, the place looked empty, devoid of life.

Breathing hard, Cams rushed in behind Amber, loaded down with a couple more bags. "I'm glad you're not into fashion." She dropped the luggage on the old wood floors. A large colorful rug rested in the center of the room. Cams looked around. "Nice."

Amber plopped onto one of the burnt orange sofas. "Not

too bad. It's even cushy."

Cams smirked a little. "Probably got these at the Salvation Army or something."

"Who cares." Amber rose from the sofa. "I've got to find my room and a place for Josh."

"Okay, I'll get your bike off my car."

Amber found a room she claimed for her own in the two-bedroom, one-bath dwelling. After she finished unloading everything and getting Josh settled in his cage, she spotted Cams opening a kitchen cabinet.

"Good. You've got a few dishes, too." Cams pulled out a glass and filled it with tap water.

"I can't tell you how much I appreciate you driving me here." Amber spread her hands over the small island counter, feeling the smooth, white Formica. At least it was clean.

"Hey, I was going in the same direction."

"Not hardly," Amber said. Cams had gone out of her way to drop off Amber at the museum before heading home to Watford City. "When are your parents expecting you?"

Cams glanced at her watch. "Not for a couple of hours. Listen, it was really no trouble to bring you here. If you change your mind, call me. I'll come pick you up."

"And then what? I can stay at your parents' with you until you go back to Grand Forks?"

A laugh escaped Cams. "Who knows, maybe I'll have changed my mind, too, and we can go back together."

"You're terrible."

"But you still love me. Besides, I'll only be there a couple of weeks."

"I know, I know. You have to get back to that part-time job," Amber said. Cams held on to a hopeless dream that her boss would ask her out. Amber would never let herself fall for a guy she worked with. That could get messy.

"You know me." Cams smiled. "Got to go. Call me if you need a ride."

"Okay." Amber waved at Cams, who climbed into her car

and backed from the small driveway, if you could call it that.

Amber sighed and sank into the sofa. Maybe she should have told Cams what happened, that she wouldn't be working in the museum like she thought. But with Cams's generosity, Amber couldn't bear to tell her she'd brought her all this way for nothing.

How could this happen? She'd come to a crossroads regarding courses for her undergraduate degree at UND. Though she'd taken classes in geology and biology, as she progressed, she became less certain about a future in paleontology. Dr. Young had strongly recommended she get hands-on experience this summer. He'd even written a recommendation for her to include in her application for an intern position at the Harrington Natural and Cultural Museum.

She'd been accepted. But with news she'd be working in the museum store?—there went her rare opportunity to intern under Dr. Selman.

❧

Brandon rushed down the corridors of the museum offices, barely aware that someone called his name in the distance. He tuned out the annoyance while he finished reading through the numbers. Though the museum was a nonprofit organization, it still had to make ends meet.

The bottom line? He needed more donors. And to get more donors he had to socialize and dine and come up with more brilliant ideas, projects, and initiatives, all within their conflict-of-interest guidelines, of course.

He entered his office and sat in his office chair, then looked up from the report to see his desk piled high with catalogs, requisitions for display materials, and the information he'd requested from a talented replica artist who'd come highly recommended. Though it was Harrington Museum's policy to avoid displaying inauthentic artifacts, at times the measure was deemed necessary. When replicas were exhibited, the authentic artifact would be kept safely in the museum's vault.

He loved his job, but at times like these he'd give anything to go back to his old love and dig in the dirt. Feel the exhilaration of discovering a fossil. Other than that, he'd often considered teaching. He'd even put an application in at UND. Then if the museum endeavor didn't fly this time, he'd have something he enjoyed to fall back on.

But right now the museum teetered on the verge of soaring, and Brandon needed to clear everything off his plate to make sure that happened. For the last three years, he'd worked toward gaining accreditation for Harrington in the American Association of Museums.

Once the museum had passed its three-year mark, they'd worked to accession, or formally acquire, the rest of their permanent collection. He sucked in a sharp breath. All that was left now before the formal application was to assemble the needed documentation.

Soon, he told himself.

After losing his good standing in the professional community, he needed this museum to gain recognition and credibility. Without validation, he had no value to anyone. *Not even God.*

His cell rang. Brandon read the caller ID and answered.

"Dad, thanks for returning my call." Not the best timing, but his parents often went to bed before Brandon even got home from work, preferring to rise very early. It was now or never.

"Your mom and I were grocery shopping. Sorry we missed your call. What's up?" Despite the fact his father was well into his eighties, his voice remained bold and strong.

"I like to check on you every once in a while, that okay?"

"You called to say you won't be coming this weekend. Am I right?"

Was he that predictable? Brandon sighed into the phone, instantly regretting it. His parents only lived an hour away. "Sorry to skip out on you again. I have too much on my plate this week. I'll have to work through the weekend."

"Son, your mother and I were talking about this today.

We're more than proud of your accomplishments. But when are you going to settle down?"

Brandon squashed his sigh this time. He was thirty-nine, and he'd heard the same lecture the last fifteen years at least. "Dad, we've been through this."

"Find yourself a wife before it's too late. Your mom wants grandkids before she dies. We need someone to carry on the family name and legacy."

Legacy? Brandon wasn't sure he had much to offer in terms of legacy given his failures. His dad, the great Chappell Selman, had been head curator of a large nationally recognized museum. Attempting to follow in his footsteps had been a daunting task. In fact, Brandon was still trying.

"Okay, Dad. I'll consider your advice. On another topic, how are you doing?"

"I'm as healthy as a horse, or so the doctor said. I know you're busy. Come see us when you can. I'm starting to think that God will have to throw a good woman in your path and make you trip over her."

They said their good-byes, and Brandon stared at his cell, wishing he had time to get away and see his parents. A stack of applications at the corner of Brandon's desk caught his attention. He slid the papers toward him.

"You're going to thank me for this." Jim Russel stood in the doorway.

In his midforties, thin and athletic, Jim had premature silver hair. Even though Brandon was younger by six years, Jim could squash him on the tennis court on Brandon's best day.

"Thank you for what?"

"I accessioned the Hamlin Exhibit. It's on loan from the Prehistoric Museum in Utah." Jim sounded energized.

Brandon squinted, trying to comprehend what Jim had said. He didn't want to get his hopes up if he'd misunderstood. "Say again?"

Jim came fully into his office and pulled out the chair across from Brandon, a victorious smile on his face. "I think you heard me. The Hamlin Exhibit. It's on its way here."

"You're talking prehistoric developmental pottery discovered in Utah, right? That's out of the provenance of our collections, don't you think?" He wasn't sure what Jim was thinking on this one. Their collections, both natural and cultural, were limited to southwest North Dakota. But maybe. . .

Jim sent him a pointed stare. "I think it's an opportunity."

Brandon leaned back as far as the chair would allow and stared at the ceiling. News of the display could certainly give him the edge he needed to solicit more donors.

"Brandon? What do you think?" Jim asked, the ring of impatience in his voice.

Probably because Brandon hadn't given him the slap on the back he was looking for. Jim was an experienced curator with a master's degree in history and archaeology. Brandon figured the man was simply doing his job. And, having worked with Brandon for years now, Jim knew better than to expect kudos.

Brandon rolled forward and sat tall, fixing Jim with a look. "We'll have to rush order the appropriate display enclosures, organize the exhibit."

Jim snorted. "Well, that goes without saying, doesn't it? I thought you'd be ecstatic."

"Oh, but I am. Can't you see the wheels in my head are already turning?"

"Sure. I hoped you'd turn a few cartwheels, too."

Brandon laughed, already visualizing the exhibit. "We'll need to create marketing materials, get the word out. I like for the displays to be as kid friendly as possible. Not sure that's going to work on this. How long do we have the collection?"

"Six months."

"What is the total value of the artifacts?" Brandon asked.

"You know that's relative, depending on who is buying." He grinned. "The museum has the exhibit insured for 150,000 dollars."

A quarter of our operating budget. Brandon whistled. That

number made him slightly nervous. "Not sure how you managed this."

"Connections are everything, as you know."

Brandon nodded, frowning. He assumed Jim referred to how Brandon had secured his current position as museum director. He didn't enjoy the reminder that his reputation alone couldn't have landed him this job.

The replica artist's materials and business card stared back at him from his desk. The way the artist's references sounded, even a museum expert would have difficulty telling the difference. Given the news Jim had shared, now would be a great time to test the artist's abilities. He grinned at the thought. At the same time, he could test Jim's ability to discern a replica from an authentic artifact, have a little fun with him. Brandon shuffled papers on his desk to hide the information packet. And. . .the way Jim acted lately, the man could probably use getting knocked down a few notches.

"I'd say things are beginning to look up." But he must maintain the foothold he had at the museum while gaining momentum. This could be exactly what he needed to accomplish that. It would mean more hours of work and even fewer free weekends.

Sorry, Dad. With the thought, the workload on his desk began pressing on him. "Was there anything else?"

"We'll need more volunteers and interns to make this run smoothly," Jim added.

At that, Brandon leaned back again and folded his arms over his chest. He gave a slight shake of his head. "I'm thinking not."

"What?" Surprised eyes stared back.

"Volunteers, yes. Interns, no. I don't have time to take anyone under my wing right now. I need to focus on making this museum a success. In fact, I've been thinking about this for a long time. Should have done this sooner."

"And what's *this*?" Jim sounded cautious.

"No more protégés." After what someone had pulled five

years ago, practically destroying his career, he wasn't sure he ever wanted to be in that position again.

Jim laughed. "Come on. You don't have to mentor anyone just because we bring them on as interns. Besides, they make better workers than volunteers who have no expertise or any interest in furthering their future."

Brandon nodded. "That's what you said last year, and I still ended up with someone expecting my time and energy." He closed his eyes, hating how the words sounded because he truly wanted to give back to others, help them if he could. He loved teaching. But not at the expense of the museum, or his time and energy.

Jim sighed.

"Just. . .not right now. I'm still in disaster-recovery mode." He'd only been museum director of the new museum for three years now. There was plenty of time in the future to mentor interns. "Right now, I have to make sure this museum gains respect and credibility." *That I have a solid future.*

Brandon avoided Jim's eyes, knowing full well the man thought Brandon should let go of the past. But Jim hadn't gone through the scrutiny that Brandon had.

At that moment, he took a closer look at the applications resting on his desk. *Intern apps.* "Therefore, we can toss these in the trash." Brandon did exactly that.

Jim jumped up. "Wait. You can't just throw them out. You have to respond to each one of them. Give them a nice rejection letter."

"Considering I didn't request them, maybe you should send out the letters."

Yanking the stash from the small garbage can, Jim rifled through them. "Do you realize how long these have been sitting on your desk?"

"No, but I'm wondering why they ended up there in the first place." Brandon chuckled, hoping to diffuse the tension and stood, moving to the credenza where he always kept a carafe of coffee.

"No idea."

He poured himself a cup. "Coffee?"

"No, thanks. I'm glad we didn't have this conversation until now because we need the additional help. Our summer months are the busiest. We already have a few extra volunteers and interns on the way."

Brandon stopped with the cup halfway to his lips. "What?"

two

Amber stood in the museum lobby. Nausea stirred in her stomach. Why did she have to follow so closely in her brother's career path when it served as a constant reminder of him? She'd spent her childhood idolizing him, following in his footsteps—but he'd destroyed everything.

The museum directory stared back at her, the exhibit listings soothing her thoughts. Maybe all things ancient was simply in the family blood.

Amber ran a finger over the directory's smooth Plexiglas surface, glad for time to peruse the museum. The directory included a floor plan, revealing the location of various exhibits.

She loved that the museum included local cultural history as well as the natural history of the region, boasting a full triceratops skull, duck-billed dinosaurs, and a full-sized model of a *Tyrannosaurus rex*—all dinosaurs that had been discovered in the nearby Hell Creek Formation. Her momentary disappointment deterred, Amber looked forward to exploring the museum.

"Excuse me." A slender college-aged girl touched Amber's shoulder. "You must be Amber McKinsey."

Amber tried not to stare at the pink stripe down the right side of the girl's black hair. "Yes, that's right. How did you know?"

"The lady in the store pointed you out. I'm Muriel Willbanks." She thrust out her hand. "We're going to be roommates." Her smile broadened. "Isn't this exciting?"

Working at the museum store exciting? But then Muriel probably wouldn't be a volunteer in the store. Amber returned the smile.

"I'm heading to the cabin now to unpack."

"Do you need any help?" Amber asked, mostly to be polite. She really wanted to explore the museum now.

"Oh, that would be great. My car is in the parking lot."

Masking her disappointment, Amber followed Muriel out to her dusty, old Honda Accord. The girl seemed nice enough, dispersing any reservations Amber had about rooming with someone she didn't know or like. At least she had wheels.

"So, what's your assignment?" Amber asked.

Muriel fairly squealed. "I'm interning under Dr. Laudan. I'll get to accompany her to the digs. Can you imagine finding a real dinosaur fossil?"

❧

When Amber woke up from a nap, her roommate was gone. Muriel's news had stung Amber in a big way, especially on the heels of discovering she'd be working in the store instead of assisting with real science or museum work. Amber had been too deflated to go back to the museum after helping Muriel unpack. And now, it was too late. Figuring she had an hour before dark, Amber pulled on her sneakers.

Running had always given her an extra energy boost and lifted her spirits. Things often looked clear where they'd been muddy. These days, with so much weighing on her, she wasn't sure she could survive without the exhilarating exercise. An ache sliced through her heart. She used to pray when she ran. Since the accident that had killed her mother and sister, she'd hardened her heart. She knew it, but what to do about it?

From his cage, Josh stared at her and wriggled his little nose. She opened the top and gently tugged him out, sending a puff of white fur everywhere. Holding the small white bundle close, she rubbed him behind the ears. Mom had always kept rabbits.

You'd really love this one, Mom. Amber held Josh up to look him in the eyes then placed him back in his cage.

Stumbling out the door, she stood on the porch. Rocky Mountain junipers and red cedars surrounded the small cabin. She took a deep breath of their strong evergreen scent, then jogged down the gravel drive lined with poplars, easily spotting the trailhead. The sign said the trail was five and a half miles and showed a diagram of a loop connecting with other trails, some nearing the Little Missouri River.

Now that was something Amber desperately wanted to see. Scientists said a glacier had forced the river into a short steep route, which created the Badlands formations. If nothing else, this summer diversion should allow her to explore the region—a huge attraction to geologists and paleontologists around the world.

Amber ran along the trail, enjoying the fresh air. With the sun quickly setting, she quickened her five-mile pace on the loop. Ahead of her, the trail narrowed between two large cedars, and another runner approached from the opposite direction. She made a longer stride between the trees and stepped on a huge rock, seemingly out of place in her path, careful to avoid stepping at the wrong angle since her injury last year.

Pushing from the rock, she propelled around another tree and collided with someone—the other runner? White and blue flashed in her eyes. She stumbled, a familiar pain ripping through her right ankle. Her balance lost, she fell forward, hands and knees catching the brunt of her fall.

Pebbles and rocks pierced her palms. She rolled onto her backside then sprawled flat on her back to stare at the canopy above. "Well, this is just a great addition to an already perfect day."

She wondered if the other person had fallen, too. "You all right over there?"

A handsome face framed with black hair hovered above her. Dark olive eyes stared down at her in concern. He offered his hand. "I'm fine. You're the one who took a fall."

"It's my family heirloom. Clumsiness." Though she wasn't sure how much value she could put on it. Amber accepted his help and stood. She dusted off her shorts. "Are you sure you're not hurt?"

The man scrutinized himself, looking over his smudged white T-shirt and dark blue running shorts. "No, I think I'm good, except that I received an elbow to the ribs." His frown spread into a V-shaped wide grin, producing large dimples. He held his side. "You pack a great punch when you're falling."

Amber stared, unsure if he was teasing. "I'm so sorry."

"Don't be. I'm not the one having a bad day."

Puzzled, it took her a few seconds to form words. "And how would you know that?"

"What? That I'm not the one having a bad day?"

"Okay, you're teasing, aren't you?"

That smile again. "Only partially. When you fell, you said something about this being a great addition to your perfect day. I assumed that was an attempt at sarcasm."

Amber's cheeks warmed. "I didn't realize I'd said that out loud."

"You want to tell me about it? We can run together."

"No, I've got an old war injury I think I just triggered when I ran into you. I should walk for a bit until it feels better."

"Okay, let's walk the trail then."

Amber considered the stranger's invitation, and feeling comfortable with him, she said, "Sure, you can walk with me. I'm heading back, though. Want to clean up these scrapes."

He reached down to grab a stainless steel water bottle with the Nike label. Uncapping the bottle, he held it out to her. "Thirsty?"

"No, I'm good."

"So, tell me about your bad day before the fall." He walked next to her when the trail would allow.

Amber readjusted her scrunchie. Did she really want to go into all that? "Oh it's nothing, really. I came here to do a certain job, only to find out I'm doing something else. Something. . .less. And the man I was planning to work under, well, I guess I'm not important enough to warrant his attention." She made it sound like she was actually employed somewhere. But how could she explain all that to a stranger?

She stopped. Through the trees she saw what looked like the breaks—the descent into the Badlands terrain of ridges, bluffs, and buttes. As Amber gazed into the distance, the man came to a stop next to her.

She took a step from the trail, thinking to head for the break in the trees and look at the terrain. "Is that—"

The man gently laid his hand on her arm. "You don't want to do that."

Warmth raced over her skin. Startled, she looked at him. "Why not?"

"It'll be dark soon. It's not called the Badlands for nothing. One misstep could land you at the bottom of a pinnacle. The Sioux Indians called it a word that meant 'land bad' and the French translated that into 'a bad land to cross.'"

Disappointed, Amber frowned. "I'm sure you're right. What was I thinking?"

"You were thinking you wanted to see something magnificent. And especially in the moonlight it truly is. Some of the structures look like ruins from an ancient city."

"Wow, really?" Amber sighed, thinking how beautiful that would be. Then she peeked at the man standing next to her. He wouldn't look a day over thirty if it weren't for the slightly graying hair at his temples, making him appear famous and distinguished.

Standing next to him, she sensed something different about him. Part of her wished there was a way she could see him again. But how?

After a thoughtful moment, the man pulled his gaze from the trees and back to Amber, returning her intense stare.

❧

Brandon held his breath, struggling to remember his father's words. Something about God making him trip over a good woman.

He eyed the young woman with raven hair—shiny and black like that of a thoroughbred—and eyes an unusual shade. Liquid gold with flecks of brown, though it was hard to be sure in the dimming light.

Striking.

An uneven rhythm thudded in his chest. *That* was new.

He'd not seen her jogging on the trails before today. Maybe Dad was right. She was beautiful, obviously loved to run, and. . . he didn't work with her.

Feeling tongue-tied as a schoolboy, he wasn't sure where to go from here.

Suddenly, he was hit with the strangest desire—he wished. . . he wished he could share the beauty of the eroded pinnacles that only appeared to look like ancient ruins in the moonlight. Asking her—a woman he'd only just met—if he could show her the sight was completely out of the question. And yet?

No—they were complete strangers. What could he say to her?

She appeared uncomfortable under his scrutiny. *Uh-oh.* He'd better say something and quick.

"I understand about disappointments and failures in the workplace, so I can certainly relate to how you're feeling."

She tilted her head just so. Cute. "You can?"

"Sure." Now what did he say? He was quickly losing his ability to communicate. But how could he tell her the rest? His job had been his life and when he'd lost it because of a vindictive young protégé. . . Brandon took a step back, feeling like he was finally coming to his senses.

"It's getting dark. I should probably go," she said.

Curious, he cocked his head. "So, where do you work? If you don't mind my asking."

She kicked the dirt around, then looked up at him as though bashful. "I shouldn't have said anything about my troubles. Really. I start at the museum store tomorrow. You should stop by some time." She smiled then took off running. "My ankle's feeling better," she called, with a quick glance back at him.

A smoldering sensation filled his gut. She must be one of the new interns Jim had mentioned. Heaving long and hard, he started running again, but in the opposite direction. He'd catch the connecting loop to burn off his frustration.

Jim insisted they needed help, and though he was right, Brandon needed to focus on the mounting work ahead of him. It was an odd twist, bringing in help, only to have to divert energy into these individuals, guiding them in the disciplines, directing their futures. In Brandon's mind, a volunteer intern was almost a contradiction.

He'd just as soon do the work himself at this point. But why had they put this young woman in the museum store? She'd been seriously disappointed.

Years ago he'd been a research paleontologist for a museum. But with a museum director father, collections had always held a draw for him, causing him to harbor the desire to follow his father. He'd forged a friendship with the director in the museum where he worked, who mentored him. Eventually, Brandon learned the process well enough to manage a small museum. When presented with the opportunity, he'd taken it. But then. . .disaster struck.

If it hadn't been for the aid of a well-respected friend, Brandon wouldn't have found his life again in the newly created Harrington Museum. Even though several years had passed, he wasn't ready to open himself up again to risk or criticism.

No more protégés. . .

The words he'd spoken to Jim came back to him. He'd stand by them. Even if she was beautiful beyond words, and he'd come within a breath of asking her on a date. Lungs burning, Brandon slowed his run as the museum complex came into view. Only two cars remained—his black Jeep and Jim's silver Lexus. He let himself in through the back, feeling the pain in his joints from the long run. After a quick stop in the men's room to wash the sweat from his face and neck, he continued on to Jim's office. Talking on the phone, Jim turned his back to Brandon, finishing the call.

Finally, Jim faced Brandon and flipped his phone shut. "Have a good run?"

"Not entirely. I ran into one of your new interns. Literally."

Jim quirked a half grin then shuffled some papers. "Sounds like Providence."

Dad would agree. "Did you personally interview them?"

"I reviewed applications and took the ones with recommendations from professors. The usual. Why? Is there a problem?"

Brandon rubbed his chin to cover his misgivings. Why was he so upset? "No, I just wished you would have talked to me before bringing on interns."

"Haven't we already been through this? What's done is done. Besides, it's a menial task you relegated to me last year, remember?" A subtle smirk slid into Jim's lips. "Though you didn't accept them, your name is on the letter. You're the director."

Brandon heaved a sigh. He was making too much out of this.

"If it makes you feel any better, I'll make sure you never see a volunteer or intern again this summer, all right?"

"An impossible promise, Jim." Scratching the back of his neck, Brandon sagged, blowing out the last of his frustration.

"So what is it about this intern you ran into that has you upset?"

How could he tell Jim he'd wanted to see this woman again only to discover she was one of the museum's interns?— a dangerous activity in which he refused to engage. "Just ignore me."

Brandon left Jim's office, kicking himself for the knee-jerk reaction.

Guilt chiseled through him. If it weren't for people willing to invest in him during his formative years as a young college student, where would he be today? He was more than obligated to pass on their generosity, despite his personal issues.

He grabbed his keys and exited the museum. Walking backward, he gazed up at the large letters. THE HARRINGTON NATURAL AND CULTURAL MUSEUM.

Everything was riding on his making this museum work. Everything. He'd been given a chance to prove himself.

An image of the young intern with dark hair flashed before his eyes, replacing that of the museum. He turned toward the Jeep and heard the telltale chirp of the lock's disengagement. She was a striking beauty, really. Good thing he wasn't one to easily fall for beautiful women.

The last thing he needed was an ever-present reminder of his past failures, lingering around the museum every day.

three

Standing on the ladder, Amber had a great view of the museum store. To add to the arrangement she was working on, she pulled another bobblehead tyrannosaurus from the box resting on the shelf below. A quick glance behind her told her Gladys had finished with her customer and would soon want to inspect Amber's merchandising skills, which were—in a word—none.

She'd spent the morning learning to operate their computerized register system as well as walking the entire floor to locate and identify each and every item. As far as she was concerned, she should be getting paid for this rather than working as a volunteer. But this was only her first day on the job.

Stocking the shelf with green felt-covered bobblehead dinosaurs was a far cry from digging in the dirt to excavate the real thing or learning the work behind accessions or collections.

Despite her disappointment, she smiled at the display and dusted off her hands. Gladys stood at the bottom of the ladder, looking up. The way Gladys smiled, Amber decided she'd convinced the older woman she had accepted her assignment without further complaint.

Gladys adjusted her glasses. "I thought you weren't sure what to do. Looks like you have a knack for display. I think you might be a keeper." She winked then turned her back to Amber, heading back to the register.

I'm a keeper? "Wait, Gladys."

A teenager stood at the register, looking around expectantly. Gladys either didn't hear or ignored Amber and hurried to assist the customer.

Amber didn't want to be a keeper. At least not in the museum store. She began descending the ladder then remembered the box on the second shelf and climbed back up two rungs. As she gripped the ladder to grab the box, her hand swiped one of the bobbleheads. It tumbled over, knocking the other toy dinosaurs over like dominoes, the clattering amplified by the store acoustics.

With an hour until closing time still left, Amber huffed, wishing the day were over already. She wasn't sure she could stick it out. And if she left, she'd have to wait until Cams could return to pick her up. She began restoring the dinosaur arrangement, wondering if the top shelf was really the best place for the display. But Gladys had insisted that children were tempted to play with the dinosaurs, leaving the toys too damaged to sell.

"The top shelf, it is," she mumbled to herself, hoping for a readjustment in her attitude.

"Hi, there." A smooth voice spoke from behind.

Where had she heard it before?

Amber turned around to see the guy she'd run into yesterday on the trail. "Oh, hi. You decided to stop by the museum store. That's nice of you." Why was she being so flirty with him? He was much older. Had to be married. But something about the way he looked up at her sent a warm, giddy feeling over her.

Please, don't let him be married. She'd hate to think a married man would look at someone besides his wife like that. A glimpse at his left hand revealed no ring. But that didn't necessarily mean anything. She made her way down the ladder without repairing the damage she'd done, stopping two rungs from the bottom. The bobbleheads weren't going anywhere.

"Looks like you're doing a great job for someone who didn't want to work here." He grinned.

Lifting the cardboard box that she'd tossed onto the shelf earlier, she blew out an exaggerated breath. "Not hardly. I've knocked these things over twice today. I'm so clumsy."

"I know. Your family heirloom."

"My family—" Amber looked at him. He remembered that?

"Starting tomorrow, you don't have to worry about arranging the dinosaur toys. You officially begin your training as an intern assigned to the digs."

She stepped down another rung, lingering on the last one, confusion whirling with panic inside. "How. . .how would you know that?"

The stranger stuck out his hand, waiting for hers. "I'm the museum director, Brandon Selman."

Stunned beyond comprehension, Amber nearly stumbled off the ladder. Embarrassment flooded her thoughts and face.

"You mean, *you're Dr.* Selman?" she asked, recalling Gladys's adamant words.

He chuckled and dropped his hand. She'd never taken it.

"I may have a PhD but there's no need for formalities. Mr. Selman will do in most cases."

As she recalled, Gladys was pretty emphatic about the doctor part. Amber wouldn't take any chances. "I was. . . expecting someone much older."

The warmth in his expression faded somewhat.

"No, I didn't mean it that way. What I meant is that you look so young. You'd think hours in the sun, digging for fossils would age a person faster, making him look older."

He cocked a brow, waiting for her to shut up, she was certain. Probably thought she was as clumsy with her words as she was on her feet.

Uncertain whether to remain embarrassed, be angry or forever grateful, she fumbled over her words. "I'm. . .I feel like such an idiot. Everything I said yesterday. Why didn't you tell me who you were?"

"Miss McKinsey, I honestly didn't know you were an intern here until you invited me to stop by the museum store just as you ran off."

"Oh, please, call me Amber." She examined her shoes while she allowed excitement to bubble inside. Had there been a mistake, or had her chance encounter with him on the trail brought her dilemma to his attention?

She smiled at him, feeling shy. Hadn't she just been flirting with the man? Hopefully, he hadn't noticed.

"I don't know what to say. Thank you." She felt humbled to think that this man with a doctorate and who knew how many other degrees, who ran a reputable museum, would have heard the cry of her heart. It seemed like even God hadn't done that. Dr. Selman had listened, and he'd done something about it.

"You're welcome. I'm sorry for the confusion about your volunteer position. As it turns out, someone who works in the digs broke her leg this morning. We've had to juggle people. So, now you get to do what you came here for."

So much for him hearing the cry of her heart. Figured. If even God didn't listen, who would?

Then it hit her. "Oh, no. I hope it wasn't Muriel who was hurt. She's one of the new interns and my cabinmate."

"Tori Gillispie was one of our returning interns working under Dr. Laudan, our research paleontologist."

Amber studied his eyes, searching for the right words. "How did it happen?"

He stared down at her, suddenly turning serious. "Remember what I told you last night about the Badlands being dangerous?"

Amber nodded, thinking about that moment. It was then that he'd talked about ancient ruins in the moonlight. At the time, it had felt almost magical.

He cleared his throat, apparently aware her thoughts were elsewhere. "The dig is along the side of a rocky outcropping. There are deep slopes and cliffs. Though it's mostly safe, especially in the amateur digs where the tourists are allowed, there are some risks involved. Tori misstepped and fell."

"I'm thinking it could have been much worse."

He studied her closely. "Are you sure you want to do this?"

"You're referring to my family heirloom."

"I won't stand in your way."

"I'd love the experience. More than you know." A thrill rushed through her. Though this wouldn't be her first time at a fossil dig, it would be her first time as an intern instead of a tourist. She smiled up at the handsome museum director.

Dr. Selman gave her a funny look. "I want your time here to be a valuable learning experience."

She thought again of the girl who'd been hurt. "I'm sure accidents are rare, aren't they?"

He nodded as he subtly glanced at the mess she'd made of the toy dinosaurs, then back to her. "Have you ever been in the field before?"

"Sure I have." Amber swallowed under his scrutiny. Michael had gone with her on amateur digs several times, but she didn't want to bring up her brother now, if ever. *Please, don't let him ask where, when, or how.*

She'd just have to keep her distance, not get too close to anyone. The last thing she wanted was for anyone to know about him. If they did, then. . .he really would have succeeded in destroying her life.

❧

"Good. Then you have some experience. And you're right. Accidents are rare."

Except in my world. . .

Brandon couldn't believe what he was doing. After a night of tossing and turning, feeling guilty over his attitude, he'd made up his mind to find the young intern he'd met on the trail last night. His previous ordeal was a once in a lifetime regret. At least he hoped.

Jim wouldn't be happy. But Brandon couldn't stand the thought of her being stuck there. Early that morning, he'd found her file on Jim's desk and read her request to work under Brandon directly. He knew that was in part thanks to his friend, Phil Young at UND. He almost laughed at the way things turned out—Jim had ended up giving in to Gladys's requests for help. Poor girl.

With the news of Tori's accident, Brandon was stepping in,

if just this once.

"Tomorrow morning, report to the certification room. It's in the basement. Jim can put you through the quick start program to ready you for a new group of tourists coming through next week. You'll be guiding the tours and eventually, maybe even assisting with amateur digs. I can't promise you that. But with Tori's injury, Dr. Laudan might request additional help sooner rather than later."

"Thank you again for this opportunity. I won't let you down." Amber flashed him a beautiful smile, her eyes filled with relief and gratitude. Then her smile faltered a bit. "I'm just sorry about Tori and hope she recovers soon."

Brandon nodded. "The museum sent her flowers, wishing her a speedy recovery." On the selfish side of things, Tori's injury could be a setback for his plans for museum accreditation. He yanked his thoughts back to the present and glanced over at Gladys, who finished up with her last customer. She wouldn't be happy about losing Amber either.

"I should at least complete this display for Gladys." Amber laughed a little nervously. "Clean up my mess."

She climbed up and began setting the dinosaurs right. Brandon picked a few off the floor and handed them to her. Despite his feelings about being obligated to tutor others, Brandon was glad he'd given Amber what she wanted for a far different reason. After only a few minutes in her presence, he sensed her enthusiasm, especially about the new assignment, and it was contagious. She'd sparked something in him he hadn't felt in a long while.

Perhaps that's what Phil had seen in her as well.

She smiled down as she took another bobblehead from him, brushing his fingers. "The basement, huh?"

He angled his head slightly. "Say again?"

"You said the certification room is in the basement."

"Hasn't anyone given you the grand tour yet?"

"Um, of the museum store, yes. Of the museum, no."

"You need a tour, then."

"Sounds like a plan." Once the dinosaurs were perfectly in place, some of the heads bobbling, she began her descent down the ladder.

Brandon's thoughts had already pushed ahead to the backlog of work on his desk. There were others to give her the tour. Like Jim or Gladys. Why hadn't Jim scheduled some sort of orientation for these people? Might as well give Gladys the news.

"Gladys?" he called, as he glanced around the store.

"I'm just locking up. Be right there."

Gladys waltzed around a shelf of dinosaur puzzles toward him and smiled. "Did you need something?"

"Miss McKinsey needs a tour of the museum, including the basement classrooms. The works. Would you. . ."

With a disapproving shake of her head, Gladys gave him her evil eye. But he saw the twinkle behind her glare. "Are you stealing this girl away from me?"

Brandon lifted his hands in surrender. "She comes to us from a colleague of mine. He wouldn't be very happy if I sent her back with only knowledge of how to run a cash register now, would he? Could you—"

"Can't do it. I have to balance and lock up the money. I'm afraid giving the grand tour, showing off your museum is your calling, talent, and gift. And considering you're taking my only help from me, and I just spent all day training her—"

"All right. Fair enough. We'll find you someone, Gladys. Don't worry."

Gladys frowned at Brandon then winked at Amber. "You kids run along. I'll put up the ladder."

"Are you kidding? I'll put it away." Brandon wasn't about to let the older woman struggle with the ladder.

After folding it, he carried it to a closet tucked away in the back of the store. He'd never regretted hiring Gladys. She was a faithful and hard worker. When he returned, Gladys was closing out the register with Amber.

When Amber saw him, she smiled.

Her smile was almost too beautiful. Suddenly, his throat turned dry. He was in unfamiliar territory.

This is strictly business. Maybe he should have accepted Jim's offer to keep interns and volunteers out of sight. But he knew that was impossible, and like Jim had said, an intern did not necessarily a protégé make.

"Ready?"

Amber grabbed her purse and moved from behind the counter. "As I'll ever be."

Brandon led her through the back of the store and down a flight of stairs. He opened the door for her. She gave him a brief glance when she walked by, stepping into the long hallway lined with classrooms.

He led her into the first room on the right. "This is the instruction room—texts, videos, and lectures created to keep the attention of adults and children alike."

They moved to the next room. "This is the lab where the tourists can learn the proper procedure for handling fossils."

She ran her fingers lightly over the counter then looked up at him, eager and full of hope and something akin to awe.

The admiration he saw in her eyes reminded him of another time and place, and someone he desperately wanted to forget. Uncomfortable, he turned away. "Next, I'll show you where we receive the collections we've accessioned."

After showing her the remaining rooms, he began flipping off the lights and making sure the doors were locked for the day. Amber chattered on about UND. How grateful she was to be interning at Harrington. He enjoyed listening to the excitement in her voice. He'd been that enthusiastic once.

"Dr. Young assured me that spending time working with you would help me better assess the direction I should take. While I love geology and have considered paleontology as my field of study. . ." She trailed off, shaking her head.

Brandon understood her very well. "You love the idea of collecting on a far greater scale." He glanced down the hallway, making sure all the lights were off and considered her words about spending time working with him. By engaging in the process, he'd already put one foot into a place he had planned to avoid. How should he handle this?

"Why, yes. . .you read my mind." She stared at him as if she had more to say but hadn't figured out how to say it. "Dr. Selman, how did you decide what to do with your life? There's just so much I want to do and I can't do it all."

As his mind filled with a million answers, he hung his head and chuckled. "You mean, how did I decide what I want to be when I grow up?"

"Yes," she laughed, softly.

There was something in her voice. Something delightful, yet unnerving. He turned his gaze to Amber. In her eyes, he glimpsed something both familiar and unwelcome.

She saw herself as his protégé.

"I didn't."

He let things happen the way they had?

Jason cleared his throat. Amber pulled her thoughts together and realized everyone was staring at her.

"You have anything to add?" he asked.

Oh yeah. Cheeks burning, she tugged the slip of paper from her pocket. Jason wanted her to become accustomed to giving the spiel. "During the tour, we'll give you time to do some collecting of your own, but remember you may only keep specimens that hold no research value to the museum."

"Hey, that's no fair," Tim piped up again.

Amber glanced at Jason, hoping for some help. He held his tongue, prodding her with his eyes. She figured he wanted her to learn to deal with problems sooner, rather than later.

She smiled at Tim then addressed the entire group. "The tour is for you to get a hands-on look at paleontology. The museum has secured our dig site through a fossil lease and proper permits. We're required to document fossils, and important collections are subject to further scientific study. We'll be digging in what we call a bone bed—parts of dinosaur bones and incomplete fossils that have been washed out by an ancient river. They're no longer *in situ*, meaning they've been disturbed. These specimens usually don't hold much value. You can add these to your personal collection after we've documented them. Are we clear?"

"Yes." Tim stuck a finger in his nose, it appeared, as a means of disrespect. The other boys laughed.

Boys.

Jason led the group out the door and to the head of the trail. "Ongoing research is currently conducted at several sites in the region, but today we'll find our bone bed near an outcropping not two miles from the museum."

Off to the left, a slightly overweight man frowned. Unhappy about the distance? Even if they drove to one of the dig sites, they'd still have to hike a mile or more over rough terrain where the researchers worked. As they moved out and down the trail, Amber brought up the back of the group.

Finally, they arrived at the end of the trail where they had to climb down a short rope ladder to the dried-up riverbed below. From where she stood, Amber could see for miles over the hills and buttes carved by the river and leaving many layers to be explored.

Her chest filled with the anticipation of being part of the paleontology dig at some point. The family heirloom was ever present in her mind as she cautiously stone-stepped over boulders of various sizes to make her way to the dirt. Though the pain was minimal and would often come and go, her ankle began to ache again, reminding her of her recent fall. She felt a small grin slide onto her lips as she recalled her run-in with Dr. Selman. Even before knowing his identity, she sensed he was someone special.

Once they arrived at the site where the tourists were allowed to dig, Jason explained what they would be looking for.

He held a rock in each hand. "Can you tell which one is bone?"

The group gathered in a tight circle. Most allowed the kids "front-row" access. One of the girls slid her hand across the rock in Jason's right hand. "This one."

"Wrong, this is sandstone. It looks smooth but when you run your hand over it, you can feel the gritty texture."

He tossed it on the ground and held out his other hand. "This is part of a leg bone. Notice the porous texture. Lots of air pockets. Bone that you find as you dig will be a tan or pink color and if you break into the inside you'll see dark brown. Also, a bone will bleach as it lies in the sun, so if you see anything that looks lighter in color than the surrounding rocks, that could be bone. When you're exploring the bone bed, you're looking for something that stands out, that doesn't look like everything else lying around."

Jason then pointed to something in the distance. "See the tarp shading the group over there? Researchers are excavating that quarry. One of our tour groups discovered bones that were weathering out but appeared to go back into the layers in the hills. That indicates the bone was in situ where it was deposited."

Ohs and ahs escaped the group. Amber suspected that, like her, they'd rather be there than here.

"Do they know what it is?" Tim asked.

"Yes, that site has yielded a young T. rex."

"Oh! Can we go look?"

Jason shook his head. "For now, the only ones allowed on the dig other than researchers are the museum interns assisting them."

Amber tried to get a glimpse of Muriel. She envied her working under Dr. Laudan on an actual fossil dig. Supposedly Amber was to work directly under Dr. Selman, but maybe it was meant to simply look that way on paper. She'd assumed she'd be working more closely with him so that she could ask questions, pick his brain, and look up to him as her mentor. This was only her first week, though, and she knew her internship didn't include giving tours the entire time. Dr. Selman had mentioned she might have the chance to assist Dr. Laudan at some point.

At least she wasn't in the museum store any longer. And she'd had a chance to speak with Dr. Selman personally, get to know him a little. Amber sucked in a breath of dusty air and stood tall. She'd do the best she could, of course, no matter where she was assigned because she really wanted to impress Dr. Selman.

Once the gathering dispersed and began walking around in search of fossils, Amber leaned toward Jason, speaking softly. "Won't we get to show them the T. rex find at some point?"

"Dr. Laudan doesn't like to mess with tour groups. But I'll ask Dr. Selman about making an appearance to show our group the discovery before the tour is over."

Amber's heart skipped a beat at the thought of seeing him again.

Hours later, the hot dry air had Amber gasping for breath. The blazing sun burned her skin despite the fact that she'd slathered on a thick layer of sunscreen and worn a hat. As Amber wiped sweat from her forehead, an errant drop burned her eye. Although she loved the digging and the excitement, sitting in a classroom for months hadn't exactly prepared her for the labor part of this field. Nor did she feel ready to conduct a tour of her own, which, according to Jason, was on the schedule for next week. She licked her chapped lips, tasting salt.

Two women found what appeared to be a bone and Amber plopped down next to them, guiding them as best as she could to dig up the fossil. With chisels and an ice pick, they gently removed the dirt from around the fossil, then brushed the soil away to get a better look. Then more digging and more brushing.

Once the women got the hang of it, Amber stood back to observe the others, which was part of her assignment—answering questions and making sure no one took something they weren't supposed to.

Amber noticed the man who'd frowned before they even started, sitting on a large rock, drinking his water. His chubby son appeared excited but tired. Though he wore a cap and she'd seen him put on sunscreen, he was already turning red.

She had her doubts that the man would come back tomorrow. What was the turnover rate on the tour? Even *she* wasn't sure she wanted to come back. Every part of her body ached like she was twenty years older. Still, she knew she'd complete her internship this summer—no matter what that entailed.

Seeing the others relatively occupied with their various finds, and Jason busy talking dinosaurs with the boys, Amber decided to grab a quick look at the surrounding land—the Little Missouri Badlands had captivated her. She'd be back before anyone knew she'd left. To get a good view, she'd need to go higher, and she could still keep an eye on the group. Amber made her way up a rise that hadn't appeared as steep as it now felt. Breathing hard, she wondered if she would actually make it to the top.

Finally, the ground flattened out. She'd made it! Still gasping for breath, she stood tall and took in the scenery. Spotting a rock she sat down while she caught her breath and poured water over her head, not caring that her face was probably now a muddy mess.

Wouldn't it be funny if Dr. Selman could see her now?

She groaned at the wayward thought. Expecting someone old enough to be her father, she'd been surprised at his good looks and that she'd been instantly attracted to him. She'd have to curb that somehow. In a moment of weariness, she let her eyes drift shut. Still the bright sun fought to penetrate her lids.

A shadow gave her a moment's reprieve until she opened her eyes. Her heart raced at the sight of him.

"Dr. Selman?"

❧

Brandon watched Amber snap to her feet like she was in the marines, and he was her sergeant. He fought the urge to give her an answering salute.

He had the strangest desire to wipe the dust and smudge from her face. Now that would go over well with a board member, donors, researchers, and tourists looking on. Instead he simply smiled and said, "Hi, there."

"What are you doing here? I thought you were busy running the museum." The sun directly in her eyes, she held her hand up to shade them.

Her question prompted him to consider why, exactly, he'd made his way up here. But their paths hadn't crossed in a few days. He was glad they did now.

"Yes, well, part of my job is to accommodate potential donors." He nodded toward the two men and a woman standing in the distance, between the tourists and the active researchers under the tarp.

Amber squinted in the direction of the donors.

"They wanted to know what you were doing sitting by yourself. Is everything all right?"

"Sorry to worry you. I'm fine, just needed a break. I was about to head back down." Amber wiped her face with a small towel she pulled from her pocket. After a glance at it, a look of horror came over her features.

Brandon chuckled. "Didn't anyone ever tell you that digging for fossils is dirty work?"

An answering smile replaced her look of revulsion, and it appeared as though she was about to slap him playfully with her towel but thought better of it. Admittedly, had he not run into her today, he would have found any excuse to see her.

Unfortunately, his rule regarding protégés had everything to do with a previous office romance. Only in his case, the affections had been one sided—the young woman whom he'd mentored had her heart set on him. Focused on his research, he hadn't seen her budding affection and the growing danger.

Wasn't there already a natural law that workplace romances should be avoided?

Regardless, he'd governed himself in this matter, and recently proclaimed the no protégé rule. As he recalled, Jim had laughed. Now he knew why. Brandon was given to helping others, teaching them. It was unlikely he would abide his own rule.

And now as he looked at Amber McKinsey—dusty, sweaty, and still beautiful—the natural law was clamoring to be broken, too.

five

"Would you like some help down?" Brandon had always said it was one thing to climb, quite another to come down. He proffered his hand.

Ignoring it, Amber scrutinized the hill below. At what should be her descent, her eyes grew wide.

Had she only now noticed how high she was?

She stared at his hand for a moment then shook her head. "No, thanks. I'm good."

As he became increasingly aware of his board member's and prospective donors' stares, his relief that he wouldn't be holding her hand as he assisted her down was almost palpable.

Amber took a timid step toward the other side of the hill where her tour group waited at the bottom. Pebbles shifted under her foot, causing her to slip on her backside. Regardless of how he felt about the onlookers, the last thing he wanted was for Amber to get hurt. Nor did he need another incident, and right in front of them.

Still sitting, she looked up at him a bit sheepishly. He cocked a brow. "You're sure I can't help you?"

Offering his hand again, he wasn't surprised this time when she took it. Soft and small, her hand felt good in his. "I'd like you to join me. I'm taking the donors to see the T. rex. That means we're going in the opposite direction from your group."

"But what about Jason? Doesn't he need my help? I was just about to go back down when you showed up."

"I won't keep you long."

"And the tour group? I'm sure they'd love to see the discovery, too."

He smiled at her enthusiasm. "I'll make arrangements

for them on another day. Including them with the donors would make too big a crowd and too many questions. But I appreciate your concern."

Amber nodded, and together, they scrambled down the steep side of the hill, over the ragged layers of sediment.

Once they cleared the hill, Brandon led Amber to the waiting threesome and introduced her to Sheila Longstrom—the only board member to oppose his hiring at Harrington—and the two potential donors, John Starks and Arnold Hammers.

"Nice to meet you, Miss McKinsey." Sheila's smile reflected no warmth. "I'm sure someone has explained to you how important it is for you to stay with the tour group. The museum doesn't need any more mishaps."

Brandon felt his jaw tighten. She referred, of course, to Tori's accident. He had the suspicion that Sheila was waiting for something to go wrong so she could prove to the board that she'd been right all along.

Amber's eyes widened as she glanced his way. "I. . .uh—"

"I'm sure Miss McKinsey, as a new intern, would benefit from viewing the T. rex site. So, I've invited her to join us."

Sheila pursed her lips, apparently unwilling to press the matter. As a board member, she should be aware the museum needed more donors, and she hadn't helped that cause today.

Fortunately, as they made their way to the tarp that shaded the research site, she joined him in explaining how the field digs opened to the public encouraged education and were one of the museum's biggest draws.

Brandon stepped under the tarp where three of the volunteers were assisting Dr. Laudan, pulling strips of burlap out of plaster of paris and wrapping a large bone.

Dr. Laudan straightened and stared at Brandon, her hands covered in plaster. Brandon didn't miss her subtle frown.

"Why don't you give us some background?" Brandon asked.

She nodded, well aware that Brandon wanted details to impress his guests. "This is called a plaster jacket. In the case of a large bone, like what you see here, we want to keep it safe as we take it back to the lab, so we encase it in plaster of paris."

Dr. Laudan continued, explaining how they would then pedestal the fossil, leaving it sitting on a large slab of rock to carry it back to the lab.

Brandon couldn't help himself. He watched Amber closely. By now she probably realized that had she asked to intern under Dr. Laudan, she very well could have joined the researchers on the T. rex find.

Guilt wound its way through his thoughts. She had to be disappointed in him as a mentor.

Like the donors, Amber appeared fascinated. But there was something else, just under the surface. What was it?

As she tugged on her earlobe—an apparent nervous habit—her eyes drifted slowly to his, then a small smile formed. She had perfect lips.

Next to him, Sheila cleared her throat. One glimpse and he knew she'd witnessed the exchange.

❧

That evening, Amber showered then made herself comfortable in the corner of the sofa. Soft lighting emanated from the lamp next to her. Today had been rough. The eagerness to discover fossils had eventually succumbed to the reality of long and arduous, backbreaking work. Amber felt sure that once her body adjusted, she'd regain her enthusiasm for the task.

Still, she couldn't shake the thought that she probably shouldn't have taken that short break from the tour group. They hadn't been out of sight, and at the time, it hadn't seemed that big a deal. . . . Dr. Selman had spotted her, and she was grateful for his help down.

She cringed as she recalled the scene. He'd appeared enthusiastic about showing her the T. rex, but when that woman had questioned her, Amber sensed her disapproval. Could her actions prove a negative mark for him, or lose the two potential donors? She rubbed her eyes and pressed her head against the cushioned sofa back. There was definitely more to a researcher's job than dusting earth off a dinosaur bone. Obtaining the necessary funds for their endeavors required the researchers to impress people. And, if *she* wanted to impress Dr. Selman, she would have to do better. No more taking her eyes from the task, no matter what.

She should pray for Dr. Selman, that her blunder wouldn't cost him. Yet, every time she thought of prayer, something she should do daily as a Christian, her heart ached. A huge, painful knot formed in her throat. She shouldn't blame God, but she couldn't help herself.

He could have prevented the accident that killed her mother and sister. They believed and trusted in Him. They'd prayed for safety for their three-hour drive beforehand. He'd let them down. Amber took a long, deep breath, hoping the tears pressuring the back of her eyes would go away.

She ran her hand over the soft maroon leather of her Bible. If she couldn't pray, at least she could read and then maybe God would answer her biggest question. . . .

Why?

Closing her eyes, she considered that she was all alone in the world—well, except for Michael. But she was angry with him, too.

She flipped her Bible open and began reading the first chapter in the book of John—her favorite and always a comfort. It was suppertime and her stomach rumbled as though she needed the reminder, but she was too tired to eat, and since Muriel wasn't there, she saw no reason to cook.

Just then, the girl flew in the front door, threw several sacks on the counter, and rushed to her bedroom, tossing a quick, "Hi Amber!" as she went.

"Hi, Muriel."

Muriel's energy after a day at the dig astounded Amber. Suddenly, Amber felt even more tired, if that were possible, and curled her legs under her. She wasn't in the mood for lively conversation.

Muriel came out from her room and plopped on the sofa next to Amber. "You're reading the Bible."

"Yes, I am."

Muriel's grin was slightly mocking as she looked from Amber to the pages of John. She and Muriel hadn't discussed matters of faith, though Amber expected it would come up at some point. It hadn't been her intent to hide her beliefs, but she wasn't ready for the great debate at the moment.

"And you want to be a paleontologist?"

Amber opened her mouth to answer, but Muriel's cell phone chirped, distracting her and saving Amber from an explanation. Amber had planned to answer that she hadn't committed to paleontology and was leaning more toward museum work in general; still, that wouldn't have answered the question Muriel was really asking.

Amber wondered how long it would take the news to spread. Paleontology was a study involving evolution, and Amber knew scientists didn't have high opinions of what they referred to as Bible-thumping Christians. Yet, here she was. Oh, how she wanted to pray, needed to pray. Yet she couldn't bring herself to speak to God. He'd failed her. But just one little cry of her heart might work.

Lord, take this anger from me. . . .

six

The next week, Amber stood with confidence as she spoke to her tour group at the bone bed where she'd assisted with last week's tour. For this group of amateur fossil hunters, however, this area was a new one to be explored, especially since it had rained over the weekend, washing out new fossils from the loose sediment.

She'd enjoyed last week's hunt. There was always a fossil to be seen, whether of a small invertebrate or a plant, and sometimes the tour group members hit the jackpot with a dinosaur bone. At one point, they'd been allowed to assist and watch the researchers as they worked to unearth the T. rex.

Nothing of significance had been discovered the previous week, but that was to be expected on most amateur digs. Amber recalled Jason saying the T. rex find had been precipitated by a tour group. She smiled to herself.

No one could see what was hidden beneath the dirt except for God.

For most of the day, Jason had kept his distance, watching her manage this new group. Being a guide wasn't as big a deal as she thought. All she had to do was give the little spiel then lead them down the path. Throughout the day she would answer questions and show them how to gently remove the fossils, which were then packaged in reclosable plastic bags for further study or turned back over to the finder, depending on the value of the fossil.

Spotting a frizzy-haired woman and her teenage daughter excitedly examining something, Amber was about to walk over to them when she saw Jason, heading her way.

When Jason stood next to her, he frowned. "Why don't you help somebody? Start digging or something."

Though startled at his cranky mood, Amber smiled. "Sure thing."

She didn't want negative reports traveling back to Dr. Selman. Leaving Jason's side, she made her way to the woman and her daughter. Amber asked about their find. She hated to be the bearer of bad news, but no, the rock they'd picked up was, in fact, just a rock.

Remembering when Dr. Selman had surprised her last week by turning up at the dig and then showing her the research site, she sighed. Watching the researchers had made her even more eager to be involved in the serious side of the museum. . . to work directly under him.

At the simple thought of him, her heart did the little flip that it did every time she'd seen him. Not a good sign.

Amber spotted what looked suspiciously like part of a bone poking from the ground. She invited the frizzy-haired woman and her daughter over and gathered the tools from the nearby bucket, placing them above hers as she sat down in the dirt. The woman eyed her like she'd planned to dig for fossils without getting dirty.

Hearing a loud yelp, Amber looked up from her digging. The shout was from a particularly rowdy group of boys that'd come with their father. She looked around for Jason, knowing she'd need his help to keep a close eye on them. She spotted him with his cell phone to his ear, approaching her.

"Amber, I think you've got it under control. Something's come up, and I need to head out."

All the confidence she imagined she'd gained bled out her feet. Amber stared. "But—"

Jason tugged her to her feet and aside, then spoke in quiet tones. "You'll be fine. I've been watching you for days now. You know the drill. Take a water break, then in a couple of hours head back to the museum and wish them all a good evening." He didn't wait for a response but patted her back and left.

She was going to ask, "But what about those boys?"

The woman and her daughter stared at her. They placed

their trust in her. Amber stood tall, and mentally reassured herself. She wouldn't let them down.

A good fifteen minutes passed before she relaxed. The earth hadn't shattered because Jason left. In a few minutes she'd dole out the water. Everything would be fine.

"Hey! What are those boys doing up there?" A short, stout man from her group yelled from a distance, looking in Amber's direction.

With the shout, Amber glanced up to the very same ridged hill she'd climbed last week. The boys didn't realize the other side was much steeper. And wouldn't you know? They were two of the-rowdies she'd been concerned about all day. How had they slipped past her?

Amber searched for their father, who knew the rules and knew he was responsible for his kids. She found him sitting with his back to the boys, drinking water and wiping sweat from his brow.

Amber marched over to him. "Your children aren't following the rules. Can you please call them down? I'm going to have to shut this tour down right now because of them, if you don't."

The man eyed her with disdain then twisted around. "They're boys. They'll be fine."

"Sir, you're not hearing me. Your boys could get hurt. This is against our policy. Please tell them to come down."

"Give me a minute, will you?"

The other tourists had stopped digging, and all eyes were on her, waiting to see what she would do. How she handled this. Why had Jason left?

"Fine, if you won't, then I will." And she had every right.

"Stay here," she called to the group as she trotted to the base of the hill. Once there, she shouted, "Boys, this area is off-limits to tourists. Come down now!"

To her relief, one of them began descending. What had they been thinking?

The other one, however, remained frozen, and whimpered. She barely heard him when he said, "I can't! I'm scared!"

Oh, great! Now what should she do? This wasn't supposed to happen. In fact, she hadn't even been told how to handle it in case it did. Feeling the stares of her group on her back, she didn't want to reveal her own fear and lack of confidence. If she blew this, she could be dismissed from her internship or worse. . .the child could get hurt.

"Stay there. I'm coming to get you." And then what? She reminded herself that Dr. Selman had easily helped her down by holding her hand.

But this was different. This was a child.

She began scaling the ribbed and rough terrain. At least it wasn't a straight-up rocky cliff, requiring any sort of equipment, but then again, that would have prevented the boys from climbing it to begin with.

Now would probably be a good time to pray for some help, except, she reminded herself, God had let her sister and mother down. She couldn't count on Him.

Focus, focus. She couldn't think about that now. When she finally made her way up, next to the boy, she looked him in the eye. Terror loomed there.

In a reassuring tone, she said, "You're going to be fine. I'll climb down with you. It's only a small distance. Okay?"

Seemingly unable to speak, he nodded, looking as if he wanted with all his might to believe her. *I can't let him down. . . .*

They descended slowly until the angle of the slope eased, though still too steep for comfort. She tugged his sleeve. "Now, turn around, sit on your backside if you have to, and make your way to your dad. The soft pebbles and dirt make this a slippery slope, so watch out." The tour would be over for the boys and their father—they knew the rules, or at least their father had signed a paper stating they did.

She watched the boy do as she said, then she started to do the same.

"Amber!" someone shouted.

Now what?

She jerked her head around and caught her foot on a rock.

Unable to stop her momentum, she tumbled forward and down the slope, rolling over and over, like a log, faster, it seemed, with every turn. Rocks scraped her, dug into her skin. Someone screamed.

Was that her? Pain seared her body.

God help me!

Blackness engulfed her.

❦

"Is she dead?" A boy in the crowd asked.

"Of course not, son," a man assured.

"It's your fault," a woman accused. An argument erupted between several in the tour group.

Brandon tuned them all out. He'd already phoned for help. Seeing Amber lying there motionless tore his gut, and he laid it wide open before God.

Lord, please let her be all right.

"Miss McKinsey. . .Amber. . ." Brandon cupped her head gently between his hands, speaking softly. She didn't appear to have any broken bones but was still knocked out cold. And God help him, he'd seen her tumble down the slope after Jason shouted her name.

Though this incident threatened to bring back a torrent of memories—the accident he'd been held responsible for—he put the unbidden thoughts aside because he only cared about one thing: that this beautiful young woman with her whole life ahead of her wasn't seriously hurt.

Eyelids fluttering, she groaned, infusing his heart with hope. Noticing her lips moving, he leaned in to listen. Soft murmuring met his ears and, at her words, he drew back in surprise.

"Amber. . ." he whispered. "Wake up. Can you hear me?"

Her eyes opened; then she squinted. Frowning, she touched her head. "Oww. . ."

Brandon didn't doubt her pain. "Amber, it's me, Dr. Selman."

"What happened?" she asked.

Brandon helped her to sit up, noting a purple knot forming

on her forehead. "Don't you remember? You took a fall."

Both hands on her head, she groaned again then focused her eyes on him. To his dismay, an apologetic look came across her face. "I'm sorry."

"*You're* sorry. Don't be." Brandon couldn't believe what he heard. "Here, let me help you to your feet, if you're able. We need to get you medical attention. I've already called."

Sirens rang out in the distance. *Finally.*

When Amber took a step, she cried out in pain then favored her left foot. Brandon wasn't about to let her walk on that. Tired of waiting for the ambulance, and knowing it would take the EMTs time to navigate the trail into precarious terrain on foot, he lifted her gently into his arms.

She yelped in surprise. "Dr. Selman, please don't think you have to carry me."

"Don't be ridiculous. You're not walking back." To Jason, he said, "Take the rest of the group to the T. rex for now." He'd give the man a dressing-down afterward. Right now, he needed to salvage this situation.

He strode carefully toward the trailhead that led back to the museum parking lot where he hoped the ambulance would be waiting. She was light in his arms, and her warm breath caressed his neck. He refused to look at her face, so near his.

"You all right?" he asked, his words breathy.

"This was my first tour to do alone. I've let everyone down."

"Jason shouldn't have left you. Especially with that group of boys when he could see they might cause trouble." He'd spotted the boys with their father in the museum earlier, attempting to touch an exhibit. Brandon had personally addressed them at the time. On his way to the digs, he'd run into Jason in a rush to leave. Of course, Brandon demanded he return to assist Amber with the tour. Museum policy was clear regarding the tour guide to participant ratio.

Once in the parking lot, the EMTs met him. Though

Amber assured them she was all right, they took her to the hospital anyway. While Brandon wanted to go along, it was probably not appropriate.

"Dr. Selman? My name is Muriel. I'm interning under Dr. Laudan, and I'm Amber's cabinmate. I was in the lab, helping to secure a specimen when I heard. I'll go to the hospital and stay by her side. Don't worry. I'll be sure to let you know what the doctor says."

News travels fast. "Thank you." He was certain he wouldn't hear the end of this.

She jogged off in the direction of the cabins, presumably to get her car.

Watching the ambulance leave the parking lot, Brandon felt a headache coming on. Clearly, several factors played a role in Amber's fall, not the least of which had to be what she termed her family heirloom.

Though relieved she appeared to be okay, he was still distraught as he continued to pace the parking lot. After a while, he noticed others looking at him, so he headed inside the museum.

In his office, he stared at the phone, hoping to hear from Muriel and wishing he'd given her his cell number. Like a fossil waiting to be unearthed, the truth had been right in front of him and he hadn't seen it. His attachment to this woman clearly exposed—he realized he'd not been able to get his mind off her since their initial collision.

Through all his years of study to achieve academic success, all his years focused on his work, he'd never had a woman distract him so. On the road to recovery from his previous misfortunes, his profession teetered on a precipice. With at least one board member looking over his shoulder, he couldn't afford another incident or even the appearance of a scandal.

What was he going to do about Amber McKinsey?

seven

Amber lay on the sofa, nursing a mild concussion. Besides that, she'd miraculously only suffered a few scrapes; and her ankle wasn't even sprained, just a tad swollen. Still, the doctor had given her a painkiller, which she'd gratefully taken—mostly to numb the pain in her heart.

She felt like such a—

Someone knocked on the door. Amber shifted on the sofa to get the door.

"Don't you even think about it." Muriel glared at her and rushed to the door.

She had offered to bring Josh out for Amber, but Amber refused her kindness, instead considering Muriel's allergies. Amber relaxed and closed her eyes, wondering who it could possibly be. No one ever came to the cabin. Whoever it was, Muriel would send them away.

Nestled on the sofa, she could easily drift to sleep.

A familiar voice resounded in the room. *Dr. Selman?* Amber's eyes popped open to see the man himself standing before her. Stunned didn't come close to what she felt. She pushed to sit up straight, sending pain through her head. She grabbed it.

"No, no. Please stay right where you are. I didn't mean to wake you."

Amber swallowed, uncertain why he was there. "I wasn't asleep. Just. . .resting."

"Good. I'm sorry I disturbed you. But I wanted to express my sincere apologies for what happened to you today."

A woozy feeling came over her. *Oh, no.* The drugs were starting to kick in. She focused hard on his face and on listening to what he'd come to say. His lips were moving. . .what was he saying? What had the doctor given her again? This felt much too strong.

He pressed his lips tight. Had he done that before? She leaned closer.

Close enough to see his stubble, some graying near his chin. His aftershave smelled great.

Amber glanced over at Muriel who sat in the chair across from the sofa. Dr. Selman sat on the edge of the coffee table and took Amber's hand. She stared at her hand. It looked so small in his. Why was he holding her hand? His touch was warm and reassuring. She put her other hand over his then smiled up at him.

He didn't smile back but frowned instead. "Maybe this wasn't the best time."

"The best thime. . . ?" she heard herself ask, the words sounding funny.

"When you're feeling up to returning to the museum, I don't want you going back to the field. We'll find you something else to do."

Had she misunderstood? "You don't want me in. . . ? Because fell?"

"Miss McKinsey—"

"Mith McKwinsey? My name Amber?" She looked at her hands, trying to recall what happened. "See?" She held the palms of her hands out for Dr. Selman. "Just a fwew scrapes."

Dr. Selman stared at her with an odd look. "I wanted to tell you in person, so you wouldn't take the news the wrong way."

His odd look turned to pity. All the hurt she'd been holding inside seemed to burst from her in a torrent of words. It felt good. Too good, and she couldn't stop them. Didn't want to. "Why?" she asked through racking sobs. "You're overweacting. I feel. . .everything wrong."

Without knowing when or how, she was against his shoulder. "Why can't I do. . .something. . .right?"

The tears continued as Dr. Selman held her. What was happening? Why was she crying on his shoulder? Oh bother. . .

"Shh. . ." Dr. Selman gently patted her back.

Though he seemed stiff, his embrace felt good. The awful tumble down the slope rattled her mind again, yet in his strong arms she felt protected and safe. The tears finally came to an end. She was quiet and felt sleepy. So sleepy. Just let her stay right where she was. . .

When Amber woke up, she was covered with a blanket, the lights were low, and there wasn't any Dr. Selman in the room. Had it all been a dream?

"Good, you're awake now." Muriel said, and handed her a cup of something warm. "Green tea. Drink up."

Feeling better and like the wooziness of the medication had worn off, Amber sat up and took a sip. "Thank you. You don't have to take care of me, you know. But I appreciate it."

Muriel sat across from her and smiled gently. "Funny thing. I want to do it. My mom is a nurse; she's a nurturing person. I got that from her, I guess. I wanted to work at the digs to see what I wanted to do with my life. Become a nurse, or a scientist."

Amber couldn't help but smile. "And now you find yourself taking care of me." God had a sense of humor, no doubt there. She took another sip and watched Muriel over the rim of her cup. Could she share that? How could she, when she was still unsure of her own heart toward God? Better to wait until everything she could say about Him sounded the way it should.

"I've got a late supper cooking. Chicken noodle soup. One of Mom's recipes."

Muriel's talk about her mom reminded Amber of her own mother and loss. Loneliness filled her with a deep cold. She needed to talk about something else. "I had the strangest dream."

"Oh yeah? What was that?"

Amber chuckled into her cup. "You'd laugh."

"Oh come on. Tell me." Muriel handed her a bowl of the soup. "Eat up. And in between spoonfuls, I want to hear your dream."

"I dreamed Dr. Selman was here."

Muriel laughed.

"See, told you."

"I'm only laughing because that wasn't a dream. He *was* here."

"What?" Amber sat up straight and quick, sending an ache through her head. She grabbed it and waited until the pain subsided. "I can't believe it. What did he want?"

"Why don't you tell me what else you think you dreamed, and I'll tell you if it happened."

Amber leaned against the sofa back and sighed. "Must have been the medication. What a time for that to kick in. I dreamed. . .oh how embarrassing. Please don't tell me I cried on his shoulder."

Muriel stood up and took Amber's empty cup. "You did, chickadee." With a grin she headed to the kitchen.

Amber groaned and rested her head against the sofa. "How embarrassing. What am I going to do now? I'm just such a mess—"

"I thought it was cute, actually."

"Cute? I feel like I'm bungling everything. And here I wanted to make a great impression. . .oh wait, did he come to dismiss me?"

Muriel laughed. "Are you serious? Just the opposite. He wants you to work with him in the museum."

Amber felt her jaw drop. He wanted her actually *with* him? This was what she had hoped for. . .but not quite like this. "Did he mention what I would be doing?"

"Something about museum displays. He was impressed with your bobblehead arrangement."

Amber and Muriel both laughed because Amber had shared about the disastrous display.

The soup was good, and Amber allowed the warmth to lull her while she considered what happened.

Muriel broke the silence. "Though I think he's just concerned, wants to make sure you're safe. . .honestly? I think Dr. Selman might have a thing for you."

❧

Later that evening, after the museum had closed, Brandon stood in his office, hitting his head against the filing cabinet.

"Looks serious," Jim said from behind.

Brandon froze. He thought the guy had already left for the day. He gave the filing cabinet a good-fisted thump then composed himself, turning to face Jim. "Can't a guy blow off some steam?"

"Sure he can. Mind telling me what's bothering you?" He cracked a half grin and grabbed a chair, making himself comfortable as if they were the best of buddies.

Brandon was in no mood to talk, even to Jim, whom he'd known for years. Funny thing, that. Jim had jumped at the chance to become curator of the Harrington Museum when Brandon began assembling his team, but they'd never been close. Still, Brandon didn't need to be friends with his employees, he just needed them to do their jobs.

He studied Jim, aware that he was waiting on Brandon to spill. So, why was it that lately Jim was getting on his nerves?

"I'm guessing this has everything to do with the new intern's accident today?" Jim asked, apparently unwilling to wait on Brandon's response.

This was going to be a long night. Brandon sat behind his desk, feeling the weight of exhaustion on his shoulders, and hung his head. "Yep, you guessed it."

"Jason said the errant boys and their father left the tour, but the rest followed him over to view the T. rex dig site, and the way he made it sound, they were all so excited about seeing it, they probably forgot about the girl."

"Fire him."

"What?"

"You heard me."

Jim stared, pausing before he replied. "But Jason's been with us—"

"He signed an at-will contract, right? You've already put him on probation for not following the rules, right? On a fossil dig, people get hurt when rules aren't followed. The guy's burned out. He messed up big-time as far as I'm concerned. He shouldn't have left Amber."

"Amber? Oh you mean Miss McKinsey?"

When Brandon didn't reply, Jim continued. "Jason has accompanied her on the tour now for several days. She should have been fully capable of taking care of the small group. If anyone needs dismissing—"

"Stop."

"We're down too many people already. Miss McKinsey clearly isn't cut out for this. Jason is experienced—"

Brandon had enough and threw up his hand. "Follow the correct procedures, but I want him gone tomorrow. And Amber. . .I've moved her from the field."

Jim's mouth dropped open. "But who's going to take their place?"

"I don't care. Find someone. Combine the groups. Figure it out, or lead the tours yourself." Brandon couldn't stop the harsh rush of words, but Jim had managed to pick the wrong time to question him about the day's events.

Jim stood. "Considering what happened before, I'd think you'd be more sensitive to how things look. And right now, my friend, it looks like your motivation—especially where this girl is concerned—is questionable. Why are you protecting her? If anything, it should be my call. You said you didn't want to be involved with the interns, remember?"

Brandon grabbed his suit coat and swung it over his shoulder then held the door in silent warning. Jim walked through and headed to his office without another word.

Once in his car Brandon sagged against the seat. The day's events had spiraled out of control and they just kept going. No matter what he did, he hadn't been able to rein things in. Then, hoping to make sure things were all right with Amber, and there wouldn't be more problems, he'd stopped by her cabin. Big mistake.

He hadn't intended to ask her to work with him. But with

her in his arms today, sobbing—though he assumed it was due to the medication—he'd heard her heart and probably much more than she'd ever intended, or ever would under normal circumstances. Then, something inside him snapped, and he'd forsaken his rule, digging in deep this time.

She most likely wouldn't remember anything, but then her roommate was there, watching him with her eagle eyes. She'd remember. Muriel would probably blather about Amber in his arms, sobbing until he quieted her, soothed her. She'd remained in his arms far too long, seemingly comforted until he finally realized she'd fallen asleep. As she rested there against him, he could feel her softness, smell her hair, but then he felt her roommate's stare.

What was he doing? What must she be thinking?

He'd then gently settled Amber onto the sofa and tucked the blanket around her. Again, under Muriel's watchful eyes. Just as well—he certainly wouldn't want rumors to fly had he been caught alone with Amber. However, they were likely to fly anyway.

He could see the small-town headlines already. HARRINGTON MUSEUM'S DIRECTOR SAID TO COMFORT BEAUTIFUL VOLUNTEERS. Brandon wasn't certain what damage control he could do now, except. . .dismiss her as Jim suggested. To protect the museum, volunteers and interns also signed an at-will contract as though they were museum employees but if someone didn't function well in the environment, he or she was simply asked to leave. He'd certainly not intended for Amber to work directly with him, but neither could he bring himself to dash her hopes and dreams because of his own past and weaknesses or to protect his own skin.

What kind of cad would he be to do such a thing? He pounded the steering wheel, noting Jim's car sitting a few spots away. Jim was wrong. Brandon was making every attempt to be sensitive to his peculiar situation. He'd do everything he could to shove aside his personal feelings for her, act like a professional, and give a budding young museum director or paleontologist the chance she needed. People had taken a chance on him, and more than once.

As he drove from the parking lot, he pondered the news about Amber that Muriel had shared with him.

eight

Two days later, Amber rolled out of bed in time to grab breakfast before heading over to the museum. The doctor had suggested she take three days off, but it only took two for her to feel better. Not to mention, she couldn't stand another day of being left alone with her thoughts. No matter how hard she tried, she couldn't forget her humiliation at having cried on Dr. Selman's shoulder—and worse—spewing her deepest insecurities.

Muriel assured her that Dr. Selman understood Amber was "under the influence" as she'd put it. According to Muriel, he admitted he'd chosen the wrong time to talk to Amber. Add to her embarrassment, she'd been waiting for this chance—but not like this. The way things had unfolded, she imagined he wanted to evaluate her rather than expand her experience.

Whenever she managed to put those thoughts from her mind, she came face-to-face with her brother's situation all over again. She'd not spoken to him since the death of their mother and sister a year ago. As Amber nuked a bowl of oatmeal, she remembered it had been about that long since she'd had a heart-to-heart with God. When she removed the bowl from the microwave, it felt heavy. . .like her heart.

Once she finished breakfast, she rushed out the door into the fresh morning air. Sucking in a deep breath, she encouraged herself with positive thoughts—like the Bible said in Philippians—she would "think about such things." This would be a good day.

She still had hope. She still had a chance to prove herself to Dr. Selman.

At the museum, she found the employees-only section and looked for the receiving room. Gladys told her she could find Dr. Selman there.

Inside the room, Amber made her way between tall stacks of boxes. When she saw Dr. Selman, she froze and watched him examine a large crate. As she observed his handsome form, she thought about how much he'd accomplished for someone she guessed to be in his late thirties. Some might call him an overachiever. Was there someone in his life who inspired him to great accomplishments?

At one time, Michael had been that someone for her.

Dr. Selman removed the batten that secured the exterior of the crate then worked to pry the top open. The top gave way, and he tossed it on the concrete floor. Peering inside, he began pulling out the material used to pad and protect the contents.

He stilled. The item inside must have drawn his full attention. To her surprise, he turned his head and looked straight at her. She pressed forward, hoping to hide that she'd been observing him.

"Dr. Selman. I was told I'd find you here. Reporting for duty, sir."

A warm smile spread across his face. "You know, this isn't the military."

She stopped in front of him, standing next to the long crate. "What do you mean?"

"I always feel as if you're going to salute me."

Amber frowned. "Oh, I. . .uh. . ." This wasn't the way she wanted to start off. "I just think of you as a very important person."

"Ha! I'm no more important than anyone else." He quirked a brow and half grinned, exposing his long dimple again.

His smile too cute for comfort, Amber blinked a few times, hoping to lessen its effect on her. "Well, in my world, you're somebody."

"Let's change your worldview, then, by dispensing with Dr. Selman. Just call me Brandon."

Call him by his first name? She tugged her earlobe, thinking. Gladys had seemed adamant about his title. And what would the others think?

"I'm sure I couldn't do that. I'm accustomed to calling my professors Doctor. Since I'm here to learn from you, it's easier for me this way."

His forehead creasing, he studied her. "Well, if you must. But this is a small museum and I'm not about titles."

His attention back on the crate, he gestured for Amber to look inside.

A life-size figure rested in the crate. Amber drew in a short breath. "Sacagawea."

"Good, that's the sort of reaction I like to see."

Uncertain what he meant, Amber considered his comment as she laid her bag against a chair. Then she stood tall, ready to work.

"You're not too disappointed about being pulled from the field?" He began pulling out the straw-like stuffing that protected the figure.

"Oh, no. I love history." Amber didn't add that she feared it was his frustration with her family heirloom that led to his decision. Then again, maybe she'd already explained that when she'd cried on his shoulder. "Um. . .before we get started. There's something I'd like to say."

Brandon dropped a handful of what Amber now saw was finely shredded tissue paper, and waited for her to continue. Wow, she was actually going to work with the man. The only downside? Her infatuation—and oh, she was infatuated with him—might actually turn into a full-blown crush. She swallowed against the tightness in her throat.

"Well?" he asked.

"You're not anything like the professors at UND."

"Is that what you wanted to say?"

"No, actually. I wanted to apologize for the other night."

"There's no need to apologize. Really. Let's just forget everything. That is, whatever you can actually remember." He quirked his crazy grin again.

The problem was that his grin was starting to make *her* crazy.

Packing material hung from the box, giving her a hare-brained idea. She snatched a handful of shredded paper.

Anticipating her next move, Dr. Selman threw up his arms as though to protect himself and smiled. "Hey, wait a minute."

Amber tossed the mass at him, but it wasn't cooperative, acting more like she'd thrown feathers. She laughed but stopped when she realized he wasn't throwing the stuff back. "Sorry, I couldn't help myself."

At least he smiled, but he appeared unsure about what to do next. His reaction reminded her of when she'd met him on the trail. He looked like a man who wanted to say something but had no words. Maybe Dr. Selman didn't know how to lighten up.

Or maybe she needed to get serious.

She cleared her throat. "So, what are we doing? Tell me what exactly you've moved me into, because honestly, I don't remember much of the other night."

"I want you to help me with the artifacts arriving in a few weeks. But in two weeks, we host Living History Week, and we have to set up a diorama. We don't want to disrupt the visitors during the day so we'll set up after. . ." He paused as though considering something. "I hope you don't mind working after hours?"

That would mean a long day.

Seeming to read her mind, he added, "You don't need to come in until after lunch, and we'll work through the afternoon and evening hours. How does that sound?"

Working long hours with handsome Dr. Selman? She'd have to think about it. Putting a finger to her lips, she said, "Okay."

"Oh, except for Wednesday nights. I teach a Bible study."

"I. . .uh. . .You teach a *Bible* study?"

Dr. Selman opened another box. "Why so surprised?"

"I think you know why. You're a paleontologist. You can't be a Christian *and* a paleontologist. And if you are, you can't let anyone know about it. "

He stopped what he was doing and placed his elbow on an unopened crate, leaning against it. "And aren't *you* considering paleontology as a career?"

The way that he said it—"How did you know I'm a Christian?"

He approached her and stood near. Too near. What was he doing? "Everyone leaves signs, little clues, of who they really are. You just have to pay attention."

He raised his hand, then touched the small cross on her neck and lifted it, holding it against his fingers. He looked from the cross into her eyes. The olive color of his appeared to ebb and flow with an emotion she couldn't read.

Did he realize how close he was?

"Sign number one."

His nearness. . . She couldn't think straight and averted her gaze. As she took a step back, he released the cross.

"Lots of people wear crosses; it's the style." She tugged on the necklace her sister had given to her.

Folding his arms over his chest, he gave her a pointed look. "After you fell, when you were unconscious, just before you came fully awake, you were praying. Sign number two."

Amber felt her eyes widen. She'd been praying? But how? Why wouldn't she know? She couldn't even pray when she was awake.

"And before you get too upset, I saw the Bible on the table next to the sofa. Your roommate told me you read it every night."

This time when Amber spoke her voice was a whisper. "Sign number three. . ."

❧

Brandon heard the distress in her voice. He hadn't meant to send her to that troubled place he'd seen in her eyes before.

"So you see? I'm not the only one who knows. I don't think it's something you can hide, do you? And why would you want to?"

For the last two days, a battle had raged inside of Brandon. Had he done the right thing, inviting her to work with him, considering the rule he'd insisted was necessary? Considering Jim had all but accused him of showing favoritism to Amber? Would he also get flak from Sheila Longstrom?

The questions had simply washed away upon seeing Amber step into the room, looking like the picture of health. Her smile had sent a flood of relief the size of a melting glacier through him.

What a joy it was to have another Christian in the museum to work beside him. She toyed with the small silver cross he'd held moments before. A deep longing gripped his heart, but he quickly buried it. "I know a handful of Christian paleontologists."

"Christian paleontologist seems a bit like an oxymoron, don't you think?" she asked.

"Not when you think about them separately. Paleontology is simply the study of prehistoric plants and animals. Prehistoric means before recorded history. And yes, to be politically correct in today's culture one must agree with the evolutionary model."

She looked confused, disappointed.

He smiled, enjoying the discussion. "I never said I was politically correct."

"Tell me, how does a paleontologist end up as a museum director?"

More precisely, she probably meant to ask how did a *Christian* paleontologist end up as a museum director. "Museum directors come in all sizes and shapes. They have an expertise in one field or another. My father was a museum director of a much larger institution. He felt it would be a conflict of interest to hire me where he worked. So I found a job working in the research department of a small museum. It was there that I became friends with the man who managed it."

As Amber watched him closely, he continued. "He was curator, collection manager, and administrator all wrapped into one. He took me under his wing and trained me. I guess you could say the work of the bigger picture fit my personality better."

"Sounds like he did everything." Amber began tugging the packing material from Sacagawea's crate. "Like you. Don't you do everything here? Well, you and Jim."

"Remember, too, this is a small museum. The bigger the museum, and the more collections, the more complicated. Here we have the fossils, the historic items that have provenance in this region, and the dinosaur dig tours."

"That seems like a lot. How do you do it all?"

"Jim is officially curator of new collections. Between the two of us, we manage collections, conservation, documentation, and administration." Brandon had often wondered why Jim had followed him here.

Suddenly, he understood his arrogance and paused. Ashamed, he peered at Amber. "And of course, let's not forget the volunteers and interns who help make things happen."

Her lips curved into a soft smile. *Pretty.*

His throat constricted. Uncomfortable with the thought, he considered what she might ask next. This line of questioning put Brandon on edge. If Amber asked the wrong one, he'd end up having to either explain or dance around the truth about what happened at the last museum where he worked. Dredging up his past failures would probably knock him down a few notches in her eyes. With that thought he'd reached the heart of the matter—he enjoyed the way she looked up to him far too much.

Disturbing.

He frowned, throwing all his attention into freeing Sacagawea. Once the life-size model was out of the crate and standing, he left Amber to clean it off while he moved to the next crate, which contained Lewis.

"Does Jim know that you're a Christian?"

The crowbar slipped from Brandon's hands. He bent over to pick it up. "Yes. He gave me a hard time at first. But not anymore."

He peered over the top of the crate. Amber gave him a questioning look that told him she was waiting for further explanation.

"Several years ago, after I was already ensconced in my career, something terrible happened. I had nowhere else to turn except to God." *Lord, please don't let her ask what happened. Not yet.*

"And after you became a Christian you changed what you believe about evolution and paleontology?"

"I met another Christian—a creation scientist. He spent hours, weeks, and months helping me through things."

"But you're still directing a museum that's in conflict with your beliefs."

Brandon removed the top off the crate. "I prayed and waited for God to lead me. Then, when I was asked to become the director of this museum, somehow, I knew it was God. He didn't ask me to leave what I do. In fact, I believe just the opposite. God is all about science—He created all the laws. I think more Christians need to enter science and biology fields. To be involved in museums."

"What about a creation science museum? Ever thought about running one of those?"

Brandon stopped working for a moment to look at Amber. "I think a creation museum is a great thing. But usually only Christians visit those. Don't you think the people who would never visit a creation science museum could be impacted by a museum that presented multiple viewpoints? So instead of seeing only facts mixed with evolutionary interpretations, they're also exposed to scientific evidence that fits with creation science, evidence that is often hidden. I'm working on initiatives that could potentially set that in motion for this museum."

"Do you think they'll go for that? I mean, really?" Amber frowned. She tucked Sacagawea's hair behind the model's shoulder and released a weighty breath. "I don't know what the answer is."

Something compelled Brandon to rush to her side, slipping between the crates. He gently lifted her face to meet his gaze. "No matter what direction you choose, you'll always face opposition to your beliefs. Don't ever let anyone take away your love for God. Do you hear me?"

"Yes." Her eyes grew wide with emotion.

Releasing her, he retreated to his work. Why had he done that? He'd seen Christians enter the science field and end up losing their faith. If it was within his power, he wouldn't let that happen to Amber.

He'd caught a glimpse of her passion for science, but it seemed already life and circumstances were threatening to snuff it out. If only he could keep that from happening. But how?

Being with her today. . .it felt like she'd somehow reignited his own enthusiasm for paleontology—the zeal he'd left dormant these years working in the museum.

While he tugged Lewis from his cocoon, Brandon prayed silently. *Lord, guide me where this young woman is concerned. I can't grow too close to her. Don't let me.*

The wrong people could use his relationship with her against him, against the museum, drawing her into a potential scandal. She had no idea what it felt like to see her face and half-truths plastered on the front page of a newspaper.

Growing close to her could end in disaster for them both.

nine

They'd worked hard on various dioramas and museum displays for the last couple of weeks, preparing for the flood of visitors during Living History Week, and still Amber had her work cut out for her.

With pride, she surveyed Harrington Museum's newest diorama, featuring Lewis, Clark, and Sacagawea. "Last, but not least," she murmured to herself. They'd only just yesterday received everything needed to finish this particular diorama.

"The store's finally closed now," Gladys said from the doorway. "Had one last customer that didn't want to leave." She smiled as she approached Amber and stood next to her, wrapping her in the scent of tea rose. "This was one of our busier days."

"What do you think?" Amber asked, looking at the display.

Gladys cocked her head. "I think that I don't know what Dr. Selman's going to do without you when you head back to that school of yours."

"Thanks. I think." Though Amber smiled at the compliment, a sense of loss coursed through her. She hadn't considered what it would feel like to leave the museum behind. Or Dr. Selman. "Looks like the museum had success long before I came on board. I'm sure he'll be fine."

"We've got a couple of months before you leave us, though, right?" Gladys straightened a photograph of Lewis and Clark on the wall.

"Six weeks, give or take. I won't leave until the end of August."

"Time flies, and I haven't even had you over for dinner. How about the week after next, when Living History Week has run its course?" Gladys winked at her. "I make a mean pot roast. I know how college students can miss home-cooked meals. Miss their families."

At the mention of home and family, Amber pictured her mother and wilted.

"What? Don't tell me you don't like pot roast?"

"It's not that. My mother and sister were killed in a car accident a year ago." She'd said too much. Hoping to avoid further discussion, she stepped onto the dais and began adjusting the display, scrutinizing where best to secure the map of Lewis and Clark's travels.

"Oh, I'm so sorry, hon."

"Not your fault, you didn't know."

"I'd love to remedy that. *Will* you join me for dinner?"

Holding the map, Amber gave a short laugh and turned her head to look at Gladys. "I'd like that very much. Thank you." She'd not wanted to disappoint the woman, but she hoped she'd be able to get out of dinner. She didn't want Gladys dragging family history from her.

Gladys nodded. "I'll leave you to it. Say, where's your sidekick?"

The woman's reference drew a chuckle from Amber. She laid the map to rest and hopped from the dais. "You mean Dr. Selman?"

"That's the one."

Somehow, Gladys had a way of cheering Amber up, reminding Amber of her mother. "I thought you knew everything around here. He's having dinner with a donor. I don't ask for details."

"And he'll be back to help you? I don't want you working here alone."

"That's what he said." Amber adjusted Sacagawea's hand, making her look more involved with the two explorers.

Though Dr. Selman had helped her remove the life-size models from their crates and set them in the area designated for the diorama, he'd spent much of his time in his office on the phone, or working in other areas.

When he first asked her to assist, she'd been under the impression she would be helping him, not designing the exhibit herself. It made her feel safe that he hung around the museum, working, as did she, during the evening hours, but she sensed he wanted to keep his distance.

At seven thirty, Amber wiped her brow. She'd been at it for two hours since Gladys left. Alone in the museum, after all. She secured the copy of the rare map of Lewis and Clark's incredible journey and stood back to study the display, featuring maps, illustrations, letters, and figures representing some of the main characters in the traveling party.

Sacagawea joined their expedition that winter in North Dakota. Amber gripped the shoulders of the brave young Shoshone woman and nudged her slightly to the right. Working on the exhibits wasn't exactly what Amber had in mind when she came to the Harrington Museum. Although, maybe Dr. Selman was right—she had a knack for the displays. She'd finished in the nick of time, too, considering Living History Week began tomorrow.

Whether the subject was dinosaurs or American history, she loved working at the museum and was grateful for this opportunity. Almost finished. As she wondered why Dr. Selman hadn't shown up, she heard keys jangling somewhere in the distance. Footfalls sounded through the museum corridors. She'd recognize that cadence anywhere.

Dr. Selman.

Her heart did the little flip again. Amber steadied her hands. It wasn't like she didn't see him every day. She stood back from the diorama to study it from a distance. Despite feeling confident regarding her efforts, especially after Gladys's compliment, Amber wanted to hear words of praise from him. His approval was important to her—and just how much, was a little disconcerting.

Dr. Selman appeared in the doorway on the other side of the exhibits and made his way through the display cases to stand next to her, a concerned expression on his face.

four

Finally, some action.

After she'd spent two days going through the museum's certification program, Amber had spent yesterday taking phone calls to register people for the tours, answering their questions. She was more than ready to make her way to the field. But she'd been assigned to accompany and assist Jason, learning from him before taking her own group out.

Inside the museum reception area, they stood together in a circle, a small gathering of mostly families with children, three single twenty-something guys, and two fiftyish women. While the digs were best suited for kids twelve years or older, children had to be at least eight years old. All had been required to sign liability waivers, including a list of rules and possible risks.

Jason began his spiel. "We're glad you joined us today. I'm personally looking forward to spending a week with you in search of fossils."

He continued on for a few minutes, explaining that the tools supplied—hammers, chisels, brushes, and more—would be available at the dig site. Sunscreen, gloves, and hiking boots or shoes were all the tourists were required to bring with them. Water and lunch, supplied by the museum, was included in the tour fee.

A freckle-faced boy raised his hand. Ignoring him, Jason kept talking. But the boy wasn't giving up. Amber figured questions were welcome at the end of his talk. Had Jason explained that?

Finally, he paused. Amber didn't miss his tight jaw when he smiled. "Yes?"

The boy revealed a toothy grin. "What about the dinosaurs?

Are we going to see dinosaur fossils?"

Jason's features relaxed. "What's your name, son?"

"Tim."

"Well, Tim, the Little Missouri River Badlands are sedimentary formations from the Cretaceous period."

The boy angled his head, apparently uncertain what Jason meant.

Jason chuckled. "This period is abundant with dinosaurs, mesosaurs, and plesiosaurs. That said, it's been heavily excavated. But there's plenty left for you to see and explore."

"Cool!" The boy bounced, apparently satisfied.

"But mixed in with the dinosaur fossils are those of other mammals like rabbits, mice, and turtles."

"Ah, who cares about them," Tim said as he appeared to wave off anything but dinosaurs.

The entire group laughed at his comment, as though everyone was there solely to get a hands-on look into a past that included the mysterious giants. Who was she kidding? Amber was there for the same reason, only she had never bought into the old earth theory or—as a Christian— evolution. She chewed the right side of her lip. Another thing she'd have to keep quiet for now, biding her time.

This experience was important to her future and career, whatever that might be. After meeting Dr. Selman, she especially looked forward to working with him. Garnering his respect and attention could benefit her in big ways. Plus, it was uncanny how he seemed to understand her, reading her mind almost like her brother.

Amber rubbed her temples. Why'd her thoughts have to go there? How would she keep her brother and his deeds under wraps? Listening to Jason drone on, she glanced around the museum. When her brother was released, could he ever work in his field again? Or in a museum?

Resentment stirred in her heart. Staring at the floor, she wanted to send up a prayer; but she couldn't get past her anger at God, either. She knew she shouldn't be angry, but. . .why had

Oh no. He didn't like what he saw. "What's wrong?" she asked.

A slight smile lifted his lips. "Nothing. Why?" He looked from her to the display.

The smile spread as he studied the exhibit, walking from one end to the other and stepping onto the dais. "You have a real passion for history."

"And you can tell by looking at that?"

"Yes. I can feel the emotion in this exhibit. Consider when someone plays a musical instrument. Are they playing by rote? Or do they inject feeling into their music, putting their very soul into it?"

Though she understood his musical reference, his comparison to her display confused her. How could he actually *see* emotion in what she'd done? "Remember, you helped with much of it."

"I helped lift the figures and directed you, nothing more." From behind the life-size Lewis, he studied her.

Embarrassed, Amber wasn't sure what she was supposed to say. "Thank you?"

He chuckled, then stepped down from the dais. "Which makes you the perfect candidate."

Uh-oh. Leery, she took a step back. "Perfect candidate for what?"

"Two of the actors for the annual Lewis and Clark re-enactment have become ill."

"I'm sorry to hear that. What's the matter with them?"

"Stomach virus. They're not sure if they'll be well by tomorrow."

"And that has what to do with me?"

Brandon smiled. "With your passion, I think you'd make a great Sacagawea."

"What?" Amber backed up farther. "Oh, no you don't. I can't act."

"Are you telling me you'd have us canceling after all the work we've done, and with the community's expectations?

The museum needs this."

"I'm not saying that at all. I'm saying find someone else."

"There is no one else." He handed a large envelope to Amber. "Here's the script. Why don't you look it over and let me know what you think in the morning. The drama isn't until the afternoon. They have a rehearsal at ten."

Stunned, Amber took the script from him. How could she say no when he'd been so convincing? "All right, I'll do it."

"Good."

Seeing the smile slip back into his eyes, she knew one thing—she couldn't stand to see him disappointed. "Who will play the other part?"

A strange look came over his face. "I'm still looking for someone to play Sacagawea's husband."

Her husband? Amber felt the panic squeeze her throat. Would she have to kiss the actor? "Any candidates?"

"Not yet." Brandon jumped onto the dais again and adjusted Clark's position, though in Amber's opinion, he was already perfect.

Watching Dr. Selman, she began to see what he meant about the passion in the display. She saw that same enthusiasm in him, and his words to her came back.

"Which makes you the perfect candidate." Should she suggest that Brandon play the part of Sacagawea's husband tomorrow?

Responding to the urgent need to splash water over her face, Amber excused herself and headed to the restroom.

﹞

Brandon stood at the back of the stage, behind most of the actors. After a frantic search, the part had ended up falling to him, after all. Dressed in period costumes, the group of actors presented a short drama regarding Lewis and Clark as they wintered in North Dakota. Brandon played Sacagawea's husband, Toussaint Charbonneau. He joined Lewis and Clark's group, the Corps of Discovery, as an interpreter along with Sacagawea, on a journey to find out if the Missouri

River met with the Pacific Ocean. Such a finding would have provided a water route from St. Louis to the Pacific.

Fortunately for Brandon, Charbonneau hadn't been a respected or infamous character, and therefore had no lines in this reenactment. Though feeling out of his element on the amphitheater stage, Brandon enjoyed the opportunity to watch Amber in action. She spoke her lines with confidence. Two long braids on each side of her head, Amber wore a brown leather costume like that seen in artists' paintings of Sacagawea.

According to history, Sacagawea gave birth to a baby that winter, which she named Jean-Baptiste. Eyes sparkling, Amber held tightly to the swaddled doll, acting perfectly the part of protective mother. Something inside of Brandon stirred. Her lines complete, she took her place next to Brandon while another actor stepped forward. With a quick glance at Brandon, Amber shot him the hint of a smile.

He returned it with one of his own and an approving nod. Her eyes shone much too brightly. And there it was again. That feeling in the pit of his stomach. He both hated and loved the way she affected him.

The short drama ended and the crowd dispersed.

"Great job, Amber!" Peter, who played the part of Lewis, squeezed her shoulder.

"You really think so?"

"Sure I do. Cindy will probably be back by tomorrow, but maybe we can find a way to fit you into the drama."

Brandon waited nearby, wanting to congratulate her on her efforts as well, but it looked like Lewis had designs on Sacagawea. That stung. But who was Brandon that he should interfere? Needing to head back to the museum, he stepped down the stairs carved from rock.

"Dr. Selman, wait." Amber rushed to his side. "I'm glad you asked me to do this. I enjoyed it. Thanks."

"You're welcome. I knew you'd be perfect." He continued down the steps.

Amber followed right behind. "What should I do now?"

"Excuse me?"

"We never got past the drama. What do you want me to do during Living History Week?"

Brandon wanted to smack his forehead. "You're right. I was so caught up in preparation...."

"You two made a great couple up there!" Muriel blocked their path while she snapped digital photos. "Let me get a picture of the happy couple."

Brandon bristled, trying to hide his irritation as he smiled for the camera. Muriel's playful teasing wouldn't have bothered him except the same errant thought had brushed his mind as well.

Once Muriel finished taking a couple of snapshots, Brandon distanced himself from Amber.

"If you'll excuse me, I have to get back to work. He smiled and turned to descend the steps.

"Hey, too bad the play didn't include a kiss between Sacagawea and her husband," Muriel said, softly.

"What are you—in junior high?"

Before Brandon was out of earshot, he'd heard Muriel, and now as he pressed through a group of teens, he could still hear Amber scolding her.

Was she merely shocked as well, or did the idea of kissing him really repulse her?

ten

"Sacagawea is one of the most honored women in American history. And that, ladies and gentlemen, ends our tour."

When no one in her group appeared to have questions, Amber rushed to the employee break room to grab a soda and a few minutes alone. Living History Week had filled her days with guided tours and answering questions about history. She rarely saw Dr. Selman except in passing, which was probably just as well.

She'd been mortified when Muriel had made her happy couple comments and wondered if Dr. Selman avoided her for that reason. Even if he wasn't avoiding her on purpose, though, the week had been too busy for words.

She put her coins into the vending machine. Nothing happened. Frustrated, she pounded the buttons and tried to shake the machine. It was no use. Too tired to remedy the problem, she slid into a chair.

Gladys entered the break room. "Can't say that I'll be upset when this week is over." She opened the fridge and grabbed a cola she'd brought. Noting Amber's empty hands, she tossed the cola to her. "Catch."

On reflex, Amber caught it. "Thanks. You're a lifesaver." The caffeine would give her a lift, especially with three more hours to go before closing.

"Think we'll make it through this week?" Gladys asked.

Amber swallowed a swig of the cool carbonation. "I hope—"

"Oh, I almost forgot." Gladys tugged a slip of paper from her pocket. "A call came into the museum store for you."

She pushed the paper across the table. Amber slid it the rest of the way and looked at the scribbled name and number.

Michael? He'd found her. Her stomach dropped as if she were on an amusement park ride. What did he want? She stared at the number. He wanted her to call him back.

"Are you all right, hon? You don't look well."

For a moment, Amber had forgotten the world around her. "I. . .uh. . .I've got to go." She rushed from the table, needing a quick exit.

Before she reached the door, Gladys called out. "Wait, Amber."

Amber leaned her forehead against the door, torn between waiting to hear what Gladys wanted and leaving. She needed to be alone. To think. "I really have to go."

"Hon, I'm worried about you."

Putting her back against the door, she faced Gladys. "I'm fine. Really."

"I've got a pot roast in the slow cooker. Why don't you come on over for dinner tonight. You look like you need a good meal. We don't need to wait until Living History Week is over." Gladys's eyes shone with concern, almost pleading.

Amber forced warmth into her smile. "Sure, that would be nice." She backed through the swinging door, resolving to come up with an excuse later.

She rushed from the museum and out into the open, gulping air filled with the scent of popcorn, cotton candy, and hot dogs. Walking along the edge of the grass, she neared the open field next to the temporary pop-up tents and canopies erected for Living History Week. Marching through the crowd, she crumpled the note with Michael's number.

Great. This was just great. He'd destroyed her life once. Why couldn't he just leave her alone? And if he were finally free, having served his time, would he stay away?

Please, God, just keep him away from me. She rubbed her arms, walking through the booths and exhibits, needing composure before returning from her break. A glance at her watch told her she should head back to the museum.

Later that evening, Amber towel-dried her hair after a

long, hot shower. Once her shift was over, she'd rushed from the museum, making certain she told Gladys she wasn't feeling well. Covering her face with the damp towel, she groaned.

Gladys was a wonderful, motherly type. Amber didn't want to hurt her. Maybe if Michael hadn't contacted her today, then she'd be able to enjoy dinner with Gladys. In fact, learning more about Gladys and keeping the conversation off Amber might even have been possible.

But Gladys could read Amber's mood, no matter how big the intern smiled. She'd want to know the reason for Amber's distress and the conversation would spiral out of control. No, it was best to call and cancel. Gladys had already put the pot roast on before she'd invited Amber, anyway.

"Amber," Muriel said through the door as she gave a light knock. "Gladys called. She asked how you were, and I told her fine. She gave her address and said to come over when you're finished getting dressed."

"What? You told her I was showering?"

"Uh, yeah? What would you have me tell her?"

That she wasn't feeling well would have been nice. Maybe she wasn't physically ill but she was mentally and emotionally distressed. "I don't know." She finished pulling on her shorts and T-shirt.

"Listen, the address looks pretty far. Do you want me to drop you off so you don't have to ride your bike?"

Amber swung the door open to face Muriel. She worked to keep the frustration from her expression. Muriel was interfering. First with Dr. Selman, embarrassing her at the drama, and now with Gladys. "Honestly, I had decided I wasn't going."

Muriel crossed her arms and slumped against the wall. "Well, that stinks. It's not every day a person gets to eat Gladys's pot roast."

A laugh escaped Amber's smirk as she pushed by Muriel, heading to her room. "What are you talking about?"

Muriel followed. "Nobody has invited *me* to eat pot roast. I can't cook one to save my life. What say, I come with you? Maybe you could say you didn't feel right leaving me behind?"

Amber tossed a pillow at her. "You're crazy, you know that?" She plopped on the bed. "All right, but as long as you promise to make sure the conversation never turns to my life as the main topic." She wasn't in the mood for full disclosure.

Pushing up on her elbows, she eyed Muriel, feeling as if she'd said too much, and given the look in Muriel's gaze? Oh yeah. . .way too much.

Amber tugged Josh from his cage and snuggled him. At least *he* didn't care that her brother was a criminal.

❧

Brandon's stomach rumbled as he pulled next to the curb at Gladys's home. He'd been putting off her invitation to dinner for weeks now. Just like he'd put off visiting his parents.

The truth? He was tired and could use a meal that didn't come from the freezer or out of a can. This week had gone smoothly and surpassed his hopes. If anything, he deserved to treat himself.

An image of Amber McKinsey in her Sacagawea garb, holding a baby, flashed before his eyes. Giving himself a moment, he leaned his head against the seatback. He thought about the young man who'd played the part of Lewis, appearing interested in Amber. Brandon had let it bother him too much, especially since he'd resolved Amber was off-limits. That he had to keep reminding himself was more than infuriating.

Opening his car door, Brandon sighed and slid from the seat. Standing on Gladys's porch, he knocked on the door and waited. Laughter drifted from inside the house. Familiar laughter. The door opened, allowing the sumptuous smell of simmering roast and vegetables to envelop him. He smiled.

"Dr. Selman, how good of you to come," Gladys said.

"Thank you for inviting me." He handed over the bottle of

sparkling cider he'd brought.

Gladys took it from him. "Oh, you didn't have to."

"It was my pleasure." Brandon listened to the voices emanating from elsewhere in the house.

"Make yourself comfortable. Dinner will be ready in a few."

"Do you have other guests?"

"Yes, I didn't think you'd mind. Two of my guests couldn't make it, but just as well. Amber brought her roommate along."

Amber. Gladys disappeared and, uncertain what to do, Brandon sank onto the sofa, growing more uncomfortable with each second. A twenty-four-hour news station played on the television set, though the sound was muted. He watched as he considered his options. Muriel, Amber's roommate, had read far too much into his visit to Amber the day she'd been injured. Then she'd suggested he and Amber made a happy couple at the reenactment. He'd never known such an outspoken person.

Brandon slumped against the sofa. If he were honest with himself—he was more wounded at Amber's horrified reaction than anything else. But these insane thoughts had to stop.

"Dr. Selman." Seemingly out of nowhere, Muriel sat next to him on the sofa. "I'm supposed to ask what you'd like to drink. Sparkling cider or tea, coffee, milk, water—"

"Water will be fine, thank you."

"Good. Why don't you wash your hands and go into the dining room?"

What was he doing here? Gladys had made it sound like days gone by, where on occasion she'd invite him over for a decent, yet private, meal.

Once he'd washed up, he strolled to the dining room, marveling that he had yet to see Amber. Covered with a country home vinyl tablecloth, the dining table was a lavish display of food, even for Gladys. Brandishing pot holders in each hand, she carried an oval turkey-sized dish laden with the roast, carrots, and potatoes.

On cue, his stomach grumbled. Amber appeared behind Gladys, carrying a large dish in each hand.

Brandon abandoned his position and rushed to her aid. "Here, let me help you." He took the green bean casserole from her, making sure to grip the potholder underneath. In the process, his hand touched hers.

"Why, thank you." She gazed at him—her eyes the very amber of her name.

"Dr. Selman," Gladys said, "you can set those here." She pointed where he could place the green beans.

Realizing he'd acted like a schoolboy, it shamed him to feel himself blushing. Grown men didn't blush.

"My, we're the absentminded professor tonight, aren't we?" Gladys winked.

The ladies took their seats, and Brandon followed, sitting where he was told. This wasn't the evening he wanted. He needed to relax, enjoy the meal, but at least two nosy women sat at the table, and Amber sat across from him.

Gladys asked him to say grace, which he did.

Once plates were loaded with food, everyone seemed too busy eating to talk much. Finally, Brandon broke the silence. "I think this is your best, Gladys." He let his fork rest against his plate for the moment.

"I'm not sure I've eaten anything this wonderful before," Amber said.

"I second that," Muriel said around a mouthful. "No, I mean I want seconds of that."

Laughter surrounded the table.

From the other end, Gladys beamed with pride. "You're all too good to me. You know, you're my family, really. I have my sister who lives up near Devil's Lake. She comes to see me on occasion. But that's it."

Her sentiments warmed Brandon's heart.

"Wait until you see what I made for dessert," she said, eyes teasing.

A cell phone rang. Amber frowned. "Excuse me. . . I thought

I turned it off." Snatching the phone from her pocket, she exited the dining room.

Gladys stood. "Dessert, you two?"

"Yes, please." Preoccupied with the frown he'd seen on Amber's face, he wasn't aware Muriel had spoken to him until she cleared her throat.

"Dr. Selman. You haven't heard a word I've said, have you?" She slid a few more carrots onto her plate.

"Forgive me, what did you say?" He stared at her plate, loaded with thirds or was it fourths?

"What? I love food, what can I say?"

"You must have a great metabolism."

Sticking another bite in her mouth, she chewed as she smiled, then swallowed. "What I was saying was, you should go check on Amber."

The idea had occurred to him, but she was Amber's roommate.

Seeming to read his mind, again, with a full mouth, she said, "Hello, I'm eating."

Brandon eyed Muriel. Though he didn't consider himself more important than anyone else, he knew that both Gladys and Jim insisted the volunteers address him with a title to ensure at least a modicum of respect. The corner of his mouth drew up. Muriel wasn't the least bit intimidated by him.

He liked that. "I'm sure she's fine. Probably chatting on her cell."

Muriel frowned and stopped chewing then shook her head as if she knew some dreadful, hidden secret.

Concern flooded him, but then he reasoned if it were true, Muriel would be the first to check on her. He'd pegged her as an overly concerned type the evening he'd spent at the cabin, talking to a medicated Amber. He sighed. What was taking Gladys so long with dessert? Maybe she had discovered what had become of Amber. He needed to excuse himself for the evening.

The front door slammed. Gladys called from the kitchen.

"Dr. Selman, can you find out who that was? Someone either came in or left. I'll have your dessert out in a jiff."

"See?" Muriel proceeded to scrape the last of the potatoes onto her plate. With larger than life eyes, she said, "I'm eating. Gladys asked you."

A niggle at the back of his mind suggested that Muriel was in cahoots with Gladys in an attempt to pair him with Amber. But he doubted Amber had left in a dramatic attempt for him to follow.

"If you'll excuse me, then." He left the table and exited the house through the front door. Amber was bent over the white railing that surrounded the small porch, looking like someone about to lose her supper.

Brandon rushed to her side. She was trembling. "Amber? Are you all right?"

She stiffened before turning to him. "Yes, everything is fine. I really have to go." Fleeing the porch, she jogged down the drive and into the street.

"Miss McKinsey, Amber, wait!" It was no use.

Brandon jumped in his car and started the engine, driving slowly on the neighborhood street. Street lamps illuminated her as she ran.

When he approached her, he opened the window. "What do you think you're doing?"

She stopped, catching her breath. "I know I must look like an idiot. I just want to go home."

"Hop in," he offered, though confused by her strange behavior.

She climbed into his car, looking wary.

"I can take you back to get your purse."

"I didn't bring one." She stared straight ahead.

"All right, then." Brandon phoned Gladys and explained that he was taking Amber home. To his surprise, she seemed more pleased than concerned.

He ended the call. "If you were that afraid of Gladys's dessert, all you had to say was, 'No, thank you.'"

His comment elicited at least a small laugh, but he noted the girl wasn't going to give up the information he wanted. "You want to talk about it? Who called that upset you?"

"Please, I. . .can't."

"Can't or won't?"

He drove in silence until he arrived at her cabin. Stopping the car, he turned to face her. She'd already opened the car door.

The dome light revealed her red-rimmed eyes. "Thank you for the ride. Look, I appreciate all you've done for me, allowing me the experience of working at your museum. It's important to me that you're pleased with my work. But, I need to keep my personal life. . .well. . .personal."

Brandon nodded. Amber shut the car door and jogged up the path to her dimly lit front door. He waited while she unlocked it and slipped into the cabin. Despite the fact that he'd not expressed an interest in her romantically, the cold stab of rejection threatened. Still, he knew that Amber McKinsey hadn't rejected him personally. Something or someone had upset her.

As he backed from the driveway, he wished that she didn't affect him. Wished that he could bury his concern. She'd drawn a line—one that should have been there to begin with.

eleven

Amber surveyed the group of fifteen children who participated in the museum's summer camp this week. In addition to the camp, Dr. Selman had worked to make the museum child friendly with interactive and hands-on exhibits. He'd incorporated live animals such as lizards, snakes, and turtles— all in appropriately contained environments in their respective exhibits, of course. The dinosaur exhibit included an area where children could don hard hats and dust sand from dinosaur fossil replicas.

His efforts revealed his obvious soft spot for the very young. The thought sent a tremble through Amber's heart. It also made her wonder if he'd ever married. But she didn't have much time to ponder the question.

Katie, a darling little girl with curly blond hair, held up a large sheet of paper covered in wet paint for Amber's approval.

"Oh, that's wonderful," Amber proclaimed.

Katie stuck her fingers into brown paint, expanding on her impression of a triceratops. So far, they'd spent the week learning about dinosaurs, doing arts and crafts, studying the exhibits. Amber even gave them a tour of the nearby digs—a day they'd enjoyed the most. The museum had created a safe path for young children, or those who simply wanted a glimpse of the prehistoric dig site. No actual digging for them.

She put a finger to her lips and smiled. That day had been her first time anywhere near the digs since Dr. Selman pulled her out. She missed it. In fact, she missed him. His company. She'd spent time working with him on the displays and then briefly participated in the Lewis and Clark drama with him.

Then, there'd been dinner at Gladys's home.

Amber recalled that night. After the crazy way she'd acted, she was surprised Dr. Selman hadn't sent her packing. But the museum had been exceptionally busy the last two weeks. They needed her help.

Hating her thoughts at the moment, she walked around the long table where the children concentrated on their art. When Muriel had made the silly reference to a kiss during the reenactment, though furious, Amber had guiltily imagined sharing a kiss with Dr. Selman. During the busyness of that week, she'd longed to see him and had been delighted when he showed up at Gladys's home. But then. . .she'd ruined everything because of her brother's call. He'd left her a voice mail that he was in town, now that he was out of prison, and he wanted to see her. How was she supposed to react to that news?

When she'd told Dr. Selman she wanted to keep her personal life to herself, her heart had screamed in defiance as she watched the hurt shimmer in his eyes.

And now, she couldn't get that image out of her mind.

If only there were a way. . .

"Now what do you think?" Six-year-old Andrew lifted his finger-painted stegosaurus.

"I think you're going to be a famous artist one day." Grateful she had the children's camp as a distraction, she tousled his hair.

He beamed with pride. "Can I take this home to my mom?"

"Of course you can. In fact, make sure you take all your creations home to show your parents what you've been up to this week."

She directed the children to begin cleaning up after themselves—a rule put in place from the beginning, thank goodness.

In her pocket, her cell vibrated, causing her pulse to race. It was sad when every phone call scared her. Tugging it from its snug hiding in her pocket, she looked at the number before answering.

"Cams!"

"Did I call at a bad time? I never know when you're working."

"I've got the museum's summer camp this week. This is the last day and we're cleaning up. I really can't talk now."

"No problem. Just wanted to find out how you're doing?" Cams's tone held subtle concern.

"What's wrong?" Amber tugged on her earlobe while watching the children. *Hurry, Cams.*

Cams sighed on the other end. "Have you heard from. . . Michael?"

The garbage can brimmed with paper and art scraps. Amber pressed the trash deeper, allowing the children to stuff more in. "Oh, Cams. How did you know?"

"He left a message here, looking for you. I arrived a few minutes ago and found it."

"Look, I know you never would have given me away, had you been there. Who do you think told him where to find me?"

"Considering you haven't told too many about your aversion to him, almost anyone could have told him where you are. My guess would be Dr. Young."

"I figured. He had no way of knowing." *And I plan to keep it that way.*

"What are you going to do? I'm worried about you."

"Keep ignoring his calls, maybe get a new number." *Hope he goes away.*

"Amber. Look, are you sure you shouldn't just talk to him? I mean, come on. He's your brother."

"That's mine!" Jonathan shouted at Greg.

"No, it's mine."

"Cams, I've really got to go. We'll talk later." She ended the call. "Boys, calm down."

❧

The next morning Amber awoke feeling grateful she had a day off. She stretched and rubbed her eyes then rolled to her side. Another half hour of sleep would be nice, especially if it kept her from thinking about all that had gone wrong. About her brother.

If she got out of bed now, she could go for her morning run, something she hadn't done in a couple of weeks. Funny how painful it could be to run, yet it made her feel great. All that oxygen pumping through her body energized her and lifted her mood. An image of colliding with Dr. Selman on her first run in Harrington came to mind. She groaned. Nope. Running would definitely not clear her mind today.

"Knock, knock," Muriel said, in a singsong voice. "Who's hungry this morning?" She waltzed into Amber's bedroom with a plate of pancakes and orange juice on a tray.

Amber pushed up on her elbows. "What are you doing?"

"I made breakfast. What does it look like?" Muriel set the tray next to Amber on the bed.

The pancakes smelled great. "Don't you have to work today?"

"No. We're off on the same day for once. It occurred to me this morning that we should do something together for fun. You seem like you could use some fun in your life."

"Gee, thanks."

"Don't thank me until you've heard what I have planned."

"Uh-oh. Better tell me now before I'm fully awake."

"Horseback riding."

Amber sat straight up. "What? You're crazy. I can't—"

"In the Badlands, Amber. You'll love it."

"I'm. . .afraid of horses."

"Have you ever ridden one?"

"Nope. And don't plan to."

"These are trained trail horses." Muriel sank to the bed next to the tray, careful not to tip the juice. "Look, Amber. You need to get out more. Please, do this with me?"

Why did Muriel care so much? Truth was, Amber could use a distraction. "Oh, all right." She grabbed the orange juice and jumped from the bed, taking a pancake with her as she headed to the bathroom for a shower.

Muriel laughed, following her down the hall. "We leave in an hour."

❧

"You sure you can handle this?" Jim asked, skimming the list of artifacts due to arrive next week. "I can reschedule my vacation if I need to."

"Come on. I don't need you to reschedule."

"It's not as if you have enough help. I wish we could hire more. At least we could bring in more volunteers."

Like Amber. Brandon frowned at the thought of her. He'd not been able to get her off his mind, or rid himself of concern for her, even after she'd drawn the strictest of lines. But she was a volunteer for the museum, a sister in Christ—shouldn't he be concerned? Nevertheless, he'd avoided her, telling the Lord that He'd have to give a sign if He wanted Brandon involved.

"I can handle it, Jim." Brandon toyed with a paperweight on Jim's desk. "Sounds more like you don't trust me to cover for you while you're gone."

"You know that's not true." Jim took the paperweight from Brandon and moved it to the credenza behind him.

Brandon laughed.

"You've been distracted lately. Might I suggest you have Miss McKinsey help you? Working under you is the main reason she signed on for the intern program. You've had her doing grunt work, nothing serious."

Earlier Jim had suggested Brandon dismiss Amber entirely. Brandon cocked his head. Could that be sign number one? No, he'd need more. "She's gaining experience in all aspects of the museum."

"Cataloging relics is part of that as well. I'd planned to have her help with that." Jim eyed him, arching his left brow. "Look, we've known each other a long time. What's really going on here? You kept her on and had me let Jason go instead, and now you don't want to use her where she's needed."

Brandon turned his back and walked to the door, then faced Jim again. "Yes, we *have* known each other for a while.

Which is why I don't understand your concern over who assists me, if anyone, in your absence."

With that, Brandon left. He tugged on his shirt collar, feeling a little guilty for his brusque response. Jim was only trying to help and yet Brandon had snapped at him simply because he didn't want to explain the odd rapport he had with Amber.

Today was supposed to be Brandon's day off, but Jim had called him in to discuss the arrival of the artifacts next week. Brandon hadn't exactly said that he *wouldn't* bring Amber in to help him, but after how she acted at dinner last week, Brandon wasn't sure working with her would be the best thing. He kept telling himself his concern was appropriate, but his feelings were anything but brotherly toward her.

Not good. Once in his office, he sank into his chair, put his feet on his desk, and leaned back. At least he admitted he *had* feelings. Still, he wasn't a professional if he denied her the opportunity because of his own weakness. He looked up the number at the cabin. He'd ask if she was willing to work with him on the Hamlin Exhibit, starting Monday.

Let *her* decide. If she didn't want the task, then he could work alone. Jim couldn't accuse him of avoiding Amber. And if she agreed, would that be sign number two? Brandon rubbed his chin. A simple phone call would give him the opportunity to ask her if she was all right. How she was doing. Never mind that he wanted to hear her voice.

He dialed the number. The phone rang twice. "Muriel here."

"This is Dr. Selman."

Quiet lingered on the line, then, "Hi. They need my help in the digs today?"

Now it was his turn to give pause. "Actually, I wonder if I could speak with Amber. . .er. . .Miss McKinsey."

"Amber isn't available."

A bad sign. "Please have her call me when she can."

"Okay. Are you working at the museum today?"

Brandon hadn't thought of that. "As a matter of fact, no. Have her call me on my cell." He relayed his number, cringing at the possible gossip that could arise. "I need to discuss a new assignment I have for her starting Monday."

"Got it. Would you mind if she calls back later today? We're going horseback riding in the Badlands, and we're running late. Hey, if you don't have plans, maybe you could join us. It's called Badland Adventures or something."

Could Muriel's invitation be sign number two?

"Thanks for the invitation, but I can't." Considering Amber wanted her personal and business life separate, he'd need more than Muriel's invitation.

"That's too bad. Because. . . ," Muriel fairly whispered, "I think she could use more friends."

At her words, his pulse pounded in his ears. Still, Brandon sighed at the news. "I'll keep that in mind." He ended the call. Ridiculous. No way would he show up at their outing.

Why had Muriel thrown a rock hammer into his thoughts? What had she meant? Most likely, nothing more than she said. Amber needed more friends. Except at Gladys's house, he'd had the funny idea that Muriel had attempted to pair him with Amber.

He rubbed his temples. He should have invited Amber to Bible study when he had the chance.

He considered himself an intelligent person and had the degrees to prove it. Yet even with all his education, he couldn't seem to figure out the right thing. He was attracted to this woman on many levels, and it was that attraction that kept him from thinking straight.

Her frazzled reaction after that one phone call had worried Brandon. Apparently Muriel was concerned as well. . . .

Okay, Lord, I'm taking that as the third sign. I need to get involved in her life. Personally.

"Whether she likes it or not."

twelve

Amber took a deep breath and smiled up at the clear, blue sky. She loved North Dakota weather in the summer. An hour ride into the Badlands would bring breathless views as well, so the guide had said.

"All right." Tom Snickett pointed at her as he led a large brown beast around. "You can have Blue."

But the horse is brown. And it looked to be twice as tall as Amber. "You want me to get on *that*?"

Another man brought a stool over and set it next to Blue while Tom held on to the reins. "Blue is one of our calmest. She won't do you wrong."

After a quick glare at Muriel who already sat astride a white horse called Black, Amber took a step. Despite her shaking knees, she forced herself to walk toward the horse. Tom lifted his hand, signaling Amber to stop.

"Try not to be afraid. Horses can sense fear."

Fantastic. If he wanted her to feel confident and douse the fear, he'd said the wrong thing.

"Chin up, chickadee." Muriel waved. "You can do this."

Amber tried to think of something else besides riding, and her thoughts landed smack on Dr. Selman. Not good. Her pulse hit high gear as she thought about his phone call. Muriel had said he wanted to speak to her. On the drive over, she dialed his cell. Getting no answer, she left a message.

Tom still stood waiting, so Amber shifted her focus to the horse.

"Okay." Tom held the reins at Blue's head. "Grab hold of the saddle horn with your left hand."

Amber stood on the stool, grateful she didn't have to figure out a way to haul herself up the side of the living mountain and somehow sling her right leg over the beast's back. She grabbed the saddle horn and stuck her left foot in the stirrup. So far so good.

"Now grab the back of the saddle with your right hand, put your weight on the ball of your left foot, then sling your right leg over the horse."

She could do this. Amber bit her lip. Hands on the saddle. Push on the left foot. Right leg over, swivel.

Once her right foot found the other stirrup, she released a sigh.

Tom lifted his hat and handed her the reins.

"Nothing to it," she said.

"Hold the reins in one hand. When you're going left, pull the reins a little toward the left side of Blue's neck. Going right, pull to the right. Not too hard, though. Blue knows the drill."

"Got it." Piece of cake.

Amber drew a long, shaky breath, keenly aware of every little movement and twitch of the horse beneath her. She wasn't sure how many riders were ahead of her in the line, or behind her for that matter, but she counted seven that she could see before the rest disappeared into the tree-shrouded trail. When the line began moving, her horse fell into step by rote, and Amber rocked with the rhythmic movement that was Blue. After a while, Amber began to relax. This wasn't bad. Not bad at all.

Though she'd mastered her anxiety over the horse, for now at least, her emotions were anything but calm as she considered Dr. Selman. He'd never called her about work before.

Again, her last words to him played over in her mind, torturing her. *"I need to keep my personal life. . .personal."* Oh, how she wished the words weren't true. That she'd never said them. How she wished she didn't have to keep to herself—especially where Dr. Selman was concerned—for fear someone would find out the awful truth.

Muriel rode Black directly in front of her and turned her head to peer at Amber. "How you doing?" she asked, while smacking her lips.

"Hey, no fair, where'd you get the gum?"

"I'd toss you a piece but you might fall off trying to catch it." Muriel's eyes grew wide as she peered past Amber. "Oh, my. . ."

Fear squeezed her chest. She took a glimpse behind her, seeing nothing unusual. "What is it?"

Muriel turned her back to Amber once again, her shoulders bouncing up and down in laughter.

"You'd better tell me right now before I spear this horse forward right next to you."

"You mean spur? Considering you're not wearing spurs, maybe a gentle nudge would be better," Muriel called over her shoulder.

"Whatever. Now, please, what did you see?" The trail began to incline and Amber leaned into Blue in order to keep her balance.

"Remember who called earlier? Did I mention I invited him to go riding today?"

"Uh. . .no." What did that have to do with what Muriel had seen?

Amber gave a quick glance behind her but couldn't see beyond the few riders following her. She had a difficult time believing Dr. Selman would spend his morning on a horseback ride. Then again, *she* was. To Amber, he seemed like the sort of person who had important things to do. Far more important than this.

Muriel's words came back to her. *"I think Dr. Selman might have a thing for you."* Amber's palms grew sweaty. Could it be true? She stroked the horse's mane absently. She couldn't believe he was interested. Not really. Any interest he expressed was purely out of concern for her as an intern at the museum, and she'd already squashed his intervention into her personal life.

No, Dr. Selman wasn't interested in Amber. And even if he

were it would all blow away like the dust once he found out about her brother.

❧

Somehow while sitting in his office, thinking over his concerns for Amber, Brandon had convinced himself that he needed to butt in to her life. When Muriel mentioned horseback riding, of course Brandon had brushed it off as ridiculous. And now, sitting on the back of a horse, his memory was a bit fuzzy. All his well thought out reasons for being here now seemed contrived.

He'd known Tom Snickett for years, and once Brandon made the decision, the deed was as good as done.

He considered his teaching at the previous Wednesday night's Bible study regarding the apostle Paul. Brandon wished he could teach it again next week, considering he now better understood what the apostle had meant when he said he knew the right thing to do but he did the wrong instead.

Brandon shouldn't be here. Yet here he was.

Why couldn't he have seen this clearly before? He had no right to insert himself into Amber's personal life. Never mind that her roommate had encouraged him. A sour taste formed in his mouth. Even without Muriel's whispered encouragement, Brandon would have found a way to interrupt Amber's day. To make sure she was all right. A week of avoiding her hadn't diminished his concern.

The only good news was that he was at the end of the line. He could turn his horse around and head back without anyone being the wiser. He'd taken Tom's ride before and knew the trail would soon open up to a field where the riders had more freedom. Amber would see him then if she hadn't already—that is, if he didn't turn around now.

He reined the horse out of line but had only ridden a few feet when he heard Tom's familiar voice behind him.

"Where do you think you're going?"

Brandon smiled. "I remembered something I need to do."

Tom caught up with Brandon, and they stopped.

"On a day like this? You don't want to miss the view now, do you?" Tom asked.

How could he get out of this? Gladys was right. He really was an absentminded professor, or rather, museum director.

At least...where Amber McKinsey was concerned.

"I guess what I needed to do can wait." Brandon followed Tom at the end of the line.

The trailhead opened up to a meadow where the riders were allowed to break the line as they headed to the other side. There they would tether the horses and hike a few yards through the trees until they came to a high bluff, offering a scenic viewpoint of the rough terrain of the Little Missouri River Badlands.

"I always get nervous at this part." Brandon drew his horse to a stop.

"Is that so?"

"Seems to me you'd get nervous, too, giving these in-experienced riders this much freedom."

"You worry too much, Doc. These horses are gentle. Besides they all know to follow Kevin's lead."

"If you say so."

Tom grinned, then urged his horse into a lope, leaving Brandon who studied the trail behind him, considering his options.

"Dr. Selman! You decided to come."

At the familiar voice, he turned to see Muriel riding up to him.

"Of course I came. What you said worried me."

Muriel's smile seemed to say she held a big secret. "I'm sure you needed some sunshine, too."

"It's a beautiful day."

"Amber isn't too good on a horse. I probably shouldn't have left her."

In his opinion, the riders should have been kept in a tight single-file line for the entire trail ride. Leave it to Tom to be creative. His trail ride was the most popular.

Brandon followed Muriel up the line and then he spotted

Amber as several riders spread out to give her space. Her horse appeared skittish, tossing its head. Amber made matters worse by tugging on the reins and kicking the horse with her heels, sending mixed signals.

Kevin and Tom were ahead, their backs to the group. Talking, they were completely unaware of Amber's predicament. When her horse bolted, Brandon kicked his into a canter, coming alongside Amber. The horse was spooked, but worse, so was Amber. Eyes wide, she clearly didn't know what to do.

Reaching across the distance between them, he grabbed her reins and brought both horses to a halt. He calmed the horse with soothing tones. Trembling and gasping for breath, Amber placed her hand on her chest.

She gazed over at Brandon, looking sheepish. "Thanks. I don't know what happened. The horse just got scared. I didn't know what to—"

"It's okay. Not everyone is experienced with horses." He grinned, hoping to inject humor into his comment. "I have an idea. Why don't we walk?"

"Huh?"

"Tom will have us tether the horses up ahead. Let's walk the rest of the way. I'll lead the horses."

Amber offered a timid smile and nodded her agreement. Brandon hopped off his horse then helped Amber off hers.

Brandon and Amber walked side by side, while Brandon held both horses' reins, leading them through the meadow. Even though they walked in silence, it was a comfortable quiet. Being next to her like this felt natural and—as he watched the soft breeze lift a few strands of her dark hair—it felt right.

"Dr. Selman, I want to apologize for what I said the night you took me home from Gladys's."

"There's no need, really. I understand. You didn't want to tell me what upset you."

She looked down, her hair swinging forward to hide her face. "It seems like every time something bad happens, you're there."

Brandon felt as if she'd struck him. What was she saying? He recalled that he'd knocked her over when they'd first met, colliding on their jog.

Eyes wide, she looked up at him. "No, that didn't come out right. I keep having trouble, and you keep being at the wrong place at the wrong time."

"Or maybe it's the right place at the right time."

She smiled gently. "Don't get me wrong. I'm grateful you've been there. I'm embarrassed, that's all. I wish you could somehow know a different side of me."

I'd love to. But he kept the errant thought to himself. "I'm just glad I could be of assistance."

"Is that why you're here today?"

"What? A man can't go horseback riding?"

That elicited a snicker. "Sure he can. I don't mean to suggest that you're here for me. It's just that Muriel told me she invited you."

Now it was Brandon's turn to be embarrassed. "Honestly, I've been concerned about you ever since that night when you were upset. I wanted to make sure you were okay."

They approached the tethering line—a rope tied between two trees. Brandon grinned and offered Blue's reins to Amber.

Looking anything but thrilled, she gave a half laugh then reached for them. Her soft fingers swept over his skin, stirring a longing inside him. He focused on the others who were already hiking the trail to the viewpoint.

"Thank you for your concern. It means a lot to me that you would go out of your way."

How could he tell her that it was no trouble at all? He inhaled the crisp air. "Would you like to come to Bible study this Wednesday?"

"Sure, I'd like that."

Warmth buzzed around in Brandon's chest where it had no right to buzz. She was his sister in Christ and an intern at the museum and. . .his protégé.

"There you are. You guys are going to miss the view if you

don't hurry." Muriel walked alongside them, appearing out of nowhere. That seemed to be her modus operandi.

"Did you tell Amber about the new assignment?"

Drawing a blank, Brandon stared at Muriel.

"You know—the reason you called today." Muriel's smile irritated Brandon. She started up the narrow trail, leading the way.

Brandon felt like an idiot. Following behind Amber as they made their way to the viewpoint, he noticed her slight form. He liked her runner's physique.

"What's the new assignment?" she asked.

Ah, yes, the phone call that had led to trail riding with Amber. "We've a shipment arriving next week—the Hamlin Exhibit on loan. I'm hoping you'll assist me with receiving the collection and cataloging the artifacts."

She stopped and turned to face him. "Really?" Her smile beamed and her eyes brimmed with joy. "Helping you with artifacts, working alongside you—it's the sort of experience I came here to do. I'd feel like a real professional."

She turned away to continue the hike.

Grand. While she might feel like a professional working beside him, beside her. . .he felt anything but.

thirteen

"Good morning, Gladys." Amber stepped through the doorway of the gift store and smiled at Gladys as the woman prepared to open her register for the day.

"Don't you look happy this morning." She stepped from behind the counter to hug Amber.

Gladys was so good to her. "I feel rested." Amber thought back to the horseback ride. Dr. Selman had come to her rescue. Again.

Did she actually *need* rescuing? She wasn't sure. All she knew was that he'd endeared himself to her, deepening what would otherwise be a strong crush.

Though she'd been timid about sitting on a horse, especially when Blue decided she had a mind of her own, Dr. Selman had been there to calm the beast and more. . .he calmed Amber's racing heart.

Gladys cleared her throat, bringing Amber back from her musings. "Looks like you feel more than rested, hon. You're fairly glowing."

Amber played with the dinosaur paraphernalia on the counter. "I went on a trail ride and saw a spectacular view." Muriel had been right about Amber enjoying the trail ride through the Badlands. But Amber knew the experience was even more memorable because Dr. Selman had shared it with her. He'd sounded eager to convey his knowledge of the Badlands with her. She could still hear the enthusiasm in his voice.

"And where will you work this week?"

"Dr. Selman asked me to assist him with the new artifacts."

Gladys lowered her glasses to peer at Amber. "I see."

The look Gladys gave was disconcerting. Was Amber's

admiration for Dr. Selman so obvious? "It's what I'm here to do, don't you know? Not crafts with children or playacting the part of Sacagawea."

"Why so defensive?"

Amber sighed. "I'm sorry."

Gladys returned her attention to opening the register. "I'm the one who's sorry, hon. You were happy when you came through the door, now I've ruined it."

"Oh, Gladys, don't let my disposition upset you. I'm just ready to be involved in serious work, that's all. Please, don't get me wrong; I enjoyed working with the children and participating in the drama, too."

The cash register drawer opened. Gladys began counting her bills. "Care to come over for dinner tonight?"

Amber almost laughed. Gladys appeared to be using Amber's guilt against her, coaxing her to dinner. "I'd love to. I didn't get to try your dessert. Is it as good as your pot roast?" In truth, she'd wanted to make up for skipping out. "Maybe I can even do the dishes for you this time."

"Are you saying Muriel didn't rave about my strawberry-rhubarb pie?" Gladys was now counting her pennies.

"Rave about it? I couldn't get her to shut up." Amber joined in Gladys's laughter, happy she'd turned the tension around.

"Tonight then. I look forward to hearing about your day off." The look in Gladys's eyes said she knew more about Amber's experience than she'd told her.

Uh-oh. "As a matter of fact I'd better get to work, too." She needed to douse her emotions where Dr. Selman was concerned.

She didn't dare ruin this opportunity. Her time here, working under Dr. Selman would be important when listing her experience on her résumé or curriculum vitae. And maybe, just maybe. . .she could get into a good grad school and finally make a break from the past.

Shaking Michael from her thoughts, she focused once again on Dr. Selman. Though she was happy he'd chosen to join her on the trail ride, his appearance more than confused her. Then, he'd invited her to his Bible study. With the way she acted around him, he probably considered her a broken fossil in need of repair. In that case, he'd better have a big bottle of glue.

In the ladies' room, she composed herself, brushing her hair back to make sure it was smooth and shiny. *Stop it.* His concern was that of her mentor and a fellow Christian—they shared that commonality, unusual especially in this field. It was nothing more.

Keeping that in mind, she could stay focused on her work. This was an opportunity to crawl from the deep hole Michael had dug for them both. Chin up, Amber pushed through the glass door into the climate-controlled room where they received collections. Wearing gloves, Dr. Selman looked up from the pottery he studied.

"There you are. You're just in time."

Amber let her backpack slide to the floor next to the wall. "What is it?" She moved next to him.

"You're looking at a Hisatsinom pot, AD 600"

Amber angled her head in question.

"The cliff dwellers of the Southwest. They're also called Anasazi, the ancestors of the Hopi."

"I'm vaguely familiar with them."

"They were basket makers but eventually made pottery. This is an early grayware piece with black on red designs. Later, they used more colors. Their artifacts are the best preserved. The Hamlin Exhibit, particularly valuable."

Dr. Selman's gaze shifted to Amber's face. "They've made a new discovery in the Hell Creek Formation."

"Of pottery?"

He chuckled. "No. What looks to be a complete triceratops."

Amber straightened at the news, wishing she could have been there, wishing her time in the dinosaur digs hadn't been so short. But. . .why was he telling her this? She realized he was studying her. Was he giving her a choice? Waiting on her to make a decision? She had the strong feeling that he wanted to know where her heart truly lay.

If only *she* knew.

His left brow arched. "I'm offering you an opportunity, Amber, if you want it."

Unsure which opportunity he meant, she considered his words. She thought of Muriel, who was sure now she wanted to study paleontology. Still, working at a new dig site would certainly mean Amber wouldn't be with Dr. Selman. "I'm here to learn everything you want to teach me."

He nodded, appearing to approve of her response. "The fossils will be brought here to study, of course. You can see them then."

"I'm looking forward to it."

He smiled. "We'll be examining each of the artifacts for preexisting damage. I'll show you what to look for. Then each item must be cataloged on the computer."

"I'm here to help," she said and studied the pot, though she could feel his gaze on her.

"Wait until you see how painfully time consuming the job can be."

"Hopefully, I won't let you down."

He placed the artifact into a specially designed box lined with Ethafoam. "In a larger museum you wouldn't be doing this without extensive knowledge of this time period. I'm here to assist you with that, considering I've broadened my education to include historical artifacts to accommodate the cultural side of the museum."

This time, Amber met his gaze. "But. . .you still love fossils, right?"

"Always." He slipped into his familiar half grin, producing that long dimple in his right cheek.

She loved his grin. Loved it.

❧

The way she smiled back at him. . .

Brandon chuckled. Was it a nervous reaction or his hopeless

attempt to shake the effect her liquid gold eyes had on him? Not only was she strikingly beautiful, she was highly intelligent. And when they'd worked on the dioramas for Living History Week, he'd admired her passion. Though there was no doubt he needed her help, his motivation went far deeper than how much she would ease his workload, cataloging the artifacts.

Working with her like this would be difficult.

Brandon explained that a digital image of each artifact was uploaded to the computer; then all cataloging information was entered, including where the artifact would be stored or exhibited within the museum. "We'll store these artifacts until we're ready to display them. And make certain that you catalog before you store."

Amber's eyes grew wide. "I can see that would be disastrous."

He chuckled. "No kidding. It took us weeks to locate an artifact that had been stored before cataloging. The volunteer stored the item then forgot to enter its location. Catastrophic for a museum."

"I can only imagine if the Smithsonian didn't keep good records—how would they ever find anything?"

At the computer, he stood behind her and peered over her shoulder as he directed her through the various components of the process. "Once you get the hang of it, it's really nothing more than data entry."

"When you put it that way, it's not something that would sound good on a résumé."

"Ah. We'll make certain your experience here shines." He shot her a grin.

Her attention focused on the computer screen, Brandon watched her, wishing he had more control over his mind. An unwelcome thought continued to accost him—he wanted Amber to give him a sign that he meant something more to her.

But Amber was young, vibrant, and beautiful. How could she think of him as anything but her mentor? Yet he'd battled thoughts of her from the moment they'd collided, and clearly, no amount of professionalism on his part would change his growing feelings for her.

Thankfully, Amber was a quick learner, freeing Brandon from hovering over her shoulder, tortured with smelling her floral-scented hair. He moved to a table at the other side of the room where he gently removed artifacts from their protective boxes, examined and cataloged them. A comfortable silence filled the room, and they spoke only when necessary.

Focusing on the computer screen, he decided he was more than pleased with the PastPerfect museum software they'd purchased six months ago. He was searching the exhibit items on loan entered so far when Amber's voice gently broke through his concentration.

"Dr. Selman."

Completing the search, he turned on the stool to face her. "What's up?"

"I'm not sure about this one. Would you mind letting me know what you think?" Brandon walked across the room to where she waited.

Her expression told him she was completely involved in the work, her mind absorbing everything like a sponge. Brandon liked to see that sort of devotion.

"This is the first damaged artifact I've had. See the edge here. How do I know if it was discovered that way, or damaged during the shipment?"

"Let's see." He ran a finger over the jagged edge of the pottery. "This doesn't appear to be new. Describe the damage and, along with the digital image, that should be enough."

Amber finished cataloging the item then placed it gently back into the protective box. She moved from the stool, stirring the scent of her perfume around him.

Near the end of the day, Brandon found himself exhausted from the wearisome tasks of cataloging.

Amber yawned from across the room. "Excuse me."

Brandon laughed. "This is definitely tedious, no question there."

"Honestly, I think I'm a field girl, when all is said and done." She covered her mouth, yawning again.

"Careful now. You know that's contagious." Brandon felt a yawn coming on as well.

"I'm so sorry. Please don't think I'm not happy to do this."

Each item took time to evaluate. However, that wasn't Brandon's problem. Could he work next to Amber for that long and keep his distance?

"You know, it could take us the rest of this week, if not two, to make it through this shipment."

She flashed him a broad smile. A beautiful smile.

"Are you saying you're willing to grin and bear it?"

"You know me too well already." A soft laugh escaped before she returned her attention to the computer screen.

In fact, he knew nothing much about her. And it was best to keep things that way. Her back to him, her shiny black hair hung past her shoulders. Was it possible to get to know her better without compromising all he'd worked for?

By Wednesday, they'd cataloged at least half the first crate he'd opened and placed the items in a climate-controlled storage room. Once they'd secured the artifacts, Brandon was ready to stop for the day; but he remembered the box of special items that had arrived earlier that morning. He mulled over whether he should open it now or wait for tomorrow.

Amber looked tired as she waited for his instructions. Considering it was nearly five o'clock, he should send her home; but he wanted her company if only for a bit longer.

He popped the crate open and dug through the packing. "Aha."

"What is it?" Amber was at his side, looking anxiously into the crate.

He liked that she seemed to always be ready for more. And he liked the feeling of her next to him, working with him.

Gently, he removed the shoe-sized box from the crate. Donning his gloves again, he pulled a beautiful pot from the foam-lined box. "This is one of the most valuable items in this exhibit. Here, you can hold it."

She pulled on her gloves, too, and took it from him, cradling yet another piece of pottery in her hands—but one of great value.

Looking at him, her golden eyes were wide and searching. In them he saw the usual admiration typical of a protégé, but there was something else. What was it?

Before he could react, the artifact slipped from her hands. Falling to the floor, it shattered. Colorful shards of clay pottery lay spread across the floor.

fourteen

Mortified, Amber stood frozen, staring at the floor. Broken pieces of pottery lay at her feet. Shock resounded through her bones. Seconds ticked by as her mind grappled with what happened.

Struggling to breathe, she finally lifted her gaze to meet Dr. Selman's. His expression reflected her own—one of dismay.

"Dr. Selman. . ." Her words came out strained. "I. . .I don't know what to say. I'm so sorry."

Amber turned her back on him and moved to the table where she'd spent most of the day. Knees shaking, she leaned against it for support.

Her eyes burned. Somehow she had to compose herself, be professional. Standing tall, she drew in a breath but it was too late. She couldn't face Dr. Selman. What would she see in his eyes? A stern expression? Would she hear reproof? What if he released her as an intern?

Hands squeezed her arms then gently turned her.

He pulled her to him, tucking her gently against his shoulder. "It was just a silly clay pot."

What? He didn't mean that, did he? What was he doing, holding her like this? It felt. . .nice. Suddenly she remembered crying in his arms the night she'd been hurt, she remembered how she felt then—safe. But this wasn't right. She couldn't—no, shouldn't—get too comfortable.

Finally, he released her and she peered into his eyes, still wary of what she'd find there. Concern flooded his gaze. He squeezed her arms again. "Amber. Are you all right?"

What could she say—that she felt much better after he'd held and comforted her? She frowned. "Of course I'm not.

How could I be?"

"Yes. . ." Dr. Selman quirked a brow. Releasing her, he pressed his clasped hands to his mouth as he looked at the scattered pieces on the floor. Dropping his hands to his side, he continued. "These things happen. You're not the first person to drop an artifact."

"I can't tell you how sorry I am."

His attention came back to her. She'd never fallen under such scrutiny before. He opened his mouth to speak, then without saying a word, closed it again as he began pacing, careful to avoid the shattered pot. What was going through that mind of his?

As he paced, she couldn't help but think about the way he'd held her. Strong, yet gentle. She shouldn't feel anything for this man. She hardly knew him. But there it was, she cared deeply for him. And her attraction to him? She shouldn't even think about it. The way he'd held her—could he possibly feel the same way?

A nervous excitement took hold, causing her jaw to quiver. Her knees trembled and once again, she used the work table for support.

At that moment, Dr. Selman looked directly into her eyes. "Miss McKinsey."

Oh, no. He'd used her last name. This was it.

He cleared his throat. "Amber. . .I've been troubled since that night I took you home. I can't help but believe there's something more going on, and that's why you're on edge. Why else would you react the way you did over the shattered artifact?"

"Why wouldn't I be upset? You just explained to me how important it was; then I let it slip from my fingers."

With a slight shake to his head, he averted his gaze.

"You don't believe me."

Pursing his lips, he looked at her. "It's none of my business. Not really."

Amber blew out a breath. Had she allowed her secret to

burden her so much, that she'd overreacted? Dr. Selman certainly seemed to think so.

He strolled closer. "Amber, please, I want to help if I can."

"I don't think there's anything you can do. Besides, it's not something I like to share."

"I understand." He nodded and left her for the broom closet. "I'd better clean up this mess."

He returned with the broom but set it aside. "How about I share a secret with *you*?" He winked then crouched to carefully retrieve the larger pieces. "The artifact you dropped was only a replica."

A replica? "You mean it wasn't even real? Then why did you let me think it was? And what about the artifacts we cataloged today?"

"It wasn't my intention to deceive you. I simply wanted to find out if, after handling the genuine items today, you could tell the difference. Your reaction was answer enough."

Still, he could have told her afterward.

"Amber."

She tugged her gaze from the pottery on the floor to his regret-filled eyes.

"I had planned to tell you. But for the time being, please keep the existence of the replicas to yourself, all right?"

She nodded, thinking about the secret she kept from him. He'd just shared one with her. Then. . .she would share hers with him. Like he'd used the replica, she would use her news to determine if he was genuine and worth the growing affection for him she harbored.

"I give."

Dr. Selman stopped sweeping and met her gaze. "Okay?"

Once she'd told him her secret, she suspected he would look at her differently. Everyone always did. "It's my brother. He recently got out of prison. He knows where I live and work." *And I don't want to see him again.*

༄

Utterly speechless, Brandon took a step back and absorbed

the words slowly. She had a brother who'd spent time in prison? And worse—he'd located Amber, who apparently didn't want contact with him. Brandon had asked, hadn't he? Offered to help if he could. He'd seen enough in his own life that he'd been arrogant in thinking she could throw nothing at him he hadn't experienced himself.

But this? This was something new. He squeezed the broomstick.

Amber appeared stricken. Brandon would have to tread carefully. He didn't want to upset her with his reaction.

To his surprise, she thrust out her chin. "You weren't expecting that, were you?"

"Honestly?" Brandon's breath caught as he searched for the words. "No. But I'm glad you told me. It was your brother who called you that night at Gladys's?"

"Yes." Amber put her hand on the broomstick, covering his hand. "Let me do this."

Her hand lingered over his. He'd wanted to know if his feelings were merely one sided. Was she finally letting him know they weren't? He released the broom to her and moved to stare at his computer, oblivious to the words on the screen. Her comment that he knew where she lived and worked made it sound like she was afraid.

Brandon grimaced. What did this mean for her?

An unwelcome thought accosted him, and he couldn't ignore it. Could such a thing have any impact on the museum? Especially since it was on the verge of applying for full accreditation.

Brandon himself was only beginning to stabilize his career. With the news she'd just shared, even if he hadn't allowed himself to care for her, could he afford to keep Amber McKinsey? Still, she wasn't her brother and, as far as Brandon knew, had committed no crime. Yet more than Brandon's personal feelings for this girl were at stake. There was Jim to consider. He'd been displeased that Brandon had requested Jason's termination and had certainly blamed

Amber. Then today she'd broken what, as far as Jim would know, was an actual artifact. And now, she had a brother who had served time in prison. Swiping a hand down his face, Brandon shoved the thoughts aside. He was overanalyzing, overreacting as usual.

While he tried to bury those feelings, he reminded himself that he'd asked her about her troubles. No matter what, Brandon would follow through on his offer to help.

"Amber, is your brother a danger to you? Is that why you don't want to talk to him?"

"No, it's not that."

He touched the sleeve of her soft blue shirt. "I'm concerned for you. Promise me you're telling the truth."

She stopped sweeping and peered at him. After a long pause, she swallowed. "I promise he's—"

Brandon's cell interrupted her. The disruption annoyed him, especially since she was most likely on the verge of telling him everything.

He tossed her an apologetic look. "Give me a sec?"

A glance told him it was one of the museum's potential donors—the call couldn't wait. He had a feeling this could take a while.

To Amber, he said, "I've got to take this. Would you mind locking up when you're finished?"

fifteen

"I want to know what happened five years ago."

The words from the phone call squeezed him like a vise as he drove home. His mind muddled with problems, he drove into the center of an intersection before he realized the light was red.

Uh-oh.

Too late to slow down. Brandon stepped on the gas, pushing all the way through the intersection while looking both ways.

Honk. Tires squealed. A blue minivan careened toward him. Brandon sped up to clear the path for the van. In his mirror, he watched the vehicle barely miss him as it skidded to a stop midintersection.

He'd already cleared the intersection himself and watched the minivan begin moving then continue through. Accident avoided. No harm done.

"Schew." He sagged in relief. *Thank You, Lord.*

A close call. Hoping to make it home alive tonight, he focused on the road ahead.

Flashing red and blue lights in his rearview mirror drew his attention. "This is just the vanilla ice cream on my blueberry pie," he said, and slowed, pulling to the side of the road.

Minutes later, Brandon sat in his car, waiting for the policewoman to finish writing on her pad.

She handed him the ticket. "Drive carefully."

"Thank you, officer." Brandon smiled and grimly pushed the button to shut his window. What a day.

His thoughts clouded, he'd been focused on anything but the intersection. Skidding breaks and a near miss had scared the living daylights out of him. Heart still racing, Brandon drove home and pulled into his driveway.

He trudged into the house and tossed his keys on the table then pulled out a frozen salmon fillet to thaw. Settling in his favorite chair, he thought about Ray Stockholm's question again. He wanted details about Brandon's previous endeavor with a museum. Brandon agreed to meet him for dinner tomorrow evening.

Would he ever escape all that had gone wrong? All his mistakes? And if that weren't enough, he had the strange feeling he'd walked into a field laden with land mines where Amber McKinsey was concerned. She promised, though, that she was in no danger from her brother.

Everything needed to run smoothly. Over the last several weeks, there had been a few incidents. Jim had pointed out that Amber didn't fit well in the environment, causing more problems than she helped solve as a volunteer. Brandon scratched his jaw. Jim was getting more difficult to read, patient with Jason's blunders—though serious in Brandon's opinion—yet intolerant of Amber.

Had Brandon not decided to mentor her after all, then Amber's fate would rest in Jim's hands alone. Brandon had stood up for her. And despite his rule to steer clear of protégés, he'd acquired one anyway. He believed in her. But he was the museum director, and his decisions had to have merit, avoiding the appearance of misconduct. He sagged at the thought, feeling as though he was already failing miserably.

Again.

Closing his eyes, he imagined her in his arms. It felt like she was meant to be there. But was he blinded by his emotions? Was he weak when it came to Amber?

He rose from the chair and prepared his evening meal.

"Lord, show me what to do."

While his salmon sizzled on the small indoor grill, Brandon checked his e-mail and found a note from his colleague Dr. Young at UND, waiting for him.

How's my star student, Amber McKinsey? I saw promise

*in her and she needed a mentor. You have too much to offer
and shouldn't keep it to yourself. Still considering teaching?*

Brandon skimmed the note, vaguely aware that his salmon
was burning.

Troubled, tonight was the first time he wanted to skip his
Wednesday night Bible study. Then he remembered—he'd
invited Amber. Would she be there?

&

Amber rolled over, stunned awake by the alarm clock. Six
thirty. She'd taken a short nap after work. Dr. Selman's Bible
study started in thirty minutes. She wove her fingers through
her hair and tugged. What was she thinking? Did she really
want to go?

Part of her didn't feel like facing him at the moment. He'd
had to rush away due to his phone call while she'd cleaned
and locked up like a good intern.

To think she'd told him everything about her brother—
well, almost everything.

She should thank the Lord for that—but she wasn't sure where
she stood with Him. He could have kept her brother away—that
would have gone a long way in helping her to get on with her life.
She sat up. If she were going to Bible study, she should start now.
It would take ten minutes to get there on her bike.

Scrambling into the bathroom, she brushed her teeth while
examining her bloodshot eyes. Toothbrush still hanging from
her mouth, she slumped. She really shouldn't go anywhere
looking this way. People could see she'd been crying. Muriel
had some eyedrops somewhere. Amber searched through the
medicine cabinet, knocking toiletries everywhere.

Muriel stood behind her. "What are you doing?"

Amber spit toothpaste into the sink and rinsed out her
mouth. "I've got to go, and I wanted to borrow your eyedrops."

"All you have to do is say please."

In her most respectful, pleasing voice Amber obliged.
"Please?"

Muriel squeezed by to look in the cabinet and drawers. "Oh, good grief. Look at your eyes, chickadee. What have you been crying over today?"

"You make it sound like I cry every day."

Muriel quirked a brow and thrust the eyedrops at Amber. "Keep it."

"Thank you, but I couldn't do that."

"You think I want it back now? Ever heard of germs?" Muriel smiled and left.

Well, when you put it like that. Amber finished freshening up. She grabbed her Bible from the side table and jammed it into her backpack then exited the cabin and hopped on her bike. Ten minutes until seven. She'd make it just in time.

The crisp air felt good against her face. Riding her bike had always been therapeutic to her—just like running. Lately though, she'd have to run a marathon a day to get the therapy she needed.

She rode her bike straight through an intersection without having to stop. If she kept this up, she'd be there early. Then she turned right into a neighborhood. Dr. Selman's little church, Harrington Christian Fellowship, was nestled in this subdivision off Cheshire Street; but the Bible study actually took place at someone's home across the street, so he'd said.

Her phone vibrated in her pocket. She hoped it wasn't her brother, but honestly, he was the only one calling her lately. Maybe that's why she'd decided to go to Bible study—she needed God to help her through this even though she blamed Him for it.

"Why, God? Why did You leave me alone in the world with only a criminal brother to care?"

The house across the street from the church was a cute pinkish color with groomed bushes. Several cars lined the driveway and curbside. Parking her bike near the porch, she tugged the cell from her pocket, ignoring her fear that it could be Michael. It might be Cams.

A text message from Michael stared back.

I NEED YOUR FORGIVENESS. PLEASE, CAN WE MEET?

sixteen

Amber's feet were glued to the ground as though she'd stepped in concrete and stayed too long. What was Michael playing at? She wished she hadn't looked at her cell, wished she hadn't even come. Her limbs began to tremble.

No. She was done with crying. Grabbing the handlebars of her bike, she prepared to swing her leg over, leaving before she gave the Bible study a chance. But Michael's text had thrown her off balance.

"Hello, there." Dr. Selman spoke from behind.

Amber winced. Not likely she could get out of Bible study now. Despite the heat in her cheeks, she spun to face him. "For someone teaching a Bible study, you're late, don't you know?"

"You're right. But considering it looks like you were about to leave, maybe my being late is a good thing." He offered his hand. "Come in with me?"

When he said it like that, how could she resist? Caught in his intense gaze, Amber wasn't sure when she'd placed her hand in his. Holding hands, they strolled to the front door, though Amber felt more like she'd been gliding. Before entering, Dr. Selman squeezed her hand and winked then released her.

Not that she believed he would actually walk into the Bible study holding her hand, but when he let go, her momentary contentment fled. He opened the door without knocking and waited for her to go in ahead of him.

Vehemently, she shook her head. "I. . .I can't. I don't know these people. Please, you go first."

"Dr. Selman." A short, stout woman appeared in the foyer, beaming warmth. "I was getting worried."

In the shuffle, Amber found herself standing in the living room. Where were all the people?

"Sorry I'm late, something came up." He grazed Amber with a glance.

The woman smiled at Amber. "I see."

"Oh, no, he was late before he saw me." What an idiot she was.

"No matter, dear." She gently touched the back of Amber's arm. "We're congregating in the kitchen. Decided to snack first since our leader wasn't here. I'm Claire, by the way."

Amber introduced herself and followed Claire and Dr. Selman into the kitchen, where the sound of soft conversation and laughter mingled with crunching chips. Come to think of it, she hadn't eaten, having taken a nap after getting home. She took the offer of a soda and began dipping chips into guacamole while she listened to the group, which included Claire and Donita, both fiftyish women and a thirty-something man who was a police officer, two guys and a girl all in their twenties. An interesting demographic for a Bible study.

Finally, the group ended up in the living room, sitting comfortably on one of two leather burgundy sofas, floral chairs, and a few large pillows. One of the guys dragged a couple of kitchen chairs into the room. A candle burned here and there, giving the room a soft glow and nice vanilla scent.

The scene brought back good memories of life before Amber's mother and sister were killed, of life before Michael had been arrested. How she longed for that time once again.

I don't know if I can ever forgive you, Michael. . . .

Everyone sat with their Bibles in their laps, either closed or flipped open. Amber did the same, opening her Bible to a random passage. The group members hadn't gotten serious yet, with several still chatting.

One of the younger guys sat next to Amber on the sofa, a little too close for her comfort.

"So, Amber, how was your day?" he asked.

"Don't I know you?" Great. Now, she was giving him a

pickup line, but he looked familiar.

"Don't you remember? I was in the drama."

Lewis. "That's right. I didn't recognize you in regular clothes." She giggled. "I never got your *real* name."

"It's Peter."

"You know Dr. Selman through the reenactment, right?"

"Actually, we attend the same church. He recommended me when the reenactors were looking for a new Lewis. I've been part of the reenactment team for three years now."

Amber smiled and nodded.

"Listen, I've been hoping to see you again. Maybe we could get together some time."

Dr. Selman cleared his throat. Amber looked around the room and noticed everyone was staring, waiting on them to get quiet.

Sitting in the large recliner in the corner, he looked different. Still authoritative and commanding like in the museum setting, but—a gentle light emanated from him. The Light was no stranger to her. Amber peered down at her Bible—it had to be the Jesus in him, she knew.

Dr. Selman led them in prayer. Guilt wrestled inside her. Even if she could forgive her brother, and God, how could God forgive her?

Vision blurring, she stared at her Bible. Gradually, the scripture became clear, seeming to jump out at her. Though Dr. Selman continued his prayer, Amber couldn't help but read the verse staring back. Matthew chapter five, verse twenty-four.

" *'Leave your gift there in front of the altar. First go and be reconciled to your brother; then come and offer your gift.'* "

And there was the crux of the matter. Whether she interpreted the verse correctly or not, she believed before she could connect with God, she needed to forgive her brother. Though torn, warmth burned in her heart—it seemed that God was nudging her in that direction. She had forsaken Him—after a fashion—but He'd never left her.

"In Jesus's name." Dr. Selman concluded the prayer. "Continuing our study in Romans. . ."

୨

Sitting in his office an hour before the museum opened, Brandon skimmed through the paperwork he'd need to complete today in addition to cataloging artifacts. Jim would return from his vacation next week. Brandon planned to have every artifact inspected, cataloged, and stored before then. They still waited on the display shelves for the Hamlin collection. Hopefully, they'd arrive soon, considering the museum had advertised the exhibit would be open to the public next month.

Adding to his tight schedule today, he needed to gather his thoughts for dinner this evening. He'd agreed to meet Ray Stockholm—a potential donor—to share his understanding of the events that ended in disaster when he directed the other museum. He'd spent five years attempting to shove what happened from his mind. And yet, he always maintained a ready defense of the facts. Though he rehearsed what he would say a million times, fear gripped him anyway.

Brandon hung his head and laughed. He grew weary of having to defend himself. Would it never end?

To make matters worse, board member Sheila Longstrom had called and asked to join them for dinner. What now?

He planted his face in his hands. Maybe that's why the Lord had him talk about forgiveness last night—he needed to forgive himself. Honestly? He thought he'd never recover from the disaster, but here he was in his own office, directing a new endeavor, a new museum and that?—because people believed in him.

He reflected again on the facts as he saw them, mentally preparing himself to talk his way through the tangled mess—an odd set of circumstances that brought a museum to its knees, and Brandon to dread facing himself in the mirror every day since.

In his first year as director of the Landers Prehistoric

Museum, he took on an intern whom he quickly began to mentor. He worked closely with her every day and trusted her with increasingly more responsibility. Focused completely on his work, he never took notice of her affections. Apparently the woman fancied herself in love with him, and one evening she surprised him with a kiss and revealed her feelings.

Taken aback by her declaration, Brandon wasn't sure what to say. But in the most tactful manner he could muster, he turned her affections aside. The moment was awkward, preventing them from returning to their daily work in a professional way.

When a large display somehow toppled, injuring her, Brandon's only thoughts were for her safety, and he blamed himself for the accident. She took his words of self-recrimination and ran with them to the courts, suing the museum for Brandon's supposed negligence. Brandon believed she exacted vengeance on him for spurning her. The museum settled with her out of court, of course, and Brandon was asked to leave. He thought he'd never work in a museum again—either in research as a paleontologist or as a director.

Thankfully, many still believed in him; and through their generous favor and recommendations, he once again directed a museum. But those days still haunted him, causing him to tread cautiously where Amber McKinsey was concerned.

Brandon shoved away from his desk and left his office. If he kept thinking on the past, he'd never move forward. And, he looked forward to seeing Amber this morning.

He'd been both happy and surprised to see her at Bible study. His thoughts went to her soft features in the dimly lit room, her face serious as she listened to the discussion. Unfortunately, he'd found it difficult to focus with her there, watching him. Somehow, he had the feeling the words were for her as well as him. But that was speculation on his part. He certainly didn't know her well enough.

He'd wanted time to speak with Amber after Bible study, but Peter had singled her out with an apparent romantic interest. Just as well. Brandon's thoughts regarding his previous experience lingered in his mind, warning him to keep his distance.

But where Amber was concerned, he was in a battle that had raged between men and women from the beginning of time, and he wasn't at all certain of the outcome in this case.

Mom and Dad must be praying for grandchildren.

Brandon sighed heavily as he crossed the hallway to the receiving room. As her mentor—if that's what he truly was—he needed to do a better job of instilling confidence in her. At the door, he unlocked it and entered to find that Amber had swept the floor clean of the pottery remnants just as he'd asked.

He considered whether or not to order a replacement, but he still had the replica for the most valuable piece. From one of the two crates he'd opened yesterday, he pulled out another box. He grinned. This artist was good, making even the packaging appear as if a *real* artifact was contained within. If Brandon didn't know better, even he could have been fooled. What was this?

The seal on the box was broken.

Brandon removed the padding.

Nothing.

In addition to sweeping up the broken replica, Amber had obviously continued cataloging more items, though he knew she couldn't have worked too much longer because she'd been at Bible study. But. . .she must have logged the replica as the actual artifact and placed it in storage.

Brandon paused, thinking it through. Since he wanted to test Jim's skills anyway, this could work in his favor.

Brandon spotted Amber on the other side of the glass door, a soft smile playing on her lips.

She pushed all the way through. "Good morning."

"I see you did more cataloging after I left. Thank you."

Amber allowed her backpack to slide to the floor next to the table where she worked. "Wait, what? I swept and straightened up then locked up like you asked."

"Well, you cataloged at least one more artifact—the wedding vase. Yesterday was slightly traumatic, wouldn't you say?" He felt a smile slip into his lips, and not yet wanting to reveal that it had been another replica, he turned his attention to his own workstation. The last thing she needed right now was for him to second-guess her.

"Dr. Selman?"

"You'll find it in the system. I'm glad you're capable of cataloguing on your own now, because I have to spend a good part of the day on other matters." He faced her again. She was too beautiful.

He'd prefer to see a smile in place of the frown, though. He'd prefer to kiss her forehead and make his way down to her lips. . . . Instead, he squeezed her arms. "Amber, forget about yesterday. Everything will be all right." His words set off an alarm inside him. While he wanted to encourage her, keep her safe—could he really back up his words?

Something in the look she gave him sent a subtle shiver through him.

seventeen

Dr. Selman had excused himself—he had a museum to run. Receiving artifacts, a small part of the work. Still, she missed his company.

Feeling the weight of the last couple of days, Amber sighed. Add to that the strange claim he'd made that she'd cataloged another item last night.

For the life of her, she couldn't remember doing it. But maybe he was right—dropping what she thought had been an artifact, watching it shatter into a hundred pieces had almost given her a heart attack. The day had been exhausting.

And then, she'd told him about Michael. Thankfully, Dr. Selman's only concern had seemed to be for her. But, he didn't know the whole of it.

Amber toyed with the artifact box he'd given her as he left the receiving room. Then she logged into her computer and searched the records. Nothing appeared after what she clearly remembered to be her last entry.

Dr. Selman had obviously found the box empty and assumed Amber had cataloged it and put it in storage.

Oh no! Maybe she'd put it in storage without cataloging it. Her heart palpitated. She placed her hand on her chest. To put an item in storage required her to leave the receiving area and tromp down the hallway to the locked artifacts storage room. The smell always bothered her in there. No. She would have remembered. Wouldn't she? She might be clumsy, but she was not forgetful.

As she worked to catalog more artifacts, she racked her brain, hoping to figure out what had happened. She recalled that she'd simply cleaned up the shattered artifact—grateful it had only been a replica—then cleared her desk. And lastly, she'd secured the door.

Clutching another piece of ancient pottery, she focused on maintaining her grip on the item. Her hands trembled, reminding her of the incident yesterday. She'd replayed the scene a thousand times in her mind. How had the pottery slipped from her hands? She shuddered. Would Dr. Selman withhold future references or recommendations for this, despite his warmth at Bible study last night?

She encouraged herself with the fact that he must place at least some confidence in her because he'd left her alone with the artifacts today. Stretching, she stood from the stool and saw him in his office through the windows on the other side of the hall. He could see her as well. On the phone, he stood and turned his back to her.

Tapping the workbench with her pen, she considered the circumstances. What would happen if she didn't find the wedding vase? Sooner or later, if it didn't turn up, she'd have to tell Dr. Selman. She knew nothing at all about it, though. He trusted her. What would his reaction be if he knew the whole truth about her brother? Would she lose his trust?

She squeezed her eyes, not wanting to entertain the obvious next thought—if the artifact was truly missing, and not simply misplaced, what were the odds Michael was involved?

He was in town, after all.

Amber leaned her head back and groaned. How was she supposed to work under these conditions?

Somewhere deep inside, despair began to rise. Michael's mistakes continued to negatively affect her life. Yet God asked that she forgive him.

She would need help with that.

Lord, please, let me find that artifact, safe and sound. With the small prayer, another place in her hardened heart grew soft.

After Bible study last night, she knew without a doubt the right thing to do was meet Michael, listen to what he had to say. On impulse, she'd texted him to meet her tonight at seven at Carl's Ice Cream Shop downtown. At the time, she'd not known an artifact was missing.

Amber finished out her day without taking any breaks, not even lunch. She wanted to plow through as many artifacts as she could. If Dr. Selman returned to receiving, she would tell him the rest of the story—doubtless, he would find out on his own soon enough.

Back at the cabin that evening, she fed Josh a few carrots to calm her nerves. Muriel rushed in and threw her things in her room. Amber headed to the kitchen where Muriel pulled out her fast-food fare.

"Sorry, I know it's my night to cook. Want some?"

"I'm not hungry, actually."

"You need to go to Gladys's for dinner more often. You're much too thin." Muriel paused and took a longer look at Amber. "What's up with the lopsided grin?"

"Can I ask you to drop me somewhere tonight?" Amber absentmindedly crunched on a carrot.

"I have plans, but I can drop you on the way, depending on what time. Then there's the issue of how you will get home."

"You've got a date?"

Muriel froze. "How did you know?"

"The faraway look in your eyes had something to do with it. Is it with that Carey guy?"

"Yes." Muriel squealed. "He finally asked me out. Sort of. I've got to get ready. When do you need me to drop you off?"

"Will six thirty mess with your plans?"

"Not at all. I'm meeting him at eight for coffee, so it's not like a full-blown date or anything." Muriel finished stuffing her face. "Can I just add that you could use a date, too?"

Amber strolled to the small living area and plopped on the davenport. "No, you cannot add that part. What is the definition of a date anyway?" Another crunch on the carrot, and Amber's appetite was completely gone. She wasn't sure she even wanted to eat ice cream.

"It's when an insanely cute guy asks you to meet him, or he

picks you up, either way."

"In that case, I have a date, of sorts."

Muriel gasped. "Don't tell me, is it with Dr. Selman?"

"Nope."

"Ah." Muriel let her shoulders droop. "I'm sorry."

Unwilling to share more details with Muriel, Amber busied herself getting ready for her "date," and as nervous as she was, it might as well have been with an insanely cute guy—or at least one who was interested in her romantically, rather than her brother.

As promised, Muriel dropped Amber off downtown. She strolled down the sidewalk, heading to the ice cream parlor. She planned to hang back, standing in the shadows of a storefront, hoping to spot her brother first. Seeing him now with all the baggage she carried would be a shock to her system.

Palms sweating and heart racing, she wanted to pound her head against the storefront. Then. . .she saw him.

Michael. . . God, please, help me.

She watched him enter the small ice cream shop and, through the glass windows, saw him go directly to the counter and order. Apparently, he wasn't willing to wait for her to arrive before getting his ice cream.

A quick glance at her watch and she knew she should walk across the street to meet him. But she was frozen. What did you say to a person whom you loved but believed had let you and your family down? Whom you blamed for the death of your mother and sister?

Amber was on the verge of shoving from the wall and forcing herself to face her nemesis because the truth was. . .she loved him very much. She knew that now, watching him. She'd always loved him. Somehow, God would help her forgive him. But, to her surprise, Michael exited the ice cream parlor.

No. . .

Where was he going? Carrying two ice cream cones, he walked across the pedestrian crossing at the intersection, directly toward her. As he drew near, his eyes grew bright, and his mouth widened into a huge grin.

"Amber," he said, his voice older than she remembered. He handed her an ice cream cone. "If I remember correctly, you like vanilla with caramel sprinkles."

૪

Windshield wipers swept the torrent from the windshield, while Brandon gripped the steering wheel and focused on the road. Figured. A day like this couldn't be complete without a hammering rain. It went right along with his mood.

Great for the digs, though, because it could uncover more fossils. However, too much and they'd have to cancel the tours altogether, which didn't bode well for his confidence level going into this dinner meeting.

Fund-raising was the one thing Brandon didn't enjoy about his job. Large institutions had an entire staff to secure funds. But in smaller museums, many jobs fell to a few people. If only he could hire a fund-raising coordinator, freeing him to do—he laughed—everything else.

He'd hoped that by this phase in his life, he could have been more successful, directing a bigger institution. Be more like his father. But like anything in life, there were pros and cons. The advantage he had now was that he could be involved in the many aspects he loved.

He drove into the parking lot and shut off the engine. Twenty minutes early, he watched patrons rush to and from the restaurant, brandishing umbrellas, paper, or plastic for cover. Some simply waited under the protective covering of the entryway until the burst subsided.

Exhaling slowly, he contemplated what would happen over the course of the next hour or two. The price had been paid for his previous mistakes, so he believed. However, the aftermath was real enough. He'd spent two years without employment until the Harrington Natural and Cultural Museum opportunity came his way.

Most donors were only interested in his management and

initiatives for the Harrington Museum. But when making a large contribution, some patrons dug deep. Leaving out the personal aspects of the situation with the woman who had sued, he would explain everything that happened. Hashing through that she'd fallen and been injured due to—as she claimed—the museum's neglect, again, wouldn't be pleasant. And considering everything that had happened at Harrington of late, his confidence was beginning to erode.

Jim had called to say he would be returning early. Brandon spent the better part of today catching up on paperwork and knew they weren't anywhere near finished with cataloging the artifacts. He wished he could have been more help to Amber, and hated every minute of being away from her.

Brandon still wasn't sure what to do with the information Amber had shared about her brother, but one thing was certain—she was skittish. He was concerned for her. She'd never actually said what crime had landed her brother in prison.

Blowing out a breath, he looked at his watch. Fifteen minutes before he was due in the restaurant.

Brandon pressed his head against the headrest and agonized over what he wanted—no, needed—to do. Because of his affection for Amber, what he was about to do riddled him with guilt. He hated to pry.

Opening his smartphone, he Googled Michael McKinsey. Pages of links stared back at him. Brandon's throat grew thick.

eighteen

Because a cloud burst had opened from the heavens, they were forced under the awning of the Christian bookstore.

"Oh Michael. . ." Taking the cone from him, a laugh-cry escaped through her aching throat. She hugged her brother, long and hard. "I've missed you so much."

Once she released him, she looked into his eyes—a dark brown, just like Dad's.

His smile exuded warmth even as he studied her. "I'm not sure about that." He gestured toward the bench and she followed, sitting next to him.

"You're my brother. So, of course I've missed you." Now that she was here with him, a wound inside her she hadn't even known about lay gaping wide open. "Although, I know it doesn't seem like it."

"Considering how hard you tried to avoid me." Though the words themselves accused her, his voice remained peaceful.

"I'm so—"

"I don't blame you. Not really," he said.

"I can't begin to imagine what you've been through."

"Only what I've deserved."

Licking her ice cream, she watched the sidewalk begin to fill with people again, as the rain subsided. *But what about me?* Or their mother and sister? Did they deserve to suffer for his actions? If it were possible, she thought she heard a ripping sound inside her heart. She'd missed her brother terribly, true—she knew that now. But Mom and Emily. . . she missed them, too. Life was so unfair.

"We can't go back to the way things were," Amber said.

It was good, sitting here with him, though she wasn't sure why he'd sought her out. Closure perhaps?

"No, we can't. I'm not asking you to."

"Then why did you want to see me?" She wished she hadn't asked the question. But it had nagged her since his first attempt at contact.

Michael's ice cream had melted much of the way down his cone. He'd clearly lost interest in it and tossed it into the garbage can near the bench. "Can't a brother see his sister?" He stared at his empty hands. "Don't answer that."

"I can't help but notice there's something different about you. What happened in prison?"

Michael stared at his hands again, then looked at something in the distance, a smile playing on his lips and a light in his eyes. "I found Christ."

Amber gasped then squeezed him. "I'm happy for you." He'd resolved his issues with the Lord. Now Amber would have to resolve hers.

"I became involved in the prison ministry there."

She'd heard people sometimes made up those stories to position themselves back into someone's life. "I can see in your eyes that it's real."

"And I can see in yours what I'd feared." Michael took her hand. "You blame me for the accident. I've always known. Everything changed because of my choices."

Tears hung in her lashes. "I can't deny it."

"I see in your eyes what I saw in the mirror every single day since making my mistake, since Mom and Emily died. I know what that can do to you. Unforgiveness can keep you from God."

Now, Amber was the one to stare at her hands, the tears slipping hotly down her cheeks.

"Amber, please forgive me."

"Oh, Michael."

He hugged her tightly as she released the anguish she'd held on to for so long. She wished their reunion could have taken place in a more private setting than in front of a Christian bookstore. "Of course I forgive you. I have to. I. . .want to."

Lord, please help it be so.

When her tears were spent, they strolled the sidewalks of downtown, peering into the shops. Few remained open in the evening. Amber detected a lift to her step, as though a weight had been removed.

"You know, I want to make sure that you're not blaming God."

She swallowed. "What makes you say that?"

He jammed his hands into his pocket. "I blamed Him when Dad died. I think that's why I ran so far from Him, that I made those terrible choices. I ended up having to find Him again. . .in prison, no less."

Despite his heavy words, she attempted to inject humor into hers. "Don't worry, brother, I'm not going to commit a crime or go to prison."

His left brow arched. "No, you're not. But we all drift away from God in our own way."

He didn't press her further, and they walked to a coffee kiosk where they ordered something to drink.

"What do you plan to do now that you're out? I mean, where will you go?" The words created an awkward moment. How did someone convicted of a crime find a job?

"A good question." Again, he jammed a hand into his pocket. "I don't suppose there are any openings at that museum where you intern." A nervous chuckled escaped him.

❧

Comfortable on the sofa, Amber had almost fallen asleep when she heard the door open.

Muriel tossed her bag on the couch, a bleak expression on her face. "Want a smoothie?"

"I'm good, thanks." From where she sat, Amber watched Muriel pull out the blender. "So, how was your date?"

"Please, don't ask."

"I already did. Come on, you know you want to talk about it." Amber tugged herself from where she sat and slogged into the kitchen. Muriel dumped ice cream and chocolate syrup into the milk already in the blender. "I thought you were making a smoothie."

"Shake, whatever."

"Well, in that case, I could use a chocolate shake, too."

"Deal, if you set me up with someone cute. Don't you know anyone?"

Michael immediately came to mind. But no, how could she set anyone up with him? She put her face on the counter. What a mess. "I'm afraid I don't."

"What about your Dr. Selman?"

Taken aback, it was a moment before Amber could respond. Jealousy stirred at Muriel's suggestion. She lifted her face to look at Muriel. "I thought you said he likes *me*. And if he's *my* Dr. Selman as you put it, why would you even ask?"

"Well, you don't seem interested."

Amber scratched her head, feeling like her life had spiraled out of control. The truth was, even with Michael's return in to her life, she could hardly stop thinking about Dr. Selman. She must be crazy.

Or. . .*in love*.

"Look, I was only teasing to see if you'd admit you have a thing for him."

"A thing for him"? Oh, Amber had a thing for him all right. In fact, her eyes were beginning to open. She had more than just a *thing* for him. But she wasn't ready to go into that with Muriel.

"I do know someone. I met him at Bible study." Oops. That might not sit too well with Muriel.

"You know, for the right guy, I could get into Jesus."

"Oh, bother." Amber knew she had failed miserably. Her blame game had cost her the ability to talk to Muriel about Jesus. But she had to try. "This is how it works. If you want to know the Truth, all you have to do is ask God. He'll show you."

Muriel chose to hit the BLEND button at the beginning of Amber's spiel and stared at her almost cross-eyed, pretending she couldn't hear a word.

Someone pounded on the door. Amber shared a look with Muriel.

"You expecting someone?" Muriel asked.

Standing there in her sweats? "Do I look like it?" Amber hurried to the door, hoping that her brother hadn't decided to pay her a visit. He'd just dropped her off an hour ago. She needed time to process everything.

Opening the door revealed a handsome and familiar silhouette. Her knees went weak.

"Dr. Selman?"

❧

Hair tousled, Amber stared up at him expectantly. Apparently, he'd disturbed her. In her eyes, he hoped he read that she was glad to see him, despite the late hour.

Brandon opened his mouth to speak but nothing came out. *I'm a first-class idiot.*

"Why don't you come in?" she stood aside, allowing him entry.

"Dr. Selman, what a surprise." Muriel smiled widely at him and held up a tall glass as if to say "cheers." Over the rim of the glass she gave Amber an amused look.

He had the funny feeling that, when it came to Amber, Muriel was the expert and Brandon a fossil laid bare.

"Can I get you something to drink?" Amber led him over to the sofa.

"No, thank you." This was more than awkward. "Can we talk?"

She brushed her long hair over her shoulder and glanced toward the kitchen. "Uh. . ."

Muriel finished her drink then set her glass down. She wiped away a milk mustache. "I hope you don't think I'm rude, but I've got a big day tomorrow. Going to hit the sack." After she leaned in to whisper to Amber, Muriel disappeared down the hall.

Amber faced him, her expression wary. "What's this about?"

Brandon stared at the coffee table. "Forgive my intrusion.

I didn't feel I had any choice but to speak to you."

"And you couldn't do this tomorrow at the museum?" Amber rubbed her arms. "Must be serious."

Fortunately, his meeting with the donor went better than expected; even Sheila appeared pleased. But he'd had to shove aside his anxiety over the news he'd discovered mere moments before dinner. Maybe he worried for nothing, but after the dinner meeting, he couldn't bear to spend the rest of the night speculating. He had to see Amber. "Please don't take this the wrong way. But I wanted to confirm that you found the artifact today." Brandon dipped his chin, waiting for her response, and feeling the weight of his question down to his toes. He'd wanted to give her the benefit of a doubt.

Amber pressed her eyes shut. As her lips trembled, Brandon felt a deep ache in his chest.

"No, I didn't catalog it. I don't know where it is," she said, her voice a hoarse whisper.

Brandon closed his eyes, too, cringing inside.

He'd give anything if nothing stood between them. All he wanted to do at that moment was hold her in his arms, but not in the same way he'd done on previous occasions when he'd simply comforted her.

No. . .he wanted to hold her in an entirely different way.

When he opened his eyes, she was staring at him.

"What do you think happened?" he asked.

Amber stood. "Look, you don't have to tiptoe around this. It's about my brother, isn't it? I told you he'd committed a crime. Then an artifact turns up missing." She turned her back on him.

He had the sneaking suspicion she was crying again and with what he was about to ask, he wasn't going to make the tears go away. "Have you told me everything?"

The knot in his throat suddenly grew larger. The last thing he wanted was for her to find out he'd hunted for information about her brother. *Cad.*

She whirled to face him, her eyes surprisingly dry. Brandon

felt everything rush out of him. He'd entertained far too much hope for something between them. "I'm not accusing you or your brother of anything."

Wasn't he?

Her expression softened. "I met with him tonight. It was the first time I've seen him in at least a year."

Brandon sucked in a breath. Her brother was in town, then?

"I could see immediately that something had changed. He told me that a prison ministry came to visit every week, and that he'd found Christ. Actually, I should say he recommitted his life to Christ."

Though the news relieved Brandon, the heaviness of the situation pressed against him. He leaned back against the couch, absorbing her words. More than anything, he wanted to believe her. But she wasn't telling him everything.

He licked his lips. "Amber. What was your brother convicted of?"

A deep frown appeared in her lips and brows. "I'm guessing you already know the answer to that."

"I'm sorry." Unable to meet her gaze, he stared down at the rug. "I know that he was caught trafficking artifacts."

Amber turned and, to his alarm, walked out the front door. Right now, he hated himself. But what choice did he have?

Needing a handle on this situation before Jim returned, he had to resolve this tonight, if possible. He followed Amber, and found her standing in the shadows of the porch, looking at the sky. Clouds skirted the moon, drifting away.

Brandon turned her to face him and lifted her chin.

"Do you want me to say I think Michael stole the artifact?" she asked. "Well, I'm not going to."

The turmoil in her face cut him deep. He hated to see her hurting. "Your brother's choices aren't your fault. They're no reflection on you. You don't pay the price for his mistakes."

She searched his eyes. "If that's true, then why are you here?"

She had him there. But her question uncovered the deeper truth of why he'd really come. He wanted to see her, be with her, make sure she was safe. At that moment, looking into her pale eyes, then down to her soft lips, he no longer cared about the artifact, the museum, or her brother's crimes. How many times had he thought about her lips? How many times had he wanted to kiss. . .

Before he knew it, his lips were pressed against hers. He lingered against their softness, while she wrapped her arms around his neck. Heart racing, he drew her closer. Her slight form fit perfectly against his frame.

"Dr. Selman." She whispered against his cheek. The way she'd said his name sent shivers over him.

He kissed her again then whispered in her ear. "Will you finally call me Brandon?"

nineteen

Sitting on the porch swing, Amber nestled against Dr.—oh wait, Brandon's shoulder.

Encircled in his arms, she rocked with him.

"I haven't felt this free in years," she murmured, "because I was holding on to resentment and bitterness. Then to see him tonight? I still can't get over the change."

Brandon kissed the top of her head. "I want to hear all about it."

"His last year in college with a double major of archaeology and museum studies, he needed additional funds. Someone approached him about an artifact. Before he knew it, he was neck deep in moving antiquities and kept at it even after graduating. My understanding is that it started small and mostly stayed that way, but there was one big item—and that's when he got caught. He served three years."

Amber thought of Michael's warning—straying from God only a little could lead her far from Him. But she had a feeling that God had a hold of her and was drawing her back. "I had planned to follow in his footsteps with my studies, then because of what happened, I ended up transferring to the University of North Dakota. I was confused about what to study. I didn't want to be reminded of Michael, but I'm drawn in the same direction he was. I was away at school when Mom and Emily went to see him in prison—that was a year ago. On their way, they were killed in an accident. Under the circumstances, and with police escort, Michael was allowed to attend the funeral. I blamed him."

Brandon squeezed her tighter, and she closed her eyes, feeling safe in his embrace.

"I'm so sorry," he whispered.

Amber sat up to look at him. "I know he's changed."

"I believe you."

Studying his face, she ran her finger over his brow and down his cheek. She knew the museum struggled. Brandon worked hard to secure new donors, kept minimal staff, and utilized volunteers and interns. She recalled Michael's question about employment at the museum. There wasn't any way she'd feel comfortable asking Brandon to hire Michael—even for the lowliest position.

"I'd like you to meet him."

He rubbed his thumb over her lips then kissed her again. Amber melted into him, overwhelmed with the joy inside. She'd only dreamed that he could care for her this way.

When he ended the kiss, he drew back and gazed into her eyes, his expression serious. "As much as I hate to say this, there's something you need to know."

Oh, no. Was her world crashing again?

"I want to believe that your brother is innocent. But I have to answer to others. The last thing I want is to bring the police in, especially now when the museum is close to gaining accreditation."

"But?"

"I know from experience that the missing artifact could very well be at the museum but has either been stored already or somehow got mixed up with the remaining artifacts. We have to finish the cataloging tomorrow. If the wedding vase doesn't turn up, then I have no choice but to call the police."

❧

Brandon and Amber worked the next day to process the artifacts, but the job was meticulous and time consuming, and they did not finish. He could tell she was tired and, he admitted, he was starting to see two of everything. They needed to break for the day. Brandon would come back and finish, even if it took him all night. Then if he couldn't find the missing piece, he would double-check everything previously cataloged. Reporting an item stolen when it was simply misplaced would draw unfavorable attention to his fledgling museum. But given the proximity of Michael McKinsey, he had every reason to be concerned and couldn't wait too long.

He sucked in a ragged breath. Whatever he did or didn't discover tonight would be the deciding factor.

But. . .however much he believed he was following the correct procedure, it was difficult to determine if he was being reasonable or not because of his feelings for Amber.

When she'd first arrived that morning, there was an awkward silence; then she appeared to understand the importance of remaining professionally detached. Still, to say it was difficult was an understatement. Every time she smiled at him from across the room, he wanted to cover her lips with his. Every time she sighed, he'd wanted to take her in his arms.

The tragedy was that she'd be leaving in a mere two weeks. How could he stand for her to be away from him? How did she feel about him? Really?

Unfortunately, he'd spent his adult life avoiding relationships to focus on his career. This was new territory for him. When on unfamiliar ground, one needed to tread slowly and carefully. But he was definitely not getting younger. Neither were his elderly parents. If he was going to give them the grandchildren they hoped for, moving slowly was out of the question.

Children with Amber? His heart skipped a beat.

Bent over a box, he felt a touch at his temple. Pulled from his thoughts, he stood tall and caught Amber's gentle smile. What would she think had she read his mind just now?

"Sorry. I couldn't help it. It seems like hours since. . ." She trailed off, blushing.

"I know. I'm finding it difficult to work with you, too. I think you should call it a day. It's getting late."

"It's only five." She looked down, her lashes shadowing her beautiful eyes. "I know what you're trying to do. You haven't called the police yet, have you?"

Subtly, he shook his head. "I have to make sure it's not here. I have no reason to think it was stolen other than. . ."

"Other than my brother."

"But after what you've told me about him, I don't believe he's involved. If there's been a crime here, why would the thief steal only one item if he'd found a way into receiving? I don't need another scandal. . . ." For the first time, he realized he'd never told her of his own past.

"Scandal?"

He wanted to kiss the top of her head, smell her hair. Reassure her. "Yes." Skipping the details, he summarized what happened before. "I can't afford any more humiliation— not at this juncture of fund-raising, not at this point in my life."

"I thought you were. . ." She sagged, leaning against the workbench.

Not caring if anyone saw him, Brandon gripped her arms and looked her in the eyes. "You thought right. I want to spare you and your brother any humiliation as well. Amber, I. . ." *love you.*

Finally, his heart had voiced the truth.

"Looks like I made it back just in time." Jim stood inside the door, hands on his hips.

Brandon quickly released Amber and shoved a hand through his hair. "Jim, welcome back."

Jim's cell rang and, to Brandon's relief, the conversation drew him out of receiving. Taking the opportunity, Brandon turned his attention back to Amber. "You've done all you can do today. I don't want Jim questioning you. Why don't you get out of here?"

Amber grabbed his hand, letting his fingers slip through hers. "Thank you for believing me about Michael."

She left him standing there and, as he watched her walk out, a morbid thought slammed him. *Oh, Lord, please don't let her be using me, playing me.*

That's exactly what Jim would think, once he found out. And he would. Brandon ground his teeth. He cared way too much about what the man thought about him. But maybe that was Brandon's biggest problem—his validation came from others.

Brandon needed time to pray.

Leaving the museum, he headed home for dinner, wishing he'd thought to invite Amber out to eat, but then again, he needed time to think. After he'd skimmed the snail mail, checked his e-mail, and eaten dinner, Brandon took a short nap so he'd be alert for the work ahead of him. Waking after dark, he wanted nothing more than a good, long run, and changed into his running shoes and clothes. Everything was happening too fast, including his relationship with Amber.

He needed a clear head and, more importantly, a clear heart.

Locking the door behind him, Brandon headed down the street, planning to jog the Little Missouri trail to add a few extra miles. The good thing—he had plenty on his mind to keep his thoughts off the ache in his legs and burn in his lungs.

Five years ago when he'd experienced a meltdown, losing everything he'd worked for, Brandon had turned to God. His mother had raised him in church, but he'd never really believed God was personal. While he might have gained knowledge during the course of his education, he'd lost his belief in God, completely. Or so he'd thought.

Then disaster happened, and he remembered the One who'd created him. Or rather, God remembered *him*. Through his desperation, he'd found a personal relationship with Jesus Christ. Always a stellar student, he'd studied and learned all he could about his Savior through the Word, enough that Pastor John had invited him to teach Bible study.

Why, then, did he feel as if he were going through it all over again—as if his life had spun out of control? God had given him another chance, as it were, and now? Would he lose everything again? He'd somehow gotten into his head, and possibly his heart, that becoming a Christian, trusting in God, meant he wouldn't have to suffer as he had before.

Breathing hard, Brandon savored entering "the zone"— that place where the endorphins kicked in. Running along the tree-lined trail, he came to the same place where he'd collided with Amber the first time they'd met.

He stopped and leaned against his legs, catching his breath. Even though he carried his flashlight, the moon shone bright enough for him to see, except when the clouds interfered.

God had given the moon to light the way for nocturnal creatures. Whether full or hidden, it was always there, watching. A raccoon moseyed past as though it hadn't noticed him, or didn't care. An idea began to form.

Why didn't I think of it before?

twenty

At the cabin, Amber sat across the table from her brother and watched Muriel flirt with him. The girl was relentless. No matter. At least it gave Amber more time to consider things, and kept Michael from noticing her complete anguish.

She'd agonized all night—all day too, but Brandon had kept her busy searching for the missing artifact. It warmed her heart that he wanted to make certain the mistake hadn't been on their part before calling the police. He'd made every attempt to believe her regarding Michael.

More than anything, she wished she could have basked in his attention. Instead the missing artifact and her brother's proximity to the circumstances, along with his appearance back in her life, eclipsed her relationship with the man she loved.

The man she loved? Despite her gloomy thoughts, she found herself smiling.

Amber suddenly noticed that both Muriel and Michael were staring at her.

"She's a million miles away," Michael said to Muriel.

"I'm sorry. I was thinking." Amber smiled.

Michael laughed and pushed back from the table. "Thanks for dinner, ladies. It's getting late, and I think I might have overstayed my welcome."

Amber stood as well. "Can I talk to you outside for a sec?"

Michael chuckled. "Sure." He said goodnight to Muriel then headed out the door.

Amber tried to follow but Muriel tugged her back. "You were holding out on me."

"What are you talking about?"

"Your brother. He's cute. You could have set me up."

"Not now, Muriel."

Looking miffed, Muriel let Amber go.

Once on the porch, she found Michael waiting for her.

"I could tell you were distracted all evening," he said.

Amber hated the gloomy look on his face. He thought it was about him—that she wasn't happy to be in his company. "Something's come up."

He cocked his brow, waiting. Muriel was right—Michael was a real catch. Except that he'd practically ruined his life. Amber sighed.

"There's no easy way to say this. A relic has gone missing at the museum. We spent all day searching for it."

Michael appeared stricken. Tightening his jaw, he turned away.

Fearing he would leave, she grabbed his arm. "Michael, please, you have to believe me. I'm not accusing you. I want to believe you had nothing to do with it. But. . ."

He stared at something in the distance, frowning. "I won't ever live down my mistake, will I?"

"I don't know."

"And the director—the one Muriel seems to think has feelings for you—he knows about me, then?" Michael searched her eyes.

The knot in her throat kept her from speaking. She nodded.

Michael released a long, slow breath. "I shouldn't have come within a hundred miles of you."

What was he saying? That he'd been tempted and fallen again? Was it like some sort of addiction?

"Say something, Amber."

Pain squeezed her chest. "I want to believe you're innocent. And so does Bran—Dr. Selman."

"You love him, don't you?"

Amber gave a soft smile. "Yes, I do," she whispered. But would her brother destroy this part of her life, too?

Lord, I forgive him. She closed her eyes. *Please, help me.*

"Tell me about the artifact."

Her eyes flew open. "Why do you want to know?"

"Maybe I can help. Find out who would want it."

"But couldn't getting involved implicate you somehow?"

"From the looks of it, I'm *already* implicated."

"All you have to say is that you're not involved. I'll stand by you." Amber held her breath, hoping.

"I promise you, I had nothing to do with it."

She released the pent-up air then told him about the artifact.

Even under the dim porch light, Amber could see Michael's face go pale.

Oh, Lord, no. . .

ð

Sitting in the small room they'd set aside for security, Brandon logged into the DVR software and selected the date in question and multiple video channels, viewing them simultaneously on the screen. He watched for any anomalies. If it turned out the artifact was in fact stolen, the police would want to view this, he was sure, once he contacted them. If he had looked right away, he could possibly have resolved the biggest question—was the artifact stolen or not?

Rubbing his neck to relieve the stiffness, he reviewed the segment from today when Amber had approached him and taken his hand. He recalled the way her simple touch made him feel. Watching it now, he relived that moment.

Then, of course, during the tender interlude they'd tried to avoid all day, Jim had walked in.

This looked very bad for Brandon. Professionally, he couldn't afford a stolen artifact, or involvement with a woman whose brother was convicted of stealing artifacts.

And personally. . .

Hands over his face, he rested his elbows on the small desk. "Why, God?"

From the beginning, he'd been against having an intern, a protégé. Yet he found himself in a similar situation as before—only this time, roles were reversed.

He'd been the one to fall in love. Thankfully, his affections were returned.

Wanting to review Jim's reaction, he played back the video, but accidentally selected to rewind the recording.

"Stupid." He began searching the video then stopped, freezing the frame.

The time and date stamp display indicated Tuesday night. Hadn't he been working late that night?

As he watched the playback of the entire segment, a sinking feeling hit his stomach. He never appeared in the video—but he'd been in the room that night.

"What the. . . ?"

Someone obviously made adjustments to the video. "Clue number one."

This was bad news for the museum. More scandal. Jim took care of security—would he bear the brunt of it this time?

Brandon attempted to sign in to the system administration in order to view the log, which recorded all system and operator activities, but he was denied access. He didn't usually keep up with password changes. Jim kept it written somewhere. Brandon left the security room to pay Jim's office a visit, uncertain exactly where he might find the password.

After unlocking the door to Jim's office, Brandon stepped inside. On a hunch, he knew it was better to search the man's office than call him for the password. Still, shame engulfed him. His cell buzzed in his pocket. Tugging it free, he found a text message from Amber.

News about the artifact. Meet me at the museum?

"Could she have clue number two?" He texted her back that he was already at the museum and would wait for her.

Standing in the dark, in another man's office, Brandon had the odd sense he was being watched. He felt like a criminal himself and flipped on the light.

A man hovered in the corner. Brandon froze.

"Jason?"

twenty-one

Amber clenched the door handle as Michael drove into the museum parking lot. Finally, he slowed to a stop. The parking lot was empty.

"That's strange. Why isn't Brandon's Jeep here?"

"You told him it was important, right?" Michael turned off the engine. "And even if you didn't, I can't imagine him not wanting to see you." He flashed a grin and a wink.

"Thanks for dropping me off." Before she opened the door, she gave Michael a side glance.

He gripped her arm. "I'm going with you."

"You can't. We've been over this. I don't want you to put one foot in that museum." Amber's heart thumped louder.

"If Brandon's car were here, sure, yeah, I could drop you off. But not like this. It isn't safe."

"I'll be all right. You don't have to do this."

"What kind of brother would I be to let you go alone, knowing the situation. Besides, I'm innocent, and. . .it's the right thing to do." He slipped from the car.

Amber did the same, and together, she and Michael hurried to the front door, discovering it was locked. Because of her late hours while working on the exhibits, she'd been given keys.

Once inside, she walked through the dimly lit museum, Michael close behind. Amber spotted light at the end of the hallway.

She started that way, but Michael grabbed her arm. "Wait. This wasn't a good idea."

"Brandon is here. He said he would be here."

Michael exhaled. "Just be careful."

They hurried down the quiet hallway. Brandon's office door stood open, but he wasn't inside. "He's got to be here somewhere. Let's split up," she said.

"Not a good idea. This could be dangerous if the wrong people are here. We'll find him together."

"Do you really think the thief is running around in the museum tonight?"

Michael's look sent shudders over her. "I don't want you to get hurt. For too long, I blamed myself for what happened to Mom and Emily. Even though God helped me to forgive myself, I'm not sure what I would do if you were to get hurt because of me."

"Because of you? This has nothing to do with you."

"We're here right now, because of me, and we're wasting time. Let's look around."

"I'll call him on his cell." The cell went straight to voice mail. "Brandon, we're here at the museum. Call me back." She texted him as well, but got no response.

After a thorough search of the museum, including the basement classrooms, they ended at the hallway emergency exit between the offices and receiving room.

Amber noticed something resting on the floor at the end of the hall. She walked to the exit and Michael followed.

"What's this?" She lifted a stainless steel water bottle with the Nike emblem. An image flashed in her mind. "This is Brandon's. Maybe he jogged here. That could be why his Jeep isn't in the parking lot."

"Who else is here, then?"

"Brandon said he'd meet us here and that he'd found something, too." Amber frowned.

"I don't like this, Amber." Michael began pacing the hallway, peering into offices. He lingered at the receiving room where the artifacts had been then peered into the windows of other offices.

"Why didn't he wait for us?" she asked.

"I think I know the answer to that." Michael motioned for her to join him, looking through the glass window of Jim's office.

Amber tried the door and it easily opened. A chair was knocked over, paperwork scattered across the floor.

Michael picked up a paperweight and turned it over. "Blood."

"I'm calling the police." Amber phoned 911 and explained the situation and that she believed foul play was at work. In her opinion, the dispatcher asked too many questions, keeping her on the phone too long. Amber squeezed the cross on her necklace, and then suddenly, an image of Brandon, holding the cross in his fingers came to mind. He'd referenced looking for little clues.

You just have to pay attention.

"I'm sorry, I have to go," she said and hung up.

"What is it?" Michael asked. "Why would you hang up on them?"

"He left the water bottle next to the door. If you go out that exit you connect directly with the trail to the digs."

"How do you know he didn't simply drop it?"

"Because I just know, all right? He meant that to direct us."

Amber shoved the door open, remembering the day she'd heard Brandon's words of caution.

One misstep could land you at the bottom of a pinnacle.

❧

Just keep him talking.

Walking down the dark trail with a gun to his back, Brandon considered every tactic to escape his predicament. He wasn't going down without a fight, and though he'd tried that in Jim's office—a nasty knot on his head to show for it—Jason had pulled a gun.

Brandon's hesitation to involve the police had been a mistake. But as they said, hindsight was always twenty-twenty. There were many things he'd change now. For one, if he had it to do over again, Brandon would have followed his heart from the beginning where Amber was concerned. But he'd been reserved, too worried about what others thought of him, how things would look to his donors. Too worried about carving out a successful career.

Now he clearly saw that Christ was the only one from whom he needed validation.

A painful jab in his back reminded him to focus on the current state of affairs. Keeping Jason talking could serve as a distraction. "You don't want to do this, Jason."

"Oh. . ." Jason sniggered. "I *want* to do this."

"Come on. You're going to add murder to your crime?"

Another jab and Brandon stifled a moan.

"Nothing would give me greater pleasure than to make you suffer. You humiliated me."

"You're going to kill me because I let you go?" Brandon asked. Did he dare remind the guy that he'd merely used his position as a means to an end?

"Who said I was going to kill you? You're going to kill yourself."

Tension jolted through Brandon's body. Still a mile to hike before they reached the digs, he considered scrambling through the wooded area. But Jason knew the terrain better.

Making me kill myself is still murder. Brandon thought he knew what Jason had in mind, and he had no plans to cooperate. If he died, it would be by Jason's hand and not some "accident."

On the chance that he made it out of this alive, Brandon thought to draw as much information as he could from Jason. "Can you at least tell me who you're working with?"

"You're really pathetic, you know that? I'd think that would be obvious by now."

Obvious? Brandon tried to wrap his mind around Jason's words while he stayed aware of his surroundings, hoping for an escape. Hoping that Amber would see the evidence of a scuffle in Jim's office, hoping she would notice the water bottle he'd left behind—*Please, God!*—and call the police. Hope and a prayer was all Brandon had.

The trail ended at the digs. If Jason planned what Brandon thought, they still had a ways to go before reaching the cliff's edge.

Brandon slowed his pace and received another sharp jab in the back. He bent over, gasping for breath. "Can we rest for a minute?"

"You've got three seconds."

Or what? You're going to shoot me here? Then it wouldn't look like a suicide, but rather a murder. Brandon wasn't about to press the man on that point. "Back to whom you're involved with. I'm afraid it's not obvious, Jason."

Brandon stood tall, waiting for Jason's answer, hoping he wouldn't hear the name Michael.

In the moonlight, Jason looked incredulous. "Jim. Who else?"

Jim? Brandon staggered back a few steps. "I don't believe you."

"Well, it doesn't really matter at this point, does it? Now get walking. I haven't got all night."

Brandon started hiking again, this time much slower. He'd grown numb with the jabs to his back and was in shock over the news about Jim. He had come with Brandon from Landers and had been in charge of accessioning the collections there. He'd known him for years. If what Jason said were true. . .how many dollars and relics had he skimmed from the museum without Brandon even knowing?

What a fool he'd been! Except. . .he was still holding one card.

When should he play it? "I don't get it, who can a person ever trust?"

"That's a good question. I'm afraid if you don't know by now, you're not going to have time to figure that out."

They'd reached the edge of the butte. Brandon refused to step too close. He wondered if he could fall off and somehow survive.

"I know who I can trust," he said.

"I don't think I'm interested. Now, jump."

"I can trust God because no matter where I go, He's there with me."

Even at the precipice of a cliff.

" 'Where can I go from your Spirit? Where can I flee from your presence? If I go up to the heavens, you are there; if I make my bed in the depths, you are there. If I rise on the wings of the dawn, if I settle on the far side of the sea, even there your hand will guide me, your right hand will hold me fast. If I say, "Surely the darkness will hide me and the light become night around me," even the darkness will not be dark to you; the night will shine like the day, for darkness is as light to you.' "

Brandon spoke the verses from Psalm 139 as though his life depended on it.

"I'm done listening. If you're not going to jump, then you can just face God now."

Brandon wondered why Jason didn't simply push him, but maybe Jason knew that Brandon would pull him over with him. Not a chance would he go over alone. Unless. . .

The card! Play the card!

twenty-two

"Wait. The artifact you have is a fake."

"You're lying."

"I'm not, actually. I commissioned an artist to create replicas of the most expensive pieces. The genuine artifact is in the vault."

"You're trying to trick me. I can tell the real thing from a replica. Now turn around and face your demise."

Fear warred with peace as Brandon did what he was told.

Every muscle in his body tightened when he heard the sound of the gun cock. A shot rang out, echoing through the Little Missouri Badlands.

Brandon jerked with the sound, believing himself shot. How was this supposed to feel? He felt. . .

Nothing. What was going on?

Was he too shocked to feel pain? He wavered at the edge of the cliff, losing his balance.

This is it.

A million regrets plunged through his soul—slowly, as though he could see each one outside of time. *Amber, I'm so sorry. . . .*

Arms gripped his body, yanking him back from the edge. He slammed into the ground next to someone.

Catching his breath, he rolled over to see the most beautiful face in the world. "Amber?" He slid his hands over his chest and abdomen. "I'm not shot?"

She smiled. "No. But I thought I'd lost you."

"You saved me." Brandon wanted to ask what had taken her so long. Grunts and scuffles drew his attention to the fight. He climbed to his feet, helping Amber to hers.

Jason struggled with another man.

Amber cupped her hands against the sides of her mouth. "Michael, be careful."

Sirens screamed in the distance, drawing closer.

Brandon came fully to his senses. Amber and Michael had come to his rescue. Michael was still fighting with Jason.

Smack. Michael landed a good punch into the center of Jason's face. The man fell back but managed to cling to the gun.

Michael stomped on Jason's wrist and kicked the gun out of his reach. Brandon scrambled for it. Jason recovered and shoved Michael to the ground, falling onto him with more punches. Clearly the stronger fighter of the two, Michael freed himself, leaving Jason groaning in the dirt.

Brandon stepped forward and took aim. "Don't move."

At that moment, four police officers surrounded them, breathing heavily, their weapons at the ready. Brandon slowly set the gun on the ground and raised his hands as instructed, as did Michael, Amber, and Jason.

Grand.

"Dr. Selman." Officer O'Riley stepped forward. He attended Brandon's Bible study. "What's going on here? We received an emergency call from the museum and then a second call explaining someone was in danger at the digs."

Amber cleared her throat. "If it weren't for Michael's call, you might not have known we were headed to the digs in time to help us."

While struggling to catch his breath, Brandon explained to his friend that Jason, and allegedly the museum curator, had stolen an artifact. Then Jason had tried to force Brandon from the cliff.

Dismissing Brandon, Amber, and Michael for the time being, the police cuffed Jason and ushered him up the trail.

As Brandon looked on in stunned silence, he tried to process everything that had happened. One second, he was on the verge of losing his life, the next, he was alive, standing next to Amber.

"Come here." He pulled her into his arms and kissed her

thoroughly. She meant everything to him. Why did it take a near-death experience to make him see how important she was? There wasn't any need for him to take his time. But did she feel the same?

As he held on to her, cherishing the moment, he realized asking her to marry him would interfere with her plans for her education. How could they make it work?

Though he didn't want to end the embrace, Brandon noticed Michael standing quietly in the dark.

Brandon walked over and offered his hand to Amber's brother. "I want to thank you for what you did."

❧

No words could express how Amber felt as she listened to Brandon thank Michael. Watching Jason holding the gun on Brandon, she'd almost crumpled.

But she'd drawn on something deep inside. Or maybe Someone. "You have no idea what a hero Michael is. He tackled a man with a gun."

"So I gathered. And apparently, just in time," Brandon said.

While Michael tackled Jason, she had yanked Brandon from the brink of death.

"No kidding. The bullet missed." *I thought I'd lost you.* Was he hers to lose, despite his kisses?

Brandon took Amber's hand as the three of them began the arduous two-mile hike up the trail to the museum.

"Earlier this evening," Brandon said, "you mentioned you discovered something about the artifact. If not for that discovery and your plans to meet me, I might be dead now. Mind telling me what it was?"

Amber started to answer, but Michael spoke up. She was so proud of him.

"I received a message from an old contact wanting to offload an artifact. He needed to move it quickly."

Brandon stopped on the trail and studied Michael in the moonlight. Amber feared he believed that Michael was involved.

"Go on," he said.

"I was furious that I'd been contacted, that word was out I was out of prison. I want no part of that anymore. I didn't respond. But when Amber told me about the artifact stolen from Harrington, I realized it was the same one."

"You realize the police will need to hear all of this information."

"Of course. I thought there was too much chaos earlier to bring it up." Amber lagged behind the two men as they continued up the trail. The police had caught their guy. At least one of them. Michael hadn't involved himself except to help, yet she feared for her brother.

Finally, the museum parking lot became visible. Lights flashing, a few cruisers had stayed behind.

Brandon turned to Michael. "You risked your life tonight in more ways than one. You might have trouble explaining your way out of this situation, considering your proximity and that you'd been contacted about moving the artifact."

Michael studied the ground, somber. "Like I told Amber, it was the right thing to do."

Brandon nodded, approval in his eyes.

"Well, I see a detective over there. I'm going to tell him the rest of the story."

"Michael, wait." Amber grabbed him and hugged him to her. "I'll pray for you."

Releasing him, she looked into his face.

"Prayer is the most important thing." He cuffed her on the chin then walked away.

A smile crept onto her lips. One day, maybe she could set him up with Muriel. She had a feeling that Muriel was close to meeting Christ.

"Are you all right?" Brandon asked as they watched Michael approach the police.

She gazed up at him. "I don't know."

Pulling her to him, he rested his chin against the top of her head.

She loved how safe he made her feel. "Dad died when I was young. But when Mom and Emily were killed, especially after Michael was taken from us by his own actions and incarcerated, I knew just how fragile life was."

Sensing that Brandon waited for her to say more, she continued. "Tonight, it felt like it was happening all over again. I was so afraid I would lose you and Michael. I'm still scared of losing Michael to this situation." And she still feared losing Brandon. She wanted to tell him she loved him, but that was for him to say first.

Wasn't it?

In two short weeks, she'd leave for Grand Forks—on the other side of North Dakota. If Brandon didn't tell her how he felt by then, she would believe she'd lost him after all.

Although, she never really had him to begin with.

twenty-three

Two days before Amber was to travel back to Grand Forks and begin another school year, she stared at the display case containing one of the earliest Hisatsinom artifacts ever discovered—the very piece that Jason had stolen under Jim's instruction—or at least he'd thought he'd stolen. Odd to think that the Anasazi wedding vase, decorated with only a few red and black designs, could create such a stir. Though the police had quickly recovered the replica, they'd sequestered it as evidence to be used in the investigation. Now, the authentic artifact was on display. All that had been disclosed to the public was that someone had attempted to steal the wedding vase.

The investigation had taken up any time she might have had with Brandon at the museum. During the evenings, his time had been consumed with dousing the rumor flames and meeting with board members.

To his credit, he'd done a brilliant job. The incident at the museum had been front and center in local and national newspapers, along with Brandon's picture. The article in the newspaper detailed the previous scandal involving Brandon, yet managed to put a positive spin on the story, making Brandon look like the hero then even though he was terminated. Regarding the Hisatsinom artifact, no one doubted his planning had prevented a great loss to both the museums involved.

Amber cut out the article to save. All the attention had increased the traffic to the museum. She stood aside while a new volunteer guided the next tour, showing the now infamous wedding vase. Though the museum hadn't officially opened the Hamlin Exhibit, board members believed it timely and in the public's interest to display the artifact.

Brandon's museum was a great success.

Michael deserved credit, too. Glad she'd forgiven him and stopped blaming him for Mom's and Emily's death, she squeezed the little cross on her neck, savoring the warmth in her soul.

She'd stopped blaming God as well.

Though she'd feared her brother's coming back into her life would destroy what little she had left, he'd not only assisted in resolving crime, but his presence had brought her closer to Brandon.

The man had actually believed in her, believed in Michael's innocence despite evidence to the contrary.

And Michael? He'd risked everything for her. Who could ask for more?

Shaking her head in awe, she whispered to herself, "Thank You, Lord."

Someone touched her shoulder. Gladys stood next to her, watching the group. "There's been so much excitement around here lately that I haven't had a chance to talk to you."

Fortunately, Gladys had been able to hire help in the museum store a few weeks ago.

"It's been a madhouse, hasn't it?" Amber asked.

The older woman ducked her head slightly, staring at Amber. "How are you doing? Really?"

"I think I'm going to live." But if she ended up leaving without getting to see Brandon alone, without hearing how he felt, she wasn't so sure.

"You know, I always thought you were a keeper."

"Thanks, Gladys. That's sweet. But I have to go back to school."

Gladys adjusted her glasses. "Leaving in a couple of days, I hear."

"Yes."

"When I said you were a keeper, I was referring to our Dr. Selman."

Brandon and Amber had been careful to hide their

affection for each other. "What do you mean?"

"Hon, Dr. Selman has always had his head in his work. That is, until you came along. Anyone with eyes can see."

What did it matter? She was leaving soon. Painful tears stirred behind her eyes. Thankfully, she kept them at bay. "I don't know, Gladys. I think his head is still in his work."

Gladys tugged her on the sleeve, backing her into a shadowed corner, away from the crowd. "Listen to me. Dr. Selman is a quiet man. He's absentminded when it comes to women and sadly, even the woman he loves."

"Gladys, you can't know that he loves me."

"Oh, he loves you. But I'm not sure he knows what to do about it. Men like Dr. Selman are thinkers. They have to analyze everything."

"What are you saying I should do?"

"You need to be the one to act."

"You can't be serious."

"I never told you about my Frode."

"Your Frode?"

"My husband of forty years."

Amber cringed. At Gladys's home, she'd seen the photographs, but somehow the conversation never turned to the woman or her life. Gladys was all about other people. A good thing and a trait Amber should consider modeling.

"Go on."

"Frode was like your Dr. Selman. A quiet man, devoted to his work and to God. Hon, I had to go out of my way to get him to notice me. And even then, I had to practically propose to him."

Amber took a step back. "You're kidding. I don't know, Gladys, that's just not me."

"When you want something, you have to work for it. Love isn't easy."

"Thanks for your advice. I'll consider your words."

"That's all I can ask."

Amber wondered if Gladys would give the same lecture to

Brandon. That might work better. No way could Amber do what Gladys suggested.

&

In his office, Brandon sat behind his desk, waiting on Amber's brother, Michael. He rubbed his eyes, hoping he didn't look like he felt after two weeks of navigating the investigation while keeping his and the museum's reputations afloat.

For what he was about to do, he could lose donors. Yet, after everything he'd been through, Brandon had now learned to conduct his life and business to please God rather than be concerned with what others thought.

He recalled what Michael had said the night he'd risked his life. It was the right thing to do.

Brandon wanted to do this for the woman he loved. The problem was—what did he do *about* the woman he loved? She still had to finish school. They would be far apart. What would he accomplish by telling her how he felt?

Michael stood outside Brandon's door and knocked lightly then opened it. "You wanted to see me?"

Brandon smiled. "Yes, come in and have a seat."

Michael sat in the chair across from Brandon's desk, looking nervous.

Brandon stood and moved to the credenza where a carafe waited. "Coffee?"

"No, I'm good. What's this about?"

Brandon refreshed his cup. "I want to make you an offer." He took a sip and waited for Michael's reaction.

Michael threw up his hands. "Listen, I don't speak for Amber. No need to ask me for her hand."

Brandon drew a startled breath while swallowing coffee and began coughing uncontrollably.

"You okay?" Michael moved to stand.

Brandon's eyes watered while he worked to regain his composure. He held up a hand, reassuring Michael. Then he sat down and cleared his throat, tugging his collar.

Michael frowned. "I didn't mean to throw you. I thought. . . sorry, I was way off, wasn't I?"

"Well, I brought you in here for something entirely different."

"Please don't tell Amber what I said."

Brandon stared at the papers on his desk and chuckled. "I won't, don't worry. I wanted to offer you a job."

Michael's mouth dropped open but he quickly recovered. "I. . .wasn't expecting that."

"No, I wouldn't think you were. I need to replace Jim."

"But why would you want to hire me?"

Brandon lifted a brow, wishing the guy wouldn't sell himself short. "I'll tell you why. It's the least I can do for a fellow believer in Christ. You need a fresh start. And from what I saw the other night—the risk you took—I can't think of anyone who deserves it more."

"But what will people say—you hiring me after the crime I committed."

"Michael. . ." Brandon toyed with an amethyst paperweight on his desk. "I know what it's like to make mistakes, believe me. God gave me a second chance, and He expects us to do the same for others. I worked with a man for years who I thought I could trust, but he fooled me. You've served your time then proved yourself trustworthy when tested, so I can't believe you'd make the same mistake again. Besides, we can certainly use your expertise—I don't think anyone is going to be stealing from my museum."

Michael responded with a big grin.

"You need to put the past behind you." Brandon should listen to his own advice.

"I appreciate your offer."

"But?"

"Will you hold it against me if I say I need to think about it? Pray about it?"

"On the contrary. I'd be concerned if you didn't."

"Can I ask you something?"

"Certainly."

"What *are* your plans regarding my sister?" Michael gave him a pointed stare.

Still, he could see the twinkle in his eyes. With a half grin, Brandon averted his gaze. So the guy had some old-fashioned protectiveness in him, after all. But why wouldn't he? He'd risked it all for Amber. Definitely a changed man.

Brandon considered his answer. He had to step carefully.

"She loves you, you know that, right?"

The man was direct. Brandon hadn't been certain of her feelings. "You can understand if I need to consider things, pray about it."

"You need to put the past behind you."

Brandon nodded, recognizing his own words used against him. "Not so easy to do, though, is it?"

Michael chuckled. "Nope."

Brandon hoped Michael would drop the subject there. He had no answers, only questions about the future. With Amber leaving for school in two days. . .

A pang squeezed his chest.

Michael stood. "Well, I think I should leave you to your thoughts. I appreciate your offer and want you to know that I'm very interested."

"Good enough."

Michael stepped out, and while pleased with the possibilities of working with the bright young man despite his past, Brandon had avoided Michael's questions.

The desk phone rang and Brandon answered. He warmed to the sound of an old friend's voice. "Dr. Young. Good to hear from you."

"There are people of influence who are more than impressed with your ability to handle crisis situations."

"Thank you."

"I have a proposition for you."

twenty-four

"Got everything packed?" Muriel trotted into the living room from the hallway.

"Almost." Leaving for UND in the morning, Amber knew she'd miss the way Muriel nurtured her like a mother. Muriel still had another week before she headed back to school.

"Don't forget your Bible." Muriel moved her hand from behind her back. "Here you go."

Amber took it from her. "Thanks, I was looking for that."

Muriel smiled. "Thought so." She sat on the sofa across from Amber.

"You know. . .I want you to have it." Amber offered it back.

"Oh, no, I couldn't take that from you." An odd expression came over her face as she stared at the book. "But I'll buy one as soon as I can."

"I have several at my apartment in Grand Forks. This is my gift. I'm afraid I've been a failure at sharing my faith with you."

"You're wrong about that. I don't think I could have been so strong if I had to deal with everything you did. Maybe you struggled, maybe you even questioned God, but you never lost hope, never stopped believing, never gave up on your faith." Muriel smiled then took the Bible back. "Thank you for this."

Amber's throat grew tight, Muriel's words touching her deeply. Amber held Josh in her lap, running her fingers through his soft fur. Since it was her last night in the cabin, Muriel agreed she could bring him out. "You've got my number, right?"

Muriel nodded. "I'm going to miss you so much. Maybe I can just transfer to UND." Muriel had been the one to cry today.

Amber laughed. "I already have two roommates."

"At least we'd be at the same school, chickadee." Muriel hopped up from the sofa. "I'm making a shake. Want one?"

"Love one."

In the kitchen, Muriel began assembling the blender and ingredients. "Any news?"

Amber knew Muriel referred to Brandon. Rumors had made their way around the museum. He and Amber were an item now. For all the good that did. Tomorrow, she'd be gone. "No," she said, her voice breaking.

Maybe she should take Gladys's advice and tell him how she felt. Find out where they stood. While Muriel ran the blender, Amber put Josh back in his cage and retrieved her cell. Sitting on her bed, she debated what to say even if she made the call. It was already nine thirty in the evening.

Palms sweaty, she found his number in her cell and pressed SEND. *What am I doing?* Heart racing, she ended the call after only two rings.

Muriel appeared in the doorway, holding her milkshake. "Here you go."

"Thanks."

Her cell rang and startled her. She dropped it.

Muriel picked it up and answered. "Amber's phone." A smile spread over her face. "Dr. Selman. Just a sec." She thrust the phone in Amber's face.

Oh no. . .he'd seen her call. What now? She took a sip of the creamy chocolate shake then traded it for the phone. She'd taken the advice from Gladys. Now, if she could just see things through. Muriel left, giving her privacy.

"Hello?"

"Did you call?"

I'm an idiot. If he was available to call her back, why hadn't he called her in the first place? "I—I hope I didn't disturb you."

"No, not at all."

Oh, this was ridiculous. "Listen, I'm leaving tomorrow."

"Yes, I know. I was just about to call you when my cell rang. It was you."

"And?"

"And do you have plans tonight?"

What was he thinking? It was already late. "What have you got in mind?"

"There's something I want to show you."

"Okay." Amber wished there was something he wanted to tell her, or. . . maybe even ask her. That was hoping for too much. She knew that now.

"Can you be ready in thirty seconds?"

"What?" Amber hurried out into the living room to see Brandon standing there.

He smiled, and when he spread his arms wide, she ran to him.

"Oh, Amber." He kissed the top of her head. "Something came up, and I couldn't get away. Change into some jeans and grab a jacket."

౭౦

Brandon gripped Amber's hand as he led her along the trail that looped through the woods near the Little Missouri River Badlands. The trail where they'd first met.

"Can you at least tell me why we have to do this at night? It's a little eerie out here in the dark. Aren't there coyotes or wolves?"

Chuckling, he said, "I'm glad you weren't worried about the coyotes and wolves the night you saved me." Shining his flashlight to guide the way, he squeezed her hand and tugged her behind him.

This wasn't going like he planned. He could tell she was irritated. Maybe he'd read her wrong all along. But there was no other way to do this.

He reached the spot he'd been searching for. "Now, follow me closely and watch your step."

"What are we doing?"

"You'll see."

"Okay. I have no choice but to trust you."

He led her through the trees and brush into a clearing. "Okay, stay close to me and watch your step."

"Have you forgotten my family heirloom?"

The playfulness was back in her voice. He loved it. "How could I forget?"

Drawing near the rocky edge, he decided that was close enough. "Okay, this will do."

"What did you want me to see?"

"Remember the first time we met, and I told you about the ancient ruins?"

In the light of the full moon, Brandon could see Amber nod and search the rolling and rocky badland formations. Her eyes slowly grew wide. "Oh, Brandon, it's beautiful. Thank you for this. I couldn't have imagined it."

"From the first moment I met you, I've wanted to show you this."

Amber turned her face to him, her eyes glistening in the moonlight. "And now?"

And now, would Brandon experience the rejection he'd doled out years before? A thick knot constricted his throat. Would she or wouldn't she?

"I couldn't think of a better place to propose to you."

She gasped, the liquid gold in her eyes muting to silver in the moonlight.

With his thumb, he lifted her chin, searched her gaze, and saw the answer to his unspoken question waiting there. "Amber McKinsey, you are rare and precious—you stand out from all others. I love you. Though I don't deserve you, would you become my wife?"

"Yes, oh yes." Lips trembling, her whispered answer resounded through the Badlands of North Dakota.

Brandon smiled, consumed with relief and joy. And her trembling lips. . .he'd looked forward to kissing them all day long. He leaned toward her, feeling her warm breath against his face. Gently he pressed his lips against hers. Her hands slid up his chest and around his neck, drawing him closer. Deepening the kiss, he surrendered his heart completely.

Amber was the one to break the moment, pulling away. A

slight frown broke into her lips.

Brandon had yet to recover from the kiss, but the look on her face worried him. "What's the matter?"

"But how will we do this? Me off at school and you managing your museum?"

"Not to worry. I plan to accept a teaching position at UND. Dr. Young contacted me."

"But I thought you loved directing the museum."

"I do, but I love mentoring and had put in my application to UND in case I couldn't make the museum successful. The accreditation should be approved within the next few weeks, and once that's done, well then, I've accomplished that goal. A change of scenery is in order."

"But you only just hired Michael," she said, the ring of concern still in her voice.

Brandon pressed his nose against hers. "What's with all the questions? Michael knows what he's doing and what he doesn't know, I'll teach him. All I need to do now is work with the board to find a new director."

Amber sighed, seemingly content with his answers. "Just one more question."

"You'd better hurry. I'm seriously close to kissing you again."

"How did you know I'd marry you?"

He considered her question, slowly. "I didn't, actually. I waited for a sign."

"A sign?"

He tilted her chin slightly. "Sign number one, the way you look at me."

Her eyelashes fluttering, she giggled.

"Sign number two. . ." Brandon leaned in and kissed her again, thoroughly. When he released her, his voice was gruff as he said, "The way you respond to my kisses."

She smiled up at him, her face aglow from the moonlight, or was it his kiss?

"And sign number three?" she asked, her voice a whisper.

"You risked your life for mine."

epilogue

Standing in the foyer of Harrington Christian Fellowship, Amber prayed she wouldn't cry from the sheer delight of the occasion. Though it took thousands of years to create fossils and only time could produce ancient artifacts, she had found something far more valuable in Brandon, and it had only taken a few short weeks.

In the same time, God had restored her relationship with Him and with her brother. Her joy was profound.

"You're the most beautiful bride in the world, Amber." Michael lifted her hand and kissed it. "I'm more than privileged to walk you down the aisle."

The special moment came and someone opened the double doors, exposing Amber to the small gathering—signaling her to begin the once in a lifetime walk. Familiar faces—Cams, Muriel, and Gladys—smiled from the pews, as well as other friends. Claire from Brandon's Bible study played the wedding march on the organ as Amber took the customary rhythmic steps alongside Michael.

In her wildest dreams, she couldn't have imagined that her summer would end with a proposal. Wearing a tuxedo, Brandon stood at the end of the aisle, looking handsome beyond words.

She'd been packed and ready to leave for the fall semester at UND, but she and Brandon decided they wanted to marry as soon as possible. So, she'd taken the fall semester off to spend time with her new husband. Brandon had been invited to teach at UND in the spring, an offer he accepted once she had accepted his proposal. She recognized it as a sacrifice of sorts that he'd made for her, to be with her. She had a feeling—or maybe she'd seen the signs—that they would both end up back in paleontology, a love they both shared. She liked the idea of digging in the dirt with their children.

Before she realized it, she stood next to Dr. Brandon Selman. In her peripheral vision, she could see his sweet, elderly parents sitting in the first row, smiling, his mother wiping her tears.

They spoke their vows, and finally, Pastor John said, "You may kiss the bride."

Brandon's lips held the promise of his love, and Amber knew that a lifetime together, refined by time and pressure, would produce a marriage beyond price.

A Letter To Our Readers

Dear Reader:

In order that we might better contribute to your reading enjoyment, we would appreciate your taking a few minutes to respond to the following questions. We welcome your comments and read each form and letter we receive. When completed, please return to the following:

Fiction Editor
Heartsong Presents
PO Box 719
Uhrichsville, Ohio 44683

1. Did you enjoy reading *Exposing Amber* by Elizabeth Goddard?
   ❏ Very much! I would like to see more books by this author!
   ❏ Moderately. I would have enjoyed it more if

   _____

   _____

   _____

2. Are you a member of **Heartsong Presents**? ❏ Yes ❏ No
   If no, where did you purchase this book? _____

   _____

3. How would you rate, on a scale from 1 (poor) to 5 (superior), the cover design? _____

4. On a scale from 1 (poor) to 10 (superior), please rate the following elements.

   ____ Heroine   ____ Plot
   ____ Hero   ____ Inspirational theme
   ____ Setting   ____ Secondary characters

5. These characters were special because? _____

_____

_____

6. How has this book inspired your life? _____

_____

_____

7. What settings would you like to see covered in future
   Heartsong Presents books? _____

_____

_____

8. What are some inspirational themes you would like to see
   treated in future books? _____

_____

_____

9. Would you be interested in reading other **Heartsong
   Presents** titles? ❏ Yes ❏ No

10. Please check your age range:
    ❏ Under 18   ❏ 18-24
    ❏ 25-34   ❏ 35-45
    ❏ 46-55   ❏ Over 55

Name _____

Occupation _____

Address _____

City, State, Zip_____

E-mail _____

"WHAT DO YOU KNOW ABOUT ME?"

Nikolas's eyes narrowed as he spoke

"What is there to know?" Candace flung back. "Just what are you trying to hide from?"

Nikolas shuddered, the convulsion racking his entire body. "I may be trying to hide from quite a few things," he said quietly. "No matter. You and I are like ships passing in the night. Soon you will be gone and meeting me will be only a memory. Perhaps I should add one more reminder before you leave."

Their eyes fused. Suddenly, Candace needed no invitation to move into his arms. His kiss was like an explosion. It rocked her to the very soul and sent her sleeping passion soaring.

No matter what happened, she could never forget Nikolas Mylonis. But could she forget he didn't trust her—and never would?

MEG HUDSON
is also the author
of these SUPERROMANCES

These books may be available at your local bookseller
or by writing to:

Worldwide Reader Service
1440 South Priest Drive, Tempe, AZ 85281
Canadian address: Stratford, Ontario N5A 6W2

MEG HUDSON
A CHARM
FOR ADONIS

A SUPERROMANCE FROM
WORLDWIDE

TORONTO · NEW YORK · LOS ANGELES · LONDON

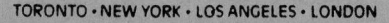

For S.H.K., who would provide any author with
unlimited inspiration and the desire to do better.
My very real appreciation for the work you do with me

———————————————◆•◆———————————————

Published July 1983

First printing May 1983

ISBN 0-373-70070-9

CHAPTER ONE

DUSK WAS SENDING FORTH exploring fingers as Candace Mayhew drove through the old central business section of Tarpon Springs, and she acknowledged with irritation that the clock had definitely got ahead of her.

After leaving the friends in Sarasota with whom she'd spent the weekend, she had opted to follow the shore route on her trip north, thus bypassing the congested area around the city of St. Petersburg. She had envisioned a pleasant, leisurely drive along Florida's gulf coast, but it hadn't been like that at all. The long miles of gulf-front communities had been choked with cars and people, the heat of the afternoon sun had been blistering and there had been road construction at two different places along the way to further impede her progress.

It had taken her over three hours to accomplish a drive of less than one hundred miles, and in the process she had lost a precious amount of daylight! She frowned, squinting slightly as she tried to make out the street sign on the corner she was now approaching, which was not a very well-lit one. She deciphered the words "Hellenic Avenue" just in time to signal left, then found herself driving down a street paved in large rectangular dark red bricks.

The street sloped gently downhill, and at the end

she saw the flashing sign of the motel she was seeking. The Grecian Gardens. Candace couldn't help
smiling. It was a euphemistic name to say the least,
and she wondered if the place would live up to its
promise. The motel was moderately priced by in-
season Florida standards, but she'd chosen it
primarily because her map of the area had shown her
it was very near Spring Bayou, where some of the
festivities she would be photographing tomorrow
were to take place.

The street curved slightly, causing her headlights to
sweep past a long low brick wall to her left. The wall
was centered with an ornate white wrought-iron gate.
Candace glimpsed a large inner yard, planted with
palms and some rather grotesquely shaped cacti, and
a huge house that seemed to be circular in shape. The
mini view was tantalizing enough to whet her curiosity. A veritable estate, right in the center of Florida's
most prominent Greek community. She wondered
who owned it.

Conjecture about the house was forgotten as she
found a parking place in front of the motel's office
and checked in. The young woman at the registration
desk was unmistakably Greek or of Greek descent.
Her English was unaccented, but her clear-cut
features could have graced an antique Grecian coin,
and her olive skin, very dark eyes and lustrous raven
hair gave further testimony to her ancestry.

She answered the telephone and began speaking in
a language completely incomprehensible to Candace,
except for the single word *kali*. In studying up on
Tarpon Springs and its Greek community, she'd
come across a few Greek phrases. *Kali*, she knew,
meant ''good.''

The young woman hung up the phone and with a smile easily switched into English again as she registered Candace and handed her the key to her room. A moment later Candace was discovering her motel room wasn't quite a Grecian garden, though it was adequate. Clean and cool, the decor was simple and the furniture functional. The draperies and bedspread were of a shade that might be called Mediterranean blue, and over the bed there was a large framed color photograph of the Acropolis by night. Another touch of Greece.

As Candace unpacked, she mentally sketched out her plans for tomorrow. She had hoped to explore some of the area beforehand so she'd be familiar with the general terrain, but her late arrival had prevented this. Nevertheless, she had a good local map, and she planned to spend some time tonight further familiarizing herself with it.

The Epiphany celebration for which Tarpon Springs was so famous would, she knew, begin at St. Nicholas Cathedral, the Greek Orthodox Church. As she understood it, the day started with the cathedral bells ringing out at dawn—literally—to summon those who would be coming from far and near for this very special occasion. And the service at the cathedral would be only the beginning, she warned herself. Candace had been over the entire list of events again and again, and now she reviewed them once more, because it was absolutely vital she cover every one of them. This was her first assignment for *Tempo* magazine, which was new and already quite prestigious. If she did a really terrific job with both her pictures and the text for her story on the Greeks of Tarpon Springs, she not only would be assured of future assignments but would have carved a nice little niche for herself in the field of photojournalism.

To verify her own recollections, she opened her briefcase and took out the sheet of paper that she'd typed in her New York apartment the week before, after a detailed phone conversation with the vice-president of the Tarpon Springs Chamber of Commerce.

There would be a procession through the streets of town after the church service, she noted, culminating at Spring Bayou. There, the climax of the celebration would come when the highest-ranking member of the clergy present would throw a gold cross into the water and, simultaneously, dozens of Greek youths would dive in to try to retrieve it. This was a scene she wanted to make sure she'd capture on film, in every detail.

The youth who recovered the cross would be honored for the rest of the day, and if legend held true, he was certain to be the recipient of all sorts of good fortune during the coming year.

Until the wee small hours of the next morning there would be banquets and balls and dances and feasting and frolicking. All absolute manna, Candace thought with satisfaction, for both her camera and her typewriter.

Tucking the sheet of paper back into her briefcase, she became increasingly aware of some sharp pangs that could only be attributed to hunger. She had not stopped for lunch along the way on the drive north and now, glancing at her slim silver-banded wristwatch, she realized it had been far too many hours since she'd nibbled that single piece of toast and had sipped a cup of black coffee back in Sarasota.

The motel did not have its own café, but the young woman at the desk had recommended two restaurants on the main street of town, both within walking distance.

Before setting forth, Candace paused to freshen her makeup and to comb out her long light blond hair, which she'd twisted into a coil at the nape of her neck. She was wearing a pale blue cotton-knit dress that was cool and attractive, but she realized as she glanced at her reflection in the mirror neither the color nor the style did very much for her. She had selected it for travel because it washed easily and was wrinkleproof. True pastels such as this, though, tended to make her look a bit too fragile—almost washed out. A richer tone would have intensified the deep blue color of her large expressive eyes, whereas this pale shade seemed to play up the shadows beneath those same eyes.

Also, she'd bought the dress the previous summer, and until she'd slipped it on in Sarasota, she hadn't fully realized just how much weight she'd lost since then. *Divorce is a much more effective way of getting thin than dieting,* she told her mirrored reflection wryly, and then she made a face at herself.

You've started on a new life, remember? She told this to the rather austere-looking young woman in the mirror. Then she stared at herself, wishing she could honestly say, "You're doing fine, Candy!"

As it was, she knew only too well her self-confidence was not as solid as she made it seem to others, or as she wanted it to be. Nor was she pleased with her reflection. She completely bypassed the excellent bone structure that made her face such an interesting one, with its rather high cheekbones, almost

classically straight nose and full, generous mouth.
Within the past few months she'd met two artists,
noted for their portraiture, who'd wanted to paint
her. She had refused them both, and she still couldn't
understand what they'd seen in her that had made
them want to translate their impressions to canvas. In
her opinion she was merely a pale and rather uninter-
esting blonde, with a figure that had been pleasantly
willowy in the past but now was getting downright
angular.

I'm going to have to make myself eat more, she
decided, and with this thought firmly in mind left the
motel and headed up toward the main street.

It was dark now, and she had to be reasonably
careful as she walked along because the sidewalk was
made of hexagonal slabs of concrete, some of which
were crumbling, so the footing was a bit precarious in
spots.

A short distance up the street she came to the
house that had intrigued her so, earlier. It was really
quite impressive, although the front area—with its
palms and cacti—looked as if it could do with a bit of
care. This, of course, was an observation made in the
rather dim, slanting light of a street lamp.

The brick wall ran across the full front of the prop-
erty, and there was another white wrought-iron gate
at the far end. This closed off a straight driveway
that ran to a porte cochere jutting out midway along
the left side of the house. Closer, a short flight of
steps with elaborate wrought-iron railings led to a
small, enclosed porch. But the rest of the first floor
was, indeed, circular in shape, as she'd thought when
she first glimpsed it, and there were wide, louvered
windows all the way around.

At the moment, both of the entrance gates were firmly closed, and through the louvered window slats Candace could see only a single light gleaming on the downstairs floor. The sparse lighting made the place look lonely, even desolate, yet there evidently was someone home. At least, there was a polished, pale gray car parked beneath the porte cochere.

Candace chuckled inwardly. Her career as a photojournalist was a fairly new one, but it had already enhanced her curiosity about people and places and things. Then she sobered, knowing there was nothing funny about this. She was grateful for her heightened sense of curiosity, her interest in others, which was exactly what she had needed since the disastrous finale of a marriage that had gone so entirely wrong.

Jeff. His name flicked across her memory, and she shivered. Jeff had never understood that expressing herself in writing had come as naturally to her as breathing. He never would have understood it. A lawyer in their hometown of Albany, he'd had his eyes firmly fixed on the New York State political scene, and he'd been possessed of scant patience toward his wife's literary aspirations.

Jeff. Candace shook herself mentally. Damn it, she was not going to think of him! There was no point in thinking about Jeff, she reminded herself sharply. It was a year since he had married the woman who had precipitated their divorce. The woman hadn't caused it—Candace had made that clear to herself from the very beginning. The rift between Jeff and herself had already become far too wide to breach. No, the lovely brunette Jeff was now married to had acted merely as a catalyst, bringing matters to a head earlier than might have happened otherwise. Nevertheless, the end result had left Candace with a nagging sense of failure. Somehow. . . .

Resolutely she shut off these negative thoughts as she turned the corner and began searching for the two restaurants that had been recommended to her.

She reached the first almost immediately to find, although it was just a little after eight, the lights had already been extinguished. In fact, this entire small business center of Tarpon Springs seemed to have shut down for the night. She quickened her steps, afraid the second restaurant might also have decided to close because of lack of business.

From her contact with the chamber of commerce, she knew there were several restaurants over in the waterfront area of the town around the sponge docks. But she was too hungry to go back to the motel and get her car and drive off in search of food unless the second restaurant, too, had closed.

It didn't become necessary. Peering through the slightly grimy window, Candace could see there were still two men sitting at a rear table, and hesitating only briefly, she pushed the front door open and went inside.

The restaurant was long and narrow, both the length and the narrowness accented by the vertically striped wallpaper in alternating panels of terra-cotta, apricot and citron. These same colors had been picked up in the tiled squares on the floor and in the varying shades of the plastic tablecloths.

A glass case on the immediate left held an assortment of Greek pastries. There was a counter to the right but evidently this was for takeout orders only. At least, there were no places to sit.

A woman came around the edge of the counter,

and looking at her Candace saw no hint of welcome and was sure she was about to be told they'd closed for the day.

She asked quickly, "Is it too late for dinner?" and was certain the woman would answer that it was. She could, in fact, virtually see the woman's hesitation. She was a fairly short woman, plump, dressed in a sagging black skirt with a loose-fitting printed blouse atop it. Her thick black hair was sprinkled with silver, her skin more sallow than truly olive, and there were deep shadows beneath her dark eyes. Candace felt a pang of sympathy toward her. She looked hot, tired, and obviously had been about to call it a day. But still she managed a smile and said in heavily accented English, "Is all right."

She waved to the nearest table and Candace sat down gratefully, scanning the limp, much used menu that was handed to her. She settled on the lamb with rice, since Greeks were noted for their lamb dishes, and a moment later was presented with a bowl of salad laden with chunks of fresh, ripe tomatoes, black olives and creamy, delicious feta cheese. The lamb came as soon as she finished the salad and was excellently cooked, flavored with a subtle blend of herbs and spices she couldn't quite identify. She topped off the meal with hot black coffee and agreed to the recommendation she try a *baklava*, which was "homemade." The pastry was wonderfully flaky, the filling rich with chopped nuts, and there was just enough honey-and-lemon syrup poured over it to make it sweet, yet not too sweet.

As she ate, Candace noticed the woman was working entirely alone in the establishment, doing all the cooking, all the serving, and washing up dishes in between.

She was also aware of the steady hum of conversation behind her, this in deep, masculine voices. The two men were still seated at the rear table and they seemed to have a lot to say to each other. Further, they were saying it entirely in Greek.

Candace was lingering over a second cup of coffee when she heard chairs being pushed back, and first one of the men, then the other came into view. Her eyes were riveted to the taller...and he was very tall indeed. Well over six feet, she would guess, with broad shoulders tapering to a very slim waistline, narrow hips and extremely long legs, clearly defined by the tight-fitting jeans he was wearing. He stood at the counter chatting with the proprietress and he laughed once, but it was a very brief mirthless laugh. She could see only the back of his head, but his hair was thick, very dark, and someone had given him an extremely good haircut. It was perfectly sculpted in a classically masculine style.

The woman behind the counter was talking to him volubly. She, too, seemed to have a lot to say, and he was listening to her with his head tilted slightly to one side, obviously giving her his full attention. The man with him was of a slighter build, tall though not as tall as his companion, with hair just as black but shaggier. He was turned slightly toward Candace so she could see his skin was deeply tanned, and he had a slim black mustache that gave him a rakish look. He, too, wore jeans and a shirt open at the throat. She caught the gleam of a gold chain around his neck, echoed in a similar chain worn by the taller man, who was bending over the counter now, looking at something the woman was holding out to him. Candace was able to catch the glint of the shimmering metal at the nape of his neck.

She found herself wishing the men would leave because she had no desire to interrupt the conversation going on at the counter in order to ask for her check. The dialogue seemed to be getting considerably more spirited, for that matter. The woman was turning her attention to the shorter of the two men, and her voice snapped with an anger she seemed unable to suppress. Candace sensed a defensiveness to his retorts, as if he were having difficulty with his explanations. And the tall man seemed to be playing the role of arbitrator. At least, he was listening to both parties with an intentness made very clear by the tilt of his head. And every now and then he said something that usually provoked a moment of silence before the woman started speaking all over again.

This, Candace realized, could go on for ages, and she stirred restlessly. And at just that moment the shorter of the two men turned and noted her movement, then spoke quickly to the woman behind the counter.

The woman nodded and called out, "Miss? You are finished?"

Candace bit her lip because she hadn't wanted to attract this sort of attention. But she merely said, "Yes," and then was further chagrined to see the woman holding out a crumpled piece of paper. Obviously, her check.

There was nothing to do but make her way up to the counter, and as she did so she was fully aware the young Greek who had noticed her was eyeing her with unconcealed admiration. His dark eyes flicked over her face, then traveled down the full length of her body, missing nothing at all, and she was glad she'd lost weight so the knit dress didn't fit nearly so snugly as it had originally.

There was a brashness to the young Greek's stare that annoyed her. At least, it seemed to her he was being brash. In an effort to avoid his overly appreciative dark glance she averted her gaze from him, only to feel as if she'd been impaled by the focus of quite a different sort of attention.

Eyes that were the color of green olives stared at her, and there was no admiration at all in their depths. She had not realized green could be such a cold color. These eyes reminded her of the frigid water at the bottom of a deep quarry she'd visited once, up in Maine.

There was an arrogance stamped in every line of the man's features that made Candace react instinctively. It was impossible not to resent it when someone looked at you like this! And those features were arresting, disconcerting. It was very difficult not to stare back at him. Oddly, he was very handsome and yet not handsome. She couldn't quite define it but knew only there was something strange about his face. This impression was derived from a single and very fleeting appraisal, for she quickly looked away.

The younger man made way for her at the counter, saying, "Excuse please, *despinís*," as he moved slightly to one side. But the other man stood his ground, so she was forced to get a bit closer to him than she really wanted to.

She could feel herself flushing as she took the check, to find her meal had been astonishingly inexpensive. Piqued with herself for being so easily disconcerted by this dark stranger who seemed to be glowering over her, she felt in her handbag for her wallet with fingers that fumbled, even though it was ridiculous that she should permit herself to become so flustered. Then, there was change to be made, and the matter of deciding upon a tip. The woman obviously ran the place; possibly a tip would offend her, yet she looked so work weary. It was this that swayed Candace. She held out two crumpled dollar bills and turned her best smile upon the tired, sallow proprietress.

"It was delicious," she said.

"Thank you," the woman answered, and then added in her heavily accented English, "Tomorrow we close for the blessing. But the next morning we are open for breakfast. Seven o'clock, okay?"

"Yes," Candace said. "I shall hope to see you then."

"*Kalinihta*, miss," the woman nodded, and Candace nodded back. Then she escaped into a night that still held more than some of the traces of the day's heat, knowing her own cheeks were far warmer than the temperature.

It seemed to her a cold, olive gaze followed her, which was puzzling. Although she was glad that the taller man had not reacted toward her as his companion had, she couldn't see why, on the other hand, he had seemed so unfriendly.

Further, she'd had the definite impression, in that brief moment when she'd looked at him, she had seen him before. There was something hauntingly familiar about him, which didn't really make sense. Certainly it would be impossible ever to have encountered this man before and then to have forgotten him. No,

Candace admitted wryly, recognition would have been instantaneous. Like him or not—at the very least, he was memorable!

Nevertheless, she found herself searching her memory as she walked back to the motel, as if she might suddenly stumble upon some hidden episode in her life she'd forgotten about. An episode in which the disconcerting stranger might have infiltrated briefly, at some point in the past.

There just weren't any hidden corners. She'd been born and raised in Albany, where her father had been an English teacher in a high school. He had died when she was seventeen, and so thoughts of going on to college and majoring in creative writing had, of necessity, been abandoned. Instead she had gone to secretarial school. Meantime she'd lived at home with her mother and an older sister.

Her mother was of English descent, and her father had come from an old-line American family. Mayhew, in fact, was a very old New England name, far antedating the American Revolution. Candace had been brought up with a deep sense of pride in her background and there had not been much that was "foreign" in her environment. The dark stranger, she thought ruefully, very definitely was foreign. For that matter, she didn't even know whether or not he was able to speak English. She had heard him speak only Greek. He would have been totally alien in the world in which she had been brought up. All the more reason why she could not possibly have forgotten him if they'd ever chanced to meet before.

After secretarial school she had gone to work in Albany. Jeff had been the lawyer representing the company she worked for. Or, rather, he had been one in the firm of lawyers and a very junior partner at the time. They had married when he was twenty-eight and she only twenty. She, at least, had been too young, too unprepared to become wife to a man who already had his aims set on a course that didn't truly appeal to her. Politics was not her forte. She tried to be enthusiastic, gave up her job to please Jeff and even campaigned with him when he ran for the state legislature. But when he was defeated he blamed her, in part, for not having been more supportive. And his failure in bringing in the vote was only a part of all he blamed her for. The physical side of their marriage had never been good; not, that is, once they'd settled into what Candace considered lovemaking by rote. Jeff had been possessed of a physical appetite that demanded regular satisfaction, but inexperienced though she was—for he was the only man she had ever known in an intimate sense—Candace was aware he was a very poor lover.

In lovemaking, as in most things, Jeff had taken without giving. If, looking back, she could think of the single thing that had been the most lacking in her marriage, Candace knew she would now, with the wisdom of hindsight, say it had been affection. There had been an initial sensual stimulus between Jeff and herself, youth calling to youth. But beyond that....

She shook her head in a silent reproach to a past that had so many dark shadows interwoven through its fabric. Inevitably, Jeff had turned to other women. Finally, there had been just one other woman, one face among the faces, and Jeff had asked Candace for a divorce. She'd still been recovering from the trauma of a miscarriage. Now she realized how much more complicated it all would have been had their child survived.

As it was, it was easy enough to say yes to a divorce by that time, even though divorce, of itself, was very much against her principles. A throwback, she supposed, to the fairly narrow morality of her childhood. But she'd faced the breakup of her marriage as she'd faced most things since her father's death—alone. Her mother had remarried, and she and her second husband had later moved to Arizona. Her sister was married and lived in Chicago, and they had never been close anyway. And there was no one else.

No, she thought, as she turned in at the motel. There was no way the dark-haired man she'd seen tonight could ever have walked his way through even a moment of her life. He would have been a raven-haired comet on her horizon, streaking across what much too often had been a very dull sky.

Where, then, had she seen him?

CHAPTER TWO

THE CATHEDRAL BELLS did herald the dawn with their pealing the next morning. Candace dressed quickly and gathered her camera equipment together, then hurried up the street toward the round-domed, yellow-stone, neo-Byzantine-style cathedral on Pinellas Avenue. Even so, the crowd was ahead of her.

She made her way up the steps, disconcertingly aware of the fact she could capture little of any real photographic merit with all these people milling around her.

Although she'd been sent all the proper media credentials for covering the day's events and was wearing a large badge with "Press" printed in big letters on it, she soon saw there was little chance of pushing through to the inside of the church. Also, she doubted picture taking would be encouraged while the service was in progress.

She could smell the wafting scent of incense and she heard voices raised in rich, glorious tones. The music they were singing was both strange and wonderful to her. Through a wedge in the mass of people filling the corridors she could glimpse tapering white candles and she could see members of the clergy dressed in lavish robes, heavily embroidered with gold. She saw one especially impressive figure raise a silver staff capped by an intricately embossed head

She noted the chandeliers in the church were magnificent, and toward the altar she could see rows of votive candles flickering in red glass holders. The stained-glass windows—depicting various saints, she guessed—were in beautiful, deep-toned colors, and there were many equally vivid paintings of other holy figures scattered across the walls and ceiling of the church. These were not considered portraits, she reminded herself, but icons. She had read that Greeks often cherished a particular saint and kept his icon in their home. The religious picture or figure could be appealed to for a special intercession with God or talked to as if talking with a beloved friend. She liked the idea of this.

As for taking meaningful photographs of anything at the moment, Candace again told herself it was an impossibility. She could write down her impressions, to be sure, but she would have to come back to the cathedral later and study it more closely when it was not packed with wall-to-wall humanity.

She slowly made her way out of the packed vestibule and started down the stone steps in front of the church, looking for potential camera material. She soon saw two little girls dressed in Greek costumes, standing with their parents along the curb as they waited for the procession to emerge from the cathedral and begin wending its way through the town toward Spring Bayou. The children were enchanting and Candace quickly sought permission to take their pictures. Then she photographed a little venerable woman dressed entirely in black, and after that she concentrated on various other individuals, entranced by the character in their faces. All of these people seemed stamped with a brand of individualism she found unique.

Finally the doors of the cathedral opened wide, the crowds began to leave and the procession started. Candace clicked her camera furiously as she saw the choir members come out in their robes, one of them walking ahead of the rest, carrying a dove. As the richly garbed priest she had seen earlier came closer, she saw that the ornate top of the silver staff he carried represented two entwined silver serpents. All these things were symbolic, she knew, and later she would have to check their precise meanings. For the moment, she kept on taking picture after picture, pausing only to reload her camera.

There were quite a number of people in the procession, and some of the little boys were dressed as miniature, make-believe versions of the Evzones— soldiers with long white stockings, frilly short white skirts and red fezes atop their heads. Other children were dressed as angels, and still others wore a variety of traditional Greek costumes, like the two girls she had photographed earlier at the curb side.

As the procession moved down Pinellas Avenue, the crowd moved with it, until street and sidewalks alike were jam-packed with people. Candace was not the only photographer in evidence. There were quite a few others, some of them undoubtedly from area newspapers, and it seemed to her all of them were obviously more adept at working in the middle of crowds than she was. Until now, she had specialized in portrait photography to accompany articles she had been writing—and selling—since she'd made the decision to turn, temporarily, from fiction to fact. She had also done a few scenic shots that were very good, and it was this combined talent for handling people and places that had brought her the assignment with *Tempo*. But this mad-scramble type of photography was something else again!

The other photographers seemed capable of running ahead of the crowd, crouching down so they could get oncoming shots of the procession without any interference. Candace felt as if she were trailing in their wake, and she made a valiant attempt to push ahead on her own as the procession swung away from the main street and started down the sloping hill toward the bayou.

She soon found herself fighting against very definite odds as she tried to round the corner in front of the crowd. Simultaneously, she noted to her chagrin the other photographers had already somehow got ahead of her, establishing their vantage points along the curb side, then moving on, as the need arose, with a facility she envied. Her one course was to speed across the hexagon-paved sidewalk and make it down the street to the bayou before they did. But a whole group of teenagers obviously developed the same idea at the same time, and the result was disastrous.

Eager young bodies thrust against her, and as Candace tried to avoid them her heel caught in one of the crumbled concrete paving stones. Pain shot through her ankle as it twisted, and her camera literally flew out of her hands. Despite the pure agony of taking a step, she made a frantic lurch forward trying to retrieve it. Stunned, she saw the camera fall to the street and bounce into the gutter. Then, as the crowd thronged forward, it was lost from sight.

Caught in the press of the mob, she was further

thrown off balance, and just as she felt certain she was going to topple to the ground and roll down the street after her vanishing camera, strong arms gripped her.

"What the hell are you trying to do?" a low masculine voice growled, and even before she looked up she knew who it was going to be.

Clutching both her arms and actually forcing her to remain upright, the dark stranger looked far more menacing—and even bigger—than he had the night before. Olive green eyes swept scathingly across her face, leaving Candace with the feeling she'd been pierced by a laser beam. Then he pulled her backward, away from the sidewalk, and the pain of moving was so intense that she closed her eyes tightly and couldn't suppress a moan.

Her rescuer gripped her still more firmly and lifted her off her feet, and she felt herself being skimmed across the surface of the sidewalk. Then she heard something clang and opened her eyes to see the arrogant Greek had kicked a gate shut—a white wrought-iron gate—and they were inside the yard of the house that had fascinated her so much the evening before.

"Can you stand?" he now demanded, making the question sound like a challenge.

"Yes!" Candace insisted promptly, gritting her teeth as she tried to put both feet firmly on the ground. She bit her lip as a new stab of pain shot through her, and despite herself she swayed.

He muttered something that could have been either Greek or English, for it was too low to be heard distinctly. But there was little doubt he was using a choice expletive.

There also seemed no doubt he was thoroughly dis-

gusted with her. He scowled and said, "I suppose
there's nothing else to be done with you," as if this
decision didn't please him in the least. Then, while
she attempted to protest volubly, he picked her up
bodily and in another moment had crossed the yard
and climbed up the short flight of steps to the entrance. He kicked the front door open as uncere-
moniously as he had kicked the gate closed and
continued through a shadowed foyer into a corridor
that seemed rather like the center of a wheel, from
which rooms spoked off. He took Candace into the
nearest room, where sheer sea green drapes had been
drawn across the windows. A ceiling fan whirred lazily. She was aware of lots of bookcases and somewhat
worn but very comfortable-looking furniture. Then
she was thrust into an armchair covered in a pale
shade of lemon. At least, she felt as if she were being
thrust, although after a moment she realized her
rescuer had actually settled her into the chair with
surprising care. It occurred to her that he could, in
fact, be very gentle. . . when he wished to be.

Without speaking, he knelt down in front of her,
pulling up a nearby hassock as he did so. In another
moment her leg had been lifted—again with astonishing care—onto the hassock, and he did have the grace
to say, "This will hurt," as he removed her shoe.

It did hurt. Candace winced and very nearly cried
out, once again biting her lip in the effort to remain
silent. The tall dark man, still kneeling in front of
her, held her shoe between hands with surprisingly
slender fingers—the hands of an artist, she found
herself thinking—and he looked at it with absolute
disdain. Actually, it was a pretty shoe. A sandal,
striped in cream and a coffee brown that matched the

sheer cotton blouse she was wearing over tan jeans. She had, in fact, chosen this particular pair of shoes because they had seemed just right for the sort of walking she had expected to be doing.

Her rescuer, however, clearly thought otherwise. ''Ridiculous!'' he snorted, sweeping her again with those searing olive eyes. ''It's a wonder you didn't break your neck! As it is, you've made enough of a mess of things.''

He was looking down at her ankle, and following his gaze Candace saw to her dismay it was already beginning to swell.

The dark Greek tossed her sandal aside as if it deserved to go straight onto a garbage heap and then got to his feet and left her without a word.

She stared after his retreating figure numbly, only wishing she could get up and be gone from here before he reappeared. But there was no chance of it. She made a tentative move with her foot just to be sure of this, and the pain was excruciating. There was little doubt she'd fall on her face long before she got to the door if she attempted to escape.

She sank back in the chair, closing her eyes, and tears of remorse came to smart against her lids. By now the procession would have reached the bayou and the boys would have dived for the gold cross. The highlight of the entire day, absolutely vital to the photographic content of her story, and she'd missed it! She'd botched the whole assignment and she blamed herself for it bitterly. It seemed to her she had been singularly inept. Certainly she should have been able to manage the whole thing better.

She told herself if she'd had any sense she would have come directly to Tarpon Springs to become bet-

ter acquainted with the locale in advance, instead of
first going to Sarasota. But the purpose of her trip
there had been to visit an elderly couple she'd known
since she was a child. They'd been friends of her
father's, actually, and had retired to Florida nearly
ten years ago Visiting them had been a link with that
part of her past that was warm and wonderful, the
time when her father was still alive—long before
she'd met Jeff.

A shuddering sigh escaped her, and she was startled when a harsh, masculine voice broke through it
to ask, "Is it really so terrible?"

He was looking down at her mockingly, and even
though reason said she scarcely knew him, she decided in that moment she hated him.

"Yes," she said testily, "it is!" She tried to be as
scathing in her tone as he'd been in most of the looks
he'd bestowed upon her, but her voice trembled and
she knew she must be appearing both stupid and
weak.

As if to further this conviction he laughed, a
derisive sort of laugh that she found very grating. It
was an abrasive sound, and it rubbed against feelings
that were not yet healed. The reasons, of course, had
nothing at all to do with this dark stranger, but that
knowledge didn't help. Dismally, she realized she
wasn't able to hold back her tears, and she flung out
blindly, "Go away, will you!"

The tears began to stream while she spoke, and
there was nothing to do but let them come. Then she
felt something large and soft thrust into her hand and
he said, "Dry your eyes. They are too lovely to be
drenched by weeping."

The comment astonished her so much she dabbed

at her eyes like an obedient child, and it was as if his words had served to stem the flow of her tears. She clutched the piece of cloth he had given her, noting it was not one of his handkerchiefs, as she had first surmised, but a napkin made of very fine linen, linen that obviously had been laundered many, many times to bring it to its present softness. Then she saw he'd stacked several similar napkins on a small table by his side, and he was also edging a bucket toward the hassock in which she could catch the glint of ice.

He smiled slightly as he looked down at her and said, "In answer to your request, there'd really be no place for me to go at the moment. And it would be rather stupid of me to leave you sitting here, don't you think? You wouldn't get very far."

Their eyes meshed, and suddenly olive green didn't seem such a cold color after all. Candace trembled, a reaction that had nothing to do with her throbbing ankle, and found herself swallowing hard. He was astonishingly attractive when he smiled—even such a slight smile—and again she felt the odd sense of having seen him somewhere before. This became such a conviction that the words "Have we met somewhere?" came very close to being spoken. Then, at the last instant, she decided without knowing why that for the present it would be better if this were a question left unposed.

He had pulled a straight-backed chair up close to the hassock, and as she watched, he sat down on it. He said, "I'm going to move your leg over so you can put your foot down into this pail of ice water. It will be a painful jolt, but nevertheless it's the best treatment."

She nodded, finding to her surprise she trusted his

judgment, but a second later she had to clutch the arm of the chair to keep from crying out. Gentle though he was in handling her foot, the shock of plunging the injured ankle into the bath of freezing water was terrific.

He was leaning forward, thoroughly intent on his task, and she could not help noticing what absolutely beautiful hair he had. It was like black satin. Then her eyes fell to the left side of his face, which was presented to her fully now, for the first time, and a silent gasp clutched at her throat.

Seen close up, there was a network of fine scars clearly visible. They crossed skin that on the other side of his face—the side, she realized now, he was careful to offer to the world whenever possible—was perfectly smooth. Another scar, deeper and more jagged than the rest, started just an inch or two above his eyebrows and disappeared into the dark thickness of his hair.

There was something else, too. There was a curious immobility about the finely scarred side of his face. Obviously, at some time, it must have been badly injured. Even when he'd smiled that slight smile, it had been only a half-smile.

She remembered that at first sight, last night, she had thought he was handsome, yet not handsome. She revised her opinion now, for she knew what had caused it in the first place. His face seemed almost more of a mask than a face. At least, half of it did. But for all of that he was not merely handsome—he was devastatingly attractive! The most attractive man, Candace thought rather weakly, she'd ever seen in her entire life, and her pulse thumped in silent agreement.

Then she saw the dark eyebrows ironically thrust upward, and she realized she'd been blatantly staring at him and he was fully aware of this.

"Well?" he asked, the single word distilled of reproach.

"I'm sorry," Candace stammered.

"No need to be," he said, shrugging slightly. "The surgeons did their best, but there are some things that can't be effaced. . . even by time."

His English was completely without accent and as fluent as her own. Last night his Greek had been equally fluent, at least as far as she could tell. She would have sworn it hadn't been long since he'd left the Aegean by boat or plane. Yet today, except for those dark, arresting good looks that were so completely Hellenic, his roots in America could have gone back as far as her own.

He said now, "I shall get you something to drink. Why don't we remove this other shoe first, though?" He quickly suited action to his words, unfastening the strap of her sandal and tossing it aside, to follow the first one. "I shouldn't think," he commented, "you'd ever want to see these things again."

"They're perfectly good shoes," Candace sputtered. They were, in fact, very good shoes. She'd paid a small mint for them.

"Most unsuitable, I would think, for a journalist such as yourself," he said. He was glancing at her press badge, and a rather derisive smile came to partially curve his lips. "You are with a newspaper?"

"No."

"What, then? Not television, surely."

"No," Candace said reluctantly. "I'm down here

doing a magazine story. At least, that *was* my assignment. Obviously I've failed.''

''Obviously?''

''I didn't get the pictures I needed,'' she said bitterly, and then was assailed by a regrettable memory. ''Oh, no,'' she said. ''My camera and my film!'' She tried to sit up, only to have her ankle protest violently as she moved it in its cold bath.

''What about them?''

''I dropped everything as I twisted my ankle. You saw that, didn't you?''

''I had a rather chaotic impression of it,'' he admitted. ''I didn't know just what it was you were attempting to do. You came running across the sidewalk as if you were trying to run your own private marathon, and then those kids bumped into you.''

''Yes, and that's when my camera flew out of my hands....''

''So,'' he said. ''Well, I doubt you'll see any of it again. Anyway, the camera must surely have been broken. Stamped on, I'd think, in the crush of the crowd. Doubtless your magazine will buy you a new one.''

''Doubtless they won't buy me anything at all,'' Candace told him. ''This is my first assignment for them and they especially wanted full coverage on this story about the Greeks here in Tarpon Springs. It fits in with an entire ethnic theme they're featuring....''

She sighed, her lovely, pale face a mirror of anxiety and frustration. ''I'm afraid I've blown the whole thing,'' she confessed unhappily.

The long, slender fingers came to touch her briefly on the cheek. ''Do not be so upset,'' he said gently. ''Surely your editors will understand when you tell them what has happened. And you will have a chance to get the story and your pictures, too, once you're able to get around again. Everything is not so easily lost, *mikrí mou*. If you have come here to study the Greeks in Tarpon Springs, I am sure you will find other ways of doing so."

"But today was the most important day of all," Candace pointed out.

"No," he contradicted. "Today was not necessarily the most important day of all."

"Epiphany...."

"A major occasion hereabouts, yes. But not everything."

"You yourself were going to the blessing," she accused.

"No," he denied coldly. "I was not going to the blessing. My intention was to go in completely the opposite direction, and that is when you started to crumple to the ground—right at my feet. Anyway," he added, "the blessing has no interest for me."

There was something about his tone that implied far more than the words themselves expressed, and there was also a bleakness to his expression that made Candace want to reach out and touch his cheek, even as he had touched hers. But she couldn't possibly have mustered the courage to do this. She imagined only too well he would be entirely capable of striking her hand away in fury, were she to make such a gesture right now.

"I must get that drink for you," he said, and once again he left her. But this time, as she sank back in the armchair, her thoughts were of quite a different nature. They involved neither the pain in her ankle nor her lost camera, complete with the film she'd taken. And they didn't deal with her depression over the assignment for *Tempo*, even though it really did seem beyond redemption. She was thinking only of the dark stranger, who appeared to her now as a singularly complex person. He'd already shown her a wide variety of moods, ranging from complete disdain to a rare tenderness and compassion, a gentle and almost sweet sort of understanding.

She wondered why the festivals surrounding the Feast of the Epiphany were so distasteful to him. He was obviously Greek, and he obviously lived here in Tarpon Springs. She would have thought all of this would be very much a part of his heritage.

She also wondered how his face had come to be scarred as it was. The scars were old ones and not to be "effaced," as he'd indicated, with the passage of time. She wondered how long he'd had them, and how old he was, for that matter. In his early thirties, she'd guess. But there wasn't a hint of gray in that raven hair, so perhaps he was a bit younger than he looked.

Candace found she was watching the door. She could hardly wait for him to come back.

CHAPTER THREE

THERE WAS NOTHING very Greek about the drink
Candace's rescuer brought to her, with a similar one
for himself.

"Gin and tonic," he said briefly. "It'll be
refreshing and will relax you without knocking you
out, as something more potent might do just now."

She had to agree. He'd added a wedge of fresh lime
to their glasses, and the drink was exactly right.

As she sipped it, she had the ridiculous feeling
she'd like to stay here for a long, long time. She was
content to cuddle in the lemon-colored armchair with
this mysterious dark stranger sitting across from her,
soaking her foot in the cold water to which he added
a new supply of ice every now and then. She'd be
content to stay here, she decided, at least until she
could learn a great deal more about this man.

A great deal more about him? She knew absolutely
nothing about him, she reminded herself. Apparently
he lived in this unusual circular house, but she wasn't
even sure of that. He had enough aplomb so that he
might simply have brought her to the first open door
and kicked his way through.

Last night, though, he had certainly "belonged" in
the restaurant up on the main street, in the sense he'd
been with another, younger Greek man and had also
known the proprietress. So it stood to reason he lived

either here in this house or somewhere else in the general vicinity unless, like herself, he was a visitor.

He didn't seem to be a visitor, though. She had the impression last night the woman in the restaurant had been both venting her opinion—or her exasperation—about a number of things and also asking for advice. This woman and the younger man had been disturbed about something, and Candace had the idea her reluctant host had been expected to resolve whatever the problem was. And it didn't seem this would have been likely unless he really was a part of the community.

Candace got a grip on herself and reasoned the only way to begin was to begin! First things first.

She said rather shyly, "I should think it's time I told you my name."

He nodded, that faint smile coming again to curve the corner of his mouth. "A good thought," he said.

She was amusing him, she sensed, and she didn't particularly like the idea. Yet under the circumstances, until she told him her name, she could hardly expect to ask him his.

"I'm Candace Mayhew," she said, and in the silence that followed forced herself to add, "and you?"

She saw him frown, and then he said rather abruptly, "Nikolas Mylonis. Nick, if you wish. Do they call you Candy?"

"Some people do," she admitted.

"I would prefer Candace for you."

"And I think I would prefer Nikolas for you."

He shrugged as if this didn't particularly matter and said, "I believe your foot has been in its cold bath long enough. I found an elastic bandage upstairs that, it would seem, has never been used. So we shall see how skillful I can be.''

He proved to be very skillful indeed. First he dried her foot with linen napkins. They were much softer than a towel would have been, and she noticed they were monogrammed, the monograms beautifully hand embroidered. She also noted the initial in the corner was *C* rather than *M*.

Her foot dry, Nikolas wound the elastic bandage around her ankle so it was tight but not too tight. This done, he secured it in place with metal clips. Then he pushed the hassock back into position and propped her foot up on it. Sitting back, he surveyed her and said, ''Well, it would seem we now have to decide what to do next.''

Candace hadn't been thinking beyond the moment. And it was difficult now to think very far beyond this particular moment, with Nikolas Mylonis so close to her. He had a definitely disturbing effect on her. She found herself more interested in learning something about him than in doing anything else. But this, she told herself quickly, was only because people were her business. Nikolas, for instance, would make an excellent short profile piece as an addition to her article. A man who was thoroughly "Americanized"—if one were to judge by his dress, his demeanor and his fluent English—yet still very Greek. She'd seen the Greek side of him first, last night in the restaurant, and she wasn't apt to forget it.

Yes, she thought, coming to terms with the situation, her interest in Nikolas Mylonis was purely professional. Not personal at all.

You've written men out of your script, remember?

There was a taunting quality to this reminder, put to her by her subconscious. But she did remember, and the thought made her stiffen slightly. Her voice was cool as she found an answer to Nikolas's puzzling question over what to do with her next.

"If you'll help me back to my motel," she said, "I will be fine."

"Fine?" The dark eyebrows were eloquent in their skepticism. "With that ankle? You're an optimist, but in this case a foolish one. I doubt your ankle will be 'fine' for a long time to come. What I was attempting to decide was whether to ask George to come here to see you or whether I should take you directly to the hospital. I imagine he will want X rays."

Candace started to sit upright and then stopped. The treacherous ankle sent out warning signals every time she so much as tried to move, and she grimaced—part in pain, part in anger over her annoying helplessness. She said tightly, "There is absolutely no need to go to a hospital. I've twisted it, that's all. By morning—"

"It is foolish to take chances when there is an accident," he said levelly. "The results of such negligence can be long lasting."

There was a heavy note to his voice, and she had the feeling he was speaking from experience. She wondered if there had been negligence involved when he had injured his face. Was that the reason there were so many scars lacing a surface that should have been smooth? She imagined plastic surgery could eradicate almost anything these days, but perhaps there were time elements to consider.

Nikolas made his decision. "We shall go to the

hospital,'' he said. ''But first I will phone George, so he will be ready to receive you.''

There was no point in arguing with him. He made his phone call in another room, but she could hear his voice. Once again he was speaking Greek, and she probably wouldn't understand a single word being said about her!

This was a new experience...and a strange one, right here in her own country. Especially so because it was all happening in Florida. Candace had always thought of Florida as a winter resort where lots of lucky people lazed around on white beaches getting tans, where a huge golden moon rose over the tropical nighttime horizon and where high-powered cars sleeked along avenues lined with palms. Different and exotic to a point but still very American.

Now, she thought, she might as well be in Athens! Or on one of the Greek islands she'd read about.

One of the Greek islands. Candace had an excellent imagination, and it was not at all difficult to picture herself on a remote Greek island, with this disturbing stranger who was so unpredictable in his moods and attitudes. Scornful one moment, tender the next. She'd known him for such a very short time, yet he'd already displayed so many different faces.

Faces. It must have been very difficult for him— after whatever happened to cause his injuries—to know he would be permanently scarred, even though there was really nothing at all repellent about his scars. Yet he must have been almost too handsome, when his face had been perfect.

Adonis, she found herself thinking.

The subject of her thoughts returned and looked

down at her from what seemed an Olympian height. "As I suspected," he said, "George would prefer we come there. I will carry you."

He suited actions to his words, lifting her up in his arms with a disconcerting ease. She was fairly tall, even though she had barely come to his shoulder when she'd been standing, and although she was a bit slimmer than usual just now, there was still substance to her. But he carried her as if she were a feather.

In a few seconds she was ensconced in the front seat of the shining gray car she'd noticed under the porte cochere the night before, and Nikolas took his place behind the wheel. She didn't have a chance to look down the street with the hope of getting a good view of the bayou, because he turned quickly in the opposite direction. Anyway, the diving for the cross and all the rest of the day's events were certainly over by now. Possibly the boy who had recovered the cross was being blessed at the cathedral, and soon the other festivities would be starting. She'd intended to leave the cathedral and go straight to the sponge docks, where there should be plenty of action during the day. Then, as a member of the media, she'd been invited to the principal banquet of the night. Now....

Candace sighed, a long, shuddering sigh, and Nikolas said sympathetically, "I'm sorry. George should be able to give you a shot that will help with the pain."

"I wasn't thinking about the pain," she told him, "though I admit it does hurt. I was thinking about the boy who got the cross...."

He glanced at her quickly, almost suspiciously.

And there was an oddly hostile note in his voice as he asked, "What about the boy who got the cross?"

"I wanted to take a few pictures of him, that's all," she said. "Pictures...I don't even have a camera...."

"Then you shall get another camera," he said. "Such matters are trivial, Candace."

It was the first time he'd used her name, and it seemed to her there was a caress in the way he spoke it, sharply contrasting with his tone of only a moment before. He was an enigma, this man. And she was attracted to this facet of him.

Candace shivered. She could not afford to become too fascinated by someone like Nikolas Mylonis. For that matter, she was amazed to think she could even reach the point where she would have to caution herself about something like this. It had been only three months since her divorce from Jeff had become final—though their marriage had been over a long time before. Finally free—legally free, at least—she had whimsically thought if she were of a different faith she might very well enter a convent. A cloistered convent, where she'd never again even have to see another man.

She had believed herself impervious to men. But the stranger at her side, who very definitely epitomized her concepts of masculinity, was raising some serious doubts about this belief—without even trying to do so! Just being near Nikolas Mylonis was enough to make her fully conscious of the fact that, regardless of all sorts of liberation movements, there would forever be a fundamental difference between the sexes that an infinite number of "amendments" couldn't alter. The phrase *Vive la différence* came to mind, and despite herself, Candace had to suppress the giggle that arrived with the thought. She didn't suppress it completely, though, and Nikolas said, "I'm glad to see something amuses you, given the circumstances. Would you care to share the joke?"

It was surely the last joke in the world she wished to share with him, and Candace said quickly, "It's nothing, really. I just feel so ridiculous, that's all."

He let it go at that, because they were approaching the hospital driveway, their short journey almost over. This time Nikolas did not carry her. He walked ahead quickly and procured a wheelchair, then he pushed her along to the hospital's emergency department. A moment later she was closeted in a small cubicle with both Nikolas and "George," whom Nikolas introduced to her as Dr. Andris.

Dr. Andris was only in his mid-thirties. He was short and stocky and not particularly good-looking. But he had the same beautiful raven hair and gorgeous dark eyes. There was a decided gleam of appreciation in those eyes as he looked at Candace—just as there had been in the eyes of the young Greek in the restaurant last night, though his appraisal had been much more brazen—but aside from this, George Andris was totally professional.

Candace was whisked to the X-ray department, and after a time the diagnosis was made that there were no fractures. "A sprain," Dr. Andris said. "But they are, of course, very painful. And they can be very stubborn. For the next few days I want you to stay off that ankle as much as possible."

When they'd arrived at the hospital, Nikolas had spoken to the doctor in Greek, and Candace had quite naturally assumed the physician had probably come to Tarpon Springs from the "old country" and he spoke little if any English. So it came as a surprise to her when he conversed with her in English as fluent and unaccented as Nikolas's, and she felt a resentment toward both men for their earlier dialogue in a language she couldn't understand.

Curiosity nagged at her. Nikolas must have elected to speak in Greek because he had wanted to say something about her he didn't want her to overhear. But what could that possibly have been?

Now she was appalled by Dr. Andris's "prescription." There was no way she could stay off her ankle for any amount of time at all, let alone a few days.

She frowned. "I'm here on a magazine assignment, doctor," she explained. "I've got to be able to get around, even if it's on crutches."

"Don't be ridiculous!" Nikolas broke in impatiently. "You nearly broke your neck just going around in a pair of simple sandals. What do you think you'd do on crutches—if, that is, you have in mind what I think you do."

It didn't seem possible she'd known him for only a short time. Candace sparred back, as if they'd been at this for years, "Are you a mind reader, among other things?"

"Perhaps I am," he replied, his green eyes glinting dangerously. "Though it wouldn't take a psychic to know you're thinking about trying to finish your silly assignment."

"My silly assignment!" Candace gasped, enraged. "Let me tell you that *Tempo* magazine—"

"I really don't give a damn about *Tempo* magazine," he interrupted. "It seems absurd to me you think you can come down here for a couple of days and do anything comprehensive at all about this community. As far as I'm concerned, what you're doing is only another example of journalistic carelessness. You people don't care what you report as long as you get a story!"

He spoke with such feeling she was completely taken back. Even Dr. Andris seemed startled by this outburst, she saw, and he said placatingly, "Nick...."

"It's all right," Nikolas Mylonis said wearily, but Candace knew it wasn't all right, not at all. "I'm sorry, Candace. I had no right to strike out at you like that. As for your injury, it would be foolish of you to try to work until your ankle is well on the way to healing. Otherwise, you're apt to have problems with it for a long time to come. Isn't that right, George?"

"She *could* have problems," George Andris amended. "Certainly it would be wiser, and a lot more comfortable for you, to do as I say, Miss Mayhew. At the moment I doubt you could get around at all, except on crutches. And even then it would be painful going. But in only a few short days, it will begin to be easier."

A few short days. A few short days could have been forever as far as Candace was concerned just now, and her eloquent blue eyes thoroughly revealed her misery.

"If that's the case," she said slowly, "I suppose the only thing to do is give up the assignment and fly back to New York." She sighed. "I'll make my airline reservation and call up the magazine when I get back to my motel," she decided then, managing a faint smile. "Thank you very much, Dr. Andris."

"Not at all," the doctor said, and then hesitated. He glanced across at Nikolas, and for a moment Candace feared he was going to lapse into Greek again, thus shutting her out entirely. But he said instead, "Look, Miss Mayhew. There's no need to be so hasty. I don't think you really have to give up your assignment because of what's happened to you. In fact, Nikolas has told me he has some ideas about it. . . ."

She turned a frosty glance toward the tall man whose face, at the moment, was completely impassive. "Does he really?" she asked them both coolly.

"Yes, as a matter of fact I do," Nikolas Mylonis said. "We'll go home now and talk it over. Maybe you could stop by in a couple of days, George, and take a look at her ankle? I may have a hard time keeping her down."

Again it sounded as if he'd known her for years. She, too, felt as if they'd known each other for years. It almost seemed natural for him to be talking about going "home."

Candace shook her head. The whole situation was rapidly getting out of hand, and she had the feeling if she didn't do something about it quickly, she'd never be able to.

"I don't think Dr. Andris will need to see me again," she said firmly. "Furthermore, for as long as I'm in Tarpon Springs, I'll be staying at the Grecian Gardens motel."

Nikolas said something in fluent Greek so fast and heated it would have taken an expert in the language to follow him. George Andris could not suppress a laugh, and he said, "At least let Nick take you back to his house for lunch, Miss Mayhew. Your motel doesn't have a café, so it would be difficult for you to get food. A person needs both food and rest, in my opinion, after an incident like the one you've suffered.''

She was tempted to ask him which incident he meant—wrenching her ankle or...meeting Nikolas Mylonis? But then Nikolas was lifting her from the examining table into the wheelchair, and her protests were silent ones.

Again the doctor hesitated briefly. Then he said, ''Go and bring your car up to the door, Nick. I'll wheel her out.''

Nikolas nodded and left the room, and it was amazing how empty it seemed without him.

George Andris guided her into the corridor, but he was moving more slowly than he needed to. Candace realized this and sensed there was something he wanted to say to her now that they were alone. Something about Nick?

Obviously, the choice of words came hard. ''Look,'' he finally said. ''Humor him a little bit, will you?''

''What?'' she demanded

''Just...go along with him.'' It wasn't much of an explanation. ''I'm no great believer in miracles, but this is....''

''You're not making any sense, doctor,'' Candace said testily.

''No, I suppose I am not,'' George Andris admitted. She realized he was deliberately keeping his voice low as he added, ''Nick and I went to high school together, Miss Mayhew, right here in Tarpon Springs. Then, of course, we took two entirely different paths. We were apart for a long time. After spending a few years in Philadelphia and then New York, I decided to return here to practice. Nick finally came back, too. But this is the first time I've seen even a glimpse of Nick as he used to be. It's the first time he's let himself become involved in anything, it's the first time he—''

"Dr. Andris," Candace cut in, "I still don't understand what you're saying. You seem to presume I know Nikolas Mylonis, but I don't know him at all. We only just met this morning, and—"

"Yes," George Andris interrupted, "I realize that. But," he added carefully, "Nick seems to think you know who he is."

Who he is.

The words seemed to burn into Candace, and the question they aroused became all-consuming. The first time she'd seen him, she'd had the curious feeling they'd met somewhere before. Well, obviously they never had, yet there was still a familiarity about Nikolas Mylonis that taunted her.

"No," she said now, growing more impatient. "Who is he?"

There was no chance for Dr. Andris to reply. Nikolas was approaching them from the direction of the emergency entrance, moving with a grace quite uncommon for a man of his height.

"Thanks, George," he said, and then took over the pushing of the wheelchair himself. He transferred Candace back into the car with a gentleness that still surprised her, and as they drove out into Pinellas Avenue again Candace thought she would surely go mad. More than anything else in the world she wanted to discover all she could about the disturbing man who sat next to her. She had to find out about him, if only for her own peace of mind!

He was watching the road ahead, and he said without glancing toward her, "You must be very hungry. I imagine you went without any breakfast this morning?"

"That's right," she nodded. "I went straight to the cathedral."

"I thought so," he said. "Well, Theone will be back by now, and she will be preparing lunch. I tell her she always makes enough for several guests, so you will not starve."

Theone. Who, Candace now wondered, was Theone? A Greek name. A Greek woman. The awful suspicion Theone might be Nikolas Mylonis's wife began to torment her.

Candace closed her eyes, not even trying to suppress the astonishingly dismal feeling that swept over her. Somehow, the last thing in the world she would have expected was that Nikolas might be married!

CHAPTER FOUR

THEONE CALLIS WAS definitely not Nikolas's wife. Candace surmised she was probably in her fifties, though she could even have been in her sixties. It was difficult to tell.

She was of medium height, neither thin nor fat, and her face reminded Candace of the woman in the restaurant last night. Theone had deep-set dark eyes that were heavily shadowed and black hair sprinkled with silver. Her skin was sallow, and although it was barely noon she looked tired. Also, she was dressed entirely in black, even to her stockings and shoes, which gave her a distinctly depressing look. But most depressing of all was the fact that there was absolutely no friendliness in her face as Nikolas introduced them.

He spoke in English as he did so but then quickly switched to Greek, this a bit sharply, and Theone left the room, evidently going back to the kitchen. Nikolas had again settled Candace into the lemon-covered armchair, and he pulled a second armchair close to it, then sank into this one himself, stretching out his long legs as he surveyed her.

"You are thinking I am high-handed," he said. "Right?"

"How could I think otherwise?" she retorted.

He chuckled. "What a direct person you are, Candace. No coquetry in your nature, eh?"

"None," she told him shortly.

His eyes narrowed. "That sounds as if there must be a reason," he said. "As if, perhaps, you have at some time been burned. Am I correct?"

She stirred restlessly. "Shall we talk about something else?" she suggested. "It's kind of you to invite me to lunch, but afterward I really must insist you take me back to the motel so I can begin to put things together."

"What things?"

"I must make up my mind what I'm to do," she said reasonably. "If it's really going to be as difficult for me to get around as Dr. Andris thinks it will be, then I haven't much choice. There would be no point in my staying on."

"You are so sure of that?"

"Of course I'm sure of it, Nikolas. . . ."

The use of his name came as naturally as if it—and he—were thoroughly familiar to her, and she saw he was aware of this, too. A faint smile twisted his mouth and he said, "You are expecting me to agree you should leave, but I don't. There is absolutely no reason why you should not stay here in my house until your ankle has at least begun to heal and you can get around fairly easily. Theone will be on the premises, and her daughter, Melina—who is taking part in the festival at this very moment—will also be here. They both live here, so you will be chaperoned night and day, if that is what you require. How old are you, Candace?"

The question came so quickly she replied automatically, "Twenty-five."

"Very well, I am thirty-four. Are you married?"

"No."

"But you have been married, eh?"

He was entirely too discerning. She avoided meeting those perceptive olive green eyes as she said, "Yes."

"So then," he said with an oddly foreign little shrug, "you have had an experience I have not had. I have never been married." He didn't say it, but it was there in his voice. *And I never will be.*

Candace looked up at him swiftly, but it was impossible to read anything from his expression. She was intensely conscious of the tension between them. Then he said, "So, it would seem we are both free to do as we please. Except I suppose like most members of your profession you feel you owe an allegiance to your editor. Well, then, call him if you wish and tell him of your mishap. But also tell him you will be able to carry on again very soon."

"On a gimpy leg and without a camera?" she asked bitterly.

"The camera, the camera. It is paramount in your thoughts, isn't it, Candace? Very well, later I will go out and see if I can learn what happened to your camera and what we can do about it. In the meantime we will have lunch, and then you must rest. There will be time enough later on to make up your mind about what you're going to do."

He rose and stretched. "Would you like another gin and tonic before we eat?" he asked.

"No, thanks, I don't think so."

"It did not occur to me when I gave you the first one it was really only breakfast time," he said wryly. "Or that you were taking it on an empty stomach. It's a good thing it didn't make you sick."

"I don't get sick that easily."

"Made of sterner stuff, eh? English?"

"American," Candace said.

He laughed. "Your ancestors must have come from somewhere."

"Very well, then," she admitted, "mostly from England. A very long time ago, though."

"They came via the *Mayflower*, no doubt?"

There was a taunting note to his voice that made her bristle. "Yes, some of them did," she said defiantly.

"Then we are at opposite ends of the spectrum," he said simply. "Your people came here in the beginning. As for myself, I am the first."

"What do you mean?" she asked curiously.

"I was born in Greece," Nikolas told her. "Ah, you look so surprised. I was born on the small island of Sifnos. It is one of the Cyclades chain, but I do not remember a great deal about it. I came here when I was seven. The town I came from was built in terraces. Most of the trees had long since been cut down for timber and for firewood. The houses were all very white—I remember them being like white cubes, stark in the noonday sun. I have learned since they were made of stone and were kept whitewashed. The mountains towered in the background and there was a church that was like a silhouette against the mountains. It had a domed top, like the cathedral here. My father was a fisherman. Probably he is still a fisherman. At least, he still lives there."

There was a harshness to his laugh. "Greeks," he said, "have been fishermen for as long as there's been history. They love the sea as much as they fear it. I think I remember Saint Nicholas, who is the patron saint of seafarers, much better than I remember my own father."

"What about your mother?" Candace asked him.

"She died when I was born," Nikolas said, his voice rough. "Anyway, my uncle used to tell me that the Greeks who went down to the sea always prayed twice. First to the ancient god Poseidon and then to Saint Nicholas.

"There is also something else I remember about the island—the fishnets, which were always being mended and left to dry in the sun. There was constant work because the living came entirely from the sea. For all of their beauty, those burning Greek islands that are beloved by so many—and I must include foreigners as well as the Greeks themselves—yield very little to provide nourishment for their people. Were it not for the fruits of the sea...."

Nikolas paused as if to catch his breath. Then he said, "I did not mean to get into my life story."

Candace disregarded this. "Have you ever gone back to Greece?" she asked him.

He shook his head. "Nearly, once," he said. "We were going to—"

He broke this sentence off as deliberately as if he were snapping a thread. It was exasperating. But she sensed the need to go slowly with him so she said only, "You mentioned your father still lives there. On the island where you were born?"

He nodded. "That's right. As I said, my mother died when I was born. My father's grief was... profound. My uncle was sure he had become crazed by it, or my father would never have come to the decision that it was I who was to blame for my mother's death. However, this is what he did decide, and when I was very small he did not even want me in his presence. Then, after a time, he married again. He married a woman who gave him more children, and I was the small outsider in the household. I think my stepmother despised me as much as my father did.

"Finally," Nikolas continued, his tone very level, "my uncle went back to the island for a visit. My mother was his younger sister. He also had an older sister there, and from her he learned of the way I was being treated. Needless to say, it was not very difficult for him to get my father's consent to adopt me and bring me back to America." Nikolas smiled ruefully. "I arrived in time to enter school here, in the first grade," he said. "I knew not a word of English, and this was in New York City. New York may be a melting pot, but even so they do speak English in the schools. What fun the other kids made of me!"

Surprisingly, he spoke without any particular bitterness, yet it didn't take much imagination to realize the effect this "fun" must have had on him. Candace's face mirrored her thoughts, recording her feelings much too vividly for he said, "So much compassion, Candace? And here I was thinking you were such a cool sort of person!"

He was testing her, and a few minutes earlier she would have risen to the bait, resenting this. But she couldn't shut the vision out of her mind. The vision of a little boy with beautiful dark hair and olive-smooth skin who, in addition to being foreign, had carried the burden of knowing he'd never been loved in the first place.

He was watching her closely, so she tried to recapture some of the coolness of which she'd been accused, but after a moment he shook his head and said shortly, "I'm sorry. It isn't like me to ramble on about myself. Excuse me, please, while I go and see how Theone is progressing with our lunch.''

He seemed displeased as he left the room, which was puzzling, and Candace leaned back and stared moodily at her bandaged foot. Her own background had been so entirely different. She and her father had been very close, and her relationship with her mother was still a good one, even though they seldom saw each other anymore. And although she and her sister didn't have much in common, there was a basic affection between them, a sense of family. Looking back at her own childhood she realized it had not been ideal, yet, closing her eyes, she could fondly remember so many things.

Christmas was one, with the fragrant, beautifully trimmed balsam tree standing in the corner of the living room. And trips to New York, for very special occasions. Once, her father had taken her to the vast Public Library on Fifth Avenue, where the famous stone lions guarded the entrance. Later they'd gone for a ride on the Staten Island ferry. She would never forget her first glimpse, on the trip back, of New York's fantastic skyline. Another time, her father had bought her an Italian ice from a street-corner vendor, and they'd gone to the Central Park Zoo, where she'd been especially entranced by the seals splashing in their outdoor pool.

During the summer, the whole family had usually traveled up to Lake Champlain, where they'd camped on an island with a steep, rocky shoreline. Her father had taught her to catch fish by dangling a long string with a hook on the end of it down through the rocks. She and her sister had loved to go wading in the cold shallows, and she remembered her mother baking wonderfully fragrant corn bread in an old iron skillet.

Now there was something else wonderfully fragrant much closer at hand. This was not a part of memory, and she opened her eyes to see Nikolas towering over her with a tray in his hand.

Placing it across her lap, he said, "There! See that you eat every morsel, or Theone will be disappointed!"

Candace privately doubted whether anything she either did or didn't do would disappoint Theone, but she only asked, "Aren't you going to join me?"

"No," he said rather abruptly. "For today, I will have something in the kitchen."

With this he left her, and she wondered how—and where—he was usually served his meals. Possibly he was accustomed to eating them with Theone, and maybe the daughter he'd mentioned, as well. Certainly, too, a house of this size must have some sort of formal dining room.

Candace turned her attention to the food Nikolas had brought her. There was an excellent lentil soup, a bowl of salad similar to the one she'd had in the restaurant the night before, and a square of an eggplant-meat mixture that she recognized as moussaka, for she'd dined a couple of times in a Greek restaurant in New York. Theone's moussaka, however, was far more delicious than the restaurant version had been, even though the restaurant in question was famous for its preparation of this particular dish.

Nikolas had also brought her a glass of chilled, slightly dry white wine, which was a perfect accompaniment to the meal, and there was a pastry for dessert. It was made with layers of the thin, flaky pastry used for *baklava*, but the filling was a fruit-and-nut mixture that was utterly delicious.

Candace did not need the memory of Nikolas's urging to devour every bit of the food that had been placed before her. She was hungry, each dish was terrific and she did full justice to them all. Whether or not Theone liked her the woman surely had to be given pluses for her cooking. She really was a culinary artist.

Nikolas came back to collect ner tray and she saw that, for the present at least, he was pleased with her. "Are you sure you've had enough?" he teased. "There's plenty more of everything."

"Not another morsel!" Candace protested, and he laughed. But when he returned a moment later, having delivered the tray back to the kitchen, he was solemn.

"Look," he said. "If you insist upon returning to your motel I shall, of course, take you there. Theone has informed me rather forcefully I have no right to keep you here against your will, and she is absolutely correct. It just seems so pointless for you to leave, although I am sure Elene would do something about having food brought in for you. But even so...."

"Elene?" she questioned.

"She is the young lady who is usually at the reception desk. Actually, she manages the motel with some scant assistance from her husband," Nikolas added rather grimly. "Elene Panagoris. She is Theone's niece, and so Theone would, of course, help her with the food for you. But as I've said, it seems pointless for you to coop yourself up in a single room when there is no need."

"It isn't really pointless," Candace corrected him carefully. "I shall only be a nuisance to you if I stay here, although I appreciate your asking me. I...I really do appreciate it, very much."

"You really do?" he mimicked. Then, raising one eyebrow, he asked, "In what way do you think you would be a nuisance to me, Candace?"

"Just having me around," she said frankly, and it was her turn to shrug. "After all, Nikolas," she said, "there's no need for you to feel responsible for me."

"Isn't there?" he asked, smiling engagingly. "Isn't it the Chinese who say if you save someone's life you are responsible for them forever after? Not that I saved your life, of course—though there's a chance, I suppose, you might have broken your neck if I hadn't grabbed you when I did."

He spoke wryly, and she had to laugh at him. His eyes reflected her amusement—it was as if they were sharing a private joke. All at once she felt surprisingly close to him, warmed by the comforting fact that he was near and she was here with him. And—somewhat incredibly—that he actually seemed to want her to stay.

He said lightly, "What I think you may fear is not that you will be a nuisance to me but that I may become a nuisance to you. You are a very beautiful young woman. I imagine men frequently make nuisances of themselves with you. I saw the way Manos Panagoris was looking at you last night...."

Manos Panagoris. He must be the young man who had stared at her so brazenly in the restaurant. She wondered if Elene and Manos were related. After all, they shared the same last name. These thoughts flickered through Candace's mind, but she was primarily conscious of the fact that Nikolas remembered her from last night. He also had noticed her in the restaurant, although he had not seemed particularly pleased at the time. Nor had there been any pleasure in his face when he'd "rescued" her today, for that matter. It had been a long while before she'd seen that first, slow half-smile. . . .

Again he was watching her closely, and he said somewhat impatiently, "Yes, of course I remember seeing you in Aliki's place last night. Furthermore, I already knew who you were. Elene had said the journalist from New York had checked in and she was blond . . . and lovely. Elene should have recommended Aliki's restaurant to you anyway, because Aliki is her mother. Aliki is also Theone's sister, which makes Theone Elene's aunt."

He chuckled. "Why look so troubled?" he asked. "Are these complicated Greek relationships too much for you?"

Candace bypassed this quip. The fact that Elene was related to two women who were sisters was not all that complicated. What bothered her was the disdainful way he'd emphasized the word "journalist." Now she said slowly, "You don't seem to have a very high opinion of my profession, judging from your tone of voice."

"No, I don't," he retorted bluntly, so bluntly that Candace felt as if he'd slapped her. This must have shown on her much too transparent face, for he added quickly, "But that, of course, is a generalization. I didn't mean to hurt your feelings."

She tried to smile. "It's a bit difficult not to take things personally when they're that . . . close to home," she admitted. She saw him make an involun-

tary movement toward her, a gesture of appease-
ment—or would it be better called consolation?

Then she sensed he was waiting for her to say
something more, and she struggled to find the right
words. "It isn't that I don't appreciate your offer of
having me stay here," she said with difficulty. "I
think I've already made that clear. But you must
understand I don't wish to feel...."

"Indebted to me?" he suggested.

"Must you always put everything so bluntly? No,
not that, really. I've already told you I don't want to
be a nuisance. It's just that I...."

She felt like a child suddenly become tongue-tied,
and as she caught the expression of amusement—a
tender sort of amusement—on his face, the balance
of the protests she'd been about to make faded away.
She was surprised at herself, for this sort of capitula-
tion was unlike her. Yet it seemed impossible not to
be affected by Nikolas Mylonis's generosity. He'd
made it clear, even at the hospital, he intended to
have her stay at his home, where she could be properly cared for. She had put this down to his sense of
responsibility, and she still did. But at the moment
she could not help but feel a guilty little sense of
pleasure because—very briefly to be sure—he did
consider her his responsibility.

"If you're sure I won't be in anyone's way," she
began stiffly, and then their eyes met. Candace
caught her breath. Amusement had vanished from
his features to be replaced by something else, an expression so intense she couldn't analyze it. Again she
had the feeling he was about to reach out and touch
her—and, what was far more astonishing, she wished
he would!

She shivered, as if she were already feeling his arms around her. She knew it would be impossible for her to push him away, were he to enfold her in those arms. And she knew this lack of physical resistance had nothing at all to do with her injured ankle. This man had the most astonishing effect on her, and it was raising havoc with all the logic she'd so carefully built into her life over these past few years.

She had to laugh at herself. Logic was a Greek word, wasn't it? Logic, the science of reasoning, originated by the Greeks? Perhaps Nikolas Mylonis could attribute this strange shimmering wave between them to logic, but, Candace thought rather desperately, she simply could not!

Those arresting green eyes were still fixed on her face, which she felt sure must be pink by now, judging from the flush she was feeling. But he said only, "It is time for you to rest in a more comfortable position, *mikrí mou*. Fortunately there is a bedroom on the ground floor, one with its own bath. Theone has fixed it for you, so if I may transport you...."

Once again he picked her up as easily as if she were a child. This time she found herself turning her face against his chest as he carried her, and she could hear the strong, steady beat of his heart much too close for comfort.

Her own heart seemed to have jumped into her throat. She felt, in fact, as if it might decide to take up permanent residence there. And she wished this journey across the first floor of his house could turn into a long safari, so she wouldn't have to be wrested away from the sanctuary of those enveloping arms.

Shades had been drawn in the room to which he took her, and there was a ceiling fan rotating slowly.

It all seemed so cool and breezy. The bed onto which he lowered her was enormous and very comfortable. Pillows were arranged so she was propped at exactly the right angle, and she looked around to see the furnishings were of light wood and the draperies and the bedspread very pale citron striped with white. Basically, despite the light colors, the decor seemed masculine to her, and she wondered if Nikolas had given up his own room for her use.

He said, "Theone will bring you a cool lemonade, and then you are to get some sleep. I will see you later in the afternoon."

He hesitated at her bedside and she was almost certain he was going to bend and kiss her, even though the thought was certainly farfetched. Yet she was very sure the idea crossed his mind just as it crossed hers, and his tone was wry as he said, "Sleep well, and do not worry."

Do not worry. Strangely, as she closed her eyes, Candace felt that seldom in her life had she been about to worry less. And given the circumstances, that simply didn't make sense.

CANDACE DIDN'T EVEN HEAR Theone come in with the lemonade, but it was on her bedside table when she awakened. It took her a moment to bring things into focus, and when they really became clear she felt a moment of pure panic.

What in heaven's name was she doing here in the bedroom of an unpredictable Greek who had virtually catapulted himself into her life and was now telling her precisely what to do with it?

Well. . .he hadn't exactly been the one who'd done the catapulting, she acknowledged. The reverse was closer to the truth. At least he had saved her from falling flat on her face.

Even so, she should have had the sense to insist upon being taken back to her motel after leaving the hospital. But then it would have meant Elene would have had to arrange for her meals to be brought to her with Theone's help or maybe Aliki's, and. . . .

Candace sat straight up in bed, exasperated with herself because she was virtually repeating word for word what Nikolas Mylonis had already said. The man really had got under her skin!

The sooner I walk, the faster I can run, she told herself grimly, and carefully slid her legs across to the edge of the bed, resting her feet on the floor for a full minute before she tried to stand up. Her ankle was already throbbing from even this much effort, but she gritted her teeth and forced herself to stand. Then she almost screamed, despite herself, as an incredibly sharp pain shot through the troublesome foot, and she sank back onto the mattress again, gasping from the force of the jolt.

As if she'd rubbed a magic lamp and he was the genie, Nikolas appeared in the doorway, folding his long arms over his chest as he surveyed her.

"You cried out," he stated.

"Yes." There was no point denying it, she decided. She didn't doubt his hearing was acute. Yet he must have been very close to her door, almost as if he were guarding it.

"What is it, Candace?" he asked. "Are you in pain? Or did you have a bad dream?"

"I tried to stand up," she confessed.

He shook his head, frowning. "I should have placed a bell by your bedside so you could ring if you wanted something," he said. "Even so, you could have tried calling out. One of us would have heard you."

One of us. Nikolas himself? Theone, perhaps? Or Theone's daughter, who had probably returned by now? Were there any others, Candace wondered.

"Do you wish something?" he asked, and the question swamped her with the realization of her present helplessness.

"Yes, I do," she said. And she did. Before leaving the X-ray department at the hospital a nurse had helped her to the bathroom, but she hadn't been there since.

She saw the light of sudden understanding in his eyes and knew there was no reason to feel so embarrassed. Yet she did, and he obviously realized this. He laughed, and as she glanced up at him she saw he was smiling. The damaged side of his face still did not respond fully. There was a certain immobility, but nevertheless it was a real smile this time and very disarming.

"So you are shy and modest among other things," he commented. "Very maidenly virtues, both, but sometimes not practical ones. Come, I will take you."

He moved to lift her, and she pulled back from him. "Indeed, you will not!" she protested hotly.

The olive green eyes were gleaming with merriment, and at that moment he looked thoroughly roguish. This was yet another facet of his personality, she found herself thinking, and a dangerously attractive one.

"Come on, now," he chided, still laughing. "You will at least permit me to carry you to the door, will you not? Then you can hop the rest of the way, if you wish.''

There was no getting around him. But Candace's cheeks were burning as he transported her across the room and then carefully placed her inside the bathroom, where, he promised, she could grab a wall rail that was strong enough to support her.

''And I shall close the door,'' he said politely.

When she emerged a few minutes later to stand in the doorway, propping herself against the frame, Nikolas was sitting on the side of her bed. He was leaning forward, his elbows on his knees, his face held between his hands, and it seemed to her he looked years younger than he had only this morning.

Again she felt that nagging sense of familiarity, and she wished fervently he had not come back into the hospital quite so quickly today, interrupting what had promised to be a very interesting revelation on the part of Dr. George Andris.

Who was Nikolas? What was it about him?

He was getting to his feet and coming toward her, and Candace raised her eyes to meet his, pulled magnetically toward the tug of his gaze. He said, ''You have washed your face with soap and water, I see. It has that shine to it that makes you look very young. Now I suppose you will want your powder and lipstick so you can dispel the illusion?''

''It doesn't really matter,'' Candace said faintly, and she would have sworn her pulse actually skipped a beat—several beats—as she looked up at him. He was so enormously engaging, this man. The word ''charisma'' could have been invented with Nikolas in mind. It was a Greek word at that. She had never before in her life felt as totally feminine as she did now. It was simply being near him. And this, she knew, was because he was so completely masculine. His virility was a force that drove the breath out of her and evoked a gnawing kind of yearning unlike anything she'd ever felt before.

A woman would not be apt to forget Nikolas Mylonis under any circumstances. But a woman would never be able to forget Nikolas Mylonis if he were to make love to her!

Candace stared at him, so staggered by this idea she was stunned. Physical love was something she didn't even like to contemplate. She'd had a full example—with her husband—of what it was like, and she had hated it. It was something she had suffered through during the early months of her marriage, only to be relieved beyond all measure when, finally, Jeff had sought her less and less. She knew now this was because he had turned to other women. But even if she had known it then it wouldn't have mattered to her. Not as long as it meant that he would leave her alone.

Jeff, she conceded, had left a very bitter taste in her mouth where so-called "love" between a man and a woman was concerned. She had sworn to herself that she would never again let a man ill-treat her as he had. She had not, in fact, wanted any man to so much as touch her—not, that is, until today. But now she knew she wanted Nikolas to touch her. She wanted very much for him to touch her.

She shivered as he came closer. Then it seemed to her something flickered in the very depths of his eyes, and he reached out to her. She thought he was going to lift her up and carry her back to the bed, but instead his arms enfolded her. And he bent over her gently, his dark hair brushing her forehead like a satin caress as his lips found hers.

His lips found hers. . . but they did not rest lightly on her mouth. Once begun, the kiss deepened, until it seemed to Candace as if Nikolas had infused her with his very essence so thoroughly she would never again be free of him.

He murmured something in her ear, something very deep, very husky. Something in Greek. And it was only then that he lifted her in his arms and took her over to the bed. But this time when he put her down he did not draw back, as he had previously.

He bent to follow her as she sank against the pillows, and she made no attempt to resist him. Her arms, in fact, found their way upward and clasped his neck. Then her hands separated, moving on so her fingers plunged deep into his lustrous black hair. She was clutching his hair when his lips descended again, his tongue probing her mouth open on a voyage of exploration. And the intimacy of his caress sent shocks of elation pulsing through her, an elation that threatened to overwhelm her.

Candace felt as if she were drowning there in Nikolas's arms, and she had no desire to be pulled back to dry land. Later, she wondered what would have happened between them if they had not been interrupted.

CHAPTER FIVE

THE VOICE WAS YOUNG, feminine, and the girl was speaking Greek. Candace felt as if she had been plunged into a nightmare, and she struggled out of Nikolas's embrace, her pulse pounding wildly.

Nikolas sat up, and for a moment he was very still. Then he said with remarkable calm, "Excuse me. There is a telephone call."

Candace could only shake her head, dazed. Her breath was still coming fast, and she felt as if she were running a fever. His calmness seemed incredible to her, and as she watched him leave the room she both envied and resented the way he had been able to achieve what seemed instant control of his emotions.

She also wondered how long the girl had been standing there watching them before deciding to tell Nikolas there was a phone call for him. The girl, she realized, must be Melina—Theone's daughter—although there wasn't much family resemblance.

Life had obviously taken its toll on Theone, as it had on her sister, Aliki, who ran the restaurant up on the main street. Both women looked old and tired, as if all their zest had been knocked out of them. But it was difficult to think either of them could ever have been half as beautiful as this girl.

Helen of Troy must have had a similar face, Candace found herself thinking. A face that could lead men wherever she wished—even to total destruction. This young beauty had exquisite features. Huge, eloquent eyes that were true black and fringed by incredibly long lashes, black satin hair that fell in long, soft waves to the girl's shoulders, and skin that was like golden honey in color and smooth as the finest silk.

And her figure was as incredible as her face. She was wearing a simple dress of white pleated cotton bordered with crocheted lace, the scoop neckline molding full, firm breasts that seemed to be straining against the confines of the fabric. Slim feet had been thrust into flat, gold kid sandals, and there was the glint of gold in the earrings that swung from small, perfect lobes.

Even as Candace took all of this in, she knew she, too, was being surveyed with an appraisal sparing her nothing, and she wished she had made use of her powder, her lipstick and her comb, as well!

"So, you're the magazine reporter," the girl said, a hint of amusement in her voice that was decidedly sultry. "I am Melina."

Candace nodded. "I thought you must be," she confessed.

"Ah," Melina said, advancing into the room. "Then Nick has told you about me?"

Her English was without accent. Like Nikolas, she must have been brought up in this country, perhaps even born here. No telling how long Theone had been in America. Candace wasn't even sure if the older woman spoke English.

"Nikolas mentioned you," she said a bit weakly. "That is, he said that both you and your mother live here."

"So we do," Melina agreed, moving further into the room. She glanced about her as she did so, and Candace had the feeling it was a room she didn't enter very often. "So, Nick has decided that you'll stay in here," she added. "The room hasn't been used much since my father died."

This statement made no sense to Candace at all, and her perplexity showed, causing Melina to nod understandingly.

"Of course," she said. "Nick probably has not explained the relationship between us. Nick's uncle, you see, was married to my mother. I am the daughter of her earlier marriage, so actually Nick's uncle was my stepfather, although he always preferred me to call him 'father.' So there is no blood relationship between Nick and myself."

There was a definite significance to the way the girl said this, and there was no problem getting her message. Candace realized Melina, in a none too subtle way, was attempting to warn her not to trespass on her territory. Melina wanted Nikolas for herself. At least, it certainly seemed so.

Candace tried to be casual about it as she surveyed the girl, wondering how old she was. Not much over twenty, she was sure, which meant Theone must be considerably younger than she looked, since this was the child of her first marriage. She tried to do some mental arithmetic and failed. With nothing to base a first statistic on, there was no point in trying to pile up numbers.

There were several more questions she would have liked to ask Melina. In fact, she was brimming with them. Yet Candace felt cautious about being overly curious and was glad she'd held her tongue when

Melina asked directly, "Is it true that you are going to stay here until your ankle has healed?"

There was no ready answer to this. The situation in which Candace now found herself had developed so quickly she'd had very little time to think it through. Ever since the moment when she'd wrenched her ankle and Nikolas had literally caught her in his arms, she'd been either with him, in the process of being x-rayed or else asleep here in this pleasant, comfortable room.

Evidently the room was not Nikolas's at all but had been occupied by his uncle now deceased. She wondered how long ago he had died, how long Theone had been married to him and how close he and Nikolas had been.

Melina was watching her curiously, and Candace knew she had to make some sort of answer about staying on in the house. The girl was probably hoping her answer would be negative, yet Candace strongly felt if she were to come right out and say she intended to leave, she'd be doing Nikolas a disservice. She could think of no logical reason why she should feel this way, but . . . .

Logic again! Her own logic seemed to have pretty well deserted her since she'd come face-to-face with her present host!

Melina was still waiting for her reply, so she said carefully, "I really don't know yet what I'm going to do. Everything has happened so quickly."

A flicker of impatience crossed the girl's beautiful face. Then she said, with more than a hint of disgust in her tone, "Nick seems to feel he's responsible for you. I suppose you do seem pretty helpless to him, lying there with your foot all taped up like that. Can't you walk by yourself at all?"

"I intend to try, as soon as I can get some crutches," Candace said stiffly.

Before Melina could reply, Nikolas reappeared. He'd overheard her last statement and he asked cheerfully, "Crutches? Why do you need crutches when you have me?"

Candace could feel herself flushing again, but he disregarded her discomfiture and went on, "You'll be late for your party, won't you, Melina? You're going with John Damianos?"

"Yes," Melina said, and her reluctance was obvious. The girl was looking at this man who was her cousin of sorts and yet not a "blood relation," and it seemed to Candace there was an actual glow in her eloquent dark eyes.

"Is he calling here for you?" Nikolas asked.

"I am meeting him at the motel," Melina answered. "Elene and Manos are going with us. Elene has a woman she knows coming over to take care of the desk for the evening."

Nikolas nodded, but he frowned slightly as he said, "Watch it with Manos, Melina."

"Oh, come on, Nick. What would I want with Manos?"

"That, perhaps, is not the question," Nikolas said. "It might be more accurate to ask what Manos would want with you. We all know Manos, do we not? And we know how reliable he is? Elene would be hurt if you paid any attention to his advances, and I do not want that."

Melina said something in Greek that was, of course, thoroughly incomprehensible to Candace. Then, with a swirl of her pleated white skirt, she flounced out of the room.

Nikolas, quite unabashed, grinned. "Women!" he exclaimed. "They love to tease, but they do not like to be caught in a web of their own making."

Candace remembered the way Manos had looked at her last night and she also remembered the question on her mind. "Are Elene and Manos married?"

She thought she detected regret in his affirmative nod.

"How can he be so...so flirtatious when he is married to someone so lovely?"

Nikolas shrugged slightly. "We could say it's the Greek in him," he suggested, but Candace was not about to rise to this. The bait was too obvious.

After a moment he smiled at her and said, "So, I must add discretion to your other virtues, eh? Don't look at me like that, Candace, or I shall have to kiss you again—if only to prove how ardent we Greeks can be!"

She wondered if this was what he really meant as she surprised a bittersweet expression on his face. An expression made all the more eloquent because it had that individual twist only his face could give it.

He clasped his hands, staring down at those long slender fingers that could evoke such surprising sensations with their touch. Candace suddenly had the feeling he'd gone a long way away from her. When he looked across at her again, it was with an expression close to sorrow. But his voice was steady and almost calculatedly unemotional as he said, "That was Paul Morrison on the phone. Earlier I found your camera in the gutter. I took it over to him to see if anything could be done with it, though I doubted it. Paul is an excellent photographer himself, and he also repairs cameras."

"Was he able to fix it?" she asked eagerly.

Nikolas shook his head. "No. Also, I could not recover any of your films. I'm afraid the ditch they fell in was wet, so your negatives were ruined. I hope you hadn't taken too many pictures."

Candace thought of the little girls who had been so adorable in their Greek costumes and of the black-garbed old lady who'd had a face she'd never forget. She thought of all the other people she'd photographed along the procession route, and she sighed.

"I'd taken quite a few," she said glumly.

"Are some of them, perhaps, things you could duplicate?"

"No," she said. "At least, I doubt it. I was concentrating on the spectators first. Then I got some shots of the procession coming down the steps of the cathedral. And...." She smiled wistfully. "It doesn't really matter," she said, which wasn't the truth at all.

Nikolas emphasized this by saying, "That's a foolish statement. Of course it matters. It matters a great deal to you. That's why I've asked Paul to come over. I think he can help you out, if you're agreeable to the idea."

"What idea?"

"Paul spent most of the day taking pictures of the celebrations," Nikolas said. "I managed to catch him when he was back at his studio. He'd gone there to pick up some more film. He also sells cameras, incidentally, and he has one that is a make similar to yours. I told him you would want it—I hope I'm right about that. He will bring it with him."

Candace shook her head ruefully. "I'm sorry, Nikolas," she said slowly. "I just don't have that kind of money with me. I have plenty to pay for my travel and food and motels, but the magazine didn't advance me any expense money. I'm to put in for that later. So I really don't have a surplus with which to replace my equipment.''

''Then I shall lend it to you,'' Nikolas said airily.

There seemed absolutely no doubt in his mind about her acceptance of such a solution, and this was a shade too macho, as far as Candace was concerned. She said quickly, ''I couldn't possibly let you do such a thing.''

''Why not?'' he demanded. ''The camera you lost was insured, wasn't it?''

''Yes, but it takes forever to collect the money.''

''I am in no hurry, Candace.''

''Perhaps you're not,'' she conceded. ''But I'd dislike feeling under such an obligation. . . .''

He raised a cynical eyebrow. ''To an overbearing Greek?'' he finished, making it more of a statement than a question.

There was mockery in his tone, but certainly nothing in his face hinted of hurt feelings. Yet she sensed she had hurt him, though there seemed no logical reason why this should be so.

Logic. There was that word again.

''Nikolas,'' she said almost despairingly. ''I appreciate your making such an offer. I really do. And you've already been very, very kind. It's just that I. . . .''

''You don't want to be under any obligation to an overbearing Greek stranger,'' he finished for her, his tone flat. ''It offends your New England pride, doesn't it?''

''Please,'' she protested.

"But you do put yourself above...immigrants like myself, don't you?" he persisted, shards of anger flickering now in those olive eyes. "We are out of your world, are we not? We people who come from the shores of the Mediterranean and the Adriatic and the Aegean? As a Greek friend of yours I would be out of place at your tea parties, your opera benefits and all the rest of your social doings, wouldn't I?"

Candace tried to respond. She wanted to tell Nikolas how wrong he was, but he cut her off.

"No...you need not say anything."

He broke off, staring at her as if she'd become a stranger, and Candace flinched. Nevertheless, she sensed what he was really saying had very little to do with her. Rather, it went back to some other time in his life and rubbed at wounds that she suspected he thought had been healed yet were still quite raw.

His face reflected a kind of agony, and she desperately wanted to reach out to him. She yearned to draw his dark head close to her and comfort him. For he was still essentially the stranger, as he himself had pointed out, despite this undeniable physical attraction that had sprung up between them so quickly and with such force.

Even greater than her urge to comfort him was her desire to learn more about him, and Candace once again fervently wished she and George Andris had not been interrupted in the hospital. Now she tried to muster the courage to come right out and ask this proud, tortured man sitting at her bedside who he really was. But she shrank from the thought of the reaction this type of confrontation might well provoke. Scorn? Condemnation? She could imagine him turning on her, lashing out at her. Even...hating her.

That is not what I want, she found herself thinking. *I only want his love.*

I only want his love. Candace lay very still, shocked by the implications of this thought.

"What's the matter with you?" he demanded harshly. "You look as if you've seen a ghost."

A ghost? Well, perhaps she had been seeing a ghost. The ghost of a woman who had thought love was an emotion she'd never know again. A passion, a real feeling that would forever be alien to her.

How wrong that woman had been!

Nikolas said, his voice low, "Again, I must ask you to forgive me. You must realize, Candace, I come from the peasant stock of Greece... there is no other blood in my veins. But there is an innate courtesy among my people that would never permit a display of the sort I've just shown you. You are a guest in my house, and I shall not forget that again. So with that in mind, may I get you a glass of wine, *despinís*?"

"Thank you," she said, forcing a smile because she really didn't care just now whether she had any wine or not. Then, as she watched his retreating figure, she knew. She knew, in a shattering instant of revelation, it wasn't wine she wanted, or anything else. It was Nikolas himself.

She wanted him. She wanted to feel the pressure of his mouth on hers again and the touch of his beautiful hands molding the shape of her body. She wanted to know all there was to know about him as a man, and this time she didn't want any interruptions. Instead, she wanted a culmination of the passion she sensed would flow between them like a river. A river ending not in the sea but in the sky.

She swallowed hard, and when she saw him returning, a glass filled with a deep red liquid cupped in each hand, she wryly thought it was not wine he should be bringing her but ice water—ice water to be dashed straight in her face, with the hope that it would bring her to her senses!

He clicked his glass to hers and said in that deep voice of his, "Let us drink to a better understanding between the Greeks and the Anglo-Saxons."

Candace forced a shaky laugh. "I'll buy that," she agreed.

"As do I," he nodded, his smile reaching clear to his eyes. Then she sensed his hesitation, and there was a hint of embarrassment in the short laugh that followed.

"I don't know how to put this," he confessed, "nor do I wish to have the whole issue develop into what might be called a 'federal case' between us. But I would appreciate it if you would take the camera Paul brings."

"Appreciate it?"

"Yes," Nikolas said. "I don't like to talk about such things, Candace, but the fact is I do not lack for money. So you will not be depriving me of a thing if it takes you a long time to collect your insurance money and repay me. Anyway, it seems obvious you must have a camera if you are to finish your assignment."

"I doubt I'll be able to finish it," she said slowly. "At the moment, I've no pictures at all."

"Ah, but Paul does," Nikolas pointed out. "That is what I have been trying to tell you. I have discussed this with him, and he is going to bring over a selection of contact prints he has already developed from pictures he took earlier today. And he will be going around to all the various festivities tonight, too, taking more pictures.''

''He is a professional photographer?''

''Yes, but he is more than that. Paul is an artist with the camera. He sells scenes—such as the ones he did today—to various newspapers and magazines from time to time. But he makes his living from his camera-repair work and from taking the usual, conventional photographs for graduations, weddings, family portraits...that sort of thing. When your ankle is better we can go to his studio and you will see the kind of work he puts his heart into. One day, I think he will become famous.''

''You said his name is Morrison?''

''Yes.''

''So he's not Greek,'' Candace said, the words emerging before she had time to think about how they might strike him.

Fortunately, Nikolas seemed to find this amusing. His teeth gleamed white as he laughed, then said, ''Half-Greek, *oréa mou*. But I would say he looks entirely Greek. Our strain does tend to predominate.''

PAUL MORRISON DID indeed look entirely Greek. He was as dark as George Andris and of much the same physical type, but he had a charming, engaging manner that made Candace feel as if he could very well be related to Nikolas. He arrived before they had finished their wine and acceded to Nikolas's request that he join them in a glass, even though he said regretfully that his time was limited. Candace was a little uncomfortable receiving Paul in the bedroom, but her painful ankle gave her little choice. Both men seemed quite at ease and soon she overcame her discomfort.

"I'll be on the go for hours yet," he told Candace while Nikolas went to get the wine. "And then I'll probably be in the mood to go back and develop my films before I turn in." He paused, then added, "Nick said you wanted to buy a new camera."

"I take it my old one is beyond repair?"

"Creamed!" Paul said eloquently. "A pity. Believe me, I know. You tend to get used to a camera, so it becomes like an old shoe. But I brought one with me that is essentially the first cousin to yours, although it's an updated version."

He reached into a leather case he'd placed on the floor as he spoke, and when Candace examined the camera he held out to her she quickly realized he was right. This camera functioned almost exactly as hers had, but not only was it a newer model, it was also much better. And, she thought, her spirits sinking, undoubtedly a good bit more expensive.

"I don't know," she said hesitantly. "It looks excellent. But as I told Nikolas, I didn't come here prepared to make an expenditure like this."

Paul grinned. "Your credit is good with me," he said. "Anyway, Nick vouches for you." It was as if that, in itself, was enough to give her a pass key to just about anything.

He was reaching for something else in his leather case, and now he handed her a large manila envelope. "Contact sheets of some of the stuff I took today," he said. "I might say the same terms go for any of these you want. I'll make glossies for you, and I've also got color shots covering the same subjects. It takes a bit of juggling sometimes, but I try to shoot the things that really interest me in both color and black-and-white. I still find black-and-white the more artistic medium, but color is definitely easier to sell for most magazine work, as you know. I'll have some good color shots of the procession, and of both the diving for the cross and the second blessing at the cathedral I can show you the slides in a day or two.''

Paul smiled. ''All I ask in return is photo credit when your article comes out. If, that is, you want to use some of my work.'' The smile became a short laugh. ''I'll admit I'd like to see my name in *Tempo*. And you don't have to worry about paying me—you can do that when the magazine pays you. Then,'' he continued reasonably, ''as soon as you're up and around again you can fill in with your own work. You could get some good shots down at the sponge docks, for instance. . . .''

Candace laughed. ''You seem to have solved all my problems,'' she said. ''But there's one major gap. Aside from a glimpse into the cathedral this morning and the beginning of the procession, I didn't see anything of the major ceremonies. The dive for the cross, especially. That's something I was really counting on.''

Paul nodded absently. ''That shouldn't be any big problem for you. Sure, I appreciate the fact you'd like to have seen it yourself, but you could hardly have a better person to explain everything that happens. Nick—''

''Nick what?'' their host asked, carrying a carafe of wine and an extra glass. Once again, he had chosen to reappear at precisely the wrong moment.

An odd expression flickered across Paul Morrison's face, and Candace had the feeling he'd just received some sort of telepathic warning from

Nikolas. Seldom had she felt so frustrated. Twice in one day she'd been on the verge of learning at least something about Nikolas Mylonis, whatever it might be. And twice he had loomed up as if he'd deliberately wanted to prevent such revelations from being made.

Paul said carefully, "I was just telling Miss Mayhew you could explain things like the diving for the cross to her because—"

"Yes, I suppose I can," Nikolas cut in, to Candace's exasperation. He poured the wine, then passed the glasses around. "Will Paul be able to help you, Candace?"

"Very much so, I'm sure," she said. "Especially if you'll. . . ."

"Fill you in on some of the details?" he finished for her. He spoke pleasantly enough, but his glance was very dark. It made her feel as if she wanted to shrink away from him. "We will get to that later." And with this he changed the subject firmly.

"Paul," he said. "When are you going around tonight, keep an eye out for Melina, will you? Also, see if you can get a shot of Elene with Manos. I should like to see the picture published in the local paper, if only to reaffirm the fact of their marriage."

Candace saw Paul's hand shake slightly, and the glass of wine he was holding very nearly spilled. She wondered at this seemingly intense reaction to Nikolas's request, but Paul only said quietly, "Elene is not a child, Nick."

"I didn't say she was," Nikolas answered. "Nevertheless, she has the heart of an innocent, which perhaps makes her even more vulnerable." He added under his breath, "And I wish to God Manos Panagoris had stayed in Greece!"

He tossed off his glass of wine, then picked up the carafe again. But before pouring a refill, he paused. Paul had not answered him, and now Nikolas said, "I'm sorry. I know I tend to ride roughshod at times. It's just that I...." He broke into Greek, and Paul responded in the same language, his own tone low and intense.

Candace sighed, feeling totally alien. It seemed to her everyone she'd met in Tarpon Springs so far was bilingual. Or, if they spoke only one language, it was more apt to be Greek than English!

CHAPTER SIX

PAUL FINISHED HIS WINE and said he had to be going, and Nikolas followed him to the front door. Candace could hear them speaking in low tones for quite a while, but she wasn't able to make out whether it was Greek or English they were using. Finally she heard the door close.

It was twilight now, and amethyst shadows were stealing their way into the room. She was reminded it had been only twenty-four hours since she'd driven down Hellenic Avenue looking for her motel. Only twenty-four hours since she'd first passed this house.

It all seemed impossible.

Nikolas walked slowly back into the room, but this time he did not come to sit on the edge of the bed. He chose, instead, an armchair at a discreet distance. He also made no move to turn on any lights and thus dispel the dimness. Candace could have reached the switch on the bedside-table lamp next to her, but she decided against this, preferring—as he obviously did—the camouflage of the encroaching darkness.

She was intensely aware of his nearness, and she knew somehow she had to get a grip on herself and again summon the self-control that normally came so naturally to her. She simply couldn't permit herself to fall apart, emotionally or otherwise, every time Nikolas was around her. Involuntarily she remembered the scene between them earlier in the afternoon when they had been interrupted by Melina. And now the mere thought of his kisses, his caress, made her pulse race. This sort of reaction to mere memory wouldn't do, she warned herself sharply. It wouldn't do at all!

The silence between them was fast becoming uncomfortable. Candace didn't know what she could say to break it, and she suspected Nikolas was having the same difficulty. But finally he made the initial attempt by asking her a very prosaic question.

"Are you hungry?" he queried.

"No," she said quickly, for food was the farthest thing from her mind.

"Well, Theone has left a cold supper for us," he said.

"Left us?" Candace asked. "Isn't she here?"

"No, she's gone out," he answered. "Aliki is catering a banquet tonight, and Theone is helping her." He laughed briefly. "When I told her it would be okay to do this I did not know, of course, I would be having a houseguest...."

He spoke as if Theone was an employee, yet according to Melina she was actually his aunt by marriage. But this wasn't the time to bring up their relationship.

Candace said hastily, "I won't need any supper, Nikolas. I ate so much for lunch I—"

"Don't be ridiculous," he interrupted. He paused as if wondering what to say next, then added, "I'm not about to devour you, Candace, so don't look at me like that. Yes, I can see those huge eyes of yours even through this gloom. Would you like me to turn a light on?"

"No," she said.

"Good, neither would I," he admitted. A heavy pause filled the space between. "Look," he went on, "this afternoon we both got...swept away. But I'll be damned if I'm going to apologize to you, though I shall take care it doesn't happen again. So you can be sure I shall not try to force my attention on someone who clearly considers herself at a disadvantage. Does that make you feel any better?"

It didn't make her feel any better at all, but she could hardly tell him this. "I wasn't thinking about that, Nikolas," she said, knowing as soon as she spoke the words they sounded incredibly lame. "I just...."

"You weren't thinking about that? Then excuse me—I was mistaken," he told her with exaggerated politeness. He stood up, and Candace could almost feel his restlessness. "I think I'd like a little more wine," he said, "and then we'll eat. How about you?"

Part of her refused, yet she found herself saying, "Yes, please."

He was gone only a moment, returning with the carafe more than half-full once again. This time he paused to switch on a dim table lamp in the corner. Its soft glow etched his profile in a golden hue. From this distance the scars were not entirely visible, and Candace caught her breath at the sight of him.

He was indeed an Adonis incarnate, yet his attraction for her went far beyond his exceptional good looks. And he was exceptionally handsome, despite the delicate network of scars on one side of his face. But his beauty was much more than simply surface deep, and it was the glimpses Candace had had of the man beneath the facade that excited her so. A man with so many moods, so many facets. . . .

Their fingers touched as he handed her her wine-glass, and Candace trembled. She knew he sensed this response, for he frowned very slightly. But he made no comment. He sat down again in the arm-chair, leaned back and looked across at her thought-fully.

"Have you examined Paul's photos yet?" he asked.

The fact of the matter was she hadn't even given a thought to the contents of the envelope Paul had left with her. "No," she said, feeling strangely guilty. She reached for the envelope, but Nikolas stopped her with a wave of his hand.

"Not now," he said. "Later I'm sure you can work things out with Paul. And he says you shouldn't have any trouble using the new camera, so you should be able to get on with your assignment very soon. Today's episode will be just that. Only an episode."

He spoke flatly, and Candace wondered just what he meant by this last statement. Was she to take it he'd acted on a purely sensual impulse today and did not intend for her to make too much of it? He'd already told her she needn't fear a repeat of the scene. Fear! Again she trembled, this time nearly spilling her wine. She wished it was fear possessing her, for there were no valid bridges between fear and desire.

She shook her head, astonished at herself. Nikolas was watching her curiously, and now he asked, "What is it, Candace? You do feel, don't you, that you can complete your assignment?"

She took the plunge. "Well. . .no," she said. "Not unless I can fill in some important details. It's not just the pictures, Nikolas. There's reporting involved, too. I didn't actually see the ceremony at the bayou or any of the other events, and there won't be a repeat for another year." She waited, then added slowly, "Paul said that you—"

"Yes," he cut in, "I know he did."

Candace bit her lip. Nikolas was staring moodily at his wine, twirling the glass between his fingers, and once again she had the feeling some preoccupation had carried him a long way off from her. Further, she was sure there was nothing at all pleasant about these mental safaris he seemed to embark on from time to time. She felt it more likely they were stirring up a past he didn't want to remember.

His memories must be very painful ones, she found herself thinking. *And it's wrong for me to ask him to relive them just for my sake.*

"Nikolas," she said quietly. "I'll make out. So don't feel you have to. . . ."

He looked up sullenly. "Have to what, Candace?"

She could feel his eyes boring into her as she stammered, "I don't want to get into anything you don't want to talk about, that's all."

"And what do you think there is I don't want to talk about?" he questioned, a rough edge to his voice.

"I don't know," she confessed helplessly. "You just seem rather disturbed, I guess."

"Disturbed?"

The challenging look he threw at Candace almost knocked her off balance. It was as if he was waiting for her to continue, just so he could refute anything she might say. She wanted to speak, but the words caught in her throat, and after a moment he rose to his feet and paced, like a caged lion, across the room to the window. He drew the drapes aside and stood there staring out, and she knew he was looking down the slope in the road toward Spring Bayou.

What was it about Spring Bayou that affected him so? This was one of a dozen questions she didn't dare ask him, and she sank back against the pillows and watched him apprehensively. But this didn't prepare her for the expression she saw on his face when he finally swung around toward her. He appeared far more hostile than he had in the restaurant last night. Far more menacing than he had when he'd grabbed her as she was falling this morning.

"What do you know about me?" he demanded, almost snarling the words.

"Know about you?" she echoed, trying not to visibly shrink away from him. "I don't know anything about you, Nikolas."

This was true enough. . . although her curiosity had reached the point where she didn't know how much longer she could go on without making an effort to solve the mystery surrounding him.

"George Andris said nothing to you?" he barked.

"No," she said. Unfortunately, he hadn't had the chance to.

"And Paul?" he persisted.

This was too much. "What is there to say?" she flung back. And without even pausing to think she added, "Just what are you trying to hide from?"

Nikolas shuddered, the convulsion racking his entire body. Then, almost as quickly, he sat down. "I may be trying to hide from quite a few things, Candace," he said quietly. "It doesn't really matter, though. You and I are—what shall I say—ships that pass in the night. Soon you will be gone from Tarpon Springs, and meeting me will only be a memory. You will have other assignments in other places. In the career you have chosen there are all sorts of possible adventures for you. So—" he shrugged "—you need not concern yourself with what I may or may not be trying to hide from."

Despite the twinge it brought to her ankle, Candace sat straight up. She tried to keep her mounting fury in check as she said tightly, "You are the most irritating man I've ever met! Do you really think I permit strange men to pick me up and literally kidnap me? And do you really think I then let them begin to make love to me, just as casually as—"

She saw his mouth curve in a slight smile and his eyes light up with amusement, and this only infuriated her more. "Oh, damn you!" she cried helplessly.

Nikolas laughed aloud. "So," he said, his inflection of the word making him sound very foreign, "I have offended your puritan sensibilities, have I? Because we both felt a perfectly natural response to each other. . . ."

"You make us sound like a couple of animals," Candace choked. "It was a lot more than a 'perfectly natural response.' It was—" She broke off, suddenly aware she was revealing entirely too much to him. She should have known he would rise to this remark, and he did.

"What was it then, Candace?" he asked. "For myself, I admit I am swayed by proximity to a beautiful woman, particularly when she has the attraction—or illusion, perhaps—of even temporary help-lessness. In our world today, the male seldom finds himself in such an enviable position. So I do not think I can be blamed if I took advantage of the opportunity to—"

It was her turn to interrupt him. "Oh, shut up, Nikolas!" she snapped.

He laughed again, but there was no mockery to this laugh. It rang free and true, and he said, "Ah, I think I've fallen in love with you, Candace. You delight me."

"Doesn't anything really matter to you?" she asked him bitterly.

He raised a questioning eyebrow. "You doubt what I just said?"

"Of course I doubt what you just said!"

"So, to all of the other things I am finding out about you, I must add you are a skeptic?" He refilled his wineglass as he said this, and she hoped he wasn't going to drink too much. It had been difficult enough handling a perfectly sober Nikolas. Candace couldn't imagine coping with an intoxicated version.

She didn't want to look at him because she knew he was studying her closely, but finally she could no longer avoid his keen green gaze. She wondered just what he was going to do next—or if she'd ever be able to anticipate this, even were she to know him for a hundred years.

Once again he surprised her by saying, "I think I've misjudged you, Candace. And if it will help with your story, I'll tell you about what goes on here on the Feast of the Epiphany."

"I think you know it would help," she managed.

"Well, good, then," he said. He stretched out

those long legs and seemed to be surveying the tips of his dark brown loafers, which looked both handmade and expensive, she noticed.

"A long time ago," he began, "I dived with the other boys for the cross the bishop tossed into Spring Bayou. In fact, I was the one who came up with it."

For some reason, this thought had never occurred to Candace. Now she had an instant vision of Nikolas as he must have been all those years ago. Slim as a reed and sun bronzed. . . an Adonis of a boy even as he was now an Adonis of a man.

"As they did this morning," he went on slowly, "the bells of the cathedral rang early that day, bringing thousands of people from different places and of different faiths to St. Nicholas's. As you know, the observance of the Epiphany is the outstanding event of the year for the people here. In fact, it was the Greek people in Tarpon Springs who really introduced the traditional Greek observance of Epiphany into this country."

Candace nodded. "Yes."

Nikolas took a deep sip of his wine, then said somewhat unsteadily, "Just now, you look like a blond Madonna. You have such exquisite features, Candace. . . ."

"Nikolas—"

"Yes, I know. You wish to hear more about the Epiphany celebration," he said wryly. "Well, in the early days, the celebration was purely a local one. Everything happened on a much smaller scale. The present cathedral was not built until the early 1940s, and in the old church there were only chairs, no pews. On Epiphany, actually, all of the people stood during the service because this was the ancient custom."

He smiled across at her. "Greeks are not inclined to change the old ways quickly," he told her. "Finally, the Epiphany celebration did become more elaborate. One of the priests of the church initiated the practice of unloosing a dove, which I'm sure you know is both the symbol of peace and the symbol of the Holy Spirit. Perhaps you saw the dove being carried by one of the choir members this morning?"

"Yes, I did," Candace nodded, and added sadly, "I even took a picture of it."

"I would imagine Paul did, too," Nikolas said by way of consolation. "Well, then, over the years the celebration grew, until now it must be admitted it has become—and I dislike using this phrase in connection with such an important event—quite a tourist attraction. But to the people who live here, it remains a symbol of unity.

"Also, this day traditionally marks the return of the sponge boats and all the other boats that make Tarpon Springs their home port. They sail into the bayou to be blessed by the bishop or sometimes even the archbishop, who comes here especially for this occasion.

"Anyway, on the day I was speaking about—the day I dived for the cross—the archbishop *was* here, and the service was very beautiful. I was only seventeen, and being so young I was easily impressed, but it seemed to me the choir sang as gloriously as angels. You heard the music this morning?"

"Yes," she said. "It was beautiful, and so different. There was a strange quality to it, but I was very moved."

"I would think it would all seem strange to you," Nikolas observed, a touch of irony tinging his tone.

"It's an alien culture, no?" He paused again and sipped his wine. "Anyway, after the service that day the procession formed to make its way through the streets, and the streets were mobbed with people, even as they were today. There were people packed all around the bayou when we finally got to it, and the bayou itself was jammed with boats. Everything in town is decorated for Epiphany, you noticed?"

Candace didn't answer immediately, and he said, "Ah, but I keep forgetting you haven't been around the town yet. You'll find both Greek and American flags flying everywhere you look and people dressed in the costumes of the part of Greece either they or their forebears came from...."

Nikolas talked on, painting for her a word picture of his town and his people, and Candace sat mesmerized by the deep sound of his voice. He spoke of himself as he'd been back then—young and easily impressed—and as he described the ornamented robes the clergy wore, she could almost feel their rich texture. She could almost smell the incense wafting through the air and imagined she could hear the solemn cadences of the liturgy being recited.

He spoke of the way the highest-ranking member of the clergy always carried a silver staff, just as she'd seen it done today. And when she asked, he told her the ornament at the top of the staff was composed of two intertwining serpents symbolizing the serpents Moses took up in the wilderness.

As he spoke, he conveyed to her the sense of excitement he'd felt as a youth when they'd neared the bayou and he and the other boys who were to dive took up their positions.

Then there was another service at the bayou—a

blessing of the boats and the men who sailed them. Finally, the words "The Spirit descended like a dove" were pronounced, and the dove that had been carried down from the cathedral was set free. At the same moment, the golden cross was thrown into the water.

"We all dived in for it at the same time," Nikolas remembered. "It made quite a splash. Needless to say, in the frenzy that followed it was each of us for himself. I can remember swimming like hell, reaching and reaching and clutching, and then—I had it! I broke back up to the surface and held the cross up high, and everyone began to cheer and applaud."

His smile was wry. "There is a heady quality to receiving one's first applause," he said.

"It really must have been thrilling!" Candace exclaimed.

"Yes. . . it was thrilling," he agreed. "Later I was to think it was very probably the highlight of my life. But at the time I was so overwhelmed I simply didn't think about it. I climbed out of the water and went to kneel before the archbishop, and then I received his special blessing. After that, all the other boys who had dived lifted me onto their shoulders, and a procession formed that went back up to the cathedral for yet another blessing. And then I was told all good things would be mine for the whole of the coming year. . . ."

"Were they?" she asked, still excited.

Again he stared broodingly at the tip of his loafers. "I suppose that depends on one's definition of 'good,' " he answered cryptically.

"To go back a bit, there is a significance to tossing the cross into the water. The cross, in this instance, represents God's message to a troubled world. And the young men who make the dive to retrieve the cross represent all the nations of the world who reach for God's aid in bringing peace and hope.

"After the religious ceremonies are over, the festivities begin. There is a *glendi*—a *glendi* is a Greek version of a fiesta—and then there are parties, banquets and plenty of outdoor dancing. You hear bouzouki music everywhere, and there is a constant open house among friends. Every person of every age gets into the act. They say nowhere else, outside of Greece itself, is there another celebration of the Epiphany that can approach the one we have here."

The thought suddenly struck her. "And all of that is going on tonight," she said seriously, "yet here you are with me. I'm sorry, Nikolas."

"Why should you be sorry, Candace? What is there for you to feel sorry about?"

"That you are missing it all and—"

He laughed, a laugh without mirth. "I am missing nothing," he assured her. "It is years now since I have been involved in such a celebration. Nor will I ever be involved in one again."

He spoke with a flatness that didn't invite questions, and this puzzled her. Despite the fact he had been the lucky youth who'd retrieved the golden cross at that Epiphany service long ago, Candace felt somehow the entire day had a very unhappy connotation for him.

As she watched, Nikolas finished his wine. Then he said, "I shall bring you in some supper. Theone has left us *dolmadákia*—these are stuffed grape leaves and quite delicious. Also, there is salad and some cold meat. Afterward we can have coffee and a dessert, if you wish."

"There's no need for you to wait on me," Candace protested. "If you could just find me a crutch of some sort, I'm sure I could hobble out to the kitchen."

He shook his head. "Not tonight, Candace. Time enough tomorrow for you to practice your hobbling skills."

He was nearly at the threshold, and there was one thing she felt she really had to ask him. "Nikolas!" she called.

He tilted his dark head slightly as he turned and look across at her. "Yes?"

"Did you keep a scrapbook or anything like that for remembering the time you retrieved the cross? Do you have any pictures of yourself?"

His face was in the shadows, so she couldn't see his expression. But she did see him stiffen. Then he said in a voice as cold as marble, "No, Candace. No scrapbook...no pictures...nothing. Nothing at all."

CHAPTER SEVEN

IT WAS A LONG TIME before Candace finally fell asleep that night. Nikolas had brought her a tray of food but nothing for himself, saying he preferred to eat a bit later. And though she was chagrined by this, there wasn't much she could do.

He'd left her to eat alone, returning to clear her tray away. Then he'd carried her across the room again, depositing her just inside the bathroom door. When she was ready to get into bed she saw he had smoothed out the covers and rearranged the pillows. He had given her a nightgown evidently belonging to Melina and a robe that looked as if it must be Theone's.

Melina's nightgown was too big for her, which was just as well. Candace had no desire to wear anything too alluring just now. Nikolas seemed to be feeling they should keep a safe distance between themselves, and Candace had to force herself to admit he was right. So she'd tried not to show any visible response when he helped her into bed and pulled the covers up over her.

He had brought her two paperback novels and a couple of magazines. Then he'd asked if she wished him to turn out the lights or if she preferred to read awhile.

She had told him she'd rather read, and so he'd

said gravely, "*Kaliníhta*, then, Candace." And with that he'd left her.

She'd not been able to concentrate on reading at all. Finally she'd switched off the light and stared miserably into the dark. She'd almost felt bereft.

Had she expected Nikolas to kiss her good-night? And would this, perhaps, have led to a reenactment of their scene together earlier in the day? Was that what she wanted?

Candace was more than slightly shocked at herself because she knew very well this was precisely what she wanted! But eventually she drifted off.

She was awakened once, at an unknown hour, by the sound of a girl laughing. Melina, she decided sleepily, returning from an evening of festivities. Candace felt the pang of a very primitive emotion. Then she told herself sharply there was no reason at all why she should be jealous of Melina. Certainly she had no claim on Nikolas Mylonis herself. Melina had an absolutely clear field. . . .

But the mere thought of Melina with Nikolas was so disturbing Candace knew unless she forced her mind off it she'd never get back to sleep. She made herself think of her article and of how she could weave into her text the things Nikolas had told her about the Epiphany celebration. However, she felt she still needed more information, so she decided as soon as possible she'd go to the Tarpon Springs library and see what was in the files.

This matter settled, she even tried counting sheep before she finally fell asleep again. . . but the sheep had a way of changing into tall, handsome Greeks with olive green eyes and enigmatic smiles.

Hers was a restless night, and when she awakened,

the sun was casting gold ribbons through the slats in the window blinds. There was a soft, perfumed fragrance in the air that came from the flowering bushes in the garden outside.

Candace sat up in bed, stretched out her arms and very carefully moved her ankle. Although it was quite sore it no longer throbbed as it had yesterday, and she conceded Nikolas had been right in insisting she stay off it for the first twenty-four hours.

She wondered if she should try to walk on it now and was deliberating over this when someone rapped on the door.

"Come in," she said.

Theone entered, and after saying something in Greek that sounded like a greeting, she smiled. Not the warmest smile in the world, but a smile just the same.

"*Kaliméra*, Miss Mayhew," she said. "You sleep well?"

"Yes, thank you."

As Theone came across the room Candace saw she was carrying a stout wooden cane. "Nick thinks you like this," she said. "It lets you keep weight off your bad foot. But he says you still must be very careful."

She spoke slowly and with a heavy accent, but her English was quite comprehensible, to Candace's relief.

Candace eased out of the bed and managed to stand, using the cane to support the offending ankle. And it really was "offending," as far as she was concerned. It was totally hampering her at a time when she needed to get around with even more than the usual amount of dexterity.

Nevertheless, she had to inch her way across the

room. It wasn't too bad as long as she remembered to let the cane do its full share of the work. Fortunately it was her left ankle that was afflicted, which would mean she'd still be able to drive with relative ease, since the car she'd rented had an automatic shift.

Theone said, "I shall bring you breakfast. You wish bacon and eggs, perhaps?"

Candace shook her head. "No, thank you. Just some coffee and toast will be fine." She hesitated, then added, "I'm sorry to be such a nuisance."

"It is no trouble," Theone replied, and this time her smile was a genuine one. "Melina still sleeps," she said, "and Nick, he has left already."

"Left?"

"Yes," Theone nodded. "He goes about the affairs of business."

The older woman did not elaborate, and Candace suppressed her curiosity. But she wondered what "affairs of business" Nikolas Mylonis was engaged in. Yesterday, of course, the whole town had virtually taken a holiday. Was this why he had been so free? She had no idea where he might work, nor what he might do. But whatever it was and wherever it was, it had probably been closed for the celebrations, and so he'd been given the day off.

"Elene Panagoris has sent over suitcase with some of your clothes," Theone continued. "Nick asked her to do this. I hope you do not mind?"

"No," Candace said. "That was very nice of her."

"She still keeps your room for you. She...." Theone waved her hands rather helplessly. "Ah, my English," she deplored. "It at times leaves me."

"Your English is very good, Mrs. Mylonis," Candace said, taking the chance this was Theone's proper surname.

Theone looked faintly surprised, but she said only, "You are kind. Nick tells me I should talk more English. He says always with me it is Greek, Greek...."

When she spoke of Nick it was in an affectionate tone, and now she chuckled. "Nick is a Greek man in every way," she confided. "Even though—"

She stopped at this, as if she'd already said too much, and again Candace was possessed by a brimming curiosity. *Even though what,* she yearned to ask Theone, yet suspected their conversation would be concluded were she to do so. Those dark eyes, remarkably like Melina's when Candace really looked at them, would become shuttered. And Theone would grow silent. Candace very definitely did not want that to happen.

No, better to keep a line of communication open with Nick's aunt. Even a slender one, rather than risk breaking this channel off by being a bit too forward.

Theone lifted the suitcase Elene had sent over from the motel and placed it across a chair so it would be high enough for Candace to reach quite easily. From it Candace selected another knit dress, this one in a soft lilac shade that brought violet lights to her eyes. She would have preferred to wear jeans today but didn't want to bother trying to ease the pant leg over her bandaged ankle.

After she had washed, dressed and put on a touch of makeup, she felt in much better spirits. She left her hair down, brushing it into a cloud around her shoulders, and Theone, glancing at it, said, "Like gold."

This comment made Candace think of the contrast—the physical contrast—between Nikolas and herself. She was so very fair, so completely Anglo-Saxon. And he was so dark, so totally Greek.

We're different in so many ways, she found herself

thinking dismally. Just about every way, probably. Except for the fire of passion that seemed to meld them together.

This fire was not to be trusted. Common sense told Candace this was true, and she had no doubt Nikolas had come to the same conclusion. This was why he'd brought her supper to her last night and then had left her to eat alone, returning only to help her into bed in the most perfunctory of ways.

Thinking about this, she chose to sit down in the chair where Nikolas had sat the evening before, and it seemed to her she could smell the slightly spicy scent of the after-shave lotion he used, still clinging to the upholstery. Even this vestige of an aroma reminiscent of him was enough to set her senses swirling. She felt a purely physical response, sensual and very evocative. And she tried to tell herself that it was just as well Nikolas was not around this morning, for she needed a little time apart from him. A little time in which to come to grips with emotions she really didn't understand.

Candace supposed she had actually come to believe she was frigid. Jeff, at least, had accused her of being frigid. He had finally moved into a bedroom of his own, leaving her to feel uncertain about her own sexuality. She had felt inadequate and confused. In fact, during the course of her marriage to Jeff she had felt so many things about herself...and almost all of them had been negative. Then, in the end, she'd concluded men simply had no place in her life. Somehow, she hadn't responded to Jeff's lovemaking the way she had expected to—and eventually she'd become glad about this. Her experience with Jeff had convinced her she'd had enough of men.

Divorce had been something she'd always detested, but in her case there had been no alternative, and admittedly her first real sense of freedom in a long time had come with her divorce decree. She'd exulted in this freedom these past couple of months, and even Barry Gehrich—

Thoughts tumbled over one another as Candace mentally brought herself up short. Barry, *Tempo*'s managing editor, had given her the Tarpon Springs story assignment, and she should have called him long before now. He'd asked her to give him a call once she had settled in so he'd have a number where he could reach her.

Theone came back carrying a tray, and Candace smelled the wonderful aroma of fresh-brewed coffee. In addition to this, Theone had grilled thick slices of Greek bread, and with them she brought a small pot of sweet, soft butter and a jar of lemon marmalade that was obviously homemade.

Candace had not realized she was hungry. Now she surveyed her breakfast with an interest that made Theone smile.

"This looks marvelous!" she exclaimed. "Perfect."

"Nick would say it is not enough for you," Theone observed.

Candace, buttering a slice of the delicious bread, sampled it and replied, "Well, Nikolas and I do not always agree." The words came out casually, as if she'd known him for years.

She saw Theone's lips curve slightly and knew the older woman was amused. But it was a kindly sort of amusement, so she ventured, "How late does Nikolas usually work?"

Theone looked surprised. "Work?" she echoed.

"Yes," Candace managed between bites. "You mentioned he had to go back to work this morning."

"Oh...the business affairs," Theone said a bit vaguely. "It depends. With Nick, one does not know."

"And your daughter?" Candace asked carefully. "Does she work?"

"Melina?" Theone said. "No, Melina does not work." She frowned. "Sometimes she helps Elene at the Grecian Gardens. Elene is her cousin, you know."

"Yes, Nikolas told me," Candace nodded.

"Melina wants to go to New York," Theone murmured. "But Nick, he is not sure."

Theone was making up the bed as she spoke, turning back the coverlets so Candace could once again slide underneath them if she wished. Though at the moment Candace had no intention of going back to bed.

"Melina is very beautiful," she said. "I can understand why she might want to go to New York. Does she want to get into modeling, perhaps? Or maybe the theater?"

Theone looked startled by this question, but as she straightened she said only, "With young girls, one often does not know what goes on in the mind. Now, you would perhaps like a book? Or a magazine?"

"Thank you," Candace said, "but Nikolas brought me a supply of both last night, and I fell asleep before I even got into them." She paused. "I would appreciate it, though, if you'd hand me the camera case Mr. Morrison brought over yesterday and that brown envelope right next to it."

"Of course," Theone said, and did so. But she still seemed reluctant to leave. "Would you perhaps like some more coffee?" she asked finally.

"No, thank you. This has been perfect. Absolutely right. But if you don't mind, could I use the phone in a little while? Nikolas said it would be okay."

"Oh, yes," Theone agreed, but she seemed slightly troubled by this request. "The nearest for you is the library. The room Nick took you to yesterday. Just out of here, one door to your left."

"I'll find it," Candace nodded. She hesitated, then added, "I'm sorry to be a nuisance, Mrs. Mylonis, but there is one other thing I'd like to ask you for in the meantime, if I may?"

"Certainly."

"Could you find me some paper? And perhaps a pen or a couple of pencils?"

"Yes," Theone said, but this was spoken woodenly, and Candace had the unhappy feeling the rapport that had been growing between them had suddenly diminished for reasons she couldn't understand.

Theone was gone very briefly. Candace imagined the older woman had found the supplies she'd asked for right next door in the library. But when she'd handed them over, she lingered once again. And somehow she looked older. The shadows beneath her dark eyes seemed to be growing deeper.

"I do not know how I should ask you," she began, the words coming slowly, her accent sounding especially heavy. "But you are not to write about Nick, are you? I do not know why he feels this way, but I do know that Nick does not want anyone to write about him. He has said this to Paul."

"Paul Morrison?"

"Yes," Theone nodded. "I overhear them. Paul does not say why this is, but I think to Nick it is something very serious."

Candace was thoroughly surprised. "I have no intention of writing about Nikolas," she said. "Why in the world should I?"

The expression of relief that crossed Theone's face was quite overwhelming. Clearly it was very important to Nikolas Mylonis's aunt things be as he wanted them to be. She smiled, and her earlier friendliness quickly returned. "That is good!" she beamed. "Do as you wish then, Despinís Mayhew. I will look in from time to time to see if you need any help. Or, if you want . . . ."

Her English seemed to fail her momentarily and Candace said gently, "Don't worry, Mrs. Mylonis. I'll call out if I really need something, but I'm sure I will be quite all right."

This seemed to satisfy Theone, but as Candace watched her leave the room she was far from satisfied herself. Why was it so important to Nikolas Mylonis no one write anything about him? And why was he so openly antagonistic about journalists?

Theone had indicated she didn't know the reason for Nikolas's aversion to appearing in print. Whether this was true—or merely a defensive move on Theone's part—was impossible to decide. But Candace had a writer's imagination, and it was easy enough to let it run rampant. All sorts of conjectures raced through her mind. It was impossible not to speculate.

It occurred to her maybe Nikolas Mylonis wasn't even his real name. Maybe he was living here in Tarpon Springs under an assumed identity. True,

Theone had answered to "Mrs. Mylonis." But when Candace thought about this for a moment, she realized this in itself could be misleading. Theone hadn't really answered to the name. She had simply not contradicted Candace's use of it.

Then, of course, there was Melina. And also Elene, the girl who ran the motel. Aliki, the woman who managed the restaurant, was Elene's mother and Theone's sister. At least, this was what Candace had been told. The other handsome, arrogant young Greek who had been in the restaurant that first night with Nikolas was Manos Panagoris, Elene's husband.

Nikolas had sketched out all these relationships, yet she hadn't really confirmed any of them. Also, this house certainly seemed to be his, and she guessed he had inherited it from his uncle. But this seemed strange, too. Theone had been married to the man. Could the house really belong to her, making Nikolas merely a guest in it, even as Candace was herself? Regardless, Theone certainly seemed more like his housekeeper than his aunt.

Candace pondered all of this and wished there were someone she could turn to, if only to find out whether or not Nikolas Mylonis was in fact hiding something from her.

Then she reminded herself there were two people who had already confirmed who Nikolas really was. George Andris and Paul Morrison. Both the doctor and the photographer not only knew Nikolas but claimed to know him very well. And each of them had been on the verge of telling her something about him, something she was sure was tremendously important. But both times there had been an interruption. . . by Nikolas himself.

Candace sighed. This mystery surrounding Nikolas both intrigued and frustrated her. And she found herself wishing he'd come back, wishing he'd suddenly walk in upon her and come to sit on the arm of her chair, bending his dark head down until his mouth came to brush against her lips. His kiss would be tantalizing at first, then would start to deepen, until. . . .

A sensuous tremor came to grip her, and Candace discovered her body's inner need—a sexual hunger, a basic kind of demand.

She gritted her teeth, resenting this intrusion because she didn't want Nikolas Mylonis—or any other man—to have this effect on her. She reminded herself how long she'd wanted to be free and out from under the yoke of any kind of male domination.

Now you are free, she told herself scathingly, *but if you don't watch it you'll be falling into a pit deeper than anything you've ever known. If you give yourself up to someone like Nikolas Mylonis there will be no getting away. You'll never be the same again.*

The same? Would she want to be the same again? Candace allowed herself to doubt this. . . even as she wondered what it would be like to have a man such as Nikolas take possession of her, claiming every inch of her as his own.

Candace knew these were questions without answers. In an effort to get both her mind and her emotions onto a different subject, she turned to the brown manila envelope Paul Morrison had brought her the night before.

The pictures were excellent. And as she pored over the contact sheets and concentrated carefully on shot after shot, Candace managed to force Nikolas out of her mind, at least for the moment.

There was the choirboy holding the dove. And pictures of the children along the curb. Amazingly, they were the same children she had photographed. There was an old woman dressed in black, too, and several other elderly people. All of their faces, carved with life's lines, were marvelous character studies. There were the members of the procession in their rich vestments and a shot of the entrance to Spring Bayou with the crowds milling around. There was a photograph of the young men ready to plunge into the water in their attempt to retrieve the cross. And another of the bishop, standing with the cross upraised. Then there was a shot of a tall, dark youth emerging from the water with the cross held high. For an instant Candace's mind raced backward, but this youth was not nearly as handsome as Nikolas must have been.

In picture after picture the composition was excellent, the subject matter just what she would have chosen herself. If Paul's color transparencies equaled his black-and-white work, and Candace had no doubt they would, she'd have everything she could possibly want in the way of photos to accompany her story. As Paul himself had suggested, she could then go ahead and fill in with a few shots of her own. She could take a look around the sponge docks and the Greek shops down along the waterfront she'd heard about. There were several picturesque waterfront restaurants, as well, and she could finish, perhaps, with some close-ups of the sponge divers themselves, since Tarpon Springs had become famous primarily as a sponge-fishing community.

There would be plenty of material to draw from, and she began to feel optimistic again about coming through on this assignment as she had hoped she might. She studied the camera Paul Morrison had brought her and noted there was no price tag attached. Well, when she talked to Barry Gehrich maybe she could make the suggestion he advance her the price of a camera so she wouldn't have to keep Paul waiting for his money. When she explained to Barry how, thanks to Paul, she would be able to save the assignment, he'd surely see the reason for doing this.

Thanks to Paul? Most of what was happening, insofar as the pictures and everything else were concerned, was thanks to Nikolas! If it had not been for Nikolas she would have fallen to the ground on her injured ankle and probably would have been hurt far more severely than she had been. She'd be either in a hospital by now or, if she'd somehow managed to reach the airport, back in bed in New York. And there would be no question of salvaging the Tarpon Springs article.

Neither Barry nor *Tempo* would have held the accident against her, certainly. But there would have been a serious chink in the magazine's editorial scheduling plans, and she would have missed the opportunity to do a really good ethnic-background article.

Thinking of this, she decided she'd better put her call through to Barry Gehrich, even though she dreaded telling him about her mishap. On the other hand, he'd been extremely kind to her, and there was no reason to assume he'd be anything less than understanding.

Barry had been an editor on a magazine she'd written for a couple of times, and he'd been impressed with her work. It had been really gratifying when he'd remembered her well enough to phone her, once he'd moved over to *Tempo* as managing editor, and suggest they have lunch together and talk over a possible story assignment.

He had taken her to a small French restaurant in the West Fifties, where they had been escorted to an upstairs dining room. There'd been a wood-burning fireplace and a delightfully Victorian decor. The building, Barry had explained, had formerly been a private mansion.

Barry obviously had been well-known in the place. The waiters had been properly solicitous, and Barry had addressed his attention to the menu with the right degree of gravity. He had ordered for both of them, and it had been an excellent meal.

Finally, over *mousse au chocolat*, they had got around to business. In the interim she had discovered that, like herself, Barry had recently been through a bitter divorce. This had given them a common bond.

She'd listened, fascinated, as he'd outlined *Tempo*'s plans for a series of articles dealing with ethnic groups in America. Articles that would be warmly human, would avoid statistics and would present the often surprising way in which old-world traditions were still maintained in so many communities across the United States—even in the midst of the jet age.

Barry considered the Greek community in Tarpon Springs a perfect place in which to start the series. Candace, listening to this, had found it difficult to believe he was actually offering her the assignment. Since separating from Jeff she had done a lot of free-lance work and had sold most of her articles and the photographs she'd so carefully taken to illustrate each one of them. Even so, she hadn't expected a plum like this to come her way for a long time.

She and Barry had met a couple of times after that to discuss the plans for the article in detail before she actually left for Tarpon Springs. He was an attractive man in his late thirties, with a weary air of sophistication mitigated by a lot of charm. Thankfully, he hadn't tried to sway her with this charm. As time went on she'd got the impression he'd like to know her better, and she didn't doubt this might very well come to pass...provided he didn't rush their relationship. Thus far, he had shown no indication of rushing anything whatsoever, and Candace had been happy with this. He was the first man she'd met in years with whom she felt comfortable.

Now there was also Nikolas on her horizon. As she carefully made her way out of the bedroom, leaning heavily on the cane Theone had brought her, she nearly laughed aloud at the thought of being "comfortable" with Nikolas.

There was simply no comparison between the two men. No comparison at all. The feelings Nikolas aroused in her were volcanic, while with Barry she merely felt pleasantly content. She didn't imagine she'd ever feel pleasantly content around Nikolas. No, there would always be that infusion of lavalike sensation running in her veins when she thought of his mouth pressed to hers and the touch of those long, slender hands caressing her body.

Damn it! As she approached the library door she firmly warned herself it was essential she regain her self-control.

It was a relief to be able to think of something other than the infinitely disturbing Greek who had

invaded her life so precipitously, and this was
achieved by dialing *Tempo*'s New York number. As
soon as the magazine's operator answered and
switched her to Barry's private secretary, she knew
she should have placed a person-to-person call. She
was told Barry was in an editorial conference and
would be going directly to lunch following the
meeting. It was doubtful he could be reached before
midafternoon.

This was a disappointment. Candace needed the
reassurance of hearing his smooth, calm voice. But
there was nothing to do except to leave Nikolas's
telephone number and ask that Barry call her back.

This done, she sat at the large walnut desk in the
library for a few minutes before starting the tedious
trip back to the bedroom. She tried to gather impressions from the furnishings of the room, anything that
might yield some sort of clue about Nikolas.

The bookshelves were well filled, and the books
occupying them looked as if they'd had their share of
use. Candace hitched herself closer and discovered
most of them were printed in Greek. Since the Greek
alphabet was an entirely different one, not even the
letters made much sense to her.

Aside from the Greek books, there was a multi-
volumed encyclopedia in English and also a large
English dictionary. The books Nikolas had brought
her last night must have come from a collection of his
own, a collection he kept outside of this room.

There were several paintings hanging on the walls,
landscapes for the most part and evidently Greek in
origin—there was a ruined temple in the background
of one. They were attractive in their way, though certainly not great art. More likely, they represented a

touch of nostalgia. Homesickness for a native land. No doubt they'd been placed here either by Nikolas's late uncle or by Theone.

Thinking about Theone, Candace realized again the strange place the older woman occupied in this household. And, as if their minds had transferred thoughts, she met Theone as she stepped out into the central hallway.

Theone was evidently coming from the kitchen. She was wearing a voluminous white apron and was drying her hands on one corner. Candace could smell something cooking, and whatever it was smelled very, very good. She told Theone as much, and the older woman smiled and said, "I am making *stifádo* for dinner tonight. That is a Greek stew with beef and wine. I think you will find it tastes good. And I have made *galaktoboúreko* for dessert. That is Nick's favorite."

"I don't believe I've ever had it," Candace said.

"It is like a—" Theone paused, seeking the right words "—a Greek custard pie," she said finally. "But we make it with the very fine layers of pastry which we call *phyllo*. It is baked in a big pan and cut in squares to serve." Theone was saying all of this slowly, laboriously, and illustrating graphically with her hands as she spoke.

"It sounds delicious," Candace said. "I'd love it if there was time for you to show me how to make some of your dishes, Mrs. Mylonis."

She meant this sincerely, because she liked to cook and was especially fond of trying new dishes of foreign origin. Theone seemed to sense this and she said, "That would be a pleasure to me. Maybe when your foot is stronger, so you can stand on it a longer time."

Theone was surveying the bandaged foot as she spoke, and she added firmly, ''I think you should lie on the bed now. Nick will not be pleased if you are not better when he returns, and to me you look tired.''

Candace was in no mood to disagree. She was glad to hand over the cane to Theone and settle back on the bed, letting Theone draw the covers up over her. She was equally glad to let Theone bring her lunch. This consisted of a delicious sandwich that was made of meat and vegetables in a rich yogurt dressing, all tucked inside a piece of warm pita bread. Theone called it a *gyro*. With this Candace was given a glass of wine that Theone proudly told her was Greek, and once again she had no trouble devouring the meal.

Lunch over, she picked up one of the books Nikolas had brought her. It was a sea story, not something she would have chosen, but she found herself becoming engrossed in it. Despite her absorption with the plot, she grew sleepy before very long. And a delicious sort of languor overtook her as she closed her eyes.

Candace slept a sleep of utter relaxation, and she awoke feeling as if she were a child again, a beloved child wrapped in a warm, protective cocoon.

She saw that the sun had moved away from her windows and toward its rendezvous with the west, but a soft apricot glow still lingered in the room. It cast a magic aura around Nikolas, who was sitting, once again, in an armchair nearby.

He said quietly, ''So you are awake, Sleeping Beauty?''

''How long have you been sitting there?'' she asked quickly.

"Long enough," he said, and smiled that odd half-smile of his. "But then it has been a pleasant task watching you. You have very long eyelashes, do you know that?"

"Not half as long as yours," she said in a dream, not thinking.

A dark eyebrow rose in surprise. "You've noticed my eyelashes, Candace?"

Again that green gaze was forcing her to look toward him as if she was being drawn by a magnet. And to her horror she found herself saying, "I suppose I've noticed... everything about you."

She saw him swallow hard. Then he said huskily, "As have I about you."

Candace felt herself melting as if she were about to dissolve. She watched Nikolas get to his feet and knew in another moment she would be in his arms. Never before in her life had she wanted anything so much! And as she fully realized this truth, she wanted his touch upon her. She wanted him to take her—all of her—in the fullest sense of the meaning.

He was of the same mind. She knew he was of the same mind. The passion mounting between them was as pure and primitive as the first man, the first woman. It wound its way through and around them. It drew them together as one. And without consciously knowing her movements, Candace lifted her arms to receive him.

His hair was satin soft beneath her fingers, as soft as his embrace was firm and sure, encircling her so that she felt encased within the warmth of his strong, vibrant body. Their lips fused, and a purely sensuous tremor shook Candace, making her feel as if she'd suddenly been wrenched free from the restraints of a lifetime of inhibitions.

The waves of desire coursing through her were strangely purifying. She felt as if she could see more clearly than she'd ever seen before, but it was Nikolas entirely who filled this new vision, a vision that was mental and emotional as well as physical.

She felt his hands move downward, and she knew in another instant he would be loosening her bra. She could anticipate the sensation of his long slender fingers touching her flesh. Then, even as she moved closer, ready to accept his embrace, the telephone began to ring, its insistent jangle a horrible, intrusive interruption.

Nikolas moved away from the bed as if he'd been stung and swore fluently in his native Greek. Candace could see the effort it took him to get a grip on himself. Then he said, his voice deeper than she'd ever heard it, "There's no use ignoring it because Theone will answer it even if I don't. And she'll only call me if it's for me. . . as it probably is."

But the call wasn't for him, which made things that much worse. Candace shrank away from the expression on his face when, having gone to the library and answered the phone, Nikolas returned. He said, "It is for you, Candace. Someone named Barry. He is calling from New York."

CHAPTER EIGHT

NIKOLAS DID NOT WAIT for Candace to make her way to the library with the aid of the cane. He picked her up and carried her, settling her into the chair back of the desk without saying a word.

She knew Barry was merely returning her call, but he could not have chosen a more inopportune time in which to do so—though he, of course, could not have been expected to know this.

She was unprepared for the warmth of his greeting. "I've missed you, Candy," he said lightly. "Why didn't you call me sooner?"

Candace was almost afraid to answer. Surely her voice was going to sound ragged, and her pulse was still thumping so violently she felt its beat must be audible even through a telephone. Nikolas had left her, striding across the room and closing the door behind him with unnecessary firmness. She kept looking at the closed door and wishing he'd stayed, because then he would have known this was purely a business conversation.

She said, "I'm sorry, Barry. I meant to get in touch with you sooner but I... I had an accident."

"Good Lord!" Barry's voice bounced through the receiver to echo loudly in her ear. "Are you all right?"

"Yes. Perfectly all right."

"Who answered the phone, Candy?"

"Nikolas."

"And who might Nikolas be?"

Candace hesitated. It was difficult to decide just how to phrase what she wanted to say. She finally decided to say only, "I'm staying at his house."

Barry sounded perplexed. "I didn't know you had friends in Tarpon Springs," he commented.

"I don't...that is, I didn't."

"Then how is it...oh, never mind. Tell me about your accident first. You're sure you're all right?"

"Yes," Candace said, "except for my ankle. I sprained it yesterday morning during the procession. But the problem is I also dropped my camera, and there's no way it can be fixed. I—"

"The hell with the camera! I'm more concerned about you."

"Honestly," she said, "I really am all right. You see, Nikolas caught me as I fell right outside his house. He brought me in here, and later he took me to the hospital for X rays. They bound up the ankle with some kind of elastic bandage, and I'm just now beginning to hobble around with a cane."

"Are you supposed to be on it at all?" Barry demanded. "If you're not careful, you could do permanent injury to something like that."

"It's okay for me to try getting around," she insisted.

"Look, Candy, if you've been told to stay off that ankle you should follow the doctor's instructions," he said firmly.

"But I don't want to stay off it," she wailed. "As it is, I lost the camera, my film and the chance to get my own firsthand impressions of the Epiphany celebrations. But I suppose you could say I did luck out, in a way. Nikolas has a friend who is a marvelous photographer, and he's going to let us use his pictures—both color and black-and-white. I've seen the black-and-white ones, and they're terrific. Also, years ago Nikolas was one of the boys who dived in the bayou on Epiphany, and he was the one who retrieved the gold cross. So he's been able to tell me all about it from his personal experience.''

She had intended after waking up from her nap to start writing down the things Nikolas had told her. But Nikolas himself, of course, had given her no chance to do so.

When she started to explain to Barry she planned to begin on her notes this evening directly after dinner, he seemed curiously disinterested. He said only, ''I hope this Nikolas is a middle-aged gentleman, safely married and with many children.''

This was so completely at variance with Nikolas that Candace nearly laughed aloud.

She said carefully, ''Well, he's in his thirties. . . .''

''Yes?''

''And he's not married,'' she said. ''But his aunt keeps house for him, and there's a girl cousin who lives here, too.''

''Too?'' Barry repeated. ''You're living at his place, Candy?''

''I've kept my motel room,'' she said quickly, ''and I intend to go back there as soon as I can. I stayed here last night, though, and I think I'd better stay tonight, as well. I'm still not as ambulatory as I'd like to be.''

Barry had obviously been thinking things over as she spoke, and he came to a swift decision. ''I'll

make arrangements for you to get a flight out of
Tampa in the morning,'' he said. "And I'll see to it a
limousine calls for you there in Tarpon Springs.
There will be a wheelchair for you at Tampa International, and I'll meet you at Kennedy myself.''

Candace forgot about the fact he was her editor.
"You'll do no such thing!" she exclaimed. "I came
down here on an assignment, and there's no reason
why I can't complete it.''

"Candy," Barry said patiently. "We'll forget
about Tarpon Springs for this year, okay? The ethnic
series is my idea, remember, and there's no reason
why the Greek story has to come first. I'll arrange for
you to do something a little closer to home. Lord
knows we have enough different ethnic groups right
here in New York you can look into.''

"It isn't the same thing at all!" Candace protested.
'You know that, Barry! I want to do the Greek
story. I'm really into it. It would be—well, it would
be tremendously disappointing to give it up now, and
there's really no need to.''

"I'm not so sure about that, Candy," Barry said.
"Who is this Nikolas, anyway? Can you tell me
something about him?''

Who was Nikolas? Barry could hardly have managed to ask her a question she felt more ill equipped
to answer.

"He's a businessman here in town," she said.
"Greek, of course. And very...very respectable.''

Amazingly, her tone actually made Nikolas come
across like a stodgy, safe sort of person, and she
marveled at this evidence of an acting ability she'd
never known she possessed.

Barry did not sound entirely satisfied, but apparently her words had mollified him, at least to a point. He said more calmly, "Okay, Candy. What's the name of the motel you're staying at?"

"The Grecian Gardens," Candace answered smoothly, not adding it was located practically next door to Nikolas's home.

"When you've checked back in there again, phone me," Barry instructed. "Do you have my home number?"

"No, I don't."

"Then take it down," he said, and fortunately Candace found a piece of paper and a pencil near at hand. As he dictated and she scribbled, the New York number gave her an oddly familiar twinge. *Home is a long way off,* she thought whimsically.

"How are you fixed for money?" he asked next.

"I'm fine," she said.

"Well, as you know, the magazine's policy prohibits me from advancing you expenses on your first assignment," he pointed out. "But, for the present, I can send you a personal check."

It occurred to Candace he was taking quite a bit upon himself. "That really won't be necessary, Barry," she said coolly.

"You'll have medical expenses," he reminded her.

"My insurance will take care of that," Candace said. Then she realized that while she was at the hospital she hadn't been asked for any information about her medical coverage, an oversight that seemed odd. She'd entered the hospital under Nikolas's aegis and then had been turned over to Dr. George Andris. If any information had been sought, Nikolas must have furnished it. And she had no doubt at all he had instructed that her bill be sent directly to him!

This was reason enough to fume, because no one had the right to be so high-handed. And Barry was giving her an added cause for concern by saying, "I shall have some money wired to you first thing in the morning, Candy. It's too late to do it today."

"If you do that, Barry, I'll simply tear it up and send the shreds back to you," she said hotly.

To her surprise, he laughed. It was an indulgent laugh and only served to nettle her further. He said, "I like your spirit, but let's be practical about this. To begin with, you'll have to do something about a replacement camera."

"I already have," she said. She almost added that Nikolas had taken care of this but caught herself short just in time. "The same photographer who will be furnishing the pictures has let me have a camera on credit," she said. "Nothing else needs to be done about it for the moment. Anyway, my other camera was insured, so the money from that should cover most of the replacement cost."

Ironically, she'd intended to ask Barry for an advance that would cover the cost of the camera so she could repay Paul Morrison promptly. But now it was too late. Anyway, he'd mentioned this was against company policy. . . .

Barry chuckled and said, "Very well, Miss Independence. Call me when you're back in your motel. And again, if you're supposed to stay off that ankle. . . stay off it!"

They hung up, and Candace sat at the desk waiting. Waiting for Nikolas, because there was no way of getting back to her bedroom without a cane, unless she could manage to hop the whole distance. Finally, when the silence seemed absolute, she decided hopping *was* her only alternative. She plotted a course from chair to chair and grabbed at each piece of furniture in turn as she tried to balance herself without going down on the injured ankle.

She nearly made it. But the last chair she clutched simply wasn't strong enough. It tipped sideways and crashed to the floor, and Candace nearly went with it.

Her left foot touched the floor briefly before she could regain her balance. So between the pain and the effort of trying not to fall as she reached for a sturdier chair, she was in no mood at all for the accusation in Nikolas's voice as he swung the library door open. He came across to her in what seemed like one giant step and demanded as he grabbed her, "What the hell are you trying to do now?"

"What do you think?" she retorted. "And where were you, anyway?"

"Where do you think I was?" he retaliated. "I was outside waiting for you to have the sense to call out you were through with your damned phone call and ready for me to come and get you. But, no, you had to try it on your own, didn't you?"

He was tight-lipped in his anger. And also, Candace felt, considerably angrier than the occasion called for. He swept her into his arms, and instinctively she leaned her head back against his shoulder. Then she felt his muscles tighten almost convulsively.

"What is it you do to me, Candace?" he asked hoarsely. There was a strange, bemused note in his voice, as if he really couldn't understand the effect she had upon him.

She was tempted to tell him he was not alone in his bewilderment. If anything, her wonder was greater than his. She was completely staggered by the effect he had on her. But then Nikolas was probably used to having women fall captive to him. He was probably used to having women make fools of themselves over him, she thought bitterly. She loathed the idea of being one in a string of followers, and it was this she was thinking about when, back in her room once again, he placed her in an armchair rather than on the bed.

Was he afraid if he put her down on the bed there might be a repeat performance? Indignation accompanied this suspicion, because she hadn't engineered this tendency they had to fall into each other's arms every time they were alone together. It was a mutual compulsion, granted. But he'd certainly done his full share toward encouraging it.

Nikolas sat down on the edge of the bed himself, and he seemed weary. His voice was emotionless, as if he'd forced himself to suppress those feelings that could be so treacherous, and was exhausted by the effort. Finally he said, "Theone has prepared a special dinner for tonight."

"Yes, I know," Candace answered, glad to get onto a neutral subject. "She told me."

"So," Nikolas continued, "we will eat in the dining room with Theone and Melina." He paused. "I hope you don't mind."

"No," she said, surprised. "Why should I?"

He shrugged. "I don't know. Theone does not mean to be impolite, but sometimes she lapses into Greek without even knowing it. Melina, however, does mean to be impolite when she lapses into Greek. But then that is something else again."

So, he was aware of Melina's hostility!

"Aliki asked after you today," Nikolas went on.

"She remembered me?"

"Yes, she remembered you. Of course, she already knew from Elene you were at the motel and that you had come to write a story about...about the people here."

Candace grinned. "How the news does travel."

"Yes," he nodded. "It is a small community, very close-knit. At least, the Greek sector is very tight." For a moment he seemed to drift, then he added, "Once, the population was predominantly Greek. Now it is down to about one-third. Still, the old associations hold. The close ties are maintained."

"But some of these people, even the younger ones, really are Greek, aren't they?" she asked, without thinking the question through.

His eyebrows rose. "What do you mean by that, Candace?"

"Only that they weren't born in this country," she replied. "Like Elene's husband. Manos, isn't it? He seems very Greek."

Nikolas smiled, but it was not a pleasant smile. "Is that to be taken as a compliment, or is it perhaps an insult?"

"Neither," she said, conscious that in his opinion she'd somehow made a gaffe. But Candace was determined not to let him rile her about it. "I was simply making a comment."

"And making a judgment?" he jabbed. "What is 'very Greek'?"

Candace sighed, an exasperated sigh. "Oh, come on, Nikolas," she said. "There's no need to make a big case out of an idle remark."

"I don't consider it an idle remark. Yes, Manos

came here from Greece. So did I. Longer ago than
Manos, in fact, so I went to school here and learned
to speak your language without an accent. But that
makes me no less a Greek than him.''

Your language. Candace gritted her teeth. Despite
an occasional intonation that had a foreign touch to
it—and a shrug, now and then, that did make him
appear intriguingly different—Nikolas seemed as
American to her as she was herself. Certainly he
considered English, as well as Greek, his language,
too.

She said stiffly, ''Manos is an entirely different
sort of person than you, as I think you know very
well.''

Nikolas's grin was wicked. ''Because he leered at
you in Aliki's restaurant the other night,'' he
taunted.

''Well,'' she said, ''you certainly would never subject a woman to an inspection such as that!''

''No?'' he challenged. But then his voice softened.
''You are so lovely I cannot entirely blame him.''

Candace felt herself beginning to blush, but before
she could respond he asked, ''Who is the man who
called you?''

''My editor at *Tempo*,'' Candace said crossly.
''Any objection?''

''No objection. Everything is all right with your
assignment?''

''Yes. Barry wanted me to come back to New
York, but I think I convinced him I should stay here
and finish what I've started.''

It was a poor choice of words. ''Do you really intend to finish what you've started, Candace?'' he
teased. For this her answer bag was empty.

THEONE'S DINNER was a veritable banquet, but the atmosphere left much to be desired.

The dining room was oppressive, the furnishings dark, the draperies heavy. Even the china was overly ornate—an overblown floral pattern thickly edged in gold. None of these things suited the Florida climate, and this was emphasized because it was very warm tonight. The room was stuffy, and even the slowly rotating ceiling fan didn't seem to be stirring up much air.

Melina was wearing a bright red dress that fitted her snugly, and large gold hoops dangled from her ears. She looked sultry and voluptuous, but like everything else in the room she was overdone. Theone, having divested herself of the white apron, again wore unrelieved black. Her dress had a high neckline and Candace felt she must be sweltering in it.

For herself, Candace had chosen a full, pale pink teardrop skirt with a matching lacy top. She'd twisted up her hair so it wouldn't feel hot on her neck, and she'd gone without jewelry. Actually, Elene hadn't included any among the few things she'd sent over, although Candace did have a case with a variety of pendants and earrings in it back at the motel.

Elene had thought to include a bottle of her cologne, though, and Candace had touched it to her wrists and to the hollow of her neck. As she ate Theone's first course of a rich lentil soup, she was glad the fragrance she was using was a delicate one. A heavy scent would have overpowered her just now.

Nikolas was wearing pale gray slacks and a fitted blue shirt open at the throat, and she noticed the gleam of the gold medallion he wore, which became visible every time he leaned over the table to spoon his soup. What did it represent, she wondered.

He was very quiet tonight. So was Theone. And Melina was obviously irritated by something. The presence of another young woman, perhaps?

Candace sighed, and Theone looked up to ask, "Your ankle is troubling you?"

"No," she said hastily. "It's hardly bothering me at all."

Was it her imagination, or did Melina seem disappointed by this statement? Whatever, she suddenly broke into swift Greek, addressing herself to Nikolas. But he only gave the girl a reproving glance, then answered her in English.

"Your mother can understand what we are saying if we speak slowly," he said. "But Candace cannot understand us if we speak Greek."

Melina's swift, dark glance in Candace's direction was proof enough she couldn't have cared less. She said impatiently, "You need not make such a fuss, Nick. I am used to speaking Greek to you. You said you wanted me to speak Greek to keep myself fluent, remember?"

"Yes, I remember," Nikolas replied evenly. "But I did not mean for you to exhibit your language skills in front of a guest, when we have one."

From the way he said this, Candace got the impression they didn't very often have guests in the Mylonis household. She wondered if this might be because Theone was still in mourning for her late husband. Theone always seemed to wear black, though Melina certainly didn't follow suit. But then the late Mr. Mylonis had been Melina's stepfather, and despite her remark he had asked her to call him "father," Candace had a strong suspicion they'd never been very close.

They progressed from the soup to a delicious salad and then to the *stifádo*, which was excellent. The meal was finished with the pastry-and-custard dessert Theone had been preparing earlier in the day, and Candace decided it was one of the best things she'd ever eaten.

As they lingered over small cups of strong Greek coffee, Candace complimented Theone on the dinner. "The dessert was especially good," she said. "Really incredible!"

Smiling, Theone said, "When you are better, I will teach."

The older woman seemed more hesitant with her English when Nikolas was around, Candace noticed. And she certainly seemed much more like his housekeeper than his aunt, even an aunt by marriage. There definitely was something almost subservient in her manner toward him. Candace had the feeling Theone was awed by Nikolas. Obviously she adored him, but she seemed to look up to him as if he were some sort of idol.

When they had finally finished Candace said quickly, "Thank you, Theone. I'd like to help you with the cleanup, but I think I'd really better get back to my room." She disregarded Nikolas's move in her direction, adding, "I can manage by myself. Good night, everyone."

As she spoke she glanced toward Nikolas. She just couldn't help it. There was a decided gleam in those green olive eyes, but he said only, "*Kaliníhta*, Candace. I hope you sleep well."

He knew damned well she wasn't going to be able to sleep at all. . .not for a long time. He had stirred her up too thoroughly. And she was surprised at her own vindictiveness as she found herself hoping insomnia was an affliction Nikolas would be sharing with her tonight.

CHAPTER NINE

WHEN CANDACE AWAKENED the next morning she stretched lazily. Then she wriggled her ankle and was pleased to find the pain had diminished considerably. She tested it gingerly and discovered she was able to stand on it without experiencing much discomfort. So, although it made sense to continue using the cane for the time being, she could see no reason why she shouldn't become a bit more active.

She was dressed and had made up her bed by the time Theone came to rap on the door. Theone did not seem very pleased by this, but she only said, "You will have eggs and bacon for breakfast this morning?"

"Thank you, no," Candace answered. "Just toast and coffee, like yesterday, will be fine."

"But Nick said. . ." Theone began.

This annoyed Candace. She didn't blame Theone, because obviously the woman took everything Nikolas said as if it were gospel. Yet there was no need for him to dictate what she was going to eat for breakfast.

"I'm seldom hungry for anything much in the morning," she said firmly, and Theone nodded unhappily and left the room to make up her tray.

Candace sat in an armchair and ate the delicious toasted bread Theone brought her. This morning the bread was accompanied by a luscious jelly Theone said was made from sea grapes. In addition to this there was a glass of grapefruit juice that, Candace was told, had been squeezed from freshly picked fruit. Several grapefruit trees grew at the back of the house.

"There are also two orange trees," Theone volunteered, "and kumquats, too. Those I cook with sugar syrup so they keep. Very good."

Theone was looking around the room as if trying to find something to do, and Candace felt as if she'd deprived her by making up the bed herself. But when the older woman came back to get her tray Candace was ready with a request, although she was not at all sure Theone would accede to it.

"Mrs. Mylonis," she began, "is Nikolas around?"

"No," Theone said. "He again had the business to do today." She paused briefly, then she said, "I should tell you my name is Callis, not Mylonis. My husband was Callis—the brother to Nick's mother."

"Oh," Candace said, slightly startled. "Well, then, Mrs. Callis. Is there someone at the motel who could bring my car over for me?"

"Your car?" Theone seemed astonished by this.

"Yes. Your niece will know which one it is. It's parked out in front of my unit, and it has a Florida license plate. I rented it in Sarasota."

Theone took all of this in, obviously understanding each sentence. But she only shook her head. "I do not think so," she said. "Not until Nick comes back."

Candace tried to restrain her impatience. Theone was acting as if she'd been kidnapped by Nikolas and was being held for ransom. The whole situation was ridiculous, and as she contemplated it she wondered how she'd ever let herself get into it. Not that she'd had much choice, she told herself grimly.

"Look, Mrs. Callis," she said carefully, "I have some work I must do today. It is very important. I can do it perfectly well because it will not require much walking. I can drive, you understand? The car is automatic, so I do not need to use my left foot."

Theone nodded, but she still looked very uncertain.

"I will probably be back before Nikolas is," Candace added encouragingly.

"For lunch?" Theone asked.

"No, I don't think so. I can stop at a drive-in for lunch, so I won't have to walk very much. Believe me, I intend to be careful."

She said this clearly, because she knew her plans were important to Theone. Theone, who was now definitely giving the impression she was accountable to Nikolas for the events that went on during his absence.

Still, the older woman wasn't satisfied. "Can you not wait?" she suggested. "Another day, and your foot will be stronger."

"No," Candace replied, "I don't feel I can wait. I wouldn't be so adamant about this if I could." She saw Theone did not understand what she meant by "adamant," so she said, "I wouldn't insist, Mrs. Callis, if I didn't need to do this. And as I've said, I promise to be very careful. Also," she ventured, "if Nikolas is angry, I will take the blame myself."

This didn't seem to impress Theone very much one way or the other. She said dubiously, "I will talk to Elene."

Candace couldn't help wishing it was Melina to whom Theone was going to talk. She was sure Melina would be perfectly happy to have her take off in the car—and never come back!

Theone left, and evidently she elected to use another telephone, for there were no sounds forthcoming from the library. And when she finally returned, she looked no happier than she had before.

By then, Candace had begun to jot down notes, starting with her impressions of her arrival in Tarpon Springs. First she detailed the curiously deserted aspect of the old downtown business district. Next she described some of the different touches that gave the place its unique atmosphere, like the brick-paved streets and the sidewalks with their hexagonal blocks of concrete. She mentioned Aliki's restaurant, which was so "Greek" it had really surprised her, and recorded the important features of the Cathedral of St. Nicholas, including its glorious choir, the clergy and the boy with the dove. Then there had also been the enchanting Greek children whom she'd photographed along the curb as the procession was about to begin.

Her pen flew over the sheets of paper Theone had given her, and she was absorbed with the task of reporting her thoughts. But Theone, who came to stand in the doorway, quickly snapped Candace back to the present. "Despinis Mayhew?" she asked.

"Yes?"

"Elene will bring the car." It was a reluctant concession. "She says she will come soon."

ELENE, CANDACE WAS RELIEVED TO DISCOVER, was a lot more positive about the idea of her driving.

"I've often been thankful for automatic transmissions because I don't have a mechanical turn of mind," she said with a smile, her English completely unaccented.

She was wearing jeans and a bright yellow shirt, and she'd used a yellow scarf to tie back her dark hair. She looked vibrant and very lovely, yet there were dark shadows under her eyes. Perhaps Elene was worried about her husband. It was easy enough to understand why she might!

She said, "Thanks so much, Mrs. Panagoris. I appreciate your doing this for me. And thanks for keeping my room. I expect I'll be moving back in sometime later today."

This bit of information was clearly a complete surprise to Elene. She seemed on the verge of questioning it, then evidently decided to leave the subject alone. She shrugged—a feminine version of Nikolas's shrug—then she said, "Is there anything I can do to help you? I suppose you have maps of the area and you know where you want to go?"

"Yes, I do," Candace said, "though I'll mostly be exploring by car today, just to get the feel of things. I'll have to postpone going to the sponge docks until my ankle is stronger."

"Ah, yes, the footing there can be difficult."

"I understand there's a boat that takes you out for a sponge-diving exhibition?"

"That's right," Elene nodded. "Also, there are films about sponge diving. I'm sure it won't be hard for you to get all the background information you want. You may run into a language problem with some of the older men if you try to interview them, though most of them do speak English...to an extent. And the younger ones, at least those who were born in the States, can always help out.''

"It seems to me you're all remarkably bilingual,"
Candace observed, shaking her head in wonder.

"Greek parents tend to insist their children learn
the language and remember their heritage," Elene
returned with a smile. "The Greeks are a very proud
people."

There was a directness to her gaze as she said this,
and Candace felt sure she was thinking about Nikolas. Was Elene trying to give her a message of some
sort? Was she trying to convey the fact that among
proud Greeks Nikolas was one of the proudest and
would not take kindly to her going off on her own today?

But that was absurd! She'd known the man for
only two days. He had no claim on her whatsoever!

She nearly said as much to Elene but decided
against it. And this, she realized, was wise. Elene
might very well go right back to Nikolas with whatever she said about him. And even if Elene didn't do
this, better safe than sorry. Candace already had the
feeling Theone was reporting back to him.

Elene, at least, wasn't afraid of Nikolas, or she
wouldn't have brought the car around. She handed
over the keys casually and said, "I've parked it under
the porte cochere. Will you need help getting down
the steps?"

"Thanks, but I think I can manage if I take it slowly," Candace assured her.

"Then I'll see you later."

After a moment Candace heard the babble of
Greek and knew Elene must have met up with
Theone. Theone, she suspected, had probably asked
Elene to stay for a cup of coffee, and she guessed

they had plenty to talk about. Manos. Nikolas. Melina. And, of course, herself. Quite a lot of ground to cover!

She'd brought along a briefcase with notebooks and other equipment, but it was at the motel. She thought of taking some sheets of paper along now, then decided not to bother. Time enough later to make notes. For the present she would spend the next few hours driving around and letting the atmosphere of Tarpon Springs seep into her.

The side door opened off the central hallway, and Candace managed to get down the steps and into the car without too much difficulty. Then she was out into Hellenic Avenue, turning toward Spring Bayou, and she felt possessed of a heady sense of freedom. Strange, what wheels could do for one's morale!

Since the traffic was light, Candace was able to park directly across from the bayou. The little bay was deserted and very beautiful just now—a deep, serene blue in the light of the midmorning sun. She saw there was an entrance of sorts right across from her. This was spanned by a shimmering arch, seemingly made of gold and silver tinsel strands woven around a frame. The arch itself was centered with a large tinsel-covered cross studded with red lights that Candace imagined would create quite an effect after dark.

A flight of steps swept down from the arch, and from her present vantage point Candace could not see to the bottom. But as she pulled out to drive along the bayou side of the street, she saw there was a concrete walkway curving along the water's edge, going all the way around.

The bayou itself was irregular in shape, somewhat

like an artist's palette, though with more curves. Across the water there was a large park area, planted with live oaks and palms.

From having studied her maps of the area Candace knew the sponge docks were to her right, and so she deliberately turned left. As she'd told Elene, this was not the day for her to visit the sponge docks. She drove around the rim of the bayou and discovered there was a wider expanse of water beyond the park. Soon she spotted a large modern building and saw by the sign out in front this was the Tarpon Springs Public Library.

She decided to stop there on her way back. This would be a smart move, because then she could give her foot a good rest while she was researching past Epiphany celebrations and other bits of local history. Meantime, she continued to drive on through a beautiful residential area of lovely homes, many of them having views of the undulating bayous. She noted that the names on many of the mailboxes out in front of these houses were Greek, proving the Greeks of Tarpon Springs had not limited themselves to either the environs of the sponge docks or the central downtown district.

As she drove she discovered that condominiums, developments and shopping complexes—with the usual supermarkets and chain stores—were becoming a part of the general area. An increasing part, she suspected. These symbols of modern living fanned out over the outlying areas of the town and undoubtedly were at least partially responsible for the fact that the old downtown center now seemed so inactive. The large, impressive city hall was on Pinellas Avenue toward the center of town, and here, also, were more than the usual number of banks, law offices and insurance companies. But Tarpon Avenue, the main crossroad, was limited primarily to a few antique shops and a couple of Greek grocery stores.

Candace became hungry after a time and found a drive-in, where she ordered a hamburger and a milk shake. But this seemed very mundane fare after enjoying the kind of culinary art Theone practiced. She threw out half of the hamburger roll because it was so soft and tasteless and felt vaguely dissatisfied as she started out exploring again.

Something seemed to be missing. She was amused at the thought Theone's good cooking had come to mean so much to her, but this empty feeling, she finally admitted, had nothing to do with Greek food. Rather, it had to do with a handsome Greek man whom she was unable to erase from her mind.

Yesterday everything with Nikolas had been so unfulfilled. Melina had put a damper on the dinner because she was so obviously antagonistic, but even before that things had gone wrong. Things had gone wrong, really, since Barry Gehrich's phone call.

Brooding about this, Candace drove back through the town and across to the library and parked as close to the main door as possible, being tempted at the moment to use one of the spaces reserved for the handicapped. Now that she was having difficulty getting around by herself she began to appreciate just how important these provisions were for the people who really needed them.

The librarian certainly wasn't Greek. At least, she had a pink-and-white complexion, fluffy white hair and very light blue eyes. Candace introduced herself, and the woman was both pleasant and helpful.

The library had a good collection of local history and excellent background material on all the special events like the Epiphany celebrations, covering many years past. Candace settled down at a table with books and papers spread out all around her and contemplated first reading a brief local history of Tarpon Springs. But then she put this aside. She knew very well before she did anything else she had to look up the Epiphany celebration of the year when Nikolas Mylonis had retrieved the golden cross.

Nikolas had told her he was now thirty-four and he'd been a teenager when he'd dived for the cross. Candace tabulated backward. Would he have been eighteen? No, she remembered him saying his day of triumph had come when he was seventeen. She quickly searched through the dates, then eagerly bent over the stories about that year's Epiphany celebration, scanning the photographs in the hope of finding his picture.

Suddenly, as she turned a page, she came upon it. There he was—holding the cross high and smiling right into the camera—but as she looked at that smiling face, Candace froze.

For a long moment, she could not even move. And as she continued to stare at the picture, her throat constricted so painfully she felt as if she were going to choke. It was impossible even to swallow. She found herself trembling violently, actually shaking, and then she felt herself going cold.

It couldn't be! He couldn't be!

Candace managed to look more carefully.

Why hadn't he told her?

But—*my God*—why should he have told her?

Nevertheless. . . .

The shock was profound. Candace raised her tormented eyes to find that the librarian, seated at a desk across the room, was looking her way anxiously. She felt sure in another minute the motherly librarian would be coming across to ask her what was wrong. And she had to force herself to turn the page, blotting out that smiling face. She made a pretense of going on as usual and even scribbled down a few notes on a pad of paper the helpful librarian had brought to her, although the words she wrote made no sense at all.

She found to her horror she was scrawling his name over and over again. Nicky Mellin, Nicky Mellin, Nicky Mellin.

Nikolas couldn't be Nicky Mellin. And yet he was!

Candace, pretending to read an article she couldn't even focus on, forced herself to try to accept this fact, but it was simply too overwhelming. For like just about everyone else in the world, she had believed Nicky Mellin was dead—which made this all the harder to believe.

He had been a meteoric cinema star—one of those blazing, youthful personalities with a fantastic impact on his fans. And many of them had been youthful, too. His appearance anywhere had been guaranteed to produce a mob scene. He couldn't even move without scores of screaming admirers trailing after him.

Candace, who had been on the threshold of her teens at the height of his fame, had been one of those fans. She'd gone to New York once with a couple of girl friends when Nicky Mellin had made a personal appearance, and they'd nearly been crushed just trying to get close to the theater where he'd been playing. Getting in for a glimpse of him had been impossible. Thinking about this now, Candace winced. Even after so many years it remained an embarrassing memory. She'd been annoyed with herself for having become one of the screaming mob.

Every detail of Nicky Mellin's personal life had been grist for the gossip columnists. Young as he was—he must have been in his early twenties at the time, she estimated—he was involved with one female movie star after another. There were endless pictures in the newspapers and magazines of Nicky Mellin escorting some glamorous beauty to a movie premiere or a Hollywood nightclub or a party at some producer's palatial home.

His movies had played to standing-room-only crowds. Candace could remember going to the Saturday matinees when she was at junior high in Albany and later, during her first couple of years of high school. She'd sat in the darkened theater with her best girl friend, both of them rapt as they munched popcorn. And their eyes had been glued to the screen, where their idol was making love to somebody else.

Then, there had been a terrible accident on the west coast somewhere. It had happened while he was on location, making a movie. The beautiful actress to whom he'd been engaged had been killed. Lila Pembroke, that was her name. Nicky Mellin had tried to save her life, but he had failed. And he'd been severely injured himself. So severely injured he had never recovered. Gradually, there had been fewer and fewer stories about him in the papers, and the items about him that were used over and over again during the first year after the accident finally became very stale news. If Candace was remembering rightly, he had suffered brain damage, and after a time he had been confined to a sanatorium, where, according to the stories she had read, he had died several years ago.

During the course of those years, her own life had changed dramatically. Her father had died, and she'd become a secretary with literary aspirations, these to be shelved for a time after she married Jeff. Then there had been the misery of three years of a marriage that wasn't marriage at all. There had been separation and finally divorce. Along the way, Candace had forgotten all about Nicky Mellin, and she supposed most other people had long since forgotten about him, too.

Still, there were thousands of her contemporaries to whom he'd been an idol. The writer in Candace forced her to become conscious of the fact that almost any magazine in the country would give a mint for a modern profile about him. The revelation that he was alive and well and living in Tarpon Springs, Florida would be a sensation!

Nikolas. Nicky Mellin. Candace simply could not connect the two. She did some mental arithmetic and came up with the year in which the accident must have occurred, and now she bypassed the stories about the Epiphany celebrations entirely and turned to another kind of search. As she suspected they would, the area papers had carried extremely detailed stories about the accident, most of them giving colorful biographies of Nicky Mellin. The same picture she'd first come across—the one in which he was holding up the cross—was published again and again.

As she perused these different stories, Candace

made notes of the dates, the pages and the issues in which they appeared. There was no way she could read through all of this material here in the library, under the watchful eye of the librarian. The experience was going to be entirely too traumatic, and she had no wish to go through it in public. So after a time she hobbled over to the copying machine and gradually began to make herself copies of the major stories. Later she could go through them slowly, in the privacy of her motel room.

As she scanned story after story, she found herself studying some of the different pictures of Nikolas. . . Nikolas as he had been back then. And now she could definitely see similarities.

Surgery had altered his face considerably. The shape of his nose was entirely different, for one thing, and his mouth was different, too. In these photographs, of course, there was no impairment of his facial muscles, as there seemed to be now. His smile was much fuller, and his mouth curved widely.

But the eyes were the same. They seemed to be looking up at her from these old printed photographs as if to ask accusingly, "What is it that you are trying to do, Candace?" And the shape of his head was the same. And that gorgeous, thick dark hair.

She shivered and carried the last batch of material she wished to copy across to the machine. Then, hobbling over to the desk with her copies, she thanked the librarian and left as quickly as she was able.

Once in the car again, she sank back against the seat while a long, slow shudder shook her body. She couldn't think clearly. In fact, she felt as if her brain had gone numb. The shock was still terribly traumatic, especially since it was overlaid with a sense of

total unreality. Nikolas Mylonis could not be Nicky
Mellin. And yet he was! There was no doubt about it.

The last of the articles on him was dated several
years ago. Possibly there had been something more
recent, maybe something when he'd returned to Tarpon Springs, but she was inclined to think not.
Nikolas, she felt very sure, had no wish to be in the
limelight again. She already realized he guarded his
privacy fiercely. Now she could see why. Yet there
were so many things she found puzzling. She'd certainly had the impression Dr. George Andris had
been on the verge of telling her something very important about Nikolas. Had he been about to reveal
Nikolas's true identity?

Pondering this, Candace tried to recall every word
of the brief conversation they'd had while Dr. Andris
had pushed her wheelchair down the hospital corridor. And now she had the impression he had
thought she already knew who Nikolas really was.
Wasn't that what ne had asked her? Hadn't he said,
"You know who he is, don't you?"

In a way, this had actually been more of an accusation than a question. Nikolas had probably told the
doctor she was a journalist, and it seemed likely Dr.
Andris had then assumed she was here in Tarpon
Springs to interview his friend, the former star.
Perhaps he thought Nikolas had given her permission
to do so, yet this didn't quite ring true. George Andris would know very well it was highly unlikely
Nikolas would give permission for an interview to
anyone, or his secret would have been out long
before now.

Paul Morrison had said Nikolas could fill her in
from personal experience when it came to details of

the Epiphany celebration. But then dozens of local boys had dived for the golden cross over the years, and there had been no reason for her to think there might have been anything unusual in connection with Nikolas's having done so.

No, she could see Nikolas had actually been able to guard the privacy that meant so much to him by coming back to this town where he'd grown up...and by trusting his fellow Greeks to keep his secret.

Candace supposed at the very beginning of his screen career there must have been some mention of his Tarpon Springs origin. She'd know better after she read through all the material she'd copied. By the time she had been old enough to become a Nicky Mellin fan, she hadn't been interested in his past. So, if she'd ever read anything about Tarpon Springs in relation to him, she didn't remember. Possibly she'd known at one time he'd come from Florida. But she wasn't even sure of that. Like most of his frenzied admirers she had been interested in the Nicky Mellin of the moment. And, like thousands of other teenage girls, she had been bitterly jealous of each and every one of the many film lovelies he'd escorted.

Certainly when Barry had discussed the concept of doing the article about Tarpon Springs and its Greek community, nothing about Nicky Mellin had clicked in her mind. For one thing, she'd never realized he was Greek. And second, she'd thought he was dead. Actually, Candace had to admit it was a long while since she'd remembered him at all.

Such was the fleeting price of fame—even fame of the caliber and magnitude that Nicky Mellin had achieved.

Candace remembered now when he'd told her

about his part in retrieving the cross during the Epiphany celebration he had said something about it being the first applause he'd ever received. A couple of other times he had stopped short when he was talking to her, as if on the verge of revealing something about himself. Once, he'd been taunting her about her own heritage and had said something to the effect he wouldn't be welcome in her social circle as the Greek he was, but....

Now that ''but'' seemed very significant. As Nicky Mellin not only would he have been welcome, he would have been sought out wherever he went.

If he was bitter today, it was easy enough to understand why. A long time had passed since there'd been any applause for him, and she wondered if after all these years he still missed it. There were no longer any fans clamoring over one another for so much as a glance from him, to say nothing of a smile. Nor were there any kings and queens or society matrons begging him to honor their social functions with his presence.

Yet she found herself thinking it doubtful Nikolas would want this kind of attention anymore. He'd certainly had more than his full share of adulation. And he didn't seem like a person living in the past.

I'd say that he lives very much in the present, Candace decided. *He's strong and capable and tender and...passionate, when he's aroused. But he would be ruthless if he were crossed, and there's no doubt his anger could be fierce and terrible. Still, to have his love would be the most wonderful thing that could ever happen to a person.*

Candace's fingers were trembling as she inserted the key in the ignition, and she still felt shaky as she pulled up outside her motel unit. The sun was scorching and the air conditioning inside her room had been turned off. Also, she was thirsty. She supposed somewhere on the premises there must be a soft-drink machine and a place where you could fill up a plastic bucket with ice, but she couldn't face the thought of walking any farther.

After hesitating only a moment, she reached for the telephone and dialed the reception desk. And she recognized Elene's voice when she answered.

"It's Candace Mayhew, Elene," she said. "Do you have someone around who could bring me over a couple of bottles of soda? It doesn't matter what kind—as long as it isn't grape or orange! And also some ice cubes? I don't want to be a nuisance, but I've just come in and—"

"It's no trouble at all, Candace," Elene cut in pleasantly. "The desk is pretty dead right now, so I'll take a break and get it for you myself."

A few minutes later there was a knock on the door, but before Candace could move, the knob turned and Elene stepped into the room.

"I hope you don't mind me using my house key, but I didn't want to make you get up," she said. She filled a glass with ice cubes and poured ginger ale over them. "I thought this might be refreshing."

Candace accepted the glass gratefully and took a sip. "It's just what I needed!"

Elene pulled out the chair in front of the dresser, then turned it around and sat down so she could face Candace. She looked tired, and she'd pulled her dark hair up on top of her head, evidently in an effort to keep cool.

"It's really hot today," she said. "I'm sorry about

the air conditioning in here. We try to practice energy conservation, so we shut the units off when the rooms aren't being used. It will be better in a few minutes, but if I'd known you were coming back so soon I would have turned it on. I didn't expect you until later.''

''I'd wanted to keep going for a couple more hours, but I'm afraid I just wore out,'' Candace admitted. She didn't add the ''wearing out'' had actually been more mental and emotional than it had been physical.

''You shouldn't push it so hard,'' Elene advised. ''Things do take time to heal.'' She smiled wearily. ''I've found that you simply can't rush nature.''

''I'm not even going to try, after today,'' Candace agreed.

''Will you be able to manage comfortably here by yourself?''

''I think so. My main problem is I wish I could take a shower, and I can't. That is, I don't think I should get the bandage wet.''

She had thrust her feet into terry scuffs before starting out this morning, and now she glanced down at her troublesome ankle. There seemed no doubt it was more swollen.

Elene said, ''I can undo it for you, and after you've had a shower I can strap it up for you again. I'm not a registered nurse, but I am a licensed practical one. I was working in a hospital in Tampa when I met Manos.''

She paused and stood up. ''Let's get you into the bathroom so you can undress,'' she said. ''Then we'll undo that bandage. I think it would be a good idea to keep the cane with you in the shower. You mustn't put any more weight on that foot than what's absolutely necessary, okay?''

"I'll do my best.''

"Good. Do you have a robe?''

"Not with me, I'm afraid.''

"Well, I have one that will fit you,'' Elene said. "It's like a housecoat—it zips up the front. We'll get you into the shower and then I'll dash over and get it for you.''

The shower felt absolutely terrific. Candace reveled in the cool water that pelted her body, and washing her hair was like a life-restoring experience. By the time she finished, Elene had returned with the robe. Candace zipped it up halfway, wrapped her hair in a turban and then made her way back across the bedroom with Elene's assistance, hopping the final few feet by herself and collapsing onto the bed. She felt so good that for the moment she almost completely forgot about Nikolas.

Elene wound the elastic bandage around Candace's ankle with considerable skill and looked quite proud as she sat back to survey her work. "That will do very well,'' she pronounced. "Now, I think you need a hair dryer.''

"Not really,'' Candace said. "I can towel dry it and let nature and the air conditioning take care of the rest.''

"That's what I usually do,'' Elene confided before going on. "About supper...I'm sure you have no desire to go out again tonight, so let me know when you get hungry—just give me a buzz on the phone— and I'll bring you something.''

"Honestly, that's not necessary,'' Candace protested. "There should be some change in my handbag. If you'd just get me a candy bar or a package of crackers from one of the machines, that will be enough.''

Elene laughed. ''Nick would have my skin,'' she said firmly. ''So if I don't hear from you by dinnertime I'll bring something over, okay?''

There was nothing to say to this but a grateful ''Yes.''

Candace got up only once from the big double bed. Soon after Elene left, she collected the photocopies she'd made at the library and spread them out carefully on top of the covers. She placed her notes alongside these, plus the assorted pencils, pens and paper Theone had given her. Then she towel dried her hair until it was only slightly damp and propped up the pillows comfortably. But before she'd turned her attention to her reading material she felt her eyes starting to close. And almost that quickly, she was asleep.

CHAPTER TEN

SOMEONE WAS KNOCKING insistently on the door. Groggy—for afternoon naps usually disoriented her—Candace wished they would go away, but the knocking persisted.

She became aware it was quite dim in the room. Time for dinner already? Elene probably had a tray in her hand and couldn't open the door with her house key.

Candace got up carefully, and using the cane she hobbled across the room and turned the knob. "Elene..." she began. But it wasn't Elene.

Nikolas stood on the threshold looking down at her, and he seemed twenty feet tall. The black slacks he wore fitted him extremely well, and the white shirt, open at the throat, served to enhance his natural olive coloring. But to Candace's dismay, she saw he was scowling, and the glint in his eyes was unquestionably angry.

"May I come in?" he asked, almost too politely.

"Yes, of course," Candace said, her voice sounding as small as she felt.

She moved back clumsily, unable to tear her eyes away from his arresting face. He strode into the room, seeming to dwarf it with his presence, and then watched critically as she lumbered across to the bed. She sat down on the edge and glanced quickly at her ankle, and to her relief the swelling had definitely subsided now that she'd been off it for a while.

She'd brushed her hair after drying it, and now it fell like a golden cloud around her shoulders. The terry robe Elene had loaned her was a lovely shade of yellow, and it complimented her coloring perfectly. She could not have known how fragile and tremendously appealing she looked to Nikolas. But she did know his gaze softened, and he said in a tone not quite so unnerving, "Why did you do this, Candace?"

She didn't make the mistake of trying to evade the issue by asking him what he meant. She knew very well he wanted to know why she had moved out of his house and back into the Grecian Gardens. So she tilted her head at a proud angle and said, "I thought I'd troubled you and your family enough, Nikolas. I can't begin to tell you how much I appreciate what you've done for me, but—"

He resorted to Greek, a short word that seemed extremely expressive even though she had no idea of its precise meaning. Then he said, "Really, Candace, was my presence so distasteful to you that you had to sneak out of my home behind my back?" He paused, visibly gathering his thoughts. "All right, maybe we rushed things, you and I. And perhaps we would have rushed them even more had we not been interrupted each time we were alone. But...you never tried to stop me."

Candace was only too well aware of this, nor did she try to deny it. There wouldn't have been any point in attempting a camouflage—and Nikolas was much too sharp for one anyway. He hadn't taken his eyes off her face, and now he said more gently,

"Theone is very upset you are not coming back to us."

"And Melina?" She couldn't resist the question.

"Melina is an adolescent," Nikolas said abruptly. "I pay no attention to her. And neither should you. Like most of the young people today she is trying to 'find herself.' I just hope she makes the discovery fairly soon. Otherwise I shall have to help her along. As for myself. . . ."

"Yes?"

"Stupid of me, I suppose," he said ruefully, "but I could not believe it when I came home to find you'd taken your car and left. First I thought of chasing you all over town, but then Elene called and confessed she'd taken your car over to you. She said you'd be returning to the motel. She thought you would probably wait until after you'd had dinner somewhere before you came back, because you were so determined not to bother anyone. Then, you returned sooner."

"Yes."

"Because you 'tired yourself out,' Elene said."

"I did get tired, yes."

"Well, Elene said you were here and she thought from the way you looked it seemed likely you were about to fall asleep. She asked me to wait awhile before I came over." Again he took a deep breath. "I waited as long as I possibly could."

Suddenly, impulsively, Nikolas came and sat down on the bed next to her, taking both of her hands in his. He said simply, "I know it's crazy, but I can't let you leave me, Candace."

"I never wanted to leave you," she said huskily, although she had not intended to say anything at all like that to him. Then she felt as if time had become suspended—and as if she and Nikolas were enveloped in a gossamer capsule entirely their own. Their eyes fused, and she needed no invitation to move into his arms. He held her back from him for only an instant, as his hands cupped her face. Then he looked down at her as if he were seeing to the depths of her soul. And he began to kiss her.

His kisses started at her forehead and anointed her nose, her cheeks and the lobes of her ears in a slow, sensual course that was completely incendiary. Tantalizingly he probed the inside of her ear with the tip of his tongue, and she shivered as her anticipation heightened. She pressed her fingers into the satin darkness of his hair as she forced his mouth to meet hers, and as their lips parted and their tongues explored, a tidal wave of pure sexuality began to crest on the horizon of a mutual desire.

Nikolas's long, slender fingers moved to the zipper of Candace's robe, and gradually he drew it down, pausing with every inch to pass his mouth over the flesh he was exposing. Finally she lay before him with her breasts bared, her nipples standing taut even before his lips came to claim them. Then he began rotating his tongue around their circumference, and soon he'd started to arouse a sequence of sensations in her she hoped would never end. And there was, certainly, an endlessness to these sensations she was feeling. Each became more exquisite than the last as his tongue roved on to brand her skin with its warmth, each touch of this vital part of him evoking a new stream of ardor that emptied into a sea of passion that surely led to emotion's own infinity.

When at last Nikolas came to probe the very core

of her, Candace cried out in sweet agony, her hands fluttering like butterflies seeking release, beating their way to freedom. Her fingers found the back of his head, becoming enmeshed with each other as they captured it. Her strength was a quivering and tenuous thing, and she knew he would sense this in her touch.

For an instant, Nikolas was very still. Then he raised his head and her fingers fell away to come to rest on his shoulders, those wonderfully broad shoulders.

Nikolas said huskily, "Candace?"

She could not possibly speak aloud. She could only nod to let him know she'd heard him.

"Candace, you know where this is leading? This is a voyage that you—that you want to take with me?"

She had thought she'd been stirred completely; now his deep, tender voice made her aware there were still depths to be discovered. Again she nodded. Then his mouth came to claim her lips once again, his fingers moving in a pattern that was pure ecstasy.

By the time the full length of her robe had been opened, Nikolas had caressed every part of her, and when finally he slipped the robe off entirely he seemed shaken by her beauty. For she was proud and lovely in her nudeness, her body a vessel of absolute desire.

His eyes seemed to glow, and he said hoarsely, "Undress me now, Candace."

She had never undressed a man before. She had never even contemplated doing such a thing. Her fingers fumbled as she began to unbutton his shirt, nor were they any steadier by the time she reached his broad silver belt buckle.

"Do to me what I did to you," he urged, and shyly at first but then with growing confidence she trailed her mouth across his flesh while her hands began their own voyage of exploration. Each contour of his virile body was a revelation to her. She caressed the swell of his muscles and felt him tense and then relax. She molded the smooth lines of his thighs beneath her fingers, then trailed those fingers across the flatness of his stomach, going on to pause, only briefly, when they came to touch the very essence of his manhood.

This was the beginning of an inevitable culmination, and their urgency increased until they'd gone well beyond the point of no return. Her eyes marveled at the beauty of his long, wonderfully formed body, while her emotions became completely chaotic. Finally, she could only thrust herself against him in a demand that was silent at first but then became a low and plaintive moan as her need grew ever more frantic, cresting to match his.

They merged in a union as old as man, their passions mounting to a mutual crescendo until at last the tidal wave that had been threatening all the while broke over them, and they drowned together in the wake of its ecstasy. Candace's pleasure peaked again and again as she was guided by Nikolas through a maze of total rapture. And when finally he let himself succumb—utterly succumb—to the glory of his own fruition, the world became transformed into an entire galaxy. And it truly was a galaxy all their own, an Eden filled with shimmering exploding stars brighter than reality.

It took a long time to come back to Earth. Candace lay alongside him, her head against his shoulder, transfixed by her love for him. He put an arm around her and she reached for his hand, then slowly drew it across her mouth, brushing kisses on his fingers.

Tears shimmered in her eyes, and she gasped as he leaned over her and began to kiss them away.

"Salt," he said in that deep, stirring voice of his. "Your salt. The salt of life. Even more vital than the sweetness."

She had savored both today, Candace thought. The salt and the sweetness.

After a time Nikolas sat up, and his laugh was shaky. "It's a miracle we weren't interrupted," he said wryly. "Any minute now, I suppose Elene will be coming to find out why I haven't returned to get your supper for you."

His leg touched something, something that rustled, and he said, "I'm afraid I've dug into your papers. I hope it won't mean doing your homework all over again!"

She hadn't given a thought to the library photocopies she'd made—copies of stories entirely about him! Now she watched in horror as he picked up some of the papers and turned them over idly as he straightened them. And she heard his involuntary gasp even before she saw his eyes narrow and his lips tighten into a thin, bitter line.

His eyes were blazing as he turned toward her, and he was so furious he could scarcely speak.

"So," he accused. "I was right about you in the beginning, wasn't I? I said I felt I shouldn't trust you. I had an idea you knew damned well who I was...though I can't begin to imagine how you found out. Incredible to think you'd actually sprain your own ankle to get to me. But you're not the first one to try such a trick! Anything for a story about Nicky Mellin, right? All mixed in with the Greek celebration in the little town where he got his start! It would have been quite a feather in your journalistic cap, wouldn't it!''

He was snarling as he finished speaking, his voice so thick with rage she was actually afraid of him. But as she shrank back he said evenly, ''You have no need to worry. I would like to kill you, I admit, but I won't. It wouldn't be worth it!''

Candace felt as if she'd been turned to stone. She was incapable of movement. She shut her eyes tightly, unable to bear watching him as he got off the bed. She knew he was putting his clothes on and it would be painful beyond belief to look at even one line of his beautiful body—the body that, just minutes before, had been so much a part of her own.

She and Nikolas had experienced something wonderful that should have lasted till eternity. Something guided by love—for it had been love. She would never doubt they had gone far beyond sensuality and into an entirely different realm. She would never doubt they had shared an incredibly strong emotional odyssey. For love was one of the strongest emotions in the world. But the other, equally strong, was hate. Now she knew how quickly the two could be interchanged. And she was shattered by this revelation.

Nikolas hated her. She dared to look at him and saw he was running his fingers through his hair as if trying to comb it into place. There was no expression at all on his face. A cold mask was hopelessly back in place.

He said tautly, ''I will tell Elene to bring you some

food after a while. As for me, Candace. . . you can go to hell before you'll ever get a word out of me.''

She watched him cross the room, she saw his hand on the doorknob and she knew she had to stop him.

She sat up, her ankle twinging in protest at the abrupt movement, and she tried to put all the feeling she could muster into a single word.

''Please!'' she cried.

He swung around and stared at her disbelievingly. ''You dare to say 'please' to me?'' he challenged.

''Yes,'' she said, swinging her legs over the side of the bed and getting to her feet. She started toward him without even thinking of her injured ankle, and suddenly it turned beneath her. The pain was agonizing, forcing her to subside back on the bed with a moan as tears began filling her eyes. But Nikolas only continued to stare at her, apparently unmoved.

''A very good try,'' he commented after a moment. ''If you fail as a journalist you might try to become an actress.''

She didn't answer him because she couldn't. And with tears streaming down her face she leaned over, almost doubled in half, and clutched her ankle in both hands as she rocked back and forth, the pain possessing her.

Candace knew he was watching her, and she wished he would go away. But right now she couldn't even summon the strength to ask him to do so. She was so racked by a mixture of physical, mental and emotional pain there was no chance of even sitting up and making the effort to get control of herself. Then, after an agonizing moment she felt his nearness, followed by a sensation of warmth as he pressed his hand against her arm.

"Candace," he said, his voice very low and so soft it was barely audible. "Look at me!"

Again there was that mesmerizing quality to his request, and despite herself she slowly raised her tear-filled eyes to confront an expression on his face she would never forget.

The damaged side appeared to be working, as if the muscles were trying to force a response to the feelings searing him. The deep scar on his forehead was more pronounced than she'd ever seen it, and now it seemed symbolic to her of all the terrible things that had happened to him.

But those terrible things were in the past. As she looked at him she knew that whether or not he had once been Nicky Mellin—an entirely different person in so many ways—was a matter of little consequence to her. He was her Nikolas, and she loved the man he was now. She didn't need to know him for another day, another week or the next twenty years to verify the knowledge there would never again in her life be anyone who could come close to taking his place.

She stared at him mutely, because she could not imagine how she could hope to convince him of either the truth or the depth of her feelings for him. And, perhaps strangely, she didn't blame him for this. She could dimly appreciate what it must have been like for him to be thrust into the role of Nicky Mellin from the very beginning. Knowing him as she did, she could imagine how his main wish, many times, must have been to escape the media, even though he had known it was vital to his place in the sun to stay in the forefront of their attention. And, after the accident, how he must have been hounded!

Now she vaguely remembered seeing a newspaper

picture of a figure in a wheelchair, his head bent forward, his hands hiding his face. A photographer had climbed the fence of the private hospital to get this shot, the guards arriving on the scene too late to divest the man of his camera, if she remembered correctly. Also, she thought, it was the last picture she'd ever seen of Nicky Mellin, and it had been a very sad one. At the time, there had been rumors his mind was so shattered he no longer even knew who he was.

When she'd heard sometime later he had died, she'd felt a deep twinge of sorrow for him, but it had also seemed a blessing. Nicky Mellin had been vital, devastatingly handsome and irresistible as a screen idol. It had been painful enough to think of him being an invalid, but to know he'd suffered mentally, as well. . . .

She drew a deep breath and brushed at her tears with an impatient gesture. "Candace," Nikolas whispered.

She shook her head, unable to speak. And she saw the agony in his eyes.

"I didn't mean the things I just said," he began unsteadily. "That's to say, I wouldn't want anything to . . . to hurt you. No matter what I . . . ."

He didn't finish the sentence. Nor did he withdraw his hand from its resting place against her arm. She wanted desperately to reach out and cover it with her own hand, but she didn't dare.

"Nikolas. . ." she ventured, her voice trembling.

His mouth twisted. "Thanks, at least, for not calling me Nicky," he said bitterly.

"I . . . I could never call you Nicky."

"Couldn't you, Candace?" There was irony in his upraised eyebrow, doubt in the tone of his voice.

And regardless of his involuntary move to her side—when he'd seen she was so clearly in pain—she knew she'd lost him.

He took his hand away from her arm and moved back until he was sitting on the floor in front of her, his legs crossed. He surveyed her carefully and with a gloomy directness that only increased her apprehensions.

The silence was intense. Then, slicing into it, he demanded harshly, "Just what do you want from me, Candace?"

"Nothing!" she said, blurting out the word. And seeing the expression that crossed his face—an expression of doubt and irony and even sorrow—she added, "But you don't believe that, do you?"

"No," he said slowly. "I wish I could."

The pain in her ankle had begun to abate. She edged herself upward across the bed and leaned against the pillows. She'd managed to slip into the terry robe and zip it up and was glad it covered almost all of her. She only wished she could pull it up to cover her head so she wouldn't have to look at his face. Especially at his eyes.

What she was seeing was pure hurt, though it had taken her a few minutes to realize this. Nikolas was not nearly as angry as he was hurt, but this did not lessen her problem. On the contrary, she was certain he'd be able to get over anger much faster than he would the conviction that she had tricked him. He, who had managed to keep his guard up against the world so carefully and for so many years.

The phone jangled, filling the silence between them with its discordant ring, but she blessed the sound of it. Any sort of interruption was welcome. Nikolas rose to answer it, a tall man who moved with surprising grace for someone his size. Candace watched him, her heart aching.

"Yes, Elene?" he said gravely. "That's okay, I'll come over and get it in a minute. We were talking about...a lot of things. I'm afraid we lost track of the time."

"Elene has fixed a tray for you," he explained after he had hung up. "She was going to bring it across to you herself, but I thought you might prefer not to have another visitor just now."

"Thank you," Candace said. Another ache gripped her as she realized they were speaking to each other like two strangers.

"George Andris came by to take a look at your ankle," Nikolas reported further. "It was his day off. Possibly he should see it now. You didn't do it any good, coming down on it like that."

She didn't care about this. At the moment she didn't care if her ankle fell off. "It will be all right," she told him.

He shrugged. "Very well, then. I'll get your dinner."

"Please," she protested, "I don't want any food. I couldn't possibly eat a thing."

"I'd appreciate it if you would make an effort," he retorted coolly. "Elene's gone to the trouble to fix something for you, and if you leave it untouched she is going to know something's wrong. You don't owe me any favors, Candace, but I wish you'd...."

Again, he left the sentence unfinished. It was frustrating, but she managed, "I'll try."

He nodded and left the room without another word. And once he'd gone, she gave vent to her suppressed feelings, and pounded her fists against the mattress.

This was impossible—but what could she do about it? True, she had sensed from their first encounter Nikolas didn't like "journalists." But then a lot of people were not overly fond of the members of the media. She'd thought he was merely following what appeared to be a currently popular trend.

Now she knew it was much, much more than that! His wounds had been patched up, and the plastic surgeons had actually created a new face for him, although they hadn't been able to obliterate all the scars. Yet she sensed there were much deeper scars in him that might not ever be healed. Nikolas, in fact, though seemingly so assured on the surface, carried within him a whole well of bitterness and hurt and suspicion.

He was not gone very long. He came back with a tray over which Elene had placed a tent of aluminum foil, and he put it down on top of the dresser.

"Everything is cold," he said. "Elene did not think you would especially want hot food tonight, it is so warm out. Though it is fairly cool in here with the air conditioning."

"Yes," Candace nodded, neither the food nor the temperature mattering to her at all.

"Would you like me to pull a chair over to your bedside and put the tray on it?" he suggested.

"No, I can get to it later. But thanks just the same."

"Candace...you will try to eat something, will you not?"

He seemed to care a great deal about whether or not she ate, but she reminded herself dully this was for Elene's sake. He was already moving back toward the door. Clearly he had no wish to linger. And she had the terrible feeling that if she let him go now, it would be over between them forever. Just the thought was something she knew she couldn't bear.

Still, short of throwing herself at his feet, she didn't see what she could do to stop him. Even if she were to throw herself at his feet, for that matter, he might just pick her up again, put her back on the bed and then stalk out anyway. At best, it would be a reprieve of only a few minutes.

Regardless of her own determination, she was certain Nikolas had the strength to keep her apart from him at a considerable emotional length. She was sure, in fact, he had no intention of bridging this chasm that had come between them.

As if to verify this, he said, "Tarpon Springs is a small place, Candace. I cannot say we will not run into each other while you are here. I almost never go out socially, and when I do it is only to the homes of close friends. The exception is that I sometimes take coffee in Aliki's restaurant. So everything considered, we are not apt to meet again. And frankly, I prefer it that way, despite what has...gone on between us." He faltered very slightly. "Since I assure you that I will never permit you to interview me, I can only hope you will respect this—and never try."

Everything within Candace was protesting. But some of that old New England pride he had teased her about stirred and came to the surface. She managed to say very stiffly, "It will be entirely as you wish, Nikolas."

"Then," he said, seeming so very Greek as he spoke, "*adío*, Candace."

And there could be no doubt at all that *"adio"* meant goodbye.

Much later, Candace hobbled across the room and put the tray on a chair and then pulled the chair over to the bedside. Her tears had finally ended—she had wept herself dry. Her eyes were red rimmed and burning, and she hoped Elene would not come back too soon to retrieve the tray. She didn't want her hostess to see the state she was in.

She forced herself to eat, but she couldn't have said what it was she'd eaten. Nevertheless, the food did infuse her with strength. Enough strength, at least, to actually make the decision. She picked up the phone and dialed the home number Barry had given her.

Candace kept their conversation brief. "Barry," she said, "I think you were right. I don't have any mileage at all with this ankle, so I think I'm going to have to give the assignment up. Could you make arrangements for a flight out of Tampa?"

"It's as good as done, Candy," he told her smoothly.

CHAPTER ELEVEN

IT WAS FREEZING in New York, and this came as a shock. Without pausing to think about it logically, Candace had assumed by now it must be summer everywhere, even though it was still only mid-January by the calendar.

Barry met her at Kennedy. As they drove back into Manhattan Candace's eyes lingered on the clumps of city-soiled snow in the gutters. They matched her mood—cold and gray.

Barry said, "Don't look so downhearted, darling. I've cleared an assignment you can get onto as soon as that ankle's strong again, and you won't have to do a lot of traveling that might stir it up."

"What's it about?" Candace asked idly.

"A profile on Yorkville, right here in the city. It used to be more German than Berlin. There are still *deutsch* touches, although now it's a much more mixed area. The theme, basically, will be neighborhoods and the changes population shifts cause in them, both for better and for worse. Loss of character, for example. At least, the kind of character that put sections like Yorkville on the map in the first place, you know? Maybe a new focus. Anyway...." He trailed off and glanced at Candace interrogatively.

"Sound interesting?" he asked.

Candace nodded. "Yes."

"But it doesn't move you?"

"I don't know," she said honestly. "Ordinarily it would, yes. But just now...."

"I don't mean to rush you," Barry said understandingly. "I just wanted you to know there's plenty on the stove for you. Matter of fact, I've been talking with the boys upstairs about the idea of putting you on staff. Would you like that?"

A staff writer on *Tempo* magazine! Ten days ago, even a week ago, Candace would have been unable to believe such a stroke of good fortune. But then a week ago a tall, dark Greek who had fallen in love with her—only to have his love turn to hate—had not yet walked into her life.

Love turned to hate? Had Nikolas ever really loved her in the first place? He'd been possessed of the same kind of desire that had fired her. That much was true. But he'd never really pretended it was anything more than that. Whereas she....

Candace realized Barry had said something to her, and she didn't have the vaguest idea what it was.

"Sorry," she said.

"You're not with me, are you?" he queried, forcing a laugh. But his voice was indulgent. "No matter, Candy," he said. "There'll be plenty of time later to talk everything over." He didn't press her into conversation for the rest of the ride, and for this she was grateful.

Her apartment was a studio in the East Sixties, and Barry let her out at the front door, then went to find a parking space. After five minutes he returned, carrying her suitcase and a couple of tote bags. In one of these Candace had stashed the material about

Nikolas she'd copied at the Tarpon Springs Public Library.

She'd been sitting on a bench in the entrance foyer as she waited for Barry. Now she looked up at him and wondered what was missing, and it came to her it was her other suitcase.

Her suitcase, the one with the things Elene had packed for her after her mishap, was still in Nikolas Mylonis's house!

"There we are," Barry said, smiling at her cheerfully. "Give me your key, sweetheart, and I'll take this stuff upstairs for you. Then I'll come back down and get you."

She was too tired, too emotionally exhausted, to protest that she could manage on her own by using the cane. The cane! She glanced down at it and realized this, too, belonged to the Mylonis household.

She had not burned her bridges as completely as she'd thought! True, she could simply abandon her other suitcase and the things in it. But the cane was hand carved. And it had a silver band rimming the curved handle. She couldn't possibly think of not returning it. It might be valuable. Very valuable.

Oh, come off it, Candace, she told herself angrily. *What are you trying to do? Think up an excuse to contact him again?*

Barry came back downstairs and carefully helped her into the elevator. It was a gray afternoon so he turned the lights on in Candace's apartment, but even so the place seemed cheerless. She hadn't done too much to the decor, and what there was revealed little of her personality.

Candace had sublet it from a girl who was with the United Nations and who had been sent to Paris for a

year. It came furnished, but evidently her lessor
hadn't had time to think much about interior decora-
tion, and the result was a bland blend of beiges, from
the color of the walls to the draperies to the floor
coverings. There was a television, a stereo and a
small but well-equipped kitchen. These things alone
had made the apartment seem more than adequate
when Candace had taken it. And the price had been
right. The rental had been accomplished through
mutual friends, so she had been screened carefully
and had passed the test.

She hadn't passed the test with Nikolas, though,
she thought sadly. He'd told her frankly he had no
faith in her and could never bring himself to believe
their meeting had been entirely accidental. He was
sure she had somehow managed to track him down,
digging up a trail buried for years, and was determined to get the real story of Nicky Mellin. Because
she was a journalist—a breed he despised—this was
all she could possibly be interested in.

"Oh, Nikolas!" she said under her breath.

Barry, who had gone out to the kitchen to make
drinks for both of them, paused in the doorway to
ask, "What was that, Candy?"

"Nothing, really."

"Your foot?"

"Yes," she fibbed. "Just a twinge, that's all."

Barry frowned as he handed her a Scotch and
soda. "I think we should have an orthopedic special-
ist look you over tomorrow," he decided.

"It's not that bad, Barry."

"You don't know that," he said patiently
"You're going on the opinion of some Greek doctor
from a fishing village in the boondocks—"

"George Andris is not 'some Greek doctor,'" Candace said testily. "He is an experienced physician. A very good one, in fact. And Tarpon Springs isn't a little hole out in the sticks. It's—"

Barry laughed. "Come on, darling," he protested. "You don't have to justify the place to me. I sent you down there, remember?"

"Yes," she said evenly, "I remember. And while we're on the subject...."

"Yes?"

"What are you going to do about the story?"

"Shelve it, I suppose. There's no need to think about it now."

"Shelve it for good?"

Barry frowned. "I haven't thought about it that much," he admitted. "Why? It is so important to you?"

"It *would* be a very good story," Candace said slowly. "I can't do it as things stand, of course." Her smile was rueful. "I never even got as far as the sponge docks," she confessed.

"But that wasn't your fault," Barry said. "I know that, and so does the editor in chief. So does the publisher. It's nothing against you."

Candace took a deep breath. "I know that you'd miss Epiphany," she began, "but I could fill in that part. I have a lot of notes, and there are pictures available...."

Pictures! She had completely forgotten about Paul Morrison and the contact prints he had brought her, to say nothing of the camera which he had been more than willing to let her take without any sort of advance payment. The camera and the prints were also in Nikolas Mylonis's house!

She'd made such a mess of things!

Candace wondered if she looked as disconcerted as she felt. But Barry didn't seem to be noticing. He'd gone to stand by the window with his drink in his hand, and she took the chance to study him.

He was a very attractive man, tall, broad-shouldered, with even features and smooth brown hair tinged white at the temples. And he was always immaculately groomed. In fact, she'd thought at first he could be a model, if he was not already an editor and very good at his job. He was also intensely masculine, and Candace was beginning to realize he was becoming a bit too interested in her as a woman rather than as a writer. It had been obtuse of her not to recognize the danger signals at that luncheon they'd shared, when he'd brought up the idea of the Tarpon Springs assignment. The fact of the matter was that despite his attractiveness she hadn't thought at all about him as a man. She'd considered him only in the context of "editor." And suddenly she was afraid Barry was not apt to let that misapprehension stand between them too much longer.

Still glancing out the window, he asked, "What is it about Tarpon Springs, Candy? I can understand your interest in doing the story, but it seems to me you've gone a bit overboard. America is pitted with great ethnic settings. We couldn't publish enough magazines in ten lifetimes to cover them all. Tarpon Springs is just one of many places. Sure, I think it would make a great story for us. Especially since we're using a new approach, as you know. But there's nothing incredibly topical about it. It's scarcely headline material. If we don't do it this year, we can do it the next. You can go down there and cover the Epiphany deal and all the rest of it next January, if you want to. Would that satisfy you?''

She said stubbornly, ''I think the story should be in your December issue, Barry. Then people who are going to Florida could make plans to detour over to Tarpon Springs. Even if they didn't, that would be the right time of year to run it.''

He laughed. ''You sound as if you've been hired by the local chamber of commerce.''

''I wasn't thinking of myself,'' Candace said, her jaw tight. ''I was thinking of your sending another writer down there. As I've said, I can put you in touch with a man who will supply pictures of the Epiphany celebrations. And I did manage to take quite a few notes on the place, mostly on the local color. But there's a lot more than the Epiphany festivities. The whole history of sponge fishing and the Greeks who came to settle in the area would make a great story. For many years they made Tarpon Springs a world sponge-fishing center, and—''

''Hold it!'' Barry commanded, laughing. ''I sold you on this assignment in the first place, remember? There's no need for you to try to make a believer out of me.'' He put his empty glass down on an end table and said, ''One thing you've done with that little speech is to thoroughly convince me you're the only person to write the story. A few weeks from now, when your ankle has healed, you can go back there and finish the job. Okay?''

Candace tried to hide her distress, because this was the last thing in the world she wanted to do.

There was no way she could go back to Tarpon Springs—ever. But this was not the moment to tell Barry that.

"Look," he asked now, standing over her with a worried frown. "Are you sure you can handle things here by yourself?"

"Positive," Candace said firmly.

"I've got one of those dinners on for tonight that I just can't get out of," he said resignedly. "It's with the chief editor and one of our top writers, who is only going to be in town for a couple of days. But I ordered some food from that Chinese place over on Lexington to be sent up to you around seven. Okay?"

Candace looked at him speechlessly.

"Also, I stashed a few groceries in the kitchen. Coffee for the morning, plus some milk, eggs and rolls. You should be set till lunchtime, which reminds me. . . will you have lunch with me?"

"Barry," she protested, "you have things to do. There's no need for you to disrupt your whole schedule because of me.. .."

"We'll talk about nothing but business," he promised quickly, but the expression in his eyes told another story. Then he bent over and kissed her lightly on the lips. "Take care, beautiful. And get some rest," he said. "Just don't go dreaming about Greeks and sponges."

THAT NIGHT CANDACE WISHED she could dream about Greeks. Particularly one Greek. She wished almost desperately she could see Nikolas Mylonis again, if only in her mind.

Her foot was better when she got up the next morning, but she'd seldom been in a more chaotic state mentally. She told herself bitterly she'd really botched it, leaving Tarpon Springs as she had. She'd waited until the last minute before calling the registration desk at the motel to tell Elene an airport limousine was coming to pick her up. Elene had hurried over immediately, obviously distressed about this, and it was a good thing the airport chauffeur had arrived when he did.

She had been whisked into the waiting car by this kind man who kept a firm grip on her arm so she wouldn't stumble. But both she and Elene had become choked up when it came to saying goodbye.

Elene had finished shakily, "Nick will never forgive me for this."

"You had nothing to do with it," Candace had assured her. And when Elene clearly wouldn't believe Nikolas would agree with this, Candace had added bitterly, "Elene...the fact is he wants me to go." Then she had departed quickly, before Elene could recover.

She'd left a check for the estimated amount of her bill on the dresser in her room and was sure she'd covered the costs adequately. But at some point in the future she would phone Elene to be certain about this, she decided. Mostly she wanted to try to make amends with the lovely Greek woman whose dark eyes had been so haunting. For Elene had been very, very kind to her.

Theone had been very kind to her, too. As for Melina's cordiality...well, that was something else again. But at this distance Melina really didn't seem to matter.

And Nikolas?

Candace tried very hard not to think about Nikolas, but it was impossible.

She made coffee, buttered a roll and then forced

herself to take the library copies out of her tote bag.
She settled down with them in an armchair by the
window, and soon she was oblivious to the street
noises outside. In a few seconds she'd become completely immersed in the stories about Nicky Mellin's
life.

At the time he had dived for the cross in Tarpon
Springs, a Hollywood film crew had been on location
there. They had been working on a documentary
about the sponge-fishing industry, which at one time
had been nearly wiped out by a blight but was
managing to make a comeback. The film crew had
shot quite a bit of footage of Nikolas, and he had
proved to be exceptionally photogenic. A trip to
Hollywood for screen tests had followed not long
afterward.

And then the rise to stardom had begun. Candace
could only guess at the behind-the-scenes maneuver-
ing that took place in a venture such as this. She was
sure that over those first few years of his film career
Nikolas must have been as carefully groomed and as
painstakingly prepared as a racehorse about to run
for the Triple Crown.

Along the way, Tarpon Springs certainly appeared
to have been forgotten. As she read about Nicky
Mellin, it seemed to Candace the studio promotion
people actually had tried to obliterate the clues to his
Greek background. They had given him a new name,
a new identity, an entirely new image. In fact, the
only stories she found connecting Nikolas with Tarpon Springs at all were the very early accounts in the
local papers.

She came across one wire-service story, dated a bit
later on, stating he had been discovered in Florida.

But the impression had been given this was in a resort setting. He had been built up by the studio press agents as an all-American youth, and he had appealed to contemporaries across the nation on an unprecedented level. Yet Candace could find absolutely nothing about his having been born in Greece or his immigration to the States as a child from a small island in the Aegean.

Nikolas, or rather Nicky Mellin—for Candace thought of them as two different people—had made his first big hit in a swashbuckling picture set in France. The script had actually been a somewhat casual adaptation of a Dumas novel, but Nikolas's youth, virility and astonishing good looks had lifted the picture from mediocrity to make it a box-office sensation. From there he had gone straight to the top, and he'd been at his zenith when the accident had happened.

Along the way, the media had been primarily interested in his romantic exploits, and he'd had a lot of them, judging from the numerous news accounts and photos. As Candace studied the various pictures, she could remember many of them from her teenage years. Back then she had been envious of the girls with him, but now she was sickened by the whole thing. One photo showed Nikolas with a stunning blonde clinging to his arm, while the next showed a gorgeous brunette. Nicky Mellin, who was Hollywood's most attractive and eligible bachelor, was evidently also its hardest to catch. And that made him all the more desirable!

Then Candace read a story about him going to a place near Acapulco for some location shots, and with a shock she learned she'd been mistaken about the accident having occurred in California.

One night there had been a party on a private yacht belonging to a wealthy Mexican. It was not a large yacht, and the owner took pride in acting as his own captain.

Reading between the lines, Candace could only assume everyone on board had got very drunk. The party had been in honor of Nicky and Lila Pembroke, the girl who was starring with him in his latest picture and to whom he was also reportedly engaged. They were returning to Hollywood in a couple of days, and rumor had it they would shortly announce a wedding date.

The weather had turned bad and the seas had begun to get rough, but no one had paid much attention to these obvious danger signals. It was late when they turned back toward the harbor where the yacht was kept berthed. Later, one of the guests told reporters Lila had been dancing out on the deck in her stocking feet—a much wilder version of a dance she'd done in the film they'd just been shooting—and in one dramatic gyration she had thrown herself against the boat railing. Incredibly, the railing had given way, and she'd plunged into the seething water.

Nicky had not wasted a second. Despite shouts of warning from his host, who knew the area very well, he had immediately dived overboard. The dangerous currents had instantly swept him up like a toy, and a moment later a violent wave had thrown him headfirst into a treacherous ridge of sharp, submerged rocks.

A hideous nightmare of events had followed. Somehow, some of the men aboard the yacht had managed to get Nikolas out of the water. And the woman who had later told her story to the media said she had taken one look at his head and had fainted.

His wounds were terrible. He had been taken first to a hospital in Acapulco and then transferred to a medical center in Mexico City. After that, a blanket of silence had been imposed over everything about him.

Lila Pembroke's body had not been recovered until shortly after dawn the following morning.

Time passed, and occasionally there was a report to the effect Nicky Mellin was undergoing further surgery. Then insidious rumors spread via the gossip columnists indicating Hollywood's most charismatic star had suffered severe brain damage and forever after would be a "vegetable."

Candace shuddered as she read the phrase.

Stories about Nicky Mellin were dug out from time to time, then were buried, only to be exhumed once again. The years passed. Then there was that one poignant shot of a man in a wheelchair. A man reported to be Nicky Mellin, his face covered by his hands.

The legend of Nicky Mellin seemed to have died completely. And Candace was sure that later she'd read somewhere the star himself had actually passed away.

Thinking about all of this as she set the copies aside, Candace could fully understand why Nikolas would have such a horror of being "brought back to life." She could imagine how the media would zero in on him today and how the cameras would focus on his face, revealing every one of the scars that lingered—and not only the physical ones. The emotional and the mental wounds would be held up for scrutiny, too, and she suspected they would be more painful than ever, once the healing balm of time had been stripped away.

No, she surely could not blame Nikolas for guarding the privacy he had so painfully achieved. She could only marvel at the way he'd been able to keep his secret. And she could only wonder at and admire the loyalty of the people who knew him in Tarpon Springs.

What hurt Candace was the thought that he could believe she would stir up all of his past. Granted, the idea of doing a story on Nicky Mellin today had crossed her mind briefly. The trained journalist in her had fully recognized the potential of the astonishing material she'd stumbled upon.

But thinking about the story didn't mean she would ever consider writing it!

For strangely enough, Nicky Mellin really was dead, as far as Candace Mayhew was concerned. The glamorous young star seemed to bear very little relation to the man she knew now. This man's character had been forged by his having been put through a living hell. And an entirely different person had emerged from the ashes.

The Nikolas Mylonis she knew. And whom she loved.

CHAPTER TWELVE

January was a miserable month in New York. It was cold and raw, with more than the normal quota of snow. And wherever the snow melted, dangerous patches of ice were left in its wake. Though Candace's ankle no longer caused her any real pain, it still had not regained its full strength, and she developed a horror of slipping on the treacherous city streets and damaging it all over again.

Barry gave her an assignment dealing with child models and their mothers, and she spent a couple of weeks going around in taxis from city apartment to city apartment, doing interviews. The magazine furnished her with a new camera, and the pictures she took of the children came out very well. Barry insisted she had an art for revealing character in her photographs and for getting a three-dimensional emotional quality of an essentially two-dimensional medium. This, he told her solemnly, was a true gift.

She welcomed the praise, but it didn't really stir her. Nothing really stirred her these days. She felt as if she were only half-alive and tried to blame at least part of her depression on the weather, but she knew very well the weather had little to do with it.

February came, and Barry asked her to go to a Valentine party with him. The party was being given by a corporate executive who could be important to

Tempo insofar as advertising went. Advertising wasn't Barry's usual area, but he had known the man's son in college, hence the invitation.

Candace was in no mood for large social affairs, and although she tried to think of a graceful way to refuse Barry, she found herself fresh out of reasons. She had refused him so many times.

Barry had been very good to her since her return to New York. He had certainly gone overboard getting her an assignment she could handle right here in Manhattan, and he had continued to keep their personal relationship low-keyed, despite her apprehensions about this. Common sense told her it couldn't last forever. Each time Barry kissed her good-night, his lips lingered on hers just a little bit longer.

Not only was he an attractive man, he was a fun person to be with, and if Candace could have been sure he wasn't going to become too persistent, she would have enjoyed his company. As it was, she decided the least she could do was go to the Valentine party with him.

She tried to put her heart into it by buying a new dress for the occasion. It was pure white and smartly styled with slashes of red. She mentioned the purchase of the dress to Barry, emphasizing it was especially for the celebration, and this seemed to please him.

On the afternoon of the party, a florist's messenger arrived with a traditional square white box. And when Candace opened it she had to give Barry points, if only for the gentlemanly way in which he acted—and courted. He had chosen to have an exquisite amaryllis fashioned into a corsage for her. It was cream white, with each petal fanning out into a series of narrow red stripes. It added the perfect touch to her costume, and she couldn't help but enjoy the effect.

The party was a lavishly catered affair. Everything was very sumptuous, but it was also very dull. Candace was relieved when Barry proposed they slip out, nor did she mind when he suggested they join a group of people going off to a popular night spot. She'd never cared much for New York nightlife—not that she'd experienced much of it—but Barry seemed to be in a heady mood tonight, and she didn't want to precipitate any emotional crises. It seemed a wise idea to party with the others for as long as possible and then to make sure his good-night kiss was a brief one.

One of the men in the group was driving his own car, although Candace couldn't imagine why anyone would want to bother driving a private car in Manhattan. The traffic was terrible and the parking considerably worse. Yet three couples crowded into the car, and as they drove through the chilly night everyone seemed to be talking at once—everyone except Candace. She wasn't really paying much attention to anything and didn't even notice where they were going.

Once inside the nightclub they were led to a table not far from the dance floor, which was about the size of a postage stamp. Barry suggested a brandy Alexander for her, and Candace agreed. One of the other women giggled and said something about being lucky not to have to think of one's diet. Candace smiled. And she was about to modestly admit weight had never been a problem for her when she found herself gazing straight into a pair of mocking black eyes.

The musicians were just coming back from a break and were mounting the small platform behind the dance floor. And Manos Panagoris—astonishingly handsome in a black tuxedo—was among them, negligently holding a guitar.

Candace couldn't believe it. Manos? Here in New York? And playing with a group in a smart nightclub? She took a deep breath. She hadn't even known he was a musician. In fact, she'd thought of Manos as something of a parasite who lounged around and did nothing while both his wife and his mother-in-law worked like dogs to support him.

The music began with a fairly slow tempo, and Barry turned to her. "Dance, Candy?" he asked.

Her ankle hadn't given her a twinge in over two weeks, and she had mentioned this earlier to Barry. So she had no excuse to refuse him.

She glided into his arms, but it was all she could do to keep her eyes away from the darkly handsome figure strumming chords with commendable ease. And as they passed the dais on which the musicians were sitting, there was no doubt at all Manos Panagoris had his eyes fixed on her!

She missed a step, and Barry asked instantly, "What is it, Candy?"

"Nothing," she said, realizing they were within earshot of Manos. She didn't know how good his English was, but there was more than just a chance it was a lot better than she'd guessed.

"That ankle bothering you again?" Barry persisted.

"No," she said nervously, forcing herself to concentrate on the beat of the music and on what she was doing with her feet.

But Barry was not about to be so easily distracted. "Darling," he said, "you have only to say the word and we'll cut out of here."

"I don't want to leave," Candace found herself responding quickly. And she added, "Anyway, I haven't finished my drink yet."

Barry chuckled and to her consternation pressed her even closer to him. She knew this must look like a very intimate bit of business to anyone watching them, and she was also quite sure Manos seldom missed a trick about such things.

The piece finished, and as Candace wended her way back to their table with Barry she told herself there was no reason she should care what conclusions Manos might come to. Nothing Manos might tell anybody could possibly hurt her. Suppose he did mention to Nikolas he had seen her in New York with another man? Even conjecturing about something like this made it seem as if Nikolas had some sort of claim on her, she reminded herself now, and that idea was a sorry joke.

But then Candace found herself thinking dismally, *if only he did!*

Evidently she'd consumed more of her brandy Alexander than she'd thought she had, for her glass had been removed from the table. Seeing this, Candace decided to suggest it might be a good idea after all if they did leave. But before she could speak Barry had ordered another round of drinks. And Candace was taking a cautious sip of hers when she became aware of someone standing at her side.

"*Despinís!*" Manos Panagoris exclaimed suavely. "How enchanting it is to see you again!"

Manos was looking down at her with such open admiration it was impossible not to be affected, even though Candace knew better! His smile was devastating, and she could sense the women at the table responding eagerly as he extended a lesser version of his greeting to each of them in turn. He was a practiced charmer, no doubt about that.

Candace had a fleeting picture of Elene. No wonder there were shadows beneath her eyes! And no wonder Nikolas had said bitterly he wished Manos Panagoris had never left Greece!

There was nothing to do but introduce him to the other people sitting around the table, and they were quick to ask Manos to join them. To Candace's dismay, he was just as quick to accept the invitation. He managed to wedge a chair in between herself and Barry, completely disregarding Barry's glare as he did so.

"You are in New York," Manos said, turning his attention entirely to her as if the others had vanished.

She didn't know whether he meant this as a question or a statement. His English was so accented it was difficult to understand him. But then, she thought wryly, someone like Manos wasn't apt to need fluency in a language to get what he wanted!

She said, "I *live* in New York," spacing the words slowly and evenly.

"Yes," he said. "Writer!" He pounced on the word triumphantly.

Candace nodded, not wanting to pursue this. She didn't know how much Manos knew about her assignment in Tarpon Springs or if he knew anything at all about what had happened between Nikolas and herself. And she had no desire to be the person to enlighten him about this or about much of anything else. She simply did not trust Manos, although there was no logical reason for her feeling this way. It was simply a gut instinct.

He beamed at her now and suggested tantalizingly, "Perhaps you write about me?"

This certainly was an invitation rather than the question it seemed to be—a fact made clear despite Manos's limited English. She chose to disregard it and asked instead, "How long have you been in New York, Manos?"

"One week," he said, holding up the five fingers of his right hand to illustrate this.

He nodded toward the dais where the musicians performed. "One guitar player gets sick. Friend in group asks me," he said, gesturing eloquently as he spoke.

The other women at the table loved him. Noting their reactions, Candace once again felt sorry for Elene. She'd said she'd met him while she was working as a nurse in Tampa. Possibly he'd been playing at a night spot there at the time. Candace imagined it must have been a whirlwind romance, and she suspected they had married before Nikolas had discovered anything about it. She didn't know how much authority Nikolas had in relation to his family, particularly concerning Elene's affairs. Elene wasn't a blood relation, but she was his stepmother's niece and Melina's first cousin. And while no one could call Nikolas a patriarch, he did seem to be very much the household head. Even Melina listened when he spoke, although not always without protesting.

One of the other women asked Manos a question, and Candace was reasonably sure he didn't understand a word she was saying. But he flashed a daz-

zling smile and nodded enthusiastically. This seemed
to satisfy the woman, as she beamed at him in return.

The musicians were sauntering back into the room
and Manos rose reluctantly. "Must go," he said, and
then he bent to raise Candace's hand to his lips, letting them rest just a fraction too long on her fingers.

She felt the urge to slap his face, again for no
justifiable reason, but she merely forced a tight
smile.

"Kaliníhta, elinítha," he said, pressing the hand
he had just released. "Beautiful girl," he translated,
and Candace could sense that Barry was bristling.

The woman who had asked the question—and had
received the wordless answer—watched him moving
back to join the other musicians. "Wow!" she
breathed heavily. "How long have you known him,
Candy?"

"I met him in Tarpon Springs last month," Candace said. "I don't really know him at all."

She glanced across at Barry to see that his eyes
were disbelieving. Him, too? This was her first experience at playing the role of femme fatale, and she
didn't like it. It seemed to breed only suspicion and
distrust.

They left the nightclub in the same car they'd arrived in, and since Candace's apartment was the first
stop along the return route, the man behind the wheel
left her off there. She was afraid that Barry was going to say something to the others so that he could
escort her all the way to her apartment and perhaps
linger, but she foiled this by mentioning that it was
almost impossible to get a taxi in the neighborhood at
this hour.

Barry got the message and walked her only as far

as the elevator. And after a rather short "Good night, Candy," he rejoined the others, who were parked at the curb waiting for him.

He was not pleased about their evening, and Candace was well aware of this as she let herself into her apartment. She knew she hadn't heard the last of Manos Panagoris's appearance at their table, and she was prepared to plead a prior commitment if Barry asked her to have lunch with him tomorrow so they could talk about things further.

The matter of her becoming a staff writer was still under discussion at *Tempo*, and as she poured a glass of milk and got a cookie to go with it, she thought about this. If she became a staffer she would be seeing much more of Barry than she was now, and they'd been together often enough lately as it was. There had been a steady buildup in the number of their engagements, both business and social. It occurred to Candace that he was staking out a claim to her in much the same way he scheduled the contents of the magazine—carefully, thoroughly and with a totally professional hand. There was nothing impetuous about Barry, and previously she had considered this a point in his favor. He was the opposite of Nikolas Mylonis in every way she could think of. But there was also a limit to his tolerance, and she suspected he could become very jealous, if provoked. Though he'd hardly said a thing, the vibes had been there tonight. And she had caught them fully.

Finishing her milk, she washed out the glass and put it upside down to drain by the side of the sink. Then she undressed and slipped into a nightgown and a warm, quilted housecoat. She turned the radio to a station that featured soft music and settled down in an armchair with a book, because although it was late she was still wide awake.

The encounter with Manos Panagoris had opened up a Pandora's box of memories. Damn it! Why did she have to walk into the one nightclub in New York City where Manos happened to be playing? And only because of a fluke! The guitar player had got sick and a "friend" had wangled the job for Manos. Candace imagined Elene had probably parted with some of her hard-earned money to pay for his air fare north.

They were playing the theme from *Never On Sunday* on the radio. A Greek movie. Greek music.

Oh, Nikolas, Candace thought miserably.

And at that precise moment, the telephone rang.

CHAPTER THIRTEEN

"PLEASE EXCUSE ME for phoning you at such a late hour," Nikolas Mylonis said.

She was so shocked at the sound of his voice she couldn't answer.

"Candace, are you there?" he asked after a second.

"Yes...."

"I thought I might have dialed the wrong number."

"No."

"As I said, I apologize for calling so late, but there is something I need to ask of you as soon as possible. A favor, I am afraid."

Nikolas—asking her a favor?

Silence stretched between them until he said again, "Candace?"

"Yes."

"Did I wake you up?"

"No."

"Is there someone there with you?"

"No."

"I'm not being suspicious. I just wondered. You are alone?"

"Yes."

"For God's sake, Candace!" Nikolas said irritably, sounding much more like her own familiar

Nikolas. "Can't you say anything except yes and no?"

"What is there to say?" she murmured.

His laugh was short, but it still conveyed a full share of bitterness. "I suppose I have that coming," he replied evenly. "And you don't have to tell me I have no right to ask any favors of you. But will you please have lunch with me tomorrow, or a drink, or anything you like? And if Manos should try to speak to you in the meantime, will you stall him until you have talked to me first?"

"If Manos should try to talk to me?" she repeated numbly.

"Yes," Nikolas said. "You needn't sound so incredulous. He couldn't wait until he got through playing tonight. He had to call me from the club to tell me he'd seen you there."

"He called Tarpon Springs?"

"No, not Tarpon Springs. I am in New York, Candace. How else do you think I could suggest we meet tomorrow?"

"You're in New York?" She felt as if she were beginning to hallucinate.

"Must you repeat everything I say? Yes, I am in New York. I live in New York a fair amount of the time."

"You live in New York?"

"There you go again! The moon is made of green cheese, Candace."

"What?"

"I just wondered if you'd repeat that for me and put a question mark at the end of it!" he said infuriatingly.

"Nikolas. . . ." she warned.

He chuckled. "It's all right, *agápi mou*," he told her. "Or is it all right? I don't think I know the difference these days. I've never been so damned confused!"

He was confused! She tried to sort things out and put them into focus. "How did you get my number?" she asked.

"You gave your New York number to Elene when you called originally to make reservations at the Grecian Gardens," he told her plainly. "It's in her record book. Next question?"

"Why didn't you tell me you live in New York some of the time?"

"Because you never asked me anything about what I did or did not do, for one thing. For another thing, we never had the chance to get down to practical issues. We were too busy driving each other crazy." He sighed deeply. "Candace, *will* you have lunch with me tomorrow?"

"I don't think so," she said carefully.

"We will meet in a public place, and I can promise you I will not force my attentions upon you."

"Don't make fun of me, Nikolas!"

"Was I making fun of you? I don't think I would dare meet you in a private place just now, Candace. I'd probably either kill you or make love to you if we were alone together. One way or another, there wouldn't be a prayer of me keeping my hands off you." He paused and then added as if speaking to himself in disgust, "What the hell am I saying?"

There was no answer to this, and she didn't try to invent one.

She heard him draw a long, ragged breath. "I would not ask you to agree to see me unless it was important, Candace. Not only to me but to Elene, among others.''

She wondered whether or not he might be using Elene as a ploy and shook her head slowly.

As if he could see her clear through the telephone line and had got the message he said, ''I take it the answer is still negative.''

''Yes, it is.''

''All right, then, I guess I will have to come to your place and we'll have to try to live with nature taking its course.''

''What are you going to do?'' she asked coldly. ''Break down the door?''

''Yes, if I have to,'' he retorted, and she had not the slightest doubt that he meant it.

''Okay, Nikolas,'' she said. ''Not lunch, though. I'll meet you for a drink at five o'clock tomorrow afternoon.''

''Do you have a preference?''

''A place to meet, you mean?''

''Yes.''

''Somewhere big and noisy and crowded,'' Candace said.

''No margin for intimacy, eh?'' he translated sarcastically. Before she could answer he went on, ''How about Rockefeller Plaza? We can divert ourselves from each other by watching the skaters. The French side at five, shall we say?''

''Very well,'' Candace agreed. Her voice was prim, but her emotions were beginning to swirl. The mere thought of seeing him again was enough to send her spiraling out of control.

''Until tomorrow then, Candace,'' he said. And with that he hung up.

SHE WAS NO GOOD for anything the next day. She tried to work on another article idea she had about career children—a spin-off of the story she'd just finished for *Tempo*—but she found herself typing the same words over and over again. Barry called and asked her to have lunch with him, as she'd been sure he would, and she stalled him by fibbing that she was meeting an old school friend from Albany who was only in the city for the afternoon. Candace didn't like to tell even white lies, but . . . .

At three o'clock she began to get dressed for her appointment with Nikolas, and it took her more than half an hour just deciding what to wear. She, who had never been overly fussy about a choice of clothes! Finally she chose a simple wool dress in a deep shade of cranberry red. It had a Russian-styled high neckline and a slightly flared skirt. With it she wore antique filigree silver earrings that had belonged to her grandmother. These were nice enough by themselves, so she wore no other jewelry.

She took exceptional pains with her makeup and tried her hair three different ways. Finally she settled for a twist coiled high on her head—a very attractive style for her. Even so, when she took a last look in the mirror, she wasn't satisfied. She was still too thin, and she was definitely too pale. There were shadows beneath her deep blue eyes that reminded her of Elene. She didn't look like someone who'd been riding a wave of happiness lately. She knew that Nikolas was going to notice every single detail about her and it wouldn't be too difficult for him to reach this conclusion. The problem was his conclusion would be right.

Candace took a taxi to the Sixth Avenue side of the

RCA Building. Then she walked through its black marble lobby and out onto Rockefeller Terrace. As she crossed the street toward the sunken plaza a cold wind swirled around her feet, and she drew in her breath at the sharpness of it. She'd always thought that this was one of the coldest places in the city—a natural spot for an icy wind tunnel—and yet she loved it. She watched the flags of nations from around the world fluttering in the February breeze and then continued on to the stairway that led down to the ice-rink level, glad the January snows had melted and the February snows had not yet fallen. It would be just her luck to slip on the ice while on her way to a rendezvous with Nikolas!

As Candace neared the restaurant a dreaded nervousness began to infuse her. *Cut it out now,* she warned herself in a whisper. But as soon as she walked through the entrance she once again felt her pulse jump. And almost immediately her eyes were drawn to him as if they'd been lured by a magnet.

Seeing her simultaneously, he stood. She noticed he had managed to commandeer a table by the window. Candace mumbled something to the headwaiter, who with a flourish bestowed an especially magnanimous smile on her and escorted her to Nikolas's side. Once again the Mylonis charm, augmented perhaps by a bit of the Mylonis money, had got its way.

It was a miracle that she was able to walk in a straight line to him. He nodded slightly and said, "Thank you," to the waiter and then drew out a chair for her so she'd be facing the rink and the skaters whirling by the glass. He took a seat just across from her so he, too, could watch the skaters.

He'd been right about choosing a place that offered some visual distraction, she decided. If, that is, she could wrest her eyes away from him.

Candace had never before seen Nikolas dressed as he was today. His gray suit, complete with vest, was impeccably tailored. His tie was a blend of chartreuse, gold and gray, the combination of which seemed to highlight the unusual olive green color of his eyes. His shirt was stark white, emphasizing the dark tone of his skin, and he must have just had his hair cut. It was contoured beautifully to the shape of a head that in her estimation was close to perfect.

His smile was wry as he asked, "Do I pass inspection, Candace? At least as a cocktail companion?"

"Please, Nikolas," she said. "Let's try not to...to fence."

"I only imagined you feared you would be confronting an uncouth Greek who—"

"Nikolas!"

He shook his head, reprimanding himself. "What is it about you, Candace?" he asked her. "What is it that provokes me to say things like that to you? Is it because, with your New England coolness, you make me feel so damned unsure of myself?"

A waiter hovered, and Nikolas broke off to ask, "What would you like?"

"A Scotch sour, please," she answered quickly, her heart pounding.

Nikolas ordered the same thing for himself, then picked up a pack of matches that had been left lying on the table. He toyed with them as he said, "Okay. I agree. Let's not fence. A truce, all right?"

"As far as I'm concerned."

"As far as I'm concerned too, *mikrí mou*," he

said softly. Then he added, his voice more normal, "It was good of you to agree to meet me. Especially after the things I said to you the last time we saw each other."

"I'd rather not talk about the last time we saw each other," Candace said steadily.

"Then we won't," Nikolas agreed. "May I say that you look exceptionally lovely?"

There was an almost wistful note to the question, and Candace glanced up in surprise. A strange expression was painted on Nikolas's face. She couldn't pin it to one word or define it by one emotion, but before she could get any further in her analysis he asked, "Has Manos tried to get in touch with you?"

She had to think for a moment. Then she asked, "Manos? Why in the world should he try to get in touch with me? You said something about that on the phone last night and it simply doesn't make sense, Nikolas."

"Manos knows you write for magazines," Nikolas replied. "He undoubtedly thinks you have connections that might be helpful to him. Also, you are a beautiful woman. Manos considers himself a connoisseur of beautiful women." He laughed. "And I might add that he also considers himself irresistible to them. He sought you out last night in that nightclub where he is playing, didn't he?"

"Yes," Candace said, "but only to say hello." Thinking back, she realized that possibly it hadn't been only to say hello. Manos had insinuated that maybe she could write about him. At the time, she'd taken it as a joke. At least, she hadn't attached any seriousness to it.

"Manos has delusions of grandeur," Nikolas said

matter-of-factly. "True, he is extremely good-looking—but there are a lot of good-looking Greeks roaming around the world."

He said this casually. If he was thinking of another extremely good-looking Greek who had gone on to become an internationally famous movie star he gave no indication of it.

"Manos also has a phenomenal conceit," Nikolas continued. "Maybe because his name is Manos he also thinks he has a great talent for composition, this in addition to his abilities in acting and music, of course."

"Because his name is Manos?"

"Manos Hadjidakis, who wrote 'Never On Sunday,' is considered one of Greece's leading composers," Nikolas told her. "He remembers the heritage of Greek folk music in his scores, and his tunes are very popular. Probably half the world can hum 'Never On Sunday.' And personally, I find his work exciting. It is so...Greek. But the only thing Manos Panagoris has in common with Manos Hadjidakis is his first name. I hasten to say that there is no relationship between them.

"So...Manos Panagoris is under the delusion that at any minute Hollywood is going to discover him. Then he will ride around in block-long automobiles, and scores of beautiful women will fall at his feet. He will live on caviar and champagne and wear only custom-tailored suits. And he can set up a theater in his own home so he can sit back and watch his films being replayed night after night.

"Manos," Nikolas concluded, "is a total damned fool!"

He was silent as the waiter set their drinks in front

of them. Then he lifted his glass to reach across and touch it to hers. "May you find happiness, Candace," he said simply.

She couldn't stem the tears that came to her eyes when he said this. And brushing at them with one hand as she lifted her glass with the other, she said, "May you find happiness, too, Nikolas."

He looked as if he was going to answer something to this. But he didn't. She couldn't help wondering what he was thinking or why he repressed these thoughts.

"Hollywood," Nikolas said then, "is not what it seems. Do not have too many false illusions about Nicky Mellin, Candace."

She was so startled she couldn't reply.

Nikolas's smile was sad as he added gently, "I don't flinch at the sound of the name, if that's what you feared. I do flinch at the thought that it should ever be. . .spoken around again. I wouldn't want him to be resurrected. So, that is what the personal favor I said I had to ask you involves. You don't owe me any consideration about this, let me stress that. You tracked me down—though I will never understand how you did it. Nor can I blame you if you're not inclined to give up easily, now that you've found me." He paused thoughtfully. "Actually, I have to admire your persistence. So many years have passed. I really thought any traces of Nicky Mellin had been covered so completely there was no longer a danger of their ever resurfacing."

"I wasn't persistent," Candace said carefully, because this was something she desperately wanted to convince him of. "My 'finding' you, as you put it, was entirely an accident. So was my meeting you. I had absolutely no idea who you were until I went to the library to look up the material on the Epiphany celebrations. I dug out all the old local papers and I might say that the stories connecting you with... with Nicky Mellin are right there, in the library files. Any other journalist could have stumbled upon them at any time."

"I don't think so," Nikolas said. "At least they haven't for about eight years now. It is simply enough to understand that at the time I went to Hollywood the studios wanted to downplay anything foreign about me. This whole thing about ethnic background wasn't as popular then as it is now. I think many people are only beginning to realize America's richness is really derived from the ethnic mixture of her people. Though I wouldn't expect you to go along with that."

"You don't expect very much of me, do you?" Candace asked bitterly.

"I know your type," he said bluntly.

This infuriated her. "Then I guess you could say I know your type, too," she replied, brimming with anger. "An overbearing, arrogant, opinionated, Greek...."

"Afraid to say it?" he taunted.

She could feel the color coming to sting her cheeks, and at the moment she hated him. "I don't usually say words like that," she retorted stiffly.

"Then for God's sake, don't soil your lips on my account," he retaliated.

The pause was electric. Then Nikolas said slowly, "Are we not able to make it through even one drink peacefully?"

"I suppose you blame me for that?"

"I didn't say I blame you. Though God knows you take offense faster than anyone I've ever met. And you are so damned defensive."

"I am not defensive at all! In your book if someone doesn't fall all over themselves to agree with you it has to be because there's something wrong with their thinking. Well, I suppose you got used to people falling all over you when—"

She broke off, horrified at what she had been about to say.

"Watch it!" Nikolas said, his voice low and dangerous. "I will not be misinterpreted by you, Candace! Absolutely not! The people of your profession misinterpreted me from the moment I first left Tarpon Springs to go to the west coast. And when I came out of the hospital I swore I'd never say another word to a reporter for the rest of my life."

"Then why are you speaking to me?" she asked nastily. "I'm here at your invitation, remember?"

"Of course I remember," he said impatiently. "As to why I'm speaking to you—well, I suppose despite myself I still had left in me an ounce or so of hope. I suppose I hoped that, your profession aside, you might also have an ounce or two of decency. If I'm mistaken...then to hell with it!"

Nikolas picked up his drink and drained it in one swallow, then beckoned to the waiter to bring a refill.

Candace had barely touched her own cocktail. And Nikolas, glancing toward it now, asked, "Are you afraid a couple of drinks might loosen you up?"

"No," she snapped, and drew a deep breath. Then she said, trying to steady her voice, "You're right, I guess. We don't seem to be able to get together without going for each other's throats."

"Or without going to bed together?"

She glared at him. "It's...it's rotten of you even to bring that up," she choked.

"Is it, Candace? You know you enjoyed it as much as I did. Don't try to tell me you did not. Right now, even though we may be at each other's throats, as you say, I would hate to put us alone in a room with a bed. You know as well as I do how we would end up."

"You're disgusting, Nikolas!"

"Disgusting, am I?" He actually chuckled at this. "That's a new name for it, *agápi mou*."

"Stop saying things to me in Greek!"

"Afraid I might be insulting you?" he teased. Then his voice softened. "*Agápi mou* means 'my love,' if you must know," he told her.

My love. Her eyes swam with those damnable tears again. The waiter returned, and through a watery mist she noted he'd brought fresh drinks for both of them. She finished her own barely touched drink in one swallow, just as Nikolas had done, and blindly handed the glass to the waiter. If the man glanced at her curiously she wasn't even aware of it. But she did know that Nikolas was intent in his scrutiny of her, and she sighed.

"I'm sorry," he said simply.

She'd taken a handkerchief from her handbag, trying to brush away the tears without being obvious. "You should be sorry," she stammered. "You're—you're horrible! You say the most terrible things to me."

"It was a shock, Candace," he said. "Can't you understand that? You've been a shock to me from the moment you stumbled into my arms. Even before that, when I saw you in Aliki's restaurant, I...." He shook his head. "I can't understand it," he admitted. "But there was something about you...."

"You don't need to act for my benefit, Nikolas," she told him flatly.

Something blazed in those green olive eyes, and he looked at her as if she'd struck him. But he recovered quickly. His face, at least, became impassive, although she sensed it was taking real effort for him to control his voice as he said, "If you think that about me then there's nothing I can say to you."

The need to strike back was a primitive one. She clenched her hands tightly and said, "Doesn't it occur to you I might distrust actors just as much as you distrust journalists?"

Fury? Hatred? A combination of both? She shrank from the expression Nikolas turned upon her.

She saw his hands clench, too, saw his knuckles whiten, and he said in a tone so low she had to strain to hear him, "Never call me an actor again, Candace. Call me anything you like, but never call me that!"

"I...I don't understand you," she said, stumbling over the words.

"No," he agreed, "you don't. I had the crazy idea perhaps you might, but now it is painfully clear to me you don't understand me at all. Regardless, let me just say I am not an actor—I have never been an actor. That, in one sense, was my problem. If I'd been an actor, Candace, I suppose I still might be working in Hollywood today. But when I lost my looks, my talent went with it. That's all I had, you see. I had the right look. And I had enough conceit and the kind of so-called charm that goes with such things. Maybe that is why Manos disgusts me so. I

see a part of my youthful self in him, except I truly
believe I was never that bad.''

Nikolas spoke with difficulty, and Candace winced
for him. She could imagine what this was costing
him, this probing into a past that could only be pain
filled. Her eyes, still shimmering with the last of her
tears, were huge as she looked at him, and her face
was very pale.

Nikolas leaned forward involuntarily and asked,
''Are you all right?''

''Yes,'' she said, but her voice sounded small and
shaky. ''And I'm sorry. I'm very sorry. I never intended to put you through anything like this.''

A dark, upraised eyebrow symbolized skepticism,
and Nikolas asked quietly, ''What do you think you'll
be doing when you write your story, Candace? Or
won't it matter by then? There is a gap between the
time something is finished and the time it is published,
I know that. And by the time your story breaks into
print you will have gone on to other things, right?
Maybe you will have decided to give up writing, for
that matter, or at least the kind of free-lance writing
you are doing now. Maybe you will have married your
'friend' from the nightclub. Manos said the two of
you seemed very. . . close to each other.''

''Manos doesn't know what he's talking about,''
Candace said tightly.

''Doesn't he? Manos isn't an authority on most
things, but I would say he has a good bit of expertise
when it comes to romance. Or shall I simply say
sex?''

She pushed back her chair. ''I'm not going to listen
to you speak like that,'' she said firmly, starting to
rise.

"Sit down, Candace," he said softly. The intent green gaze was commanding.

"Nikolas—"

"Sit down. Or, by God, I'll make you sit down."

"Brute force?" she grumbled as she sank back into her chair. "Damn you!"

"You can damn me all you want," he assured her. "I'm damning myself for being such a fool as to think that if we talked to each other you might be able to understand."

He shook his head and said, "It's no use. Thank you for coming, Candace. That, at least, was generous of you."

He was dismissing her!

Candace glared at him. There was no limit to his audacity! She said, her voice as low as his had been, "I'm not leaving, Nikolas."

"Then I will."

"All right, I can't stop you. But if you try to walk out on me I'll...I'll scream, that's what I'll do!"

For a moment he stared across at her as if she'd taken leave of her senses. Then he grinned. It was a lopsided grin, because the damaged side of his face could not respond fully to impulse. "Would you really?" he queried.

"Try me," Candace challenged.

"I wouldn't dare," he laughed. "God, but you are beautiful when you're angry."

"Nikolas!"

"Excuse me, Candace, but facts are facts. In your profession, you should know that. You can't expect me to shut off all my senses when I'm with you."

"Nikolas!"

"What in hell can we talk about that is safe?" he asked wryly.

"You might tell me why you wanted to see me, for starters."

"You think *that* would be safe?" He shrugged, and as it always did, this made him seem more foreign to her—and even more attractive. He said, "Okay, let's begin again with Manos. He is not brilliant, but he's not stupid, either. He knows you were staying at the Grecian Gardens. He could very well figure out Elene might have your home phone number."

"And you think she'd give it to him?"

"Manos could get anything out of Elene if he really tried," Nikolas said dryly. "He's her Achilles' heel. Appropriate, isn't it? Very Greek."

Candace could only stare across at him.

"Stop looking at me like that, please. It has a strange effect on my concentration."

"I just wish you wouldn't be so caustic when you talk about things being Greek," she said.

"Am I? I wasn't aware of it. I am proud of being Greek, actually. A terrific heritage. We go back thousands of years. Way before Americans were even thought of."

"Nikolas. . . ."

There was a moodiness about him, and Candace had the feeling he was skirting close to the edge of all sorts of things he didn't want to get into. But he said only, "You do like the sound of my name, don't you!"

"Nikolas!"

"See? You are saying it again."

"If you can't discuss anything sensibly," she began, "then there's just no point—"

"Sometimes there doesn't seem to be, does there?" he agreed. "I think we do much better in bed. And, for God's sake, don't say, 'Nikolas!' again."

His laugh was bitter. Then he said slowly, "*Agápi mou*...I wish I could tell you all the things I would like to tell you. But even I do not like the thought of living that dangerously. I would have to trust you completely, and I simply do not."

Candace felt her heart twist, and the pain was intense. She wanted to cry out to him. She wanted to demand how he could possibly think that she, of all people, would ever want to do anything to hurt or betray him. But she forced herself to say carefully, "Trust is a strange thing. It can't be forced on anyone. It can be neither ordered nor inflicted. What I mean to say is there's no way I can make you trust me. There's nothing I can do to convince you I may be worthy of your trust."

"Oh, I wouldn't say that," he replied surprisingly. "There are ways in which you could prove yourself."

"I don't think I especially like the idea of having to prove myself. It shouldn't have to be like that."

"No, I agree," he said. "It shouldn't have to be like that. But then our circumstances are not exactly normal."

"True," Candace said, then opted for what she thought might be safer ground. "Go on about Manos," she urged.

"I am surprised he didn't try to get in touch with you this morning," Nikolas admitted. "Last night when he phoned me he was exuberant about having seen you. Maybe it was because you were there with another man. I think Manos occasionally enjoys sticking the knife into me. He knows I disapproved of Elene marrying him. Too bad her father was not still alive. Aliki says her husband would have thrown Manos out of the house.''

''So Theone and Aliki are both widows?''

''Yes. Theone has been married twice. My uncle was her second husband. But I guess you know that.''

''Yes. Melina told me.''

''And it surprised you, I imagine. I don't wonder. Theone still acts more like a housekeeper than an aunt to me, but then she kept house for my uncle for a long time before she married him. I was gone by the time she came to this country. She never met me until I went back to Tarpon Springs. Uncle Nikolas had sent for me because he was dying, and although I had never intended to go back there after what had happened between us, I couldn't refuse him when the time came.''

''What had happened between you, Nikolas?''

''He wanted no part of me after I went to Hollywood. You might say he put me out of his life. And I was actually glad when the studio wanted to downplay my Greek background. But in the end, blood proved to be thicker than water. I was his namesake . . . and he wanted me with him during those last few weeks.''

''Weren't you afraid the whole Nicky Mellin story would come out if you went back?''

''No,'' Nikolas said. ''I trusted my friends in Tarpon Springs. Paul Morrison, George Andris and one or two others. Over the years, my name was not mentioned in my uncle's household. Whether justified or not, he felt I had been a traitor to him. He had brought me here from Greece and raised me as if I were his son. He wanted me in his business—he owned a fleet of sponge boats. He never gave up hope the industry would come back and one day be as thriving as it was years ago.''

''The sponges were destroyed by a blight, weren't they?'' Candace asked.

''At one time, yes.''

''And didn't the arrival of plastics here hurt the industry, too?'' She remembered reading something about this in the material she had gathered before her trip down.

''The competition from the plastics factories didn't help,'' Nikolas said. ''But it was something else that kept the sponge industry down. It was a lack of manpower. The young Greek men do not want to dive for sponges anymore. The work is too hard. The divers are away at sea for days at a time, sometimes for weeks. And they don't make all that much money. Can you imagine Manos Panagoris being a sponge diver?''

''Only in a movie,'' she said automatically, and Nikolas had to laugh.

''Yes, only in a movie,'' he agreed. ''Funny, isn't it? I dived for my uncle when I was in my teens, but they never cast me in that kind of a role. Generally speaking, I was pure American in Hollywood. Once or twice I had a touch of French or Italian in my ancestry, but they never wanted me to be a Greek. It is good to see that more recently Greek actors have come into their own. Now they can be Greek and proud of it. Flamboyant about it, in fact. It was not that my studio had anything against Greeks. It was the way they wanted me to appear, that's all. And I have to admit it worked. They made a myth out of me. But that's all it was, don't you see, Candace? The myth was never me.''

"Who were you then, Nikolas?''

"A callow kid who did not know any better. I learned the hard way. I learned exactly how much fame and success and money really mean," he said bitterly. "But I guess you could still say at one time I had everything in the world that mattered. Except, perhaps, the most important thing.''

"What was that?''

"Love," Nikolas Mylonis said simply.

Candace recalled that his mother had died when he was born and his father had hated him. He'd come to America as a small boy, and in the intervening years his uncle had evidently tried to bring up Nikolas by himself. He had wanted him in his business. She could imagine a crusty old Greek who wouldn't know how to show affection to an impressionable child in a new land.

"Again, Candace," Nikolas said. "Please do not look at me like that. I will not be responsible for myself if you do. We keep getting away from Manos, don't we?''

"Yes, we do.''

"All right, I suppose I must tell you this." He paused. "It is more important to me than I can possibly explain that Manos Panagoris never finds out anything about my past.''

Candace was puzzled. "I don't know what you mean," she hesitated.

"You see," Nikolas said slowly, "Manos has no idea that once upon a time I was Nicky Mellin.''

CHAPTER FOURTEEN

IT WAS INCREDIBLE. Neither Manos Panagoris, Elene nor Aliki knew anything about Nikolas's illustrious past. Nor did Theone or Melina have any idea at all that the tall, dark man now living in their midst had once been one of the most famous entertainers in the country.

The waiter came to hover at their table again, and Nikolas asked Candace if she would like another drink. When she shook her head negatively he requested the check and, this paid, they walked out together into the winter evening.

Rockefeller Plaza, with the great golden statue of Prometheus poised above the ice rink, looked like a movie set. Prometheus, too, was Greek. A Greek god. Like the man walking beside her. Candace had thought of Nikolas as an Adonis before, and now she did so again. The undamaged side of his face was turned toward her, and although he looked very different from Nicky Mellin, she knew that no one else in the world could ever seem half as attractive to her.

She hadn't put on her gloves, and now Nikolas reached for her hand. She pressed it into his, her heart pounding at the touch of his palm against hers. They stood outside the rink enclosure and watched the skaters whirl around, their costumes splotches of bright color against the white gray ice. And the music that filled the air seemed to echo inside Candace's heart with a poignant sweetness.

She was with Nikolas, and that was all that really mattered. She felt as if she should snatch this moment in time, because there might never be another one. But that idea was too painful even to contemplate. She found herself leaning into him, as if she wanted tangible, physical evidence of his closeness.

"Cold?" he asked, glancing down at her.

Candace shook her head. "No," she answered. She wanted to add, *how could I possibly be cold when you're this near me?*

"Shall we walk for a while?" he suggested.

"Yes," she nodded, because walking with him would postpone the moment when she'd have to say goodbye once again.

People scurried along Fifth Avenue. The cold was bitter—it was not a night for strollers. But Candace felt as if she'd become impervious to the weather, while Nikolas laughed softly by her side.

"If it were spring we could linger all along the way," he said. "We could window-shop, and when we wound up outside the Plaza we could sit by the fountain and watch all the people...if, that is, we could manage to take our eyes off each other."

He released her hand, and Candace decided to put her gloves on. They were warm gloves, yet her hands felt cold in them in comparison to the warmth of his touch.

"Is your ankle up to so much walking?" he asked after a time.

"Yes."

He frowned. "I've never known you to go in for one-word responses, Candace."

"I suppose I'm afraid I might say the wrong thing to you," she admitted.

"My God! Do you have to be that edgy with me? You give me the feeling we are walking on a verbal eggshell. I like it better when you are blunt."

"All right then, Nikolas, I'll be blunt. You leave such gaps in everything you say to me. You skirt around the subjects we discuss. You've told me that all of these people who surround you, with the exception of a couple of old friends, have no idea you were ever...Nicky Mellin."

"That is true."

"Then can't you accept the fact I didn't know it, either? I still wouldn't know if your picture hadn't been in the local paper back at the time when you dived for the cross. Even then, I didn't recognize the picture as you."

"What do you mean by that?"

"I knew I was looking at a picture of Nicky Mellin, that's all. Or someone who looked so much like him that he would have been his identical twin. You'd told me how old you were when you dived and retrieved the cross. There was no one else to choose from that year. So, incredible though it seemed to me, I began to realize that you and Nicky Mellin had to be...the same person. The eyes were very definitely the same." She didn't dare look at him as she said this. "And...well, there is a certain similarity to the names, at least when one's looking for a tie-in."

"Yes," he said almost diffidently. "I suppose there is."

"That's what started me looking for all the material I could find about Nicky Mellin, and I began to put two and two together," she said. "But most people researching the Epiphany celebrations would never have stumbled onto it. When I think it through I can see why you've been safe all along. As it was...I found it very difficult to relate any of the material to you. I still do."

He was silent, and again Candace avoided looking at him. But after a moment she ventured to ask the question she had wondered if she would ever dare to ask him.

"Nikolas," she began, "the last clipping I could find about Nicky Mellin showed him—showed you, that is—in a wheelchair in a private hospital out in California. It was dated more than ten years ago."

"So?"

"Well," she went on slowly, feeling a lump in her throat, "where have you been during all those missing years?"

"Trying to interview me, Candace?"

There was a caustic edge to the question, and she looked up at a profile that could have graced a coin and seemed equally metallic. There was no compromise in the set line of his jaw, and she forced herself to face the truth. Wherever he'd been for the major part of these past ten years, one thing was certain. Nikolas had learned how to protect himself. He'd layered on a veneer that was not apt to be chipped. He telegraphed the message he'd been hurt and intended never to be hurt again.

They walked in a silence that grew increasingly uncomfortable. Then suddenly he asked, "Well?"

"Well what?"

"Are you trying to interview me?"

"Would it make any difference if I said I wasn't?"

"It might."

"I don't think so," Candace said, and as she spoke she could not keep the hurt out of her own voice. "It— it might ruin your whole concept of the media if you found out I'd been honest with you," she said bitterly.

"Candace—"

She didn't let him finish. Just at that moment she saw an empty yellow cab edging near the curb. Quickly she flagged it down.

Before Nikolas fully realized what she was doing Candace blurted, "There's no point to any of this. There's no point to our even trying with each other. Thanks...thank you for the drinks."

She covered the stretch between sidewalk and curb in an instant and was inside the cab before he could rally. Slamming the door she said to the driver urgently, "Please...I don't want him to come after me."

The cabbie obliged with a squeal of tires as he took off down Fifth Avenue and accelerated through a yellow light at the first intersection. Only then did Candace expel her breath and manage to give him her address.

As the cabbie turned left on the next crosstown street he gave her a sympathetic glance in the rear-vision mirror and said, "Was he giving you a hard time, lady?"

"A very hard time," Candace agreed.

CANDACE WAS PREPARED to fight. If Nikolas came to her apartment house she was ready to tell the door-man—who would announce him on the intercom—

not to let him come upstairs. If he phoned she would hang up, she decided firmly.

But the time passed, and Nikolas did neither.

The evening elapsed while she paced the floor waiting for him to do something. And when it became evident he didn't intend to do anything at all, her frustration mounted.

Finally she heated a can of soup, ate it and went to bed. But she had one ear attuned to the possible ringing of the telephone, and she had a very poor night's sleep as a result.

It started to snow the next day—a mushy city snow that did nothing to enliven her descending spirits. Barry called and suggested they get together for lunch and talk over her next story assignment for *Tempo*. He added he expected the offer of a staff job to come through for her any time now. But even this wasn't exciting. She told him she had a slight sore throat and didn't think she'd better go out, and he at once offered to come to her place. Candace, clutching for a way to prevent this, said she'd taken a couple of pills that had made her drowsy. She intended to "sleep in," she said. Then, to placate him, she managed to wax enthusiastic for a few minutes over the prospect of being on *Tempo*'s staff.

Once she'd hung up, she was left with the feeling she was getting herself tied up in a cobweb. What was the old saying? "Oh, what a tangled web we weave when first we practice to deceive...."

She tried to get back to work on her article about career children, but it was impossible to concentrate. She found a soap opera on TV, although she rarely watched in the daytime, but she couldn't sit still long enough to get into the plot's slow development. After this she tried a book, only to find herself reading the same line over and over again.

The apartment became confining to the point of threatening her with claustrophobia. But it was miserable outside and senseless even to consider going for a walk. A wet snow was still falling, and later the gutters would be choked with slush.

Candace seldom minded being alone. She'd been alone during the major part of her marriage, so she was used to it. Actually, she'd always welcomed having time to herself because it gave her the chance to write.

But this was different. Possessed by cabin fever, she decided to put on some warm things and go out. The likelihood she'd get soaking wet and the possibility of falling and spraining her ankle all over again were simply overshadowed by the need to escape from inside four walls. But before she could translate this resolve into action, the phone rang.

Nikolas. It had to be Nikolas!

But it wasn't.

"Candace?" The voice was deeply accented, and she knew at once that it was Manos. "You will have breakfast with me?" he suggested.

Candace glanced at the clock on the kitchen wall. "Manos," she protested, "it's after noon!"

"I sleep late, I eat late," Manos said reasonably. "I come and get you."

"No!" she answered sharply. "I'm sick, Manos. In bed. I'll be in bed all day." She coughed as if to emphasize this and said very clearly, "Sore throat."

"Sore?" Manos asked.

"Yes. Very bad."

"Then tomorrow," Manos said. "We eat breakfast tomorrow."

He rang off before she could tell him that she didn't intend to have breakfast—or anything else—with him today, tomorrow or any other time. And though she admitted she was being foolish and more than a bit paranoid about it, she felt slightly panicked by his phone call. She really didn't need Manos Panagoris on her plate, whether he viewed her as a potential publicity source or as yet another in what must be quite a line of conquests.

Peering through her windows again at the disastrous weather, Candace decided to wait it out inside instead of embarking on a trek to...to where? And for what? She wished Nikolas would phone. The hours ticked by and the silence was getting on her nerves to the point where she wanted to scream, if only to hear the sound of her own voice.

She went through the Manhattan phone directory three times looking for Nikolas's number, but he certainly did not have a listed phone. He'd told her he spent a lot of time in New York and so it stood to reason he must have a place somewhere in the vicinity. She asked information about possible Nikolas Mylonises in Brooklyn, Queens, the Bronx and Richmond—New York's four other boroughs—and drew a blank in all of them. In a couple of instances there were names with similar spellings. But when she tried them, none of the men who answered was Nikolas.

Finally Candace realized she had been overlooking the obvious. Since it wasn't likely that Nikolas would have given Manos her phone number, he must have got it from Elene. And Elene must also have

Nikolas's New York number. At least, it was worth a try.

She dialed the Grecian Gardens with feverish haste and held her breath when she heard the phone ringing at the other end of the line. It would be just her luck to have the motel closed for vacation or repairs! But she recognized Elene's voice immediately when she answered. Candace felt as if she were throwing herself across the miles as she said, "Oh, Elene, it's so good to hear you! This is Candace."

"Who?"

"Candace Mayhew."

"Candace!" Elene's excitement was both beautiful and contagious. "Where are you?"

"In New York," Candace said. "Elene, I had cocktails with Nikolas yesterday and I really need to get in touch with him again. Do you have his number here?"

Pray he is still in New York, she added silently.

"No problem," Elene said smoothly, and in another instant was reading it off to her.

Then Elene said, "Candace, I'm so glad Nikolas called you. He was terrible after you left. Like a bear. He didn't even want to talk to me. He seemed convinced I could have stopped you."

"That's ridiculous."

"Try telling Nick so! When he was about to take off for New York I got up my nerve and said to him, 'Why don't you call her up?' He just glowered at me, but when I wrote your phone number down on a card for him he took it. I've been keeping my fingers crossed ever since."

So that's the way it had been! Nikolas had not asked for her phone number. Elene had given it to him. Even so, he finally had put it to use. Not because he'd wanted to. Rather, he'd thought it essential to get in touch with her on account of Manos Panagoris.

She very nearly blessed Manos!

After she and Elene hung up, Candace paced the floor for fifteen minutes before she could summon enough courage to dial Nikolas's number.

Then, when the phone rang and rang and there was no answer, she succumbed to the anger of pure frustration.

By five o'clock she was ready literally to tear her hair out. And this time, when there was a click at the other end of the line after only two rings—and a deep, masculine voice said, "Hello?"—she was so startled she couldn't respond.

"Hello?" the voice repeated testily. It was Nikolas, unmistakably. She recognized that note of contained impatience.

"It's Candace," she said slowly, and was rewarded by a low, throaty chuckle.

"Well," he said. "Since Muhammad would not go to the mountain, it looks as if the mountain decided it wasn't so immovable after all!"

"Don't go allegorical on me!" she snapped.

He laughed. Then he said, his amusement still lingering, "How did you get my number, Candace?"

"I called Elene."

"I should have told her unlisted means unlisted," he teased, but Candace didn't think this was very funny.

She held the phone receiver out from her ear, staring at it as if it had suddenly taken a human form. Then she slammed it down, and the noise it made echoed in the sudden stillness.

The tears came. Candace buried her head in her hands and let them come, rocking from side to side as she cried it all out. There were a lot of things she had never let herself cry about until now. This was a purging that went way back. She even touched upon grief for her father. And there was also the shame she could still not help but feel sometimes over the ruin of her marriage. And now Nikolas....

Oh, dear Lord, Nikolas!

The phone jangled, and it was second nature to pick up a phone when it was ringing at her elbow. She sniffed a "Hello" into the receiver and heard the quick intake of his breath at the other end of the line.

"Dearest," he said, "please...do not hang up! Candace, I'm sorry. That was a very bad joke."

She could only sputter something unintelligible.

"Oh, *agápi mou*," he said. His deep voice was, in itself, a caress. "We've got to do something about the way we treat each other."

"Please, Nikolas," she managed. "I'm not in the mood for fun and games."

"Nor am I, Candace."

"Nikolas, I called you because of Manos," she said, her voice getting steadier. "You were right about him. He got my number from Elene and he phoned me. I stalled him, but I have the feeling he's going to be a nuisance. I suppose I could have my number changed...."

"I would not put it past Manos to haunt the entrance of *Tempo* magazine's building until he saw you entering or leaving," Nikolas said grimly. "When Manos wants something, he can be astonishingly persistent. Too bad he never puts this quality to a good purpose.''

''What should I do?'' She'd got sufficient control of herself to speak clearly, but she still felt shaky inside.

''I must think about it,'' Nikolas said. ''Precisely what did Manos want?''

''He wanted me to have breakfast with him. I pointed out it was already past lunchtime, but Manos said he sleeps late so he eats late, something like that. He said if we couldn't breakfast together today he'd make it tomorrow. I get the impression he doesn't think there's a woman in the world who could refuse the pleasure of his company.''

''True,'' Nikolas said. ''Manos is a combination of pampered child and scheming adult. His father died when he was quite young, so his mother raised him. She still dotes on him, even though she lives in Greece. Manos says he's going to bring her to this country when he is rich and famous. At least, that is what he promised her.''

''When did he come over from Greece?''

''Only a year or so ago. He has relatives in Philadelphia. Through them he made some connections and got a job playing at a place in Tampa. It was not a long engagement, but Elene met him during the course of it, worse luck. When he found out that Elene was related even indirectly to me, he was about to let her go.''

There was an edge of bitterness to Nikolas's voice, and once again Candace was puzzled. What he'd just said to her didn't make sense, if Manos wasn't aware Nikolas and Nicky Mellin were one and the same person.

She said, "I thought Manos didn't know about your...previous career. Or Elene, either."

"They don't. Manos knows me only as Nikolas Mylonis."

"Then why...?"

Nikolas didn't answer, and the silence between them seemed to speak for itself. Its tension was elastic, and Candace felt as if it were about to snap in her face and flinched from an imaginary sting.

"It is very difficult for me to believe you, Candace," he said then. "I am trying, but I can't help saying you seem as if you carry your naiveté to quite an extreme sometimes."

"Nikolas," she said, touching on despondency, "I don't know what you're talking about. Do you have to be so mysterious? We barely get through one cloud when you fly right ahead and disappear into another."

"I'm not trying to obscure issues, if that is what you are suggesting," Nikolas said slowly. "I just find it hard to believe you....."

She could imagine him shrugging that slightly foreign shrug of his.

Then he said, "It would be better if we talked about this face-to-face."

"You think if you're looking at me you can gauge truth from deception, is that it?" she challenged.

"Perhaps," he evaded. "Regardless, this is not the sort of conversation to continue over a telephone. Do you want me to come to your place or do you want to come to mine? I would remind you it is miserable out, but the choice is entirely up to you."

"I'd prefer to meet on neutral ground," she said stiffly.

Nikolas chuckled. "Are you really that unsure of yourself, Candace? Suppose I swear I won't touch you?"

"Why should I believe you any more than you believe me?"

"Touché," he laughed. "But there is only one way of finding out whether I can be trusted, isn't there? You will have to test me!"

CHAPTER FIFTEEN

NIKOLAS DIVESTED HIMSELF of his fur-lined gloves, storm coat and boots and then started unpacking the contents of the two big brown paper bags he'd brought with him.

"The makings for omelets and a Greek salad, among other things," he told Candace. "I will cook our supper."

He seemed to fill her kitchenette, yet it was so natural to have him there. He flashed her a smile that was unexpectedly sweet and said, "You look tired. Go prop your feet up and I'll bring you a drink. I bought some Greek brandy for us, incidentally, and there is no need to wait to sample it."

Candace could think of a lot of reasons why they probably shouldn't sample it at all, but she decided to hold her tongue. She had no desire to do anything that might spoil this peaceful interlude between Nikolas and herself. She suspected the peace might be short-lived anyway, because that's the way things always were between them.

She walked into the large studio room that served as living area by day and sleeping area by night and paused at the window to look out onto a winter-in-the-city scene. Somehow it seemed a little less depressing now that Nikolas was in her kitchenette pouring Greek brandy for both of them. The bleakness had gone out of things.

It was still snowing, and Candace watched the flakes drifting past the big white globes of the streetlights. Across the way she saw a young girl in a bright red coat trudging hand in hand with a boy who was considerably taller. *Just as Nikolas is considerably taller than I am,* Candace found herself thinking. On an impulse, she opened the window. Wet snow pelted her cheeks, but she heard what she wanted to hear. The peal of laughter. The laughter of two young people in love, in love on a chilly winter night. Watching them, she felt a pang of envy.

Nikolas, coming into the room, asked, "What are you trying to do now? Catch pneumonia?"

"No," Candace said, shutting the window. But for reasons she didn't attempt to define, her heart felt considerably lighter as she turned to face him.

He was wearing a dark green shirt without a tie, and his hair was slightly tousled. He looked big and capable and enormously virile. And once again her heart began to play tricks on her.

"Come on," he said, indicating an armchair and pushing a hassock over to it with one extended foot. She sat down, afraid for a moment he was going to sit on the hassock, which would bring him much too close to her for safety. But he said, "Put your feet up, Candace. Good. Now, sip this slowly."

"Yes, sir," she said with mock obedience as she accepted the glass he held out to her. She sipped, and fire trickled down her throat. But it was a delicious fire.

Nikolas chose a chair that was at a definitely conservative distance away, and it occurred to Candace he was as cautious about proximity as she was. And this, despite her attraction to him, left a rather good feeling!

He said, as if they were at a board meeting and getting down to the agenda, "Now, about Manos."

"Yes."

"He hasn't called you again, has he?"

"No," Candace answered modestly. "I doubt he will until tomorrow. I told him I had a sore throat and was going to try to sleep the day away."

"Good thing he did not suggest he join you."

"Nikolas!" she protested.

"Don't look so shocked. It is not you I am casting aspersions on, it's Manos. And I certainly cannot fault his taste." His glance was brooding. "You are so lovely, Candace," he said. "I suppose you're a classic example of the old saying that one can't tell a book by its cover."

She sat up straighter. "What's that supposed to mean? It has all the earmarks of a dirty crack!"

"I only meant that one would not expect you to be a clever journalist or an expert at ferreting out secrets that were supposed to have been buried forever."

Nikolas stared defiantly at her. "See what I mean?" he challenged. "You are looking at me as if I have outraged you. All that innocence in those huge blue violet eyes. Honestly, Candace, there is no need for you to pretend with me. It's a waste of talent."

She reacted instinctively. She got to her feet and in another moment had strode across to him and dashed the contents of her brandy glass straight in his face. Then she looked around, desperately, for some place to flee. In her studio apartment she had three choices: the kitchenette, the bathroom or the great outdoors.

She opted for the outdoors, not giving a damn it was snowing and she'd be soaked through to the skin in a few minutes. But he caught her just as she grabbed the doorknob.

"I will not let you leave here," he said, his voice tightly contained. "Also, I will be damned if I am going to kiss you into wanting to stay! Go back and sit down and behave yourself!"

Kiss you into wanting to stay. Each word was a slap, and Candace's mind reeled from the accumulation of their impact. But she had no intention of letting Nikolas see how he had affected her. She summoned up all the pride inherent in that New England heritage he had teased her about more than once, and she said icily, "You seem to forget this is my apartment, Mr. Mylonis. And that I am asking you to leave."

He moved back, still watching her. He had taken out a handkerchief and was mopping his face. "A waste of perfectly good Metaxas," he commented. "I must have hit close to home in my appraisal, Candace."

"Pat yourself on the back if it makes you feel any better, Nikolas," she retorted. "I really don't care. Now, your things are out in the kitchen. Please take your groceries with you. All right?"

Candace felt as if she were holding herself together with paper clips and bits of glue, and she wanted only for him to take his things and go. If he didn't do so soon, she was afraid the emotional patch-up job she had hastily effected would crumble. No, something was bound to come undone, but she'd be damned if she'd ever again let Nikolas Mylonis see her with so much as a single tear in her eyes!

Without moving, he said negligently, "I have no intention of leaving."

"Then shall I ask the doorman to have you evicted?" Candace suggested.

"I wouldn't advise that, Candace."

"I don't care what you'd advise, Nikolas. This is my apartment! Please get out."

"I love you," Nikolas said, without even changing his tone of voice or taking his brooding eyes away from her face. "God help me, Candace, I love you...and I don't see what the hell I can do about it!"

Anger sparked. And this, at least, helped to hold the glue together. "No wonder you were so successful in Hollywood!" Candace told him. "Acting's as natural to you as breathing, isn't it?"

"No," he said calmly, "it is not. I've already told you that. And anyway, I am not acting."

"Honestly, Nikolas!" She could not have been more disdainful. "You expect me to believe you?"

"Not necessarily," he said quietly. "I am a realist, though you may not believe that, either, and also I respect your intelligence. The bomb has fallen on me, not on you. It is an invisible bomb, and you can't be expected to know what it's done to me. I will have to convince you in time of the extent of the damage, that's all. And—"

"Oh, stop prattling!" she interrupted irritably, totally annoyed with him.

The echo of her words was followed by stillness as each of them stood eyeing the other mutely. Then Nikolas managed a mere shadow of a smile.

"Perhaps you should try to estimate the number of times I have already apologized to you," he suggested. "And you should keep an accurate count from now on. One day I will have a necklace made for you with a pearl to represent each 'I am sorry.' I only hope the strand will not be so long that it reaches to your toes."

He spoke with a note of chagrin in his voice and she looked up at him in surprise. An expression of wistfulness bordering on sadness met her gaze.

"Once again," he said, "please forgive me, Candace."

There was a charisma to him that made her shiver. Manos Panagoris could take lessons from Nikolas, who was a master at the art of exerting charm when he chose to do so.

He said, "If you really want me to leave I'll go. But I would prefer to stay and pour you another brandy and talk to you about why I came here in the first place. I swear to you I will not get out of line again in my conversation."

Candace shook her head. "It's no use," she said. "It just doesn't work with us. We both should realize by now that this is true. I'm not saying you may not have good intentions, but in five minutes...."

"In other words," he interpreted, "you are saying we have two options open to us. Either we can fight with each other...or we can go to bed together."

"That's not what I'm saying at all!" she objected hotly.

"On the contrary, that is what you have suggested, Candace, whether you realize it or not. All right, let's try again, shall we? We're adults, and we have something between us that should be discussed. Let's try to get back to it and stay on the subject.''

Candace was afraid in another minute he'd be holding out his hand and offering to shake hers in agreement, but he didn't. Not at all convinced, she moved back to her chair and accepted a fresh glass of brandy when Nikolas gave it to her. She was waiting for him to make a blithe comment as he did so, and although his eyes twinkled, he managed to refrain.

''To get back to Manos,'' he said. ''As I've already mentioned, he can be persistent. Also, I think he must see a dual attraction in you. A very lovely young woman who would be a sufficient allure in herself. And also a writer who may be able to do a profile of him that would give him the big chance he is looking for. With two such incentives, you are not apt to get rid of him so easily.''

''Thanks a lot.''

''Well. . . facts are facts.''

Candace was thinking about something Nikolas had said when he'd first phoned her. Something about why he needed to see her for his own sake, in addition to what was important to Elene. She asked about this now, and Nikolas frowned.

''What involves Elene, as I'm sure you must have guessed, is Manos,'' he said. ''He has tried to get Melina to go out with him, but Elene doesn't know about this. And I have told Melina I will deal with her severely if she starts to brag about it and the stories get back to Elene. Elene took quite a liking to you in the brief time you were in Tarpon Springs. It would hurt her very much if you were to encourage Manos.''

''*Me* encourage Manos?'' The mere idea was so

repellent Candace couldn't believe he was suggesting it. "Are you out of your mind, Nikolas?"

"I don't think so," he said. "But I like your reaction to the idea anyway. So...Manos really doesn't appeal to you?"

'Why would I covet someone else's poisonous snake?" she said by way of an answer.

"He is very good-looking," Nikolas said quietly.

"Isn't he, though!" She didn't bother to spare the sarcasm. "Is that all you think of, Nikolas? Someone's looks?"

"I must remind you," he said slowly, "for a number of years my own looks were my stock-in-trade. When my face went down the drain, my career went with it."

She glared at him. "Don't you ever look in the mirror?" she demanded impatiently.

"Yes, of course I look in the mirror. When I shave."

"Then you must know, damn it, that you're...." Candace's voice faltered as she groped for the right phrase.

The momentary pause was a taut one. Then, as if looking for the answer, Nikolas stared into his brandy rather than at the woman sitting across from him.

"Far more attractive than Manos Panagoris could ever hope to be," Candace said, angry because he needed her to say the words. And yet, she couldn't have left them unsaid.

Then she felt that magnetism again, a tug that forced her to look into his green olive eyes.

"Thank you," he said, and added wryly, "Despite what you may say, Candace, I am well aware my face is a mess. There are scars—'' he touched them lightly with those long, slender fingers ''—and one side that can't entirely respond to the other side. So if you honestly do find me attractive—aside from the crazy biological urge we seem to have for each other—then I can only think it goes beyond my looks, beyond the surface. And that means a great deal to me. For so long I got by on my looks alone. Now, even if I could have Nicky Mellin's looks back by snapping my fingers, I would never again want to get by on physical appearance alone. In that respect, I have learned a full lesson.''

''And in other respects, Nikolas?''

The question was out before she could stem it. But he didn't hedge. He said, ''I am beginning to think all the other things I thought I'd learned may perhaps not be so valid after all. You see, I was left with a bad case of bitterness and a pretty profound distrust of most people. Especially people of your profession. Sometime, maybe, I will tell you about Nicky Mellin. The whole damned story. Then you can judge for yourself.''

She had the feeling that as he was saying this Nikolas was throwing down a symbolical gauntlet. It was up to her to pick it up, and she knew whatever she did with it was going to be very important to both of them.

Did she want Nikolas to tell her ''the whole damned story'' of Nicky Mellin? If he were to do so and anything ever came out in print that touched on it, he would blame her, whether or not she was responsible. But as a writer how could she learn anything about Nicky Mellin. . .and hope to resist recording it?

Temptation? Yes, she had to admit the temptation would be close to overwhelming. It would be very, very hard not to put such a story down on paper.

Nikolas, she thought ironically, was making an Eve out of her. Except that the apple in this particular garden of Eden was a journalistic plum!

The phone rang, and she blessed the interruption.

Nikolas said, "Shall I get it? It could be Manos."

Candace shook her head. "He's not the only person who might decide to call me," she said, being a bit snippy about this.

And, in fact, it wasn't Manos. It was Barry.

"Oh," Candace said in response to a question about her sore throat, "it's much better. I needed a day of rest, that's all. No, I don't want you to bring over hot chicken soup, Barry. No, you don't have to pretend to be a Jewish mother." She tried to laugh and couldn't.

She saw Nikolas walk across the room and switch on the stereo to full volume. He grinned across at her wickedly, and she wanted to slap him. And in answer to yet another question on Barry's part, she said, "Yes, I do have company. Unexpected. My old friend from Albany."

They brought the conversation to a close and she faced Nikolas, outraged.

"You didn't have to do that, damn it!" she sputtered.

"I imagine he said he hoped the friend was female," Nikolas taunted.

That was exactly what Barry had said. But before she could think of a suitable answer Nikolas refilled her brandy glass again. "Why don't we get back to business, okay?"

"Look," Candace said. "I'm not about to get sloshed with you on Greek Metaxas or whatever it is."

"Afraid we'll wind up going to bed?" Nikolas teased. Then he sighed elaborately. "Honestly, Candace," he complained. "Have you no faith in me at all? Have you forgotten that I told you I wouldn't touch you? A promise is a promise, *agápi mou*."

He didn't touch her for the rest of the evening, even though before very long she was shaking inwardly with the desire to have him do so and suspected he was well aware of this. He instructed her in the art of making a Greek salad, finger-tearing pieces of chicory and romaine, adding halved cherry tomatoes, wonderful Greek olives, chunks of creamy feta cheese and slices of a huge, juicy onion and tossing this all together with pure olive oil and just the right amount of salt. Then he made a mixture of mushrooms and some sort of sausage and used it as an omelet filling, and his omelets were like clouds. He'd had a bottle of Greek white wine chilling in her fridge, having put it there immediately upon his arrival, and it went perfectly with the meal. She decided whatever else she could manage to find fault with in Nikolas could not be extended to his cooking.

He was suspiciously cheerful all the time he was fixing the food, and now and then she couldn't help looking questioningly at him. He was being too good to be true! He caught a few of these glances and laughed as if he knew a secret she didn't, and this, of course, was infuriating. But all in all it was a good evening. A very good evening.

Nikolas insisted upon washing the dishes, so Candace dried them and put them away. Once, their fingers touched as he was putting a plate into the dish rack at the side of the sink, and she felt a tremor go through her as if she'd been shocked by an electric current. She was careful after that to avoid skin-to-skin contact. It looked as if Nikolas had the strength to hold to his promise of keeping his hands off her, but Candace wasn't sure she had the stamina to maintain her own distance from him, under these circumstances. So very near. . . yet so very far.

The dishes done, she poured coffee for both of them, and as he stirred sugar into his, Nikolas asked, "What are you working on at present?"

"A story about career children."

"For *Tempo*?"

"No. I did a different sort of thing for *Tempo* involving something on the same subject, and this one is a spin-off. I don't have a specific assignment for it, I'm just doing it free-lance."

"And what about *Tempo*?"

"It looks as if I'm going to be offered a job as a staff writer."

"Oh?" Candace saw an eloquent eyebrow rise, but Nikolas only said, "Are you going to take it?"

The question made her stir restlessly. "I don't know," she confessed. "I suppose I'd be a fool not to. Yet I'm not all that crazy about the thought of just writing for one magazine. I'm not sure I want to tie myself down like that."

"To the magazine or to Barry Gehrich?"

"Both, I suppose," Candace admitted. But she added hastily, "I really should say that Barry's a good friend. He's been very helpful to me."

"Yes, I imagine he has," Nikolas said dryly. "It would be easy enough to be helpful to you, if one had the opportunity.'' He paused, then said, ''Do you care for Gehrich?''

''Really, Nikolas. . . .''

''Please don't evade me, Candace. It's important.''

''Well, then, yes. I like Barry—to a point.''

''But, like Manos, he can be persistent?''

She smiled. ''Certainly not in the same way,'' she answered lightly, and amended, ''No, never in the same way.''

Yet there was a grain of truth in Nikolas's suggestion. Barry had been increasingly persistent of late. And he had been angry about Manos Panagoris's appearance at their table the other night. She suspected if the others hadn't been with them when he brought her home there might have been a scene. A scene that she had no desire to star in.

''Second thoughts?'' Nikolas asked perceptively.

''Not exactly.''

''Is Gehrich in love with you?''

''What is this, Nikolas? An inquisition?''

He shook his head. ''No, it's merely a thought that has come to me. A possible solution for our problems—mine as well as yours. Both Manos and Gehrich would be thwarted, and I wouldn't have to worry about Elene in connection with Manos and you. Maybe I could even think of something to do about Manos that would get him on the right track. I admit I've got to give considerably more attention to that. For the present, though, this would take care of everything.''

Candace laughed. ''You sound as if you've invented a wholesale panacea,'' she told him.

''Not quite. But it is one that would serve the purpose on a temporary basis.''

"I can't wait to hear what you have in mind, Nikolas."

"Can't you?" Nikolas said, a gleam in his eyes. "Well, then, how about you and I pretending we are engaged?"

CHAPTER SIXTEEN

How ABOUT YOU and I pretending we are engaged!

"I thought you were going to be serious," Candace said resentfully. "I suppose I should have known better."

"I am serious," Nikolas said, and she looked up quickly, surprised by the solemn sound of his voice. The surprise was reinforced by the expression on his face. "It would be useful to me to have a fiancée just now," he explained. "And not only because of Manos Panagoris."

"Oh? Are some of the women on your string becoming too persistent?"

Nikolas shrugged. "Perhaps. As I say, it would be a solution to our problems. Certainly Manos would be out of your hair."

"He hasn't even tried to get *in* my hair yet," Candace pointed out.

"Would you prefer to wait until he does?"

"No!"

"Okay, then. It would also give you time to take a breather from Barry Gehrich. Who knows? Absence may make the heart grow fonder."

"Absence?"

"I thought you might want to go back to Tarpon Springs and finish your assignment," Nikolas suggested with suspicious casualness.

"And where will you be?" Candace queried steadily.

"I have business here in New York that will keep me occupied for the rest of the month," Nikolas said. "Then I will need to be in London for a week or so during the first part of March. Of course you could come with me if you like."

"I think not, thank you just the same!"

He laughed. "What a trusting soul you are, Candace. May I say our temporary engagement would carry with it the guarantee I made to you earlier today? In other words, I would not attempt to force my attentions on you. You would be as safe as if I were your brother."

Candace felt a surge of hysteria at this and had to fight the impulse to laugh wildly. She'd never had a brother, but she knew that fraternal feelings and the emotions Nikolas aroused in her had absolutely nothing at all in common.

She was also beginning to feel as if she'd stumbled into the midst of a puzzle. There were too many things involving Nikolas she didn't understand. Some of them went back to the time of Nicky Mellin. Others were much more recent.

"Just what business are you in, Nikolas?" she ventured.

"I have my fingers in a number of things," he evaded.

"Here in New York?"

"Some in New York, yes. Some in other places." He grinned. "Nothing illegal, if that is what you're worrying about. At least, no more illegal than the businesses of most people."

"And you say you live in New York a lot of the time?"

"I have lived in New York most of the time for several years," Nikolas answered. "I came here as soon as I was able to...to function again. It can be a remarkably anonymous city, Candace. I found I could literally get lost here—and that is exactly what I wanted to do for a long time. Get lost...in a personal sense, that is. Fortunately, the first agent I had when I went to Hollywood was a great help to me. Through him, I met a lawyer who became my business manager and a very close personal friend, as well. He was a wonderful person—you would have liked him. He died five years ago. I was with him until his last hour, and he told me he'd had the immense satisfaction of seeing me come back and be all the better for it. I will never forget those words."

They'd kept the lamps on low, and in the dim light Nikolas's face had the appearance of being etched with dark brush strokes. Watching him, Candace felt this to be symbolic. There had been so many shadows for Nikolas. So many shadows.

She tried to suppress the pang of pity that threatened, because it would be dangerous for her to soften toward Nikolas. Emotionally she was always on treacherous ground with him. Yet at such a moment as this, it was impossible not to yearn to go to his side, to bend and kiss his forehead, and then....

Nikolas said, "Gerry, my lawyer friend, handled the transfer of my assets, so when I was ready I had the funds to launch a new career. He instructed me during those earlier years when I was making pictures. *The Wall Street Journal* and some of the financial magazines became my required reading. A strange twist of fate, wouldn't you agree, for a Greek kid who thought he was going to grow up and fish for sponges all his life? In many respects, I was very lucky.''

He stirred restlessly. ''That's enough about me,'' he said. ''Let's get back to the subject at hand. I have proposed to you, woman, and you haven't said a damned thing about it.''

''I don't think that's very amusing,'' Candace replied. ''Nothing is sacred to you, is it? Not love, not marriage, not anything else. Well, mock proposals are not exactly my sort of thing.''

He took her up on this quickly. ''You would prefer a real one, Candace?''

''Don't be ridiculous!''

''That is what I thought you'd say. Although. . . .''

''Yes?''

''Contrary to what you may think, marriage *is* sacred to me. That is why I never married. If I ever do, it will be for life. Divorce is something I do not believe in.''

Candace drew back as if he'd stung her. ''Thanks,'' she said bitterly.

''I wasn't speaking about you!''

''I was married. . .and divorced, Nikolas.''

''Yes, I know. You told me so at the very beginning of our somewhat precarious relationship. But you didn't tell me why.''

''Why I divorced?''

''Of course I am curious,'' he said. ''Though I am not suggesting you tell me now. You don't owe me any explanations about anything, Candace.''

''Suppose I want to tell you,'' she said, and the surprising thing about it was she did.

"Then, please do," he urged.

"Okay," Candace said, feeling a slight nervousness. "I married Jeff when I was very young. I was twenty but young for my age. I'd been my father's little girl. Looking back, I can see he overprotected me. I didn't know much about men when I got married. And I knew even less about sex."

Her eyes were shadowed, her unhappiness visible. Nikolas said impulsively, "Candace...."

"No," she said, shaking her head. Now that she'd started she had to get it all out. "I married a man who was a few years older than I was in years and a lot older in experience. I think he knew we'd made a mistake long before I did. I merely thought the reason I couldn't respond to him was because I was...frigid. That's what he told me. So you see, I'm not at all the way you think I am, Nikolas."

"Dearest—"

"No," Candace said. "Hear me out. I hated the thought of divorce as much as anyone could possibly hate it. It went against everything I believe in. Also, Jeff was content to let our marriage ride because he wanted a future in politics. So he didn't press for a divorce because he feared his name would be tainted, even in this liberated day and age. But then he met a woman who meant enough to him to risk it. And, maybe conveniently—though I know this really does sound bitter—she had excellent political connections through her family. I think Jeff knew he couldn't go wrong with her. Our divorce became final over a year ago, and Jeff married her almost immediately."

Nikolas was sitting back and looking at her thoughtfully, and he didn't say a word.

"I went back to work," Candace said, expelling a

breath of relief. "I got a secretarial job in Albany, and I began to write articles on the side. I was fortunate to have some success, and when I started selling to better markets I moved to New York last fall. Just before that, my mother had remarried. Then she, my sister and I decided the only sensible thing to do with the old family home in Albany was to put it up for sale. We got a good price for the house, and my mother insisted we divide the profits three ways. That's given me enough of a nest egg to be able to keep going until I can support myself fully with my writing. We had a lot of nice old things in the house. I suppose you'd call them family heirlooms. Furniture, china, glassware—that sort of thing. We divided them up, too. My share's in storage and will be. . . until I have a place of my own one day. But I don't expect that to happen for quite a while. You have to sell a lot of articles to make a real living."

"Suppose you were to go on staff at *Tempo*?" Nikolas asked now.

"I'd still be cautious, I guess," Candace answered. "Perhaps I've learned to be cautious. One day, though, I'll have a place of my own."

"When you marry again?"

"No. I don't intend ever to marry again."

Candace's voice was flat as she said this, and she didn't dare look at Nikolas. Because in these few minutes of going into a past she hated to discuss, an overwhelming truth had swept over her. It was true that she hadn't intended to marry again. And suddenly she knew the chance of her doing so was more unlikely than ever. The only man she could imagine marrying now was this tall, dark Greek who was looking at her with a strangely puzzled expression in his beautiful eyes.

She loved Nikolas Mylonis. If nothing else, he'd proved to her she certainly was not frigid, whatever else she might be! But her love went way beyond the sensual, as she'd already realized. And tonight, here in her apartment, he had underlined the role he could play in her life. Tonight they had shared a curiously domestic little scene. There had been humor and affection between them and an ease of communication such as she'd never before known with a man.

She'd had a glimpse of what it would be like to share all the trivialities that would be a part of daily living with Nikolas. There might be a lot she didn't understand about him, mysteries to be solved, but already he'd come to be so dear to her she couldn't face the thought of spending the rest of her life without him.

"Candace," he said slowly. "If you are trying to make me feel like a heel, you have succeeded. I had no right to make you dig up things best forgotten. Your husband must have been the most consummate of fools, but he is behind you now. You have your whole wonderful life ahead of you."

Nikolas came across to her now, tall, graceful and enormously beloved. He lifted her chin in the curve of his fingertips and bent to kiss her lips. There was no passion in his kiss, no fire, but it was so exquisitely tender that it brought tears to Candace's eyes.

He said huskily, "I'd better get out of here before I go back on my word. One thing, though. Are we engaged, quote unquote?"

An eventual separation between them was inevitable. Candace knew that. But a mock engagement would at least stave it off.

She nodded and tried to make light of it. "Under the circumstances," she said, "why not?"

"THERE IS THE MATTER of a ring," Nikolas said over the phone at ten o'clock the next morning.

It had stopped snowing, and through her window Candace could see a Department of Street Cleaning truck pushing the slush into a grimy pile along the curb.

She had been trying again this morning to do some work on her career-children article and so far had succeeded in writing the same half-page seven times. Now she asked, "What about a ring?"

"No one will believe we are engaged if I don't put a ring on your finger," Nikolas said. "I have a conference at ten-thirty, but I can meet you for lunch after that. We could go to Tiffany's and choose something."

"Tiffany's no less!"

"Only the best for you, *agápi mou*."

"Nikolas," Candace said seriously, "I've slept on the idea, and the more I think of it the more ridiculous it seems. No one's going to believe we're engaged."

"And why not, may I ask?"

"Because we won't act engaged, for one thing."

He laughed and said, "I will if you will."

"Nikolas, honestly...."

"You are protesting too much. Look, you can certainly stand to keep my ring on your finger in order to accomplish all our goals, can't you? Why don't we say for March, April and May. Up until the end of May. What about right through to Memorial Day?''

''Lovely connotation,'' Candace said wryly. ''Anyway, that's more than three months.''

''You're going to quibble about a few days?''

''All right, then. Memorial Day.''

''Come to think of it,'' he said, ''let's pick the ring first. Then you won't be so likely to change your mind again. Tiffany's at noon, okay?'' And before she could answer, he hung up.

It was crazy, utterly crazy. Candace kept telling herself this for the next hour. Nevertheless, she found herself taking special pains with her makeup as she prepared to dress. She decided to wear a deep green wool suit with a matching plaid cape, a present she'd bought for herself after the sale of her first major article. It was the most expensive item of clothing she owned.

Even so, when she met Nikolas at Tiffany's she knew after a quick glance at him that one sleeve of his suit had probably cost as much as her whole outfit. He was very much the smart executive this morning, and there was no hint of the young Greek boy who had come from a remote Aegean island not all that many years ago. He carried a black leather coat, and his superbly tailored suit was a deep tone of charcoal with a gray-and-white pattern. His shirt was light yellow, and the tie he wore picked up the other colors nicely. Even his gold-strapped wristwatch looked expensive.

Candace had never been inside Tiffany's before and she was duly impressed by the store. But she was even more impressed by the attention shown to Nikolas. She soon realized he must have phoned ahead, for an assortment of rings had obviously been selected especially for them to look at. The mundane matter of price wasn't even mentioned.

Candace was staggered by all the rings, and finally she said, "They're a bit overpowering, Nikolas."

"You don't care for diamonds?" he asked quickly.

"It isn't that. But I...."

"When is your birthday, Candace?"

"September."

"Sapphire is the stone for September, is it not?" Nikolas asked the clerk. And when the man nodded, he said, "Then that is perhaps what we should look at. A sapphire would match my fiancée's eyes."

The sapphire they finally selected was square cut and a deep, incredible blue. Nikolas insisted on slipping it onto her finger himself, and the fit was perfect. It was a simple ring and all the more glorious because of this. As Candace stared down at it, she remembered hearing a good sapphire could often cost more than a diamond.

She started to say she thought they should look at something smaller, but with an imperious wave of his hand Nikolas decided the matter was settled.

Twenty minutes later they were seated at the best table in a popular English grill on East Fifty-fourth Street, and the waiter was bringing champagne.

After he'd toasted her, Nikolas said, "I thought we should, today, go in for a touch of your national heritage, cuisinewise, Candace." He looked around the room with a satisfied expression. "All very British, wouldn't you say? Matter of fact, it was an associate of mine in London who recommended this place to me."

An associate of his in London. And he'd had some sort of mandatory business conference this morning. He'd also told her, more than a bit vaguely, he had his "fingers" in an assortment of different enterprises. Her curiosity was piqued once again, but she refrained from asking questions. This, of all moments, was not the one in which to be inquisitive, she warned herself decisively.

Nikolas was in an exuberant mood, and Candace realized she'd never before seen him so carefree. She had the feeling he'd be content to sit and sip champagne all day. Finally she suggested she was getting hungry. Then she wondered how she was going to manage to eat all the food that was placed before her.

The food was indeed very British and very good. They were served a succulent mixed grill of thick lamb chops, kidneys and bacon, accompanied by brussels sprouts. There was even a trifle for dessert, laden with whipped cream.

Candace was amused by Nikolas's choice of a luncheon place for ethnic reasons, much as she was enjoying it. And it occurred to her he seemed to mix "England" with "New England" when it came to heritage. She was tempted to tell him at one time her ancestors had fought the Crown in order to achieve American independence but thought better of this. She had a greater desire not to do anything that would affect Nikolas's mood. It was the first time she could remember there having been no conflict between them. And although she had the uneasy feeling this was a situation that couldn't last, she was determined to enjoy it for as long as she could.

Finally he looked at his watch and said, "I have to get back at four for an important overseas phone call, or I wouldn't break this up.'' He paused briefly, then asked, "Dinner tonight?''

"I couldn't possibly eat another thing before morning," Candace answered hazily.

"Did you have some other plans for tonight?'' Nikolas pursued.

"None, to be honest.''

"I'll call you later then,'' he said. "In the meantime, Candace, why don't you get some rest? You've been looking rather tired lately.''

"I think I may just do that,'' she agreed sweetly.

They parted outside the restaurant, Nikolas brushing her lips lightly in farewell. And as she watched him stride off in the direction of Madison Avenue she remembered he hadn't said where it was he had to get back to. Thinking about this, Candace also realized she had absolutely no idea where he might actually live.

As she slowly walked up Park Avenue, opting to get a little exercise by going home on foot despite the cold of the afternoon, she felt strangely at odds without Nikolas by her side. What an effect the man had on her! When she was with him she had the feeling she was surrounded by him—but it was a feeling she liked. Although he was dominant, he wasn't domineering, and there was quite a difference. She felt warmed by him, safe with him.

Safe with Nikolas? She had to laugh at the thought, and yet primarily it was true. The only thing that she was in real danger of where Nikolas was concerned was losing her heart. And that would be an irretrievable loss.

As she neared her building she stopped on a street corner for a red light. All at once the gloomy truth of the situation struck her. Losing her heart to Nikolas Mylonis was something that had already happened!

Candace waited by herself in the lobby for an elevator and wondered in silence how it would be to go on living without a heart once her three-month engagement was over.

CHAPTER SEVENTEEN

DARKNESS CAME EARLY on these winter afternoons, and the apartment seemed dim and cheerless. After a time Candace brewed herself a cup of tea and then tried to get back to her career-children article, but it was slow going. The dinner hour came and passed, and because she was not used to eating so much at lunch Candace decided tonight she'd just settle for toast and hot cocoa before going to bed. She forced herself back to the typewriter, managed one good sentence and then another. But one ear was listening for the telephone, since Nikolas had said he would call.

The ring that finally interrupted her was not the telephone—it was the house intercom. Candace's pulse skipped a beat as she realized Nikolas must have decided to come to see her in person. She knew this wasn't wise, regardless of his promises to her. Neither of them could tolerate such proximity without emotional danger.

Was he already going back on his word after only a nine-hour "engagement"? Approximately that much time had passed since he'd placed the shimmering sapphire ring on her finger in Tiffany's.

He has no right to do this, she was thinking angrily as she crossed the room and answered the intercom. But then she discovered it wasn't Nikolas being announced. It was Barry Gehrich.

Barry was probably the last person Candace wanted to see just now, with the possible exception of Manos Panagoris. Yet there seemed nothing else she could do except say, "Send him up, please."

As she met him at the door, she knew immediately she was in for trouble. There was an unaccustomed grimness to Barry's expression, and he didn't even smile as he greeted her. She took his coat, offered him a drink and decided she'd better fix one for herself, too, so she poured Scotch on the rocks for both of them.

Barry was sharp. As she gave him his glass his glance fell to her hand and to the beautiful blue jewel that adorned the proper finger.

She saw his eyes narrow and his mouth tighten. But he said casually enough, "I see something new has been added."

"Yes."

"When?"

"Today."

"An engagement ring, I take it. Even though it's not the conventional diamond."

Barry made the question sound more like an accusation, and this annoyed Candace. But she only said levelly, "Yes. It's an engagement ring."

"You got up from your sickbed to go and get yourself engaged?" he asked, not without a trace of sarcasm. "Who is it, Candy? Not that Greek musician you met in the nightclub, I hope."

"No," she said swiftly, "of course not."

Barry sat down in the nearest armchair, his eyes morose as he surveyed the Scotch. "I should have known there had to be a reason why you were stalling me," he said. "Sore throat, hell!"

"It wasn't my intention to stall you, Barry." Now Candace sat down herself, hating every minute of this. It really hadn't been her intention to be unfair to him. She'd welcomed his friendship these past few months and she was grateful to him for his many professional kindnesses. True, she'd been getting worried lately about the personal side of things between them. But even so. . . .

"My fault," Barry said, downing half of his drink. "I thought we had a...well, a better relationship than this. You know, something between us. Was it all on my side, Candy?"

"You've been a very good friend," she said carefully.

"I think you know I'm not talking about friendship. God, I've been an idiot."

"Please, Barry. Talking like that isn't going to get us anywhere. . . ."

"Get us anywhere? I've never had a chance of getting anywhere with you, have I, Candy? What was it you really wanted? The staff job at *Tempo*?"

She flinched, but before she could deny his accusation, Barry shook his head sadly. "I shouldn't have said that," he admitted. "Let's keep business out of this. What you do or don't do as far as *Tempo* is concerned has nothing to do with what I'm talking about now. I went at it easy with you, Candy, because I knew you'd had a rough time with your marriage. We'd both been burned. I'd had longer to get over it, of course. Hell, I was over it well before I met you. But there was still something so frightened about you. . . ."

He surveyed her unhappily. "I guess I found your vulnerability appealing. But that isn't there anymore, is it? You've been different since you came back from that damned Greek place in Florida. That's why I wondered if the fellow the other night...."

"Nothing I've done has had anything to do with him," Candace said truthfully. But then she realized this was not entirely so. Nikolas had suggested this mock engagement to thwart Manos—and to thwart Barry, as well. She felt a faint touch of shame as she remembered their plan.

"Well, are you going to enlighten me?" Barry asked.

"What do you mean?"

"Who is he? Do I know him?"

Candace shook her head. "No, you wouldn't know him," she said. "I did meet him in Tarpon Springs, though. And...he is Greek. His name is Nikolas Mylonis."

Nothing could have prepared her for Barry's reaction. His face ran a gamut of expressions as he slammed his now empty glass down on her coffee table. He looked at her loathingly and said with an open nastiness, "Well, you do go for the jackpot, don't you, baby?"

Candace was stunned, and a horrible feeling began to come over her. She could think only of Nikolas having said he had his fingers in all sorts of pies, or words to that effect. But what kind of pies? Organized crime, maybe? She suppressed the thought— she hated it—yet it would explain a lot of things. Including the look on Barry's face as he stared at her.

"Oh, my God, Candy," he said, disgusted. "I don't think I can bear up under all the innocence you're turning on me. What the hell did you expect me to think?"

"I had no idea," she said. "And that's the truth!
Nikolas's name certainly means something to you
that it doesn't mean to me. I told you I only met him
recently, in Tarpon Springs. In fact, he was the man
who caught me when I twisted my ankle."

"How fortunate!" Barry said. "You didn't manage to stage that fall by any chance, did you? You
couldn't have tumbled into better arms."

Candace was reminded of an accusation Nikolas
had made and felt herself flushing. Then Barry
laughed, a short and very unpleasant laugh.

"Am I hitting too close to home?" he demanded.

"No," she snapped. "You're entirely wrong about
all of this. The name Nikolas Mylonis means absolutely nothing to me except it happens to belong to
someone I know. . .and love."

The conviction in these last two words rang true
and even made an impression on Barry. Candace
hadn't intended to speak them aloud, and now she
could only hope they wouldn't get back to Nikolas.
She would put nothing past Barry, judging by his expression at the moment. He looked as if he'd take
any chance for retaliation he could get.

He said harshly, "Love! Well, I suppose it's easy
enough to fall in love with someone when you know
their pockets are lined with gold. Don't you ever read
The Wall Street Journal, Candy?"

"No," she said steadily, "I don't. The world of
business and high finance has never interested me."

"Then you'll have to alter your life-style," Barry
said abruptly. "A good wife should at least know
what her husband does, shouldn't she? Yours—your
intended, I should say—plays in a very exalted
league. International finance, banking, shipping, im-

porting. . . you name it. I guess you could say Nikolas Mylonis heads his own conglomerate, and one that stands up pretty well to the giants. There is even talk of his acquiring *Tempo*, provided we do well enough through our first year. Maybe he'll give the magazine to you for a wedding present.''

Candace couldn't believe what Barry was saying. She stared at him numbly, wanting to challenge everything he was telling her. Yet she knew in her heart he was telling the truth. Nikolas had mentioned his lawyer friend had safeguarded his assets after the terrible accident had ruined his career in pictures. Later he'd been able to transfer these assets in some anonymous way so all traces of their ever having belonged to Nicky Mellin had been covered. Then, when he was well enough, Nikolas had started on a new kind of career. He certainly had the purpose and the ruthlessness necessary for big business, she thought weakly. Yet he also had so much compassion. . . .

''You look as if you're seeing ghosts,'' Barry accused. ''Have I conjured up images to haunt you, Candy?''

''I don't know,'' she said wearily. ''I just don't know, Barry.''

''Why so unnerved?'' he taunted. ''Is it so upsetting to find out you're going to marry a man who's worth millions? You'll never have to touch a finger to a typewriter again for the rest of your life.''

Wouldn't she? In three months her engagement masquerade with Nikolas would be over. So there were no gold-paved corridors in her future. She needed to make money from her writing now, and she'd need it just as much once Nikolas walked out of her life.

Suddenly she knew she couldn't bear to have Nikolas walk out of her life. And yet, especially now, there was no way at all anything between them could ever be permanent. The tremendous physical attraction would always be there, to be sure, but that simply wasn't enough to make their relationship last.

What really hurt Candace, though, was realizing that even as she'd agreed to Nikolas's proposal in jest, she had cherished the secret hope that somehow, over these next three months, things would change between them so that what had started as a joke would become genuine. Now she knew this could never be.

She brought her thoughts to a quick stop, appalled by the truth. She'd actually imagined three months from now there was going to be a wedding in her life! She had been picturing herself walking down the aisle with Nikolas by her side. . . .

Candace nearly cried aloud from the pain of it all. Folly, pure folly. *Oh, you fool,* she chided herself.

Barry got up abruptly and said, "I think we could both use another drink." A moment later he thrust a glass into her hand filled with Scotch and very little ice, but she didn't care. She took a gulp, then grimaced.

Barry looked at her curiously. "I'm beginning to believe you really don't know who Mylonis is."

"You might as well," Candace said dully.

"My, my. . . wouldn't one of the national scandal sheets go for this one!" Barry mused. "You're lucky I'm an editor and not a writer, Candy. Although this would hardly be *Tempo*'s sort of thing."

"Thanks a lot, Barry," she said, still abstracted yet able to react to the position he was taking. "How can you possibly think about such a thing as a story?''

"Because it's the kind of material that sells," he said plainly. Barry had got a grip on himself, she could see that. He was already addressing the situation factually. The thought occurred to her he would be a terrible lover. He would analyze every emotion, every move. Whereas Nikolas....

"You look pale as hell," he said, assessing her now. "So, okay, I believe you, Candy. But it's insane. You can see it's insane, can't you?''

"Yes, I suppose so.''

"Does Mylonis come from Tarpon Springs?" Barry frowned. "I can't remember ever hearing that about him. It seems to me he came to New York from London, or maybe it was Chicago. I don't know. By the time he really got into the business news he had already made it big.''

A flag of caution began to wave. She didn't like the idea of Barry probing into Nikolas's Tarpon Springs background. Not that he'd be apt to uncover anything connecting Nikolas Mylonis with Nicky Mellin. Although there was always a chance....

"He was born in Greece," she said, which was true enough.

"Another story of someone coming to America and taking the pot of gold from the end of the rainbow right in front of us natives," Barry said wryly. "Well, I suppose you have to hand it to him. He must be brilliant.''

He flung this out as if it were a question, but Candace evaded answering. For one thing, she didn't really know whether Nikolas was brilliant or not in business or financial matters. She knew him on such an entirely different level. As a person, as a lover....

She reached for her Scotch, and Barry finished his own drink. Then he said almost cheerfully, "Well, at least he can't ever claim you said you'd marry him because of his money. You can always call me in as a witness and I'll testify that you nearly passed out from the shock. Are you going to tell him, Candy?"

"Tell him what?" she asked, her mind elsewhere.

"That you know you'll be Mrs. Moneybags."

"I'd never thought you could be so crass, Barry," she said distinctly, the whiskey giving her an edge of false courage. "Now it's late, and I think you'd better go."

"Your wish is my command," he replied, slightly tipsy. He struggled into his coat, but she was not to be let off so easily. At the door he reached for Candace before she had a chance to evade him, and in another moment his mouth was pressed against hers with a force that was unmistakable in its intent. She struggled against him and stepped back hard on her ankle, which was still not all that strong. The pain shot through it, causing her to cry out sharply.

Barry said, his face flushed, "My God, you hurt easily. Does Mylonis wrap his fingers in velvet before he touches you?"

Candace stared up at him, her eyes huge and dark in a face stark white. Barry had the grace to look ashamed as he dropped his hands to his side, but he didn't apologize—and she was just as glad.

She closed the door behind him and put the chain across it, then leaned against the wall and shuddered, chill waves of anguish sweeping through her body.

Time stood still for a few minutes, and then the phone rang. Candace was sure it was Nikolas. But just now she couldn't bear to talk to him. She let it ring, and when it rang again fifteen minutes later she still forced herself to refrain from answering.

For the next two hours the phone rang at regular intervals. Then finally the ringing stopped, and after a time Candace fell asleep in the armchair where she'd retreated.

THE INTERCOM BUZZED and the impersonal voice at the other end said, "Mr. Mylonis is here to see you, Miss Mayhew."

"Send him up," Candace said, deciding it was going to be absolutely essential to keep calm in this session with Nikolas. But her pulse was already beginning to race.

She was almost afraid to open the door for him. And when she did, he stood on the threshold for a long moment, surveying her narrowly.

"Your mouth is swollen," he said brusquely. Then he stalked ahead of her across the room, pausing to shrug off his heavy overcoat and throw it on her daybed.

He turned to watch her walking away from the door and said sharply, "You are limping, Candace. Why? What happened last night? Why didn't you answer the phone?"

"Three questions in a row!" she sparred. "Which one shall I answer first?"

"Don't play games with me," he said tightly. "I didn't get home until later than I thought, and I lost track of the number of times I tried to reach you after that. Were you out all night?"

"Who were *you* with?" she countered. "It must

have been someone interesting to keep you out so late yourself.''

"I was with business associates," he snapped. "As I've said, don't play games with me. I have enough on my mind. I thought I wouldn't need to go to London so soon, but now certain things have come up that require my presence there. I am taking a plane out tonight, and I will be away for two weeks."

"Tonight?" Everything else faded away as Candace considered this. Nikolas going to London tonight? Nikolas going to be away for two weeks? Two weeks suddenly became synonymous with eternity.

"Yes," he said shortly. "I'd thought originally that you could go with me. I mentioned it to you, in fact. Now there is no time to arrange such matters. Do you have an up-to-date passport?"

"No," she said, and smiled faintly. "I've never owned a passport. I never needed one."

Nikolas nodded absently. His mind was clearly not on the amount of traveling experience she'd had. "Where were you last night?" he demanded again.

"Here," Candace returned.

"Then why didn't you answer the phone?"

It had always been difficult for Candace to dissemble. It was particularly difficult with Nikolas playing the role of inquisitor. But she tried to anyway.

"You would have done well in the Middle Ages," she found herself saying.

"What the hell am I supposed to derive from a statement like that?"

"You've no right to. . .interrogate me."

"Haven't I, now?" He towered over her, and a cynical smile tugged at his mouth. "I come in here after trying to reach you by phone half the night, and I find you looking like someone has mauled you. What are you going to try to tell me? That you retwisted your ankle in a dream? If so, did I catch you in that dream, Candace? Did I take you in my arms?''

He was advancing on her, and she froze. There was no tenderness in this Nikolas. Instead, there was a fury suppressed—and a passion that matched it. She sensed them both as his arms came to clutch her, and he drew her to him in a swift, rough movement, pinning her so close she could scarcely move.

Candace was wearing a sheer wool caftan, and through the material she could feel the contours of Nikolas's powerful, muscular body. His physical need for her was so evident she could not fight back her own arousal, and she responded by pressing even closer, so obsessed by her involuntary reaction to him that even his short, bittersweet laugh of triumph failed to halt her. Nikolas knew her weakness. Oh, how well he knew it! He crushed her, forcing his burgeoning maleness against her, then slowly gyrated in a way that enflamed her with a sensuous frenzy she couldn't possibly stem. His lips came hard against her swollen mouth with deliberate force, and the response they aroused brought hot tears to her eyes. Nikolas kissed her tears away as if they were trifles not to be bothered with, while his long hands swept down the length of her caftan. And in one expert movement he drew it up over her head and flung it aside.

Candace knew she had nothing on underneath it, and she was thoroughly aware her body was giving her away. His knowing eyes raked her breasts and took note of the taut, rosy nipples. Now her breath was coming so fast she was close to panting. And this time he didn't ask her to undress him. He was divesting himself of his clothes even as he drew her toward the daybed and reached down impatiently to brush his heavy overcoat off onto the floor. Then he stood before her, fully revealed in the morning light.

Candace moaned, biting her lip to suppress the sound as she looked at him, shaking inwardly with her need for him. Nikolas was indeed an Adonis, his body close to male perfection. There was a magnificence to him from the width of his shoulders to the narrowness of his waist, from the smoothness of his hips to the powerful masculinity of his thighs. Candace could not keep her eyes from running the whole length of him, and she could not fail to have them become riveted on the essential core of his manhood.

Something basic and primeval twisted inside her, and even before his arms reached out to claim her she flung herself toward him, consumed by a desire for him so intense it swept away the last vestige of anything remotely related to logic. Her response was total, more total than it ever had been before, her fingers entwining themselves through his hair as her body arched to meet him, her thighs parting to make his way easier.

As flesh touched flesh their mutual urgency communicated like a flow of molten lava and the surge of Candace's rising passion was, indeed, volcanic in the heat of its eruption. She felt Nikolas enter her and she gave herself up to his mastery, even as her hands roamed over his skin, pressing against him in a mounting expression of frenzy. He seemed to fill her, there was nothing of her that he was not possessing, and as if to underline this he raised his head briefly, to lower it again only so that he could claim her mouth, his tongue invading her lips to enter yet another part of her, its probing a trailing distillation of pure rapture.

Candace could no more have broken away from him than she could have forced herself to die at that very instant. Yet, today, he plundered her. As his hands roved roughly across her body his fingers became absolute in their strength, while he continued to press his hardness into her with a force that was shocking. Her passion became laced with confusion at first, then soared, until she was meeting him fully, moving to become fused with him, frantically twisting toward him as she sought to meet him, to rise with him on the same current. And this she did. Desire, merging, became a hot torrent, a geyser of emotion spiraling upward to cascade into an explosion of colors that went beyond the spectrum and reached out past the planets into infinity.

Candace came back to reality ever so slowly. She lay at Nikolas's side, feeling as if she'd been fragmented, as if she must grope carefully to reclaim the scattered pieces of herself if she was ever to be whole again.

She turned to meet his beautiful olive green gaze. But she could read nothing in his expression.

Then she drew herself together, feeling herself filled with the sweet essence of him. And she forgot he'd taken her, in the beginning at least, in a way that was close to barbaric.

Her eyes misted, and she smiled. "I love you,

Nikolas,'' she told him, her voice even and sweet.

Something flickered in the depths of those unusual eyes. And he said, his voice harsh, ''Don't confuse love with lust, *agápi mou* .''

CHAPTER EIGHTEEN

THERE WAS NO QUESTION of making peace. She had
suffered both physically and emotionally. Candace
had never been ashamed of her body, but now she
felt she could not stand Nikolas's eyes upon her for
another minute. She reached blindly for her caftan
and rushed to the bathroom.

She was physically ill, retching miserably. There
was nothing to vomit because she'd had nothing to
eat this morning. She'd been about to make coffee
when Nikolas had arrived. Now she splashed cold
water on her face and then started to brush her hair,
as if doing ordinary, mundane things might somehow
put her world back in focus again.

After a time Nikolas began to pound on the bathroom door. At first she ignored him, but finally he
shouted, "Open up, or I'll break the damned thing
down!"

He would. She knew he would. He would do anything that suited him in order to get his own way. She
recognized this fact with a sinking heart, only beginning to realize what kind of adversary he could be.
Then she threw the bathroom door open so swiftly it
nearly knocked him off balance.

"You've got to let me talk to you," he insisted.
His face was rigid, his nostrils pinched.

She shook her head. "I think you've said everything," she told him. "There's no need to take it back. What you said was true enough."

"Candace, for God's sake, don't be an idiot. I've been going crazy for the past twelve hours with...."

"With what?" she demanded sourly.

"With plain blind jealousy." He spoke as if it were an admission being wrenched from him, and again Candace reminded herself that despite his disclaimer about his talents Nikolas had once been an actor, and a highly successful one.

She brushed past him and went out to the kitchenette. Her fingers began to do things by rote, putting coffee into the pot, adding water to the right gauge level. The familiar things. The ordinary things. *Keep with what you know,* she cautioned herself.

Only when the coffee started to perk did she dare to turn and face him. He was wearing snug-fitting black slacks and a dark green crew-neck sweater. Casual clothes. He looked much as he had the first day she'd met him. None of the successful executive about this Nikolas Mylonis.

He leaned against the doorjamb, his face stark, and said, "I suppose it would be stupid to say I'm sorry."

"Very stupid," she agreed.

Candace had never considered herself one for dramatic gestures, and it was hard to keep her hands from trembling as she wrested the sapphire ring off her finger. She covered just enough of the distance between them to thrust it at him.

Nikolas grasped it involuntarily, raising an eyebrow. "No more engagement?" he asked her.

"I think you know the answer to that."

"It was a promise, Candace."

"Who are you to speak to me about promises?"

"I suppose you are right. And I suppose there is nothing I could say or do that would make any difference to you, either, is there? You've made up your mind not to listen to me...and you're the most stubborn person I've ever met!"

"Too bad," she said. She poured out a cup of coffee for herself and added indifferently, "If you wish coffee, help yourself."

"Thank you," Nikolas said, his eyes still riveted on her face. "But there's a chance I might be poisoned by thought transference if I were to drink any of it, don't you think?"

"I'm not thinking. That's up to you."

He said something under his breath, something short and angry and very Greek. But then he moved across to the counter and poured coffee into a mug.

"Look," he said, "can't you even begin to understand how I felt? If you'll tell me what happened last night—"

"I don't owe you any explanations about anything, Nikolas," she cut in coldly.

"I'm well aware of that. But I still think you might realize how it looked to me when I walked in here. I had no intention of seducing you, Candace, I swear to that! Not that we could really call it seduction, could we? Once we got going you surely were as avid as I was—" He stopped short and then said bitterly, "There I go again. Why the hell is it you inevitably bring out the worst in me?"

"You tell me," she challenged.

"Candace, this will never happen again. I swear it to you. Not unless you tell me it's what you want. Also...I had no right to take you the way I did. I am deeply ashamed of myself for doing so. But please...take the ring back. Let's start over again from this minute on. I won't ask you any questions...."

He was coming toward her, holding the sapphire out to her, and she shook her head violently.

"You can swallow the damned thing for all I care!" she choked.

Nikolas's eyes seemed to be made of green stone. She could not help but be daunted by the cold anger that etched his face. "You mean that, don't you?" he said.

"Very definitely."

"Okay, then," he finished with a calmness she mistrusted. And as she watched he pocketed the ring, then turned and walked back into the other room.

Soon the quiet became so intense Candace could not help herself. She had to follow him.

He was standing at the window, a strangely dejected tilt to the line of his proud head. Then he swerved to look her directly in the eye. "So, Candace," he said, his voice strained. "You have fooled me not once but twice. First, you discovered Nicky Mellin. Now, although you've evidently taken pains to make it seem otherwise, I would gather you also knew all along about Nikolas Mylonis. Is that going in your story, too? How you managed to break down the resistance of one of the world's richest confirmed bachelors?"

She could only stare at him, dumbfounded.

"You've missed your vocation, Candace," he told her, his voice very low. "On the other hand, perhaps it still isn't too late. There seems little doubt to me you could become a really great actress."

She shook her head impatiently. "You're wrong," she insisted. "Absolutely wrong. The name Nikolas Mylonis meant nothing to me until last night—aside from the fact it belonged to you. It must seem strange to you that everyone isn't versed in your world of business and finance. And I suppose this makes me appear hopelessly naive. But...that's the way it is."

"Ah," he nodded, "last night. Now perhaps we can get down to what really happened."

"Not at all what you suspect," she said hotly. "Barry Gehrich stopped by to see me because he was concerned. Then he noticed the ring, so I admitted I'd become engaged. He asked your name and I told him. And he, as I'm sure you realize, knew very well who you are."

"Who I am." Nikolas turned the words over slowly. Then he asked almost lazily, "Who am I, Candace? Do you wonder at all?"

She'd been possessed of curiosity about him since the first moment she'd met him, but she was not about to tell him that. Not now. And there were still so many frustrating gaps to be filled in about this tall, dark man who was standing before her, actually looking tormented.

"You said when you came in here you didn't want to play games," she reminded him. "Well, I don't want to play games, either. But your endless distrust of me has brought me to the conclusion you will never tell me the whole truth about yourself. Nor can I hope to convince you otherwise."

Nikolas said slowly, "I've had very few reasons to have much faith in people. I think I could count on the fingers of one hand those I have ever trusted—and a couple of them are dead."

Something thudded deep within Candace. He had never spoken of the beautiful actress who had died in the boating mishap where he'd been so severely injured.

Lila Pembroke. Suddenly Candace saw pictures of this glamorous young woman before her eyes, and they came to loom larger than life between Nikolas and herself. How could she ever have hoped to compete with such an image?

He said now, "I suppose that sounds as if I'm making a bid for your sympathy, but that is not my intention. I don't expect your sympathy, nor would I want it. But I could use a...a little understanding. I'm as bewildered by these clashes between us as you are, Candace. Maybe I still do not trust you—but this goes only to a point. Because—don't you see—I don't trust myself, either. Not where you're concerned. I'm pretty levelheaded about most things. I've had to be. As you've indicated, I have made the trip from relative rags to...wealth." The words came out reluctantly. "That much is true, but it hasn't been an easy journey. Making money can be a very lonely business. Also, until I met you I'd blocked out everything that had happened in my life prior to...a certain date. I'd relinquished every connection with the past."

"Yet your uncle was able to find you when he wanted you," she pointed out.

"No," Nikolas said. "I went to him. George Andris told me of the condition he was in and how much he had wished to make peace with me before I died."

"Before *you* died?"

"I was dead, as far as the world was concerned," Nikolas said. "Dead, as far as my uncle was concerned. In fact, he'd written me out of his life long before my death was officially announced. He did that soon after I went to Hollywood. It was all the more reason why I thought the door to my past had been sealed—forever. Then you came along and managed to reopen it.''

Candace said steadily, "It wouldn't have been opened again if you hadn't told me how old you'd been when you dived for the cross. My discovery about you was accidental, Nikolas. After that, the rest just fell into place...."

He sighed heavily. "Maybe I'll be able to believe that someday. I hope so. But as it is...."

He shrugged and seemed so very alien to Candace. "As it is," he said, "I must leave. I have a great deal to do before I take off for London tonight. I'll call you when I get back."

He slipped on his overcoat, looking older and quite stern. The dark fabric made him seem very austere. Candace felt as if he'd withdrawn completely from her. He was a stranger, this man. Yet she also sensed a desperation about him. She felt as if he were wordlessly imploring her to do something to stop him.

There was only one weapon with which she could stop him—her body. She could run to him and press herself against him. She could entwine her arms around him and kiss him to arousal, her fingers tugging at his black satin hair. She could lure him to her bed again, where everything would be forgotten except their mutual need for each other. But it would all be so temporary. Afterward there would again be a reckoning. With things as they were between Nikolas and herself there would always be a reckoning.

Candace forced herself to say stiffly, "I hope you have a good trip."

He paused on the threshold. "I think you know very well that I won't have a good trip!"

The door closed and Nikolas was gone. And Candace wanted to pummel her fists against the wood. She wanted to scream his name and beg him to come back to her. Even so, her shocked senses allowed her only to walk to the window in a trance. She was hoping he'd cross the street. Then, at least, she might get a glimpse of his tall figure walking along the other side. But this didn't happen.

Noon came and she sat quietly, trying to think things out. It was such a muddle, all of it. Somehow she had to pull the threads together and once again get her life into a pattern she could live with. For as long as she was beset with thoughts of Nikolas, there would never be anything approaching tranquillity.

Time passed, and finally Candace came to a conclusion. Begin at the beginning, she told herself resolutely.

The beginning, in this case, was the New York Public Library. Candace walked over that afternoon, stayed until the library closed for the evening and was back when it opened the next morning. And it was not until nearly noon that she came upon what she was looking for.

She had started by researching Nikolas Mylonis. And she'd been staggered by her findings about him. Despite the fact he'd never granted an interview to anyone there had been a great deal written about him. But there were very few pictures. Obviously he had become adept at avoiding photographers—even when they did occasionally capture him on film he usually managed to avert his face. In the pictures, she recognized Nikolas primarily by his figure and by the shape of his head.

Nikolas Mylonis was a natural gold mine for journalists. He was young, interesting, handsome and very rich. Seemingly he had come out of nowhere, yet enough background had been provided to fit an entirely new life and at the same time allay any suspicions of what came before. As she read about him, she realized some of the information had been contrived. The implication was that Nikolas had come to New York from the midwest and had for a time worked for a firm in London. So, she could see why Barry Gehrich had remembered this about him. The stories were calculatedly vague, yet not too much so. She had to admire Nikolas for covering his tracks as he had. His lawyer friend had undoubtedly advised him, and this had enabled him literally to begin all over again.

Journalistically, Nikolas had been painted as a man with a single-minded purpose: that of making money. There was no doubt he was an antisocial loner. Nevertheless, he was sought after eagerly by hostesses who seldom succeeded in getting him to attend a function, unless it was for charity. For charity he did make an occasional appearance, although the inference was he much preferred to make his major contributions monetary ones.

Something was said about his owning an island retreat off the coast of Maine. Evidently there was also a country place in England, in Devon. And one article mentioned he maintained a pied-à-terre condominium in Manhattan.

When Candace had finished reading all about

Nikolas Mylonis, she was left with the feeling she surely had never met this man. Certainly she didn't know him at all. In fact, judging from the newspaper and magazine accounts she didn't think he was a person she'd even want to know!

Finally she turned her attention back to earlier years and the meteoric story of Nicky Mellin. This time she went past the poignant picture of the figure in the wheelchair, until finally she came upon the story of Nicky Mellin's death.

It was there in black and white. Nicky Mellin, whose career had ended so tragically, had died at the age of twenty-six at the ranch he owned near San Bernardino. The story of his death was released by his close friend and business manager, Gerald Fraswell. Aftereffects of the accident were given as the cause of death, and Fraswell had verified for the press the fact that the film star had existed in a twilight world since the moment when he'd plunged from the deck of a friend's yacht in the unsuccessful attempt to rescue his beautiful colleague.

Nicky Mellin, the story went, had been cremated, and his ashes had been scattered by Fraswell on the grounds of the ranch, which he described as the film star's "personal oasis."

According to the story, there were no surviving relatives. And the lawyer announced that aside from a few personal bequests, the proceeds of the estate Mellin had amassed during his few brief years of stardom would go entirely to charities he had designated a long time before.

The story showed a photo of Nicky Mellin as he had been at the peak of his career. It was a head-and-shoulders shot, and looking closely at it Candace wondered how she could have been so blind as not to have recognized Nikolas before. Now she clearly saw the resemblance between the two faces. Many of the features had remained the same, and there was something about that smile. Even though Nikolas Mylonis could not match the smile Nicky Mellin had displayed in this newspaper picture, the same charm somehow came through.

Candace had a copy of the clipping made and then left the library with it in her possession. And as she wandered up Fifth Avenue, her thoughts were spinning like the colors on a whirling pinwheel.

Nikolas and Nicky Mellin were one and the same person. This was fact, she told herself. Or was it? Despite the facial similarities, was there a chance that Nicky Mellin really had died on his California ranch? Maybe the obituary story was true. And if not, was it really the fabrication of a clever man who hoped to make a wrecked life whole once again? Was it possible that Nikolas had dived for the cross but had not been the boy to retrieve it? Was it possible that Nikolas's uncle—Nikolas Callis—had actually had two nephews? And they had both dived for the cross on the same day in Spring Bayou and they'd both come up grasping it and...?

Oh, come on now, Candace told herself impatiently. *Let's get a little logic into the picture. Let's argue things both ways.*

She first tried to assume Nicky Mellin really had died and the obit was true. If that was the case, maybe Nikolas Mylonis was a relative. Perhaps he had even been the recipient of a large bequest, and with this money he'd been able to lay the groundwork for making his own fortune.

Then she reminded herself that the obituary clearly stated that Nicky Mellin had left no relatives.

But he'd had an uncle. Certainly he'd had an uncle. An uncle who had disowned him—who had cut him off as if he were dead. Yet when this uncle had been dying himself, he wanted nothing so much as to see his namesake nephew again.

In the final analysis then, Nikolas Callis had claimed relationship to both Nicky Mellin and Nikolas Mylonis.

Brooding over this, Candace came to the turn-in to Rockefeller Plaza, and her footsteps lagged. It seemed to her that whenever Nikolas came into her life things telescoped. In a matter of hours, she lived lifetimes. Hadn't she just been here with Nikolas, sharing a rare kind of intimacy with him as the skaters went whirling around? And hadn't a benevolent Greek god watched over them? Once again, in such an incredibly brief space of time, so much had happened. She'd even become engaged to Nikolas, although the engagement had been a mockery. And now....

"Oh, damn you, Nikolas!" Candace said aloud without realizing it, even as several passersby stared at her curiously.

CANDACE FIXED A CAN OF SOUP and heated up some rolls for her supper that night, but she didn't even taste what she ate. Eating had become purely automatic. She had the sense to know she needed sustenance, and she responded to instinct.

She'd reread the obituary story at least two dozen times and thought about it all again and again, and nothing made sense to her. Washing up her few dishes, Candace shook her head wearily.

Her mind was creating one scenario after another trying to solve the mysteries surrounding Nikolas. And so far she had succeeded only in becoming ridiculously bizarre. She was, in fact, becoming paranoid on the subject of both Nicky Mellin and Nikolas Mylonis...and she knew these were two ghosts that had to be laid to rest.

She also knew there was only one way to do this. She would have to go back to Tarpon Springs and try to pick up the pieces all over again. Nikolas would be in London for at least two weeks, so she would have a clear field, provided she didn't waste any time.

She thought fleetingly of Manos Panagoris. But he had not tried to get in touch with her at all. So much for Nikolas's conjecture—although it was possible he had spoken to Manos and had advised him about their "engagement."

Probably nothing about this farce of a betrothal had got back to either Elene or Theone, and that was to the good. Candace wanted to go back to Tarpon Springs as a journalist, not as Nikolas's make-believe fiancée. She wasn't even that, anymore!

To accomplish her task, she would need a reinstatement of her assignment for *Tempo*. And that, of course, depended upon Barry.

What a time to have to ask him for anything!

Wait a minute, Candace thought practically. *This is entirely a professional matter.* And Barry himself had said their personal relationship should have no bearing upon her work for *Tempo*. She only hoped he would hold to that.

She thought of calling him at home and asking for an appointment, but that would seem a bit too eager.

No, better to call him in the morning. She'd even meet him for lunch, if he suggested it.

Then she thought of the ring!

Barry would notice at once she was no longer wearing Nikolas's sapphire. She decided she'd somehow have to manage to talk the assignment over with him on the telephone and convince him to let her go ahead with it.

This proved to be surprisingly easy. Barry was about to go into an editorial conference when Candace phoned him the next morning. Of necessity he was in a hurry, and this obviously distressed him.

"Damn it all," he complained. "Let me call you back, Candy. It shouldn't be more than an hour or so, unless we really run into some snags. We can have lunch...."

She took the plunge. "I'm going back to Tarpon Springs to finish the story," she said. "I'm taking a plane out today, so I'm afraid I can't meet you."

"Tarpon Springs?" He was wrestling with this, and she could picture the frown creasing his forehead. "What the hell, Candy?"

"I want to do it, Barry," she said. "It's nagging me to death. The story is a good one, and we really shouldn't wait on it."

"What does Mylonis think of your doing this?"

"I haven't told him," she said, forcing out the words.

"Trouble in paradise?" Barry suggested, sounding more cheerful. "Okay, sweetheart, I'll arrange for expense money. And you'll need another camera...."

"I'll catch up on that later," Candace answered. "Anyway, there's a brand-new camera waiting for me down there just like the one I lost.'' She added a fib. "No time to tarry,'' she said. "I've made my plane reservation and I have a thousand and one things to do. . . . ''

Candace didn't have a thousand and one things to do before she left, but there were enough of them. Ordinary details to be taken care of, like stopping the newspaper and notifying the management she'd be away. She did this, but the duration of her absence remained a question mark.

One thing was certain. Candace had no intention of being in Florida come April. By April she would have bested her ghost—or ghosts—or done whatever it is one does with ghosts. Much more important, she would have written her story. And when it was done—when it had been accepted—she would make sure a xeroxed copy reached Nikolas Mylonis.

Just for the sake of the record.

This was the thought she kept uppermost in her mind as her cab sped out to Kennedy. And as she boarded the jet that would take her to Tampa International Airport, a bittersweet smile crossed her face.

Nikolas Mylonis, or Nicky Mellin—whatever name one called him or thought of him—was going to be taught a lesson!

CHAPTER NINETEEN

IT WAS SO strangely familiar to Candace. Driving a rented car into the oddly deserted business section of Tarpon Springs was like stepping back into another life, and yet she felt so alien here.

This was Nikolas's terrain, not hers. She was painfully aware of him as she drove past the circular-sided house and over the long, deep red bricks that paved Hellenic Avenue. She more than half expected to see him stride through the wrought-iron gate, peremptorily halting her to demand where she thought she was going.

She drove past the Grecian Gardens motel and felt a nagging sense of guilt. But she could not face seeing Elene tonight and certainly not either Theone or Melina. Maybe tomorrow, but not now.

She remembered the name of another motel she'd seen the day she'd taken her drive around the town. The motel was to the west of Spring Bayou, so Candace phoned there from the airport. Fortunately there was a vacancy, and she booked a room without giving the matter a second thought.

A middle-aged woman was on duty at the registration desk. She was pleasant, friendly and very definitely not Greek, and this gave Candace a funny feeling. Suddenly Nikolas, and everything else Greek about Tarpon Springs, seemed curiously remote.

The units in the motel were furnished a bit better than the ones at the Grecian Gardens. Modern, up-to-date, impersonal. There were framed floral prints on the walls. No pictures of the Acropolis by night.

Candace unpacked her things, then got out all her research material—the notes she'd made on her first visit and the miscellany of books, articles, photocopies and pamphlets about Tarpon Springs she'd amassed. Then she cleared everything superfluous off the dresser and set it up as a desk. She'd carried a portable typewriter along with her, and a supply of paper, carbons, and all the other traditional tools of her trade. As she arranged everything into a convenient working order she tried to keep her mind strictly on business, but the attempt was not a successful one.

Thoughts of Nikolas kept intruding. He would be in London by now. Maybe at his country place in Devon. Candace wondered if he was alone. Despite all the emphasis on his being antisocial and a loner, she knew from her own experience he occasionally took refuge in the company of a woman.

Thinking about this, Candace felt something twist inside her. It was a very physical feeling, a wrenching pain, and it took her a moment to realize what it was. It was jealousy, transmitted by her body to her mind. Incredibly, it was a new sensation for her. She'd never been truly jealous of anyone. But then, she thought sadly, she'd also never really loved anyone before.

Candace bit her lip and winced at the resulting pain. Then she forced herself to go to work and planned a tentative agenda for the next few days. Tomorrow would be exploratory. She'd visit the sponge docks and drive around the area again. What she wanted was an overall impression, a mental picture done in broad sweeps. Then she'd get down to details, one frame at a time.

Finally she felt the strains of hunger and decided to settle simply for a takeout order from the hamburger stand she'd been to before. Aliki's was the only real restaurant she was familiar with, but this was the last place she wanted to go to just now.

Back at the motel again, Candace switched on the TV absently and thought about all the people she really couldn't avoid seeing. It wouldn't be fair not to visit at least briefly with both Elene and Theone, and there was also the matter of Paul Morrison and the camera and prints. She'd somehow got the impression that Paul was in love with Elene. Too bad he hadn't married her before Manos Panagoris had arrived on the scene!

Too bad about a lot of things, Candace thought dismally.

Inevitably the hours passed. And when morning finally arrived, Candace was anxious to get started with her work. She dressed quickly and then drove over to the sponge docks. And as she parked her car in a dusty lot and then walked out onto Dodecanese Boulevard, she soon realized the pictures she'd seen of this area hadn't captured too much of its reality.

Dodecanese Boulevard was an imposing name for this fairly narrow street that bordered the Anclote River just to the north. At the head of the street, there was an enormous, ultramodern restaurant built on several levels, and initially this building dominated the entire scene. Candace remembered reading the place could serve something like three thousand diners simultaneously.

Past this, she could see a forest of masts, these belonging to the boats tied up along the docks. Between the street and the docks there were parking lots, departure points for boat tours featuring sponge-diving exhibitions, places where people could arrange deep-sea fishing trips and also the "Spongeorama" exhibit center. Films about sponge divers were shown here, in addition to a small museum and a "working" sponge factory. There were also a few restaurants and several gift shops.

The "land side" of the street was lined almost entirely with more gift shops and restaurants. Baskets placed outside almost every store brimmed with honey-colored sponges of various sizes and shapes and were also filled with strings of shell beads and other curios. And of course there were the ubiquitous displays of T-shirts emblazoned with pelicans, sea gulls, palm trees and bright orange Florida suns. As Candace walked slowly along she heard Greek music being played in some of the shops. The cadences were lively and sounded faintly Oriental in tone. Then she could smell the aroma of rather spicy fresh-baked goods and the heavenly scent of strong coffee.

Candace had forgotten about breakfast, and now she stopped and indulged. She was served coffee and honey cookies called *phournákia*, the name imparted to her by a short, plump woman who was every bit as Greek as Theone.

As she ate, Candace tried to sort out her mental impressions of the sponge docks. But a tall, dark man intruded constantly on her thoughts. She asked herself sadly how she ever could have hoped to return to Tarpon Springs without Nikolas coming along to haunt her! And her eyes misted with tears because she missed him so unbearably much.

There was a wall phone in the little restaurant, and after she paid her check, Candace paused to consult the phone book alongside it and was relieved to find that Paul Morrison was listed under Morrison's Photo Shop. She'd brought a small map with her and quickly located his street, which was only a block or so off the dock area.

Before heading over, she walked along Dodecanese Boulevard for a couple of blocks and visited several of the gift shops. Some really lovely items were interspersed with what Candace privately termed "tourist trash." She saw some fine Greek pottery, an assortment of very attractive costume jewelry and several imported Greek dresses and blouses. She was especially attracted by one blouse in a lovely soft shade of blue. It had embroidered trimming around the neck and sleeves, and Candace couldn't resist buying it.

She was becoming fascinated by the sound of the music many of the shops played, much of it featuring Greece's famous stringed instrument, the bouzouki. There was an excitement to the beat, a pulsating quality that accelerated to a dizzy climax. She imagined dancers spinning in an abandonment that mounted with the tempo until, frenzied, they succumbed to passion....

Passion! Candace didn't even want to think about passion.

Then, as she was admiring a necklace featuring a single, pearly shell edged with a band of gold, the tempo of the music changed. It became slow and haunting, and a man began to sing in a low, sensual voice. She couldn't understand the words he was saying, but there was no doubt as to their meaning, and she felt as if Nikolas had come to stand beside her. Quickly, Candace was caught up in a wave of sensuous emotion that made her giddy. Dazed, she put the shell necklace back on the counter and walked out of the store blindly, while the saleslady who had been waiting on her looked after her in astonishment.

She was trembling by the time she was standing out on the sidewalk again and totally dismayed by her own behavior. She had no control at all and was only beginning to realize what a mistake it had been to come back to Tarpon Springs.

Why, then, had she come back? Because she wanted to prove something to Nikolas Mylonis, she reminded herself. She wanted to prove to him she could be trusted, and there was only one way she could think of doing this. Even so, she felt she was fighting a losing battle. Would Nikolas Mylonis ever really trust anyone again?

Candace bypassed the rest of the gift shops and at the next corner walked away from the waterfront, following the mental route she'd sketched to Paul Morrison's photo shop.

It was a small place, the window offering a display of cameras offset by photographs of smiling brides and grooms. The brides were lavishly dressed in satin and lace, while the grooms wore formal clothes in pastel shades piped with black and huge oversize black bow ties. They all looked very Greek.

It was a hot day, the sunlight was dazzling and the inside of the shop seemed so dark in contrast it was a moment before Candace could see clearly. There were glass cases on either side of the room, arranged with cameras and photographic supplies, and a glass-top counter case at the far end. A number of other portrait photos, mostly of babies and young people, lined the walls. But there was also a photo of an elderly couple that caught her attention—an old man and an old woman, garbed quite elegantly. The woman wore a high-necked silk dress with a cameo pin fastening the ruching that edged the collar. And the man was handsome, with a proud thrust to the tilt of his head, his hair thick and white, his eyebrows still startlingly dark. Candace decided it was probably a fiftieth wedding anniversary picture, and it was charming. There was character etched in every line of those intensely Hellenic features.

Nikolas will look like that when he's old, she found herself thinking, and felt a sad twinge. By the time Nikolas was as old as the man in this picture he probably wouldn't even remember the young, blond girl from New England he'd once caught as she was about to fall to the sidewalk outside his house.

The beautiful photo portrait had captured her attention completely, and as Candace turned away she realized for the first time the store was empty. Paul Morrison, she thought dryly, surely had faith in his fellow man to go off and leave his place unattended like this. But at that precise moment he appeared in the doorway holding a cup of steaming coffee, and he stopped and stared at the sight of her.

"Candace!" he exclaimed. "Miss Mayhew, that is."

She couldn't help smiling. "Candace sounds nicer, Paul," she told him.

"Does Nick know you're here?" he asked.

"No, he doesn't. He's in London."

"I know," Paul said. "He phoned me before he left." He hesitated slightly, then added, "He didn't say you were coming back...."

"He didn't know," Candace replied. "Paul, I have an apology to make. I left both your camera and your contact prints at Nikolas's house. I should have got in touch with you long before now, but it's been... well, it's been kind of a crazy winter."

Paul smiled, and Candace felt her throat tighten. Although he could hardly be called handsome, there was a unique charisma to his smile. And again she was forcibly reminded of the tall, dark Greek who had plowed such a furrow through the path of her life.

He said, "Nick mentioned something similar."

Candace's mouth quirked. "In Greek?" she asked.

Paul laughed. "Yes, in Greek. Nick is certainly as American as anyone, yet at times he does revert to Greek. Especially when he talks about certain things...." He put his coffee down on the counter, and now he said, "Would you like some? I can go next door and get another cup."

"Thanks, no. I just had coffee and some marvelous cookies over at a place by the sponge docks."

"You like Greek food, Candace?"

"Yes," she said, and added involuntarily, "It seems as if I like... everything Greek."

As soon as she said this she felt the blush of surprise course through her cheeks. What a thing to say, she told herself! She looked up quickly at Paul, but he only said gently, "Well... that's good to hear."

He hesitated once again, and Candace had the feeling he was definitely holding back. Holding back what, she wondered. Then Paul quickly switched the subject.

"About the camera and the prints," he said. "Nick returned them to me. I sold the camera, but I got another just like it earlier this week. And the contacts are still available if you want them."

"I was hoping you'd say that," Candace said, relieved.

"Then you're going to write the article?"

There was a wariness to the way Paul asked this, a guarded look to his very dark eyes. She realized he was one of the few people in the world who perhaps knew the entire story about Nikolas Mylonis. And she felt convinced he belonged in the handful of those Nikolas trusted.

She was tempted to tell Paul she knew about Nicky Mellin. Yet an inner sense of caution prompted her to hold her tongue. She'd yet to win Paul's confidence, and she was also sure his loyalty to Nikolas was absolute.

No, Candace thought silently. Better not say too much.

"They'd suggested at *Tempo* we might hold off on the article until next year," she said, "so I could come back and cover the Epiphany celebration myself. But I persuaded them not to wait that long. Too much can happen in a year."

"True," Paul agreed. "Even so, for the sake of your story it might be better if you did wait." He spoke carefully, but Candace could sense his edginess.

"Why?" she ventured.

"Nick said you did a lot of research while you were here, despite your bad ankle," Paul volunteered.

"Yes, I did," she replied. "But there's nothing to beat on-the-scene observations. I really need to talk to a lot of people and delve into a lot of things. I've gathered background material about sponge fishing and sponges, for example, but I want a far more personal approach. I'd like to talk to some of the divers."

"Sponge fishing isn't what it used to be," Paul reminded her. "You do know that?"

"Yes. But it's still done."

He shrugged. "To a relatively limited extent," he said. "Most of what you see now is more for the tourists than anything else. The younger men . . . well, they don't really want to dive anymore. It's a hard life, and they have their educations to pursue, among other things. But the older divers still take pride in their work. They have it in their blood. Some are in their seventies, you know. The sponges they bring back to Tarpon Springs are their life. Have you seen those baskets outside the gift shops over by the seawall?"

"The seawall?"

"Along Dodecanese Boulevard," he explained. "It's geared to the tourists, but the sponges really are impressive. Anyway, who knows how long it will last? Times change . . . people come and go. . . ."

"Do you think some of the older divers would agree to be interviewed?"

"Perhaps. They are not unfriendly, and—" Paul smiled "—every Greek man responds to a beautiful woman. There might be a language difficulty, however, because with some their English is very limited. And many of the women do not speak English at all, though they've lived here for twenty or thirty years. They are Greek to the core, these people."

"Was Nikolas's uncle Greek to the core?"

Paul was startled, but he recovered quickly. "Yes, he was. He was a good man, Mr. Callis, but a hard one in some ways. The girl he loved—this was in Greece—died a short time before they were to be married. That was one reason why he came to this country. He was a very intelligent man, he worked hard and he succeeded. He built up a good business with the sponges here, and he owned a fleet of sponge boats. He married Theone only a couple of years before he died. She had been his housekeeper...I guess you know that. I would say the marriage was to protect her, to make sure she would get something after he died. He didn't want to think of her living out her years in poverty."

"Did he leave her his business, then?"

"No. What was left of the business went to Nick. The house, too. Mr. Callis left trust money for Theone and made Nick the administrator of the estate. Nick will make sure Theone is never in want. Or Melina, for that matter."

The phone interrupted him, and Paul excused himself. In another moment he was speaking Greek as easily as he had just been speaking English. When he was finished he said to Candace apologetically, "More baby pictures. There is to be a christening at the cathedral and a party afterward. Not too much of a party because it is Lent, and really Orthodox Greeks frown on festivities during Lent. Which reminds me—you should visit the cathedral. Besides its beauty, there is, of course, the story of the icon."

"The icon?" Candace asked curiously.

"The icon of Saint Nicholas," Paul told her. "Saint Nicholas is the protector of all seafarers, and so he is the patron saint of Tarpon Springs. When the first Greeks came here to fish for sponges, they built a church to honor Saint Nicholas. Much later, the present cathedral was built. An icon, as you may know, is a holy figure. And the portrait of Saint Nicholas is obviously very important to the cathedral. It is kept behind glass in a very elaborate wooden screen that looks like a small altar.''

Candace remembered her introduction to the cathedral. ''I was there on Epiphany,'' she said, ''but it was so crowded I couldn't see very much.''

Paul nodded. ''You have to look closely at the icon to really appreciate its story,'' he admitted. ''It was quite a few years ago—December, 1969, to be exact—when it was first noticed the icon was weeping. Tears had formed around the halo over Saint Nicholas's head and on his eyes and cheeks. And each time the pastor said prayers in front of the icon, those tears disappeared. The pastor was not about to label this a miracle, though. There were investigations and everything was considered, including the possibility the tears were being formed by moisture getting into the case. The icon was moved outdoors and also to different locations within the cathedral, but nothing had any effect on the tears when they occurred. They first appeared on the day before Saint Nicholas's name day, which is December 6. Thereafter, sometimes they would flow profusely. Other times they would abate until they were barely visible.

''So...the tears appear from time to time, and they have been witnessed by thousands of people Many theories have been offered—some scientific, some theological—yet nothing definite has been concluded. Meantime, the faithful who believe in miracles come to touch the icon, to kneel before it and kiss it and to place lighted candles by its side.''

"That's amazing," Candace breathed.

"Yes, it is," Paul agreed. "You would be interested to know that Nikolas Callis contributed generously to the construction of the new cathedral. He was named for the saint. So was his nephew. In fact, I have seen Nick, who is not at all Orthodox in his thinking, deeply moved by the story of the weeping icon."

"He does wear a gold medallion around his neck," Candace pointed out. "Is it of Saint Nicholas?"

Paul nodded. "Yes. But then a lot of us wear similar medallions. Is it religion or merely superstition? Who's to say?"

Candace had listened raptly to Paul's story about the weeping icon and she, too, was moved by it. Saint Nicholas, the protector of this small Greek-American community, the protector of men who lived with the sea, was also the protector of her Nikolas. They bore the same name, although one still spelled his in the Greek way.

Keep him safe, she found herself whispering under her breath. Then she rallied and said, "Thanks for telling me the story, Paul. I'll certainly visit the cathedral again now." She paused. "Do you think they'd mind if I took a picture of the icon?"

"I'm sure the pastor would give you permission," he answered. "Or, if you'd like, you can look over some of the ones I've taken. I've always meant to write a short piece about the weeping icon myself. I'd sure have enough illustrations to go with it."

"You write, then?"

"Not really," Paul smiled. "My talent is primarily

with the camera. You're lucky that yours is two-fold.''

"Thanks," Candace managed, reddening slightly again. "But I knew the moment I saw your contacts you were really good."

"Well, thank you," Paul returned. "Why don't you take me up on my offer, then? Within the next couple of days I'll get together some material that may interest you. And I'd be happy to drop it off. Where are you staying this time, Candace? At the Grecian Gardens or with Theone?''

"Neither," she said. "I'm staying at the Bayou Vista."

Paul didn't try to mask his surprise, and a strange sense of disloyalty crept over Candace. She tried to suppress this nagging feeling as she left the photo shop, new camera in hand. Paul had insisted she try it out before she paid for it, and laughingly she'd told him he was a terrible businessman. But to this he had replied rather gravely, "One has to have faith."

Now, as she walked back toward Dodecanese Boulevard, Candace could hear the echo of those words, and she knew Paul was right.

If only she could convince Nikolas to have faith.

CHAPTER TWENTY

CANDACE TOOK A DEEP BREATH, summoned her courage and then walked through the swinging glass door into the small lobby of the Grecian Gardens motel.

Elene looked up from the registration desk and gasped aloud, then hurried out and hugged Candace as if she were a long lost sister.

"Where have you come from?" she beamed. Then she laughed shakily and said, "What a silly question! As if it really matters. You're here, so who cares where you came from?" The shadows seemed to have deepened beneath Elene's lovely eyes and in just these few weeks she'd got noticeably thinner. But her smile was still beautiful, and before Candace could speak, she exclaimed, "Oh, I'm so glad to see you! Nick called the night it happened and told me, and I'm so thrilled about the two of you. Where's the ring? Let me see the ring!"

She grasped Candace's left hand, but when she saw the bare finger where the sapphire should have been, her smile faded. "What happened?" she asked, looking stricken.

Words came, as if prompted by some invisible force. "It was a bit too large so...so Nikolas took it back to have it fixed before he left for London."

"Oh, yes...of course." Elene's relief was manifest.

And Candace was appalled. What had she done? Why did it matter so much that she and Nikolas were engaged? Why should Elene care as much as she obviously did?

Elene's smile was tremulous. "He is such a wonderful man," she said, "and he has suffered so much. I can't think of anyone who has been through even a fraction of what Nick has been through." Then, seeing Candace's astonished expression, she added quickly, "Yes, I know about Nick. But he has no idea."

Elene stepped back and took a deep breath. "One night Paul told me everything because he wanted to make me understand that no matter how terrible things seem to be, there is always a reason to hope. You see, I...I was going to kill myself."

"What?" Candace felt stabbed by the shock.

"Don't look like that!" Elene implored. "Please...don't. Oh, this is no place to talk about such things. Melina is coming to take over the desk in a few minutes, and then you and I can go to my apartment, where we'll be alone."

"Melina?"

"Yes." There was mischief in Elene's smile. "Nick told her she was going to have to go to work and suggested I give her a job. Surprisingly, when you consider how much she sulks, she's not half-bad. It gives her a discipline she needs, coming to work here, and it keeps her out of trouble. She actually went to the movies with John Damianos on her own volition last Saturday. So, who knows? A miracle could happen.

"Now," she went on, swiftly changing the subject, "where are your suitcases? You left one behind, you know. I was going to send it to you in New York, but

Nick said to keep it here. He said you'd be back."

"Nikolas said I'd be back?"

"That's right," Elene nodded. "He said you hadn't finished your story yet."

"I see."

"Why are you looking like that, Candace? It's true, isn't it?"

"Oh, yes. It's true, but . . . ."

Elene was glancing at the clock behind the registration desk, and now she said, "Well, as usual Melina is going to be late. In all fairness, though, she's never really bad. She's just not punctual, that's all. Ah, you see. . . here she is now."

Candace turned to see Melina saunter through the door. She was wearing bright yellow shorts and a matching lacy blouse, and she had on enough makeup for two girls her age. Nevertheless, she was beautiful. Rich, ripe, she could probably go to Hollywood herself. Yet there was a certain pathos to the role she was playing.

"So," Melina said flatly. "Welcome back."

"Thank you," Candace replied, realizing that Melina had expected to see her, too.

"Well, Melina," Elene said, "now that you are here, Candace and I are going to have some coffee." She turned to Candace. "Shall we get your suitcases first?"

"No," Candace answered quickly. "They're okay."

Elene led the way through a doorway at the back of the reception foyer and then up a short flight of stairs to her apartment. It was surprisingly pleasant, the picture window in the large living room revealing a beautiful view of Spring Bayou.

"Sit down and make yourself comfortable," she urged. "The coffee will take only a few minutes."

To Candace's delight, Elene brewed Greek coffee and also brought a plate of delicious buttery cookies, thickly edged with powdered sugar. "Is the coffee sweet enough?" she asked after Candace had sipped it.

"Perfect."

"Then what is wrong? You look as if you have a sour taste in your mouth."

Candace put her cup down slowly. "Elene. . . I've checked in at the Bayou Vista."

An expression of hurt immediately crossed Elene's emotional face. "Why?" she asked directly.

"Because—oh, it isn't so simple that I can say it all in one sentence," Candace said, feeling miserable herself. Then she decided to plunge. "Elene, downstairs you—well, you confided in me. May I confide in you now?"

Elene looked startled. "Does it involve Nick?" she asked sullenly.

"Yes, it involves Nikolas. But I'm not asking you to tell me anything at all about Nikolas. You must understand that."

"Listen, Candace," Elene said. "Before I say anything about anything, I have to ask you a very personal question."

"Yes?"

"Do you love him?"

Candace's blue violet eyes met eyes as dark as a Grecian night. "Yes, I do," she said firmly.

Tears actually filled Elene's eyes, but despite them and the fatigue that etched her face, her smile was vivid. "If that is so," she said, "then there's no danger of what I might say to you, because Nick... Nick is safe with you.''

"Nikolas will always be safe with me," Candace replied, "but he refuses to believe that. His experiences with other journalists have been awful. And, Elene, he's told me several times he doesn't know if he'll ever trust me. So, there's only one thing I can do that might possibly change his mind.''

"And what is that?''

"Write the article about Tarpon Springs—and leave Nikolas out of it. He told me he thought I'd tricked him from the very beginning just so I could get a shot at a big story. Well, he's wrong. And whatever else happens, I want to prove that to him.''

"I believe you, Candace.''

"So Nikolas told you I'd be back, did he?''

"Yes," Elene nodded. "He said you were sure to return, although he couldn't say exactly when.''

"Did he say why he thought so?''

"Because of your story," she admitted reluctantly. "But I knew nothing of what might be involved. I'd only been told originally that you were here to write a story about Tarpon Springs and its Greek heritage.''

"That's the truth," Candace said. "That's all it is.''

Elene refilled their coffee cups, then asked, "How is it that you and Nick became engaged?''

"It was only a mock thing because—" Candace stopped in mid-sentence. She could hardly tell Elene the false engagement had been invented, at least in part, because of Manos! "Elene," she continued carefully, "Nikolas thought it would solve a couple of problems... for both of us. It was only a joke.''

"But Nick said he bought you a ring....''

"Well, he did," Candace hesitated. "And I fibbed to you when you asked me about it. The ring isn't at the jeweler's. I gave it back to Nikolas."

Elene was momentarily startled but regained her composure quickly. "So, Nick has gone off to London, and you are here, and you didn't want to get in touch with any of us, is that it? You were simply going to write your story and leave, hoping none of us would ever know you'd come back?"

"No, Elene, I wasn't going to do that," Candace denied. "I planned to stop by and see all of you. In fact, I've already seen Paul Morrison. I picked up a new camera from him." She paused as the enormity of what Elene had said downstairs washed over her. "How did Paul know...?" she asked in a whisper.

"About me? About what I intended to do?" Elene, too, lowered her voice and then sighed deeply. "Ah," she said, "you must think I imagine myself playing a role in a Greek tragedy. But, as you say, things often are not simple. This was not simple. I had just found out that Manos had been unfaithful— and not for the first time, I'm sure.

"The doctor had given me pills because I'd had a miscarriage not long before, and I wasn't sleeping well. One night, when I was here all alone, I switched out the lights downstairs and came up fairly early. It was only about eleven o'clock. Paul was driving by on his way home from some sort of meeting. Anyway, when he passed the motel and saw it was dark, he thought this was odd. We always leave a light on by the desk, you see, in case someone comes in late looking for a room.

"Anyway, Paul decided to come in, and then he came upstairs. I had laid out all the pills in little rows on the kitchen table, and I'd started taking them. He caught me as I put number ten in my mouth, and he. . . he forced me to vomit. Then he stayed with me until dawn. We talked and talked. And because he knows I love Nick so dearly—like the brother I've never had, Candace—he told me the truth about him. It saved me, it really did.''

Candace was thoroughly shaken as she said, ''But, Elene, did Paul also warn you about the consequences that could occur if you betray his confidence?''

''Yes,'' Elene said, the shadow of a sad smile coming to cross her face. ''In fact, he said he'd kill me. Very Greek, isn't it? It could be right out of Euripides. But there is a deep bond between Paul and Nick. It may seem like a primitive emotion, yet I have a feeling for it. I respect it.''

''So do I,'' Candace said quietly.

''So you see,'' Elene finished, ''Paul taught me I must not give up, and he used Nick as an example. I often look at Nick, knowing all I now know about him, and I marvel he could go through such hell and come out so strong. And I have prayed time and time again that love and happiness will come to him, because no one I've ever known deserves these blessings more than Nick. He has had so very little happiness. . . and nothing at all of love.''

Candace could not speak. There were no words left to speak. She was totally drained by Elene's simple eloquence.

''If you have broken this engagement, Candace, think again,'' Elene said softly. ''Think again. . . when Nick comes back.''

When Nick comes back. Later, when Candace was

alone in her room at the Bayou Vista motel, those words echoed again and again in the silent spaces of her mind.

She had come to feel a tie with Elene today that went beyond mere affection, although she had demurred when it came to the idea of returning to the Grecian Gardens. "Maybe," she'd hedged. "I did tell the people at the Bayou Vista I'd stay there at least four days." This was true enough. She had estimated it would take her approximately that long to cover everything she wished to cover in Tarpon Springs. Now she realized she'd already spent one full day researching, and most of what she had discovered could never be put into print!

The next morning Candace found she really wanted a good breakfast and decided there was no point in skulking around back corners, hoping no one would recognize her. She had braved facing Elene yesterday, and she planned to call on Theone later this morning, so now she drove up Pinellas Avenue and walked into Aliki's small cafe.

Her eyes were immediately drawn to the table at the end of the room—the table where she'd first seen Nikolas as he sat talking to Manos Panagoris. Only now it was vacant.

Aliki still stood behind the counter and still looked tired, and Candace realized how much the old woman probably worried about Elene, her unhappy daughter. She wondered if Aliki had any idea of just how desperate Elene could become over Manos. Was it possible Paul had confided in Aliki about that one terrible episode he had prevented from becoming a tragedy?

Aliki smiled at her and said, "I am glad the *despinís* returns."

"Thank you," Candace answered.

There was a lot more she would like to have said to Aliki. She wished they could sit down over a cup of strong coffee and talk, for she felt an affinity with Elene's mother, too.

As it happened, however, there was no chance at all to talk to Aliki. A party of tourists swamped the restaurant soon after an order of bacon and eggs had been placed before her, and watching Aliki, Candace marveled at how she handled both the cooking and the serving single-handed. Finally, after a second cup of coffee, she said goodbye to Aliki and walked out onto Pinellas Avenue. It was time to visit the cathedral.

Candace found Saint Nicholas's icon in the vestibule. The face was entrancing, even though the colors in which it had been painted—and which the Greek people obviously favored—seemed overly bright to her. Saint Nicholas was depicted as having classical features and a gray beard, but it was his eyes that held most of Candace's attention. Large, dark and eloquent, they seemed to symbolize his wisdom, compassion and knowledge. There were no tears at the moment, though.

After a while she wrenched her eyes away from the icon and entered the cool interior of the cathedral. Then she sat down in one of the beautiful gold brown pews and let the peacefulness of the place soothe her.

As her eyes adjusted to the subdued light, Candace began to discern the vivid paintings of holy figures that dominated the walls and the ceilings. Similar figures were also depicted in the jewel-toned windows. By contrast, almost everything in between had been done in a soft, creamy white. Candace again noticed the magnificent crystal chandeliers and the rows of twinkling votive candles in red glass holders banked on both sides of the altar. She had first glimpsed these on Epiphany as she had strained to see through the crowds involved in the service prior to the procession.

It was strange to her, this church with its exotic colors, yet Candace did not feel like a trespasser. As she got up to leave, a small, white-haired woman, obviously Greek, brushed past her in the aisle. Dark Hellenic eyes appraised her knowingly for the "foreigner" that she was, yet the woman gave her a sweet smile that was almost like a benediction.

Back in the vestibule, Candace paused again by the icon, and it seemed to her as if the eloquent eyes in the picture were looking directly at her. She found herself saying, "Please keep him safe." And she hoped this would not be considered blasphemous because she wasn't Greek Orthodox by faith. Then she picked up one of the slender white candles and put a dollar in the box left for offerings. And gripped by an emotion that made her fingers tremble, she lit the candle carefully and placed it by the icon.

Back out in the sunlight, Candace drew a very long breath. This interval in the cathedral, with its unexpected feeling of peace, had strengthened her conviction about the article she was going to write. If she could do nothing else for Nikolas, perhaps she could at least erase some of the bitterness he still harbored deep inside. Perhaps she could convince him the elements of life called love and trust really did exist—even among journalists!

CHAPTER TWENTY-ONE

By THE END OF THE DAY Candace was steeped in the history of Tarpon Springs and the Greeks who in earlier years had made it one of the world's great fishing centers. It had been a surprising day, because the people she'd talked with had been quite different than she'd expected. And Theone had been no exception.

After she'd left the cathedral and before she'd embarked on anything else, Candace had decided to call on Theone. She'd worried a little about how Theone would welcome her—after all, she'd left Tarpon Springs without even bothering to say goodbye to the woman. And Theone had been so kind to her. She wouldn't blame Nikolas's aunt if she now got a cool reception.

To her surprise, though, Theone actually reached out to embrace her, saying in her deep, accented voice, "Ah, it is good that you have come back, Candace."

Theone had never called Candace by her first name before, and this was unexpectedly warming. It also seemed natural to be led out to the kitchen, where she sat at the big round table, sipping coffee and eating delicious Greek pastry.

Theone seemed more relaxed. She said, "Nick will be so glad when he gets back and finds you have returned. Elene called last night to say you have come. It is good. Very good.''

Yet it didn't seem right to Candace to let everyone go along with the supposition that she and Nikolas were going to have some sort of glorious reunion when he returned from London. She said carefully, ''I'm only going to be here a few days, Theone. I have to finish the article I started when I was here before.''

Candace spoke slowly, for she was never quite sure whether or not Theone understood everything she said. This time, however, the older woman certainly seemed to grasp the gist of what she was saying. She frowned and said doubtfully, ''But you cannot leave, if that is what you mean. You must wait for Nick!''

She seemed agitated about this, and Candace decided there was no point in upsetting her any further. ''We'll see how things go,'' she said vaguely. This seemed to satisfy Theone, for she smiled and reached over to pat Candace's hand.

''You are very good for him,'' she said.

Candace felt a lump in her throat, because there was no doubting Theone's sincerity. Yet if all the facts were tallied, she couldn't see how anyone who cared for Nikolas would consider her ''good'' for him. Their relationship, from the outset, had been entirely too explosive.

She heard a door close and started in panic. *Oh, my God, he's come back!* The thought was involuntary, and she felt like getting under the table and trying to hide. But it was Melina who came into the kitchen.

Melina was dressed very conservatively—for Melina—in a trim, light blue cotton dress. The change of style was profound. Her dark hair had been tied back into a ponytail with a blue scarf that matched her dress, and she looked almost like a schoolgirl. And even she was not hostile today. She smiled at Candace and said gaily, "Hello." Then she spoke to her mother in Greek.

Theone nodded and said in her carefully worded English, "When you come back you can bring some butter." Then she explained to Candace, "Melina goes to help Aliki, my sister, in the restaurant. Each day she works there for lunch."

So, Melina was working part-time for Aliki and part-time for Elene! Candace had no doubt this was all Nikolas's doing and that he must have read the proverbial riot act to Melina and at least symbolically taken her over his knee in order to effect such a reformation. But working seemed to be doing her good. She had already lost a fair share of her petulance.

After Melina left, Theone said quietly, "He makes the miracles, Nick. Now maybe he can do something with Manos Panagoris." Surprisingly, Theone seemed to take it for granted Candace was aware of the problems with Manos.

She was being treated as if she was one of the family! Nikolas's family. She wondered how much Theone actually knew about Nikolas. According to what he himself had said, she was unaware of his earlier "identity." So were Aliki and Melina, as Elene had been, too, until Paul had chosen to confide in her. Nikolas must have come into Theone's life only during her husband's last illness, but obviously she had a deep regard for him. There seemed no doubt Nikolas had been very good to her—and was now still very good to her. Nikolas, Candace realized, really was something of a patriarch to his family. He had taken on the handling of both Theone's and Melina's affairs, and he seemed to feel himself pretty much responsible for Aliki and Elene, as well.

He'd taken these four women and made them his family. Two widows, two fatherless girls, none of them related to him by blood. Yet they were fortunate in that they could not have been left in safer hands...nor with a finer person.

Her emotions must have shown plainly on her face for Theone said, "What is it, Candace? I do not like to see you so sad."

"I'm not sad, really. I was just thinking...." she evaded.

"Will be all right," Theone said insistently.

Candace didn't know exactly what it was Theone thought was going to be all right, but she decided it was wiser to keep quiet about this. She also decided to try a bit of interviewing with Theone, although that had not been her purpose in making this visit. But Theone was Greek, and she did live in Tarpon Springs.

This proved to be hard going. Theone was willing enough to talk, but in trying to get into a discussion of any depth they approached a realm in which her English was much too limited to do justice to what she really wanted to say.

"We need interpreter," Theone finally said. "Nick, he should be here."

Candace did learn Theone had come from Greece with her first husband and they had lived in the Boston area.

"Greeks are everywhere when you come to

States,'' Theone had said, waving her hands in a big circle. "You meet Greeks, little neighborhoods. That is problem. You do not learn to speak English good enough because always there is someone who speaks Greek.''

Theone's first husband had been in what she called the "fish business." Candace took this to mean he had worked for a seafood wholesaler. He had been plagued with arthritis and had come to Tarpon Springs nearly ten years ago, seeking the relief promised by the milder Florida climate. And he had found work with Nikolas Callis, who had dealt with fish as well as sponges.

"He died when Melina was thirteen,'' Theone reported. "Bad age for girl to lose father. Nikolas Callis give me job as housekeeper, a place for Melina and me to live. He was a good man, but not used to young people around, you know?''

Candace knew. Years before, from what she could make of things, Nikolas Callis had tried to dominate a young Greek boy. . . and it hadn't worked. She suspected that for the rest of his days—most of them, anyway—he had harbored a grudge against young people.

"So,'' Theone said, "after time passes, Nikolas Callis and me, we marry. Then, when he gets very sick I know what is in his heart. He wants someone of his own blood to be here with him. I ask Paul is there anybody? And he tells me there is one nephew in New York. So I say to Paul, ask him to come. Beg that he comes.''

Nikolas.

"He was so good, so big, so kind, Nick,'' Theone said. "At first I think, what does he do with Melina and with me after my husband dies? Does he throw us out? No. Instead he makes sure we are all right. He talks to Melina like he is big brother. She needs this. And to me—'' Theone's face was wonderfully expressive ''—to me, he is like my son,'' she said proudly.

Tears stung Candace's eyes. ''He will always take care of you and Melina,'' she said softly.

''Yes,'' Theone said. 'And you, too.''

It was nearly time for lunch when Candace broke away. At the door, Theone asked, ''You will be back for dinner?''

Candace shook her head. ''I really can't tonight, Theone. I have to make notes and write down a lot of things. But . . . thank you for asking.''

''Tomorrow night?''

''Maybe,'' Candace promised. ''I'll be in touch.''

Paul Morrison's photo shop had been next on her list. She didn't want to push him about getting his material together, yet she hoped he still had the contact prints of the Epiphany procession easily accessible. She wanted to go through these to recreate her own mood. Then she would write the beginning of her article, based on this highlight of the Tarpon Springs year.

Paul was on his way out as Candace entered the shop. But he flashed her a grin and said, ''Just in time for lunch. I was going across the street for a *gyro*. Join me?''

''I'd love to.''

He took her to a restaurant that bordered the sponge docks, and they sat at an outdoor table overlooking the water. Part of the menu was written in Greek, and Candace wished she could read the intriguing Greek alphabet. Obviously Paul could.

"Can you write it, too?" she asked him.

"Sure," he nodded. "I learned most of my Greek from my mother, the rest at parochial sessions at the cathedral. Today they have an even more bilingual program available. The population is still over one-third Greek, and a few years ago a special language program was started in the schools here. The kids begin to learn Greek right in kindergarten. They even get two report cards, one in English and the other in Greek! This is very pleasing to the parents, of course. Even some of the Anglos—the non-Greeks, that is—enroll their children in the Greek-language program. Actually, it almost works the other way. Many of the Greek kids don't learn very much English until they enter school. They've heard nothing but Greek in their own homes."

"Even today?" Candace asked, finding this amazing.

"Even today. Greeks do tend to marry Greeks—the idea of perpetuating the heritage is a pretty strong one. My mother was an exception, although there is nothing that rigid about it. She fell in love with a Scot who came down here on a fishing holiday. He stayed and went to work for the local newspaper. He was a journalist, too. So you see, Candace, I am more than slightly familiar with your line of work."

"I should have known, Paul. Anyway, what about the cathedral? Do they still have the parochial classes?"

"Yes. Perpetuating the Greek language, culture, heritage—that's all a big part of the church plan. Classes are held in St. Nicholas's every afternoon, after the kids finish at their regular school. The Greek Orthodox theology is taught, but they also learn Greek history, mythology, music, dancing. . you name it. And only modern Greek is used in the classroom.''

"So," Candace said thoughtfully, "Tarpon Springs should be a sort of Greek-culture citadel for a long time to come, wouldn't you say?"

"I'd agree with that," Paul beamed.

"I'd love to get pictures of some of the classes. Especially the children dancing."

"Easy to arrange. I'll just speak to the pastor. He's a good guy."

They were interrupted by the arrival of the waitress. Their *gyros* were accompanied by glasses of a slightly tart red wine.

Candace munched and said, "This must be one of the world's best sandwiches." The waitress, who knew Paul, smiled at the compliment.

As they ate, Paul said, "You'll notice most of the activity around here deals purely with the tourist trade."

Candace nodded. There seemed to be a constant procession of white boats going in and out of the river channel, and all of them were laden with people. They were sturdy boats, trimmed with an array of small, bright pennants in rainbow colors, and as one docked nearby and the people disembarked, she saw an elderly man wearing a diver's suit get off last. He paused on the dock to put down the heavy helmet he was carrying. Then he lit a cigarette, squinting against the sun as he blew out the first stream of smoke. His hair was sparse and gray, his wrinkled skin the color of chestnuts. Watching him, Candace wished she could paint. He would have made a terrific study in oils.

She couldn't resist saying, "He looks as if he should be sitting out on his front porch taking it easy."

"Thanos?" Paul said, following her gaze. "Yes, he is an old-timer. He will soon be seventy-five, and his friends say they are going to try to persuade him to retire on his birthday. He no longer goes out into the gulf to dive. He works here, for what I shall call the sight-seeing boats. Have you been out on one?"

"No, not yet."

"You mustn't miss it. A short trip only takes half an hour or so, but you do get an idea of what sponge fishing is like."

"No chance of going out on a regular trip in the gulf?" Candace queried.

"I don't think so. If anyone could arrange such a thing I suppose Nick could, but actually you'd get enough of what you'd need for an article just by doing the tourist bit."

Candace let it go at that. Paul was glancing at his watch, and he said regretfully, "I have a man coming in to look at a movie camera at two o'clock, so I'm afraid I'll have to be getting back."

As they left the restaurant, she thanked Paul for an especially enjoyable lunch, then remembered to ask him about the contact prints. He'd kept them together as she'd hoped he would, so she stopped at the shop and picked them up.

There was still time to go back to the docks and take one of the boat trips, but she decided to defer it until another day. Now she had a lot of material to put together, and the logical thing was to go back to the motel and begin.

As Candace cut across town, the route took her past Spring Bayou, and she could not resist stopping. It was a lovely place, with white walkways paralleling the curving aquamarine water and live-oak trees spreading welcome shade throughout the quiet, palm-studded park. Candace wanted to take the exotic walk she hadn't been able to take before, but her discipline told her to do otherwise, so she motored away slowly.

After several hours of concentrated typing she paused briefly to patronize the drive-in once again. And midway through the evening Elene called, asking her to come for dinner the next night. When Candace explained Theone had also issued a similar invitation, Elene laughed.

"You are so popular," she teased. "But Aunt Theone will not mind if I ask her to let me have you first. Then you can go to her the next night."

They hung up, and Candace returned to her work with a warm, happy feeling. And this feeling seemed so strange, given the circumstances. Nikolas was far away, and despite the rather mysterious friendliness his family had extended to her, Candace could only wonder at how their relationship stood. She had not expected to be happy at all during this sojourn in Tarpon Springs, but at the moment she was. She'd almost forgotten she'd left New York behind in the slush of winter.

She settled down to read about how the first Greek spongers had come to Tarpon Springs not long after the turn of the century. Sponge fishing in Florida had been going on for a long time by then. Its history actually dated back more than a hundred years, when it was recorded that fishermen around Key West picked up the sponges that washed up onshore after a storm. Then, still in the Florida Keys, a form of sponge fishing called "hooking" had been initiated. In this method the sponges were retrieved from the shallow waters by boats using long hooks.

A bit later it was discovered that in the gulf waters, and especially in the area off Tarpon Springs, there was a veritable forest of sponges. And late in the nineteenth century, a Greek named John Cocoris was sent to Florida by a Greek-owned New York sponge company. He came to Tarpon Springs to buy sponges that were still being harvested by the Key West-type hooking boats. But Cocoris was sure there was a better way of getting the sponges, or "yellow gold," from the Gulf of Mexico waters. It was he who brought the first Greek divers to the area. The special boats and diving equipment that had long been used successfully in Greece soon followed.

Candace was intrigued by the story of the first sponge boat to put out to the offshore beds. A diver had jumped overboard and had reportedly stayed down ten minutes. Then he had surfaced, laughing wildly. A bag full of wool sponges—the most prized of all species—was clutched in each hand, and he had yelled up to the deck, "There are enough sponges out here to supply the entire world!" When his boat, named the *Elpis*, had returned to Tarpon Springs that night flying both the Greek and American flags, it was literally laden down with sponges.

As the years passed, the sponge business had continued to grow and expand. And more and more Greeks moved to Tarpon Springs with their families to take part in it. The community flourished, for which the Greeks were primarily to thank.

Then, in the early 1940s, the sponge beds fell victim to the dread organism known as "red tide" and were all but wiped out. It took years for the beds to become healthy again, but eventually about half a million dollars' worth of sponges was again being harvested in gulf waters each year. This happy state had continued for more than two decades, until the production figures had begun to take the dismal fall from which they had yet to fully recover.

Candace remembered Nikolas had explained to her that the availability of good sponges was no longer the problem. It was the readiness of manpower. The young men didn't want this rugged, solitary sort of life. The computer age simply offered too many interesting alternatives.

With the decline of the number of boats going out to fish for sponges there was another potential peril, too. It was a vivid illustration of nature's law of supply and demand. Now there were almost too many sponges, and if the beds were not harvested they would overgrow and finally become dormant. And if this were allowed to happen, there was a chance they would die out completely.

Could love, untended, wither in a similar fashion?

Candace, alone in her motel room, thought sadly about that possibility.

CHAPTER TWENTY-TWO

CANDACE NEVER FAILED to be astonished by the volume of material she accumulated each time she researched background for an article, but now the time had come to begin writing. She wanted to get a first draft that could be filled in later with the remaining color she hoped to acquire by visiting the Greek classroom and perhaps taking one of the boat excursions.

She got up early and faced a warm morning that threatened to develop into a really hot day. Breakfast was at Aliki's, and again she wished that Aliki might be free enough so they could talk together. But, as before, the small restaurant was thronged with tourists.

Back in her motel room, Candace was grateful for the air conditioning, despite its annoying hum. She set to work quickly and soon found she had the framework of the article well in mind. The phrases came easily, and when she paused during her lunch break and read over some of her copy, she was pleased to find she was actually capturing the Greek essence of Tarpon Springs exactly as she had wanted to.

After a half-hour respite she went back to work and didn't pause again until midafternoon. By then she had the beginning of a headache and she'd sat at her makeshift desk so long she was getting stiff. The chair she'd had to use was not the proper height for typing, and her muscles were starting to ache as a result. Candace rubbed her temples wearily. Definitely, a change of pace was in order.

Even as she thought this, the phone rang. "I hope I'm not interrupting your creative processes," Elene said quickly.

"No, you're not," Candace assured her. "As a matter of fact, I'd just decided to stop for a while. I thought I might go for a walk, maybe around Spring Bayou. I've wanted to do that ever since the first time I saw it."

"Why not come directly here afterward?" Elene suggested.

Candace hesitated. "I really should put in one more hour before I quit for the day."

"Does your story have to be done in such a hurry, Candace?"

She had to laugh. "Not really, Elene. It's just that when I get into something like this I tend to become possessed by it, that's all."

"Well, I shall not try to dissuade you. As it is, I have to be at the registration desk myself until at least five. Then Melina arrives to take over. Anyway, dinner is something that will keep. So you can come over whenever you're ready, okay?"

"Okay. May I bring something?"

"Only yourself," Elene said firmly.

This was very well, but Candace wished she could think of something that might help to erase some of those worried shadows that seemed to haunt Elene's face. She wondered where Manos was. Still in New York, probably. Elene had not mentioned his whereabouts, nor did Candace have any desire to ask.

Outdoors, it was still very hot in the sun, but there was a breeze sweeping in from the gulf. Candace parked her car near the gate with the tinseled cross and then slowly walked down the broad white steps that led to the walkway bordering the water. She could not help thinking of the blessing of the fleet that had taken place here sixteen years ago. She imagined she could see the young, eager, dark-haired boy whose perfect body must have curved in an arc of pure symmetry as he dived into the water to retrieve the golden cross.

She walked to the left and followed the bends in the bayou along the perimeter of the park at the far side. Here the oak trees offered shade, and Candace discovered that once you were out of the direct Florida sun it could be surprisingly cool and pleasant—at least when there was a breeze blowing, as there was now. She sat down on a white stone bench and watched a large egret mincing daintily along the water's edge on tall, spindly legs. There were not very many people around today, and for a moment she felt as if she had this beautiful oasis all to herself.

But only for a moment.

Nothing could have warned her of his approach—no intuitions or awkward footsteps. And she was looking in the other direction, lost in her thoughts, when he suddenly came to stand directly in front of her.

He was wearing old deck sneakers, faded blue jeans and a white cotton shirt open at the neck. She saw the gleam of the gold medallion he always wore and looked up to his eyes, which were hidden behind dark glasses. Nothing, though, could have camouflaged the weariness etched in his face, a weariness emphasized by the stubble of beard on his cheeks and jaw and by his slightly tousled hair.

Candace got to her feet involuntarily and blurted out the first thing that came to her mind.

"You're supposed to be in London!" she stammered.

"I was in London."

"But you weren't due back for another week."

"I'm aware of that," he said testily. "Is it so disconcerting to have me change my plans?"

It was very disconcerting to have him suddenly appear like this, but she wasn't about to give him the satisfaction of telling him so.

She sat down again, forcing calm. "Did you finish your business?" she asked.

The damaged side of Nikolas's face seemed especially immobile as he answered her, his mouth twisting crookedly. "Which business? There are several that need my attention, but only one can be finished at a time. The question became which I should finish first—my business in London or my business with you. It seemed the better choice to postpone matters in England."

Candace had no idea what these "matters" might involve. But she knew from reading about him that Nikolas must be concerned with very big business indeed. How could she possibly have taken priority over the demands of whatever it was that had sent him to London on such short notice?

He sat down beside her but at the opposite end of the bench, moving deliberately as if to get the message across to her that he intended to keep his distance. And with the dark glasses still in place, he was more inscrutable than ever.

Just now he was virtually impossible to read.

"So," he said. "You couldn't wait until I got back to come down here!"

Her chin jutted upward defiantly. "Did you expect me to?"

He sighed. "I wouldn't be so foolish as to expect anything of you, Candace. Let us say I hoped you might."

"Why?"

"So that I would have the chance to speak my own piece, I suppose. For once in my life, I would like the facts to be straight."

She shook her head. "Nikolas, I don't know what you're talking about."

"The hell you don't! I think I've made my feelings about the media plain enough. I think I've made it clear to you how much I detest distortion. Living in the kind of glare your sort of people can turn on did enough of a job on me years ago."

Your sort of people. The words leaped out of context so strongly Candace nearly missed the import of what he was saying. But then it came to her, and she couldn't believe what she was hearing. Unless she was completely off base, Nikolas was suggesting he tell her his story. No need to assure him she had no intention of ever printing it. What would be the use? He'd never believe her!

Your sort of people. Candace tried to wring the hurt out of her voice as she said, "I don't think I've ever misquoted anyone. Certainly not deliberately." She didn't give him time to answer. "How did you know I was here, anyway? Elene?"

"No, not Elene," he replied. "Paul called me right after the first time you went to his shop."

"He called you in London?"

"Yes, in London. They do have telephones in London."

"And you felt you had to rush right back here because of me?"

He slowly removed the glasses, and to her surprise Candace saw a flash of amusement in those familiar green olive eyes. "Isn't that a good enough reason?" he chuckled.

That really stung, but Candace only said, "I don't think that's very funny. In fact, I don't think anything about this is... is very funny at all!"

She turned away, knowing only too well she was on the verge of tears once again. She hated herself for being so weak. Lord knows Nikolas had made it clear what he thought of her profession—and he'd been nothing less than downright insulting in doing so. Yet for all of that he still made her feel as if she was a pawn in his hands.

Well, maybe she was... emotionally. But she was damned if she was going to let his sexuality undermine her this time.

Your sort of people, indeed! Those words showed her exactly where she really stood with him. The fact he enjoyed going to bed with her was something else entirely.

At her side he asked quietly, "What is it, Candace?"

She shook her head, bit her lip and barely managed a muffled "Nothing...."

Two long, slender fingers tilted her chin toward his face, and the tears spilled out of her eyes. And in the moment before he drew her head against his shoulder she saw him wince, as if her tears were hurting him.

"Oh, *agápi mou, agápi mou*," Nikolas said. "Why do we do this to each other?" He was holding her tenderly, stroking her hair lovingly, and gradually her cheeks began to dry. Then he touched her eyes with a folded white handkerchief and said resignedly, "They are still a woman's greatest weapon."

"If you think I was trying to cry..." she began angrily.

"No, my dearest, I do not think you were trying to cry. I know only too well you have entirely too much pride to cry in front of me unless you can't help yourself. It is my fault. But why is it you always seem to make me put things in the worst possible way? I admit I am very tired right now. Jet lag, you know...it always does this to me. But I am willing to start, if you are. The sooner we get this over with, the better."

Again, Candace didn't know what he was talking about. "Start what?" she asked.

"Your interviewing, or whatever you want to call it," he said, looking out across the bayou. "Strange, isn't it, that this particular spot should be our point of rendezvous? In a sense, it all began here."

"Nikolas—"

"No, it's okay. I may find it difficult to break the habit of silence I've imposed on myself for over a decade. But, as I've told you, I would rather have the story come out as it really happened. The truth... without distortion. Let's start at the beginning, Candace."

"Nikolas..."

Again he appeared to ignore her, and Candace made the decision—the momentous decision—to let him talk freely. She thought to herself, *maybe if he gets it out of his system....*

"You already know about the Epiphany celebration," he said, "and you know that I dived for the cross and was lucky enough to get it. And I guess you must know about the film crew that was here doing location shots. Somebody took some footage of me, and that's what led to my being offered the chance to go to Hollywood for screen tests.

"I wasn't even eighteen, but I went to California during the Easter vacation from school, and...I came back to Tarpon Springs with a movie contract. I finished high school here, and then I went back to the coast, even though my uncle told me he'd disown me if I did this. He was a strict old Greek. He'd worked hard as hell to build up his own business, and he wanted me to follow in his footsteps. As a teenager, I just didn't understand what he was offering me. I didn't understand it at all, and I had no idea how deeply I was hurting him when I left.

"Youth is cruel, Candace, in part because it is so callow. You can imagine that I was on a rising tide and determined not to let anything hold me back. Even though the last thing that would have entered my mind—of my own accord, I should amend—was the thought of being a film star.

"My uncle was bitter, and I left under a cloud. I think when this happens to a kid he reaches out for reassurance wherever he can find it. Often he reaches in the wrong directions. I certainly did my share of turning in the wrong directions. I had no one to keep my values straight once I got out to the coast.

"It probably would have been better if I had completely flopped in my first part. Yes, that would have been the best thing that could have happened to me. But it didn't. I played a poor young guy who's a swimming champion. A rich girl falls in love with him despite her father's disapproval. It was a trite picture, but it went over. I went over. Ironically, I came across as an all-American boy. When I look back, it is frightening to see how the whole thing mushroomed after that.''

Nikolas smiled wryly. "It all came too fast, too soon," he said. "I wasn't ready for it. I didn't know how to handle fame, and I had no one to advise me. It went to my head. Later, Gerry told me that when we were first introduced he thought I was the most obnoxious brat he'd ever met!"

Candace remembered reading about Nikolas's lawyer friend when she'd done her research at the New York Public Library. It seemed like years ago now.

"Gerry—Gerald Fraswell—was the greatest thing that happened to me over those years. I had a hell of a fight with the first agent who handled me after I got out there, and it was through my second agent, just a short time later, that I met Gerry. He was old enough to be my father. In fact, he *was* like a father to me. A father, a friend, my business manager and my attorney, as well. When I met him, I was living it up to the hilt with every cent I was making. Gerry sat me down one day and said frankly, 'Let's face it, Nick. You've got a body and a face...and about fifty cents' worth of acting ability. You're like an athlete. One of these years your professional time will be up, and unless you can become a hell of a lot better actor than you are now, you will be all through. And unless you start thinking about providing for the future—,''

"You took comments like that from Gerald Fraswell?" Candace interposed.

"Yes. I may have had my full share of conceit, but I wasn't an idiot. I knew Gerry cared about me, and I knew he was right. Kind of a sixth sense, you might say. It's hard to put it all into words, Candace. Also, this is only scratching the surface, at best. But what I'd really like to get across to you is what actually happens to a person under circumstances like those. Anything you can say about it becomes an oversimplification, because when success comes too early in life it can be a disaster. Especially when it is built on a foundation as shaky as mine was.

"Let's assume my ambition in life had been to be an actor. I'd worked toward it, I'd studied and finally I'd managed to get a small part somewhere—I'd showed a spark of talent. Working my way up would have provided a foundation of experience under me, so that if I ever approached the so-called top, I would have been prepared to handle the phoniness of life out there in Cinema City. I might have been able to handle all the adulation, the exposure and...the fraud.

"A successful actor, perhaps more than most people, needs to be able to come to grips with himself. He must be able to separate the image from the individual, or he will always be as two-dimensional in life as he is on the screen. I was entirely two-dimensional, and there was nothing to fill me out. As I've said, it all came too easily. I didn't know what it was like to struggle as an actor. Gerry was right—I had about fifty cents' worth of talent. But he was the first person who motivated me to try to do better. I also had a couple of directors who were very, very good. I think they could have got emotion from a stone. But my stock-in-trade was this," Nikolas said, lightly touching his face. "Somehow I projected on the screen, and you know what happened. America...young America, especially...was crazy about me. And in my so-called private life I was built up as a great romantic image. I think the studio publicity people teamed me up with half the women in Hollywood under forty."

"I've seen the pictures," Candace said downheartedly.

"So have I," he reminded her. "And as time went by, I got more and more fed up with them—and with the fact that I couldn't go anywhere without being besieged by fans. I appreciated the fans. Any celebrity is a damned fool who doesn't appreciate his fans. You have got to be gracious, you've got shake hands and give autographs. And that smile must always be there, no matter how you are feeling inside.

"Sometimes, and this may sound funny, what I used to do was get lost in a crowd myself. I'd put on some old clothes and wouldn't shave for a couple of days, and I'd go out to a county fair or something like that. Almost always I'd get by without anyone recognizing me. I think that's what gave me the idea of going to New York to live. I'd learned you can be your most anonymous self when you've got a lot of people around you.

"Anyway," Nikolas continued, "back in Hollywood Gerry had started investing for me. He helped me find the ranch, which we bought under another name, so it was quite a while before some bright journalist discovered it was my place." He paused wistfully. "I loved that ranch, Candace. Until the media zeroed in on it I could go out there and get away from all the insanity."

"With your current love?" She couldn't refrain from asking the question.

"No, not with my current love. Gerry and his wife often came out to visit. She's a wonderful person. She's the only person from that phase of my life with whom I stay in touch, and when she occasionally comes to New York we always get together. I wish she'd marry again, but I doubt she will. Gerry was her only love."

Nikolas stared moodily out over the bayou and added, "It's rare, I know. But some people really do have only one love."

Candace felt her throat tighten. Was he referring to Lila Pembroke? She was almost afraid to have him tell her about the accident that had ended the lovely actress's life. . . and his career.

As it was, he turned toward her to say simply, "I have the feeling I'm going about this in entirely the wrong way. You haven't asked me a single question. Wouldn't it make more sense if I just told you what you want to know?"

"What I want to know?"

"That's what I said. For God's sake, Candace, don't start echoing me. You seem to have a habit of doing that."

"I don't mean to echo you. I. . . I don't know what I mean to do." Candace felt herself tightening up and wrung her hands nervously. "Nikolas, I. . . ."

"Yes," he said dryly, "I can see. You are about to burst into tears again. Sometimes I can't figure out the effect I have on you."

"Then that makes two of us."

He laughed and put his arm around her shoulder in an almost brotherly fashion. "Don't look so unhappy, *mikrís mou*. Once we've got your story behind us...."

Candace shut her eyes tightly. "Nikolas," she said, "I didn't come to Tarpon Springs to interview you."

"Yes, I know that," Nikolas told her levelly.

"I came here to get information about Tarpon Springs," Candace persisted, "not about you. You don't seem to want to believe that, but the article I am writing for *Tempo* is about the community and the people who live here. It's about sponge fishing, the Greek culture, that sort of thing. It is not about you!"

"All right, if you say so," Nikolas nodded, his face impassive.

Candace sighed. It was a beautiful day, such a beautiful day. This would be a wonderful place to be, with Nikolas by her side, were it not for the thorn of his distrust. "You still don't believe me," she said, discouraged. "What can I do to convince you I'm telling you the truth?"

He considered this, gazing out over the bayou, his eyes remote. Then he said slowly, "I suppose time is the only thing that can really build trust between two people, Candace, when you get right down to it. Also, as you already know, my faith in people of your profession was seriously damaged a long time ago. Please," as he saw the expression on her face, "don't misunderstand me. I want to believe you, Candace. You can't imagine how much I want to believe you...and to believe *in* you, as well. But wanting to do something doesn't necessarily make it so. I think it is only honest to say that in many ways we are going to have to prove some things to each other.

Agreed? Now...let's talk about something else, shall we?''

She fought back a nagging sense of defeat. She had wanted desperately to have Nikolas tell her she'd already proved herself to him, but obviously this was not to be. She asked, "How did you know where to find me?''

"I stopped at the Grecian Gardens. Elene said you told her you were planning to take a break from work and go for a walk along the bayou. She said you are to have dinner with her tonight and she asked me to join the two of you. I hope you don't mind.''

"Why should I mind?" she asked a bit testily.

"It seems that Theone is also expecting you for dinner tomorrow night and she, too, has asked me to be present. But I had to refuse, so at least you won't have to suffer my presence two nights in a row!''

"Oh, stop it!" Candace said, annoyed.

But Nikolas only laughed, a lazy and surprisingly indulgent laugh. Then he stretched and said, "This would be a good afternoon for the beach. It's just a short drive over to the gulf. You have a bathing suit with you, don't you?''

"Yes. But just for sunning and pool splashing. I don't swim.''

"Not at all?" he asked incredulously.

"No, not enough to count," Candace answered. "We lived in Albany, and summers when I was little we did go up to Lake Champlain on vacations, but my sister and I used to just splash around in the shallow water. My mother didn't swim, and although my father always intended to teach us, he never got around to it. I suppose I could have taken lessons...."

"No need to take lessons," Nikolas said. "I will teach you."

The mere thought of having Nikolas teach her to swim was unnerving. The mere thought of being around Nikolas, who would be more of an Adonis than ever in bathing trunks, and of having him hold her....

A wave of desire so unadulterated it was jolting in its intensity swept through Candace, and she actually trembled. Then she said, "If I'm going to make it to Elene's for dinner, I should really be getting back to my motel."

He raised a mocking eyebrow. "Very well, then. I will go with you."

"You will not go with me!" she contradicted swiftly. "Believe it or not, Nikolas, I'm on a schedule, and I...I've got to keep to it. Before dinner, I need to put in another hour's work."

"I, too, was on a schedule, Candace," he reproved, "and I inconvenienced quite a few other people when I changed it—because of you. I am not about to let you start playing your silly games. I want to get this over with more than you do, believe me. So I don't give a damn whether we keep on talking here or whether we finish up in your room. I intend to go back to London tomorrow, so the main thing is not to waste any more time."

"You're going back to London tomorrow?"

"You're echoing me again," he said impatiently.

"No. What I mean is...are you telling me you flew all the way across the Atlantic for just one day?"

"It seems obvious, doesn't it? It was important enough to me you hear the truth, but I am the first to admit I'm not doing a very good job of telling it. I have muddled along without really conveying what it was I wanted to convey. But...this isn't easy for me."

It wouldn't be easy for him! He'd buried Nicky Mellin years ago. Now, to have to exhume the memories and emotions and pain....

"Nikolas?" Candace asked tentatively.

"Yes?"

"Why was there a story printed that said Nicky Mellin had died? And that his ashes had been scattered over the San Bernardino ranch?"

She saw the muscle twitch in his jaw, and it was a few long seconds before he answered. Then he said slowly, "Because Nicky Mellin had to die, Candace, if Nikolas Mylonis was ever to have any chance of living. Can you understand that? Nicky Mellin was a legend...like the Beatles, like Presley, like a lot of others I could name. And there was no way he could play the part of a phoenix rising from the ashes. The past would always be there to haunt him. He'd been created out of whole cloth in the first place, can't you see that? He was an illusion, built up out of nothing. Sometimes I wonder if there ever really was a Nicky Mellin."

He fell silent for a moment, his face dark and brooding. Then he said, "Gerald Fraswell stuck his neck out as few people would when he issued that obituary story. He laid his reputation on the line, and it was a very fine reputation. He and his wife, Mary, knew what it would mean if it were ever discovered he had faked Nicky Mellin's death...and had also managed to have the estate handled in a way that would allow Nikolas Mylonis to begin living again. That was eight years ago. Gerry's dead now, so it doesn't matter so much if the truth comes out. He and Mary didn't have any children, so there is no problem there. But...exposure will hurt Mary. It is bound to hurt Mary. We have talked about it, though, and she would still do anything to protect me. She even said I could plead amnesia." His smile was wry. "She said I could plead that I don't remember a thing about ever having been Nicky Mellin, that his life is all blacked out. I only wish to God it were!"

"Did you love her very much?" Candace barely whispered the words.

"Did I love who very much?"

"Lila Pembroke. Did you love her very much?"

Even the breeze that had been blowing gently through the palms seemed to stop. It was a silent moment, an intense moment. Then Nikolas said, "That is a question I am not going to answer right now. Later, maybe, but not now." He exhaled deeply. He had finished, and now he said, "Come along, Candace."

"Come along where?"

"We'll go over to the docks and have some coffee at Mike Lekakis's place. You can breathe in some authentic Tarpon Springs Greek atmosphere. Okay?"

His mood had changed that suddenly. And strange as it seemed, he was acting almost lighthearted. Candace decided it was doubtful she'd ever be able to understand Nikolas, but nevertheless she nodded.

"Okay," she said. "You lead the way."

CHAPTER TWENTY-THREE

SOMEONE WAS POUNDING on the door. Candace awakened with a start, her heart hammering. She glanced at the luminous dial of her traveling alarm clock and saw that the hands stood at four.

Four o'clock in the morning! She crossed to the door, caution making her call out, "Who is it?" before she opened it.

"Nikolas," came the answer. "For God's sake, Candace, open up!"

She fumbled with the chain and turned the bolt. He brushed past her unseeingly, then sank into the small armchair in the corner.

He looked terrible. His face was putty gray, making the scars seem more pronounced than she'd ever seen them, and he was carrying a pint bottle of whiskey. Now he held this out to her and demanded abruptly, "Would you mind?"

She could sense his anxiety, so she asked, "How much?"

"Just a straight double shot."

Candace got a glass from the bathroom and poured a generous measure of whiskey into it. At the same time, she plugged in the small portable coffeepot she had carried along in her travel case. *A cup of coffee wouldn't hurt either of us just now,* she thought sleepily.

She'd left him not four hours before They had spent a wonderful evening with Elene, eating a delicious Greek spinach pie and playing Greek music. Both Nikolas and Elene had said the music was to put Candace in a totally Hellenic mood.

Candace had driven to the Grecian Gardens herself, having returned to her own motel to change after she'd had coffee on the sponge docks with Nikolas. And even that had been a very pleasant experience. He had introduced her to one of the divers, and the man had actually joined them for a while. Nikolas had acted as an interpreter, since the man's English had been limited.

Nikolas had been a charming companion both at the docks and at Elene's, and he had seen Candace out to her car when the time had come for her to leave. Then he had bent down to kiss her on the lips before he'd said good-night. It had been a tender kiss, and love for him had suffused her. The quicksilver attraction between them was not in the least diminished, but it seemed to Candace that today she and Nikolas had inexplicably entered a new dimension.

In parting, he had suggested they meet for breakfast at Aliki's at eight o'clock the next morning. And she had agreed, so mesmerized by him she would have been apt to agree to anything he suggested just then. Then she'd gone to bed wondering how she could bear having him go back to London so soon.

Now, four hours later, this was happening, and as Candace glanced down at Nikolas's dark, tousled head she knew something was terribly wrong. He looked up at her, his green eyes haunted, and didn't wait for the question. He said simply, "Manos is dead."

Manos Panagoris had been the last person in the world on Candace's mind. So she could only stare at Nikolas, stupefied. Finally she wrenched out the word, "How?"

"He cracked up a car out on Long Island late yesterday afternoon, and I guess the cops had a hell of a time making an identification. He was with a woman. In fact, it was her car—one of those expensive sports jobs. Manos was driving. He had no business trying to handle a car like that. He went off the road on a curve and plowed into a concrete post. Evidently they were both killed instantly. Needless to say, the woman's husband—once they'd called him to come to the morgue—didn't know who the hell Manos was. For that matter, from what I have learned since, his own mother wouldn't have been able to recognize him."

"Oh, God!" Candace moaned. "Poor Elene!"

"Yes, poor Elene," Nikolas said grimly. "I wish there had been some way of keeping the circumstances from her, but it was a cousin of Manos's who called from Philadelphia. He came right out with all the details, the damned fool. The dead woman's husband knew she had gone out with friends. And the friends knew she had teamed up with Manos at a nightclub. That's how they traced him. I guess there was a letter in his room from this cousin in Philadelphia. It doesn't make much difference," Nikolas said wearily. "These relatives in Philadelphia are the people Manos lived with when he first came to the States."

Candace was shaking, and the only thing that brought her back to reality was the sound of the water boiling. She made coffee for both Nikolas and herself, and as she handed him a cup, his fingers closed over hers. For a moment he pressed them tightly, then he said, "Thanks, Candace." She bent to kiss him on the forehead and realized he was struggling to keep control of his emotions. He closed his eyes under those long dark lashes, lashes almost too beautiful for a man.

"Is there someone with Elene?" she asked.

"Yes," Nikolas managed, gaining control again. "Theone is there. Elene called our house and I answered the phone. I don't think it has really hit her yet. I went right over and Theone came with me."

"And Melina?"

"We didn't wake Melina up. Morning will be time enough to cope with Melina...and to see how Melina copes with something involving someone other than herself. We didn't call Aliki, either. Theone said to let her sleep a couple of more hours. Aliki hated Manos, but that may make it worse instead of better. Greeks, in case you haven't noticed, tend to be as intense as hell when it comes to emotional issues. There is going to be a lot of moaning and pure black mourning, because that's the way it is when there's a death. But I'd like to spare Elene some of that, if possible. That is why I came to get you."

"You want me to be with her?"

"Yes. The two of you are close in age, and it seems quite an empathy has built up between you. Elene is essentially a shy person. It is rare for her to respond to someone such as she has with you. Even with everything else she had on her mind tonight—mostly Manos—she was almost lighthearted there for a while."

"Have you called Paul?"

Nikolas's glance was curious. "No," he said. "Time enough for that in the morning. George Andris is coming over, though. I imagine he will want to give Elene a sedative, even though she's probably going to insist she doesn't need one. But at some point she is going to shatter. She will have to. The grief will have to come out if she's to be. . .healed."

Their eyes met. Candace was thinking of Nikolas's own tragedy. He had lost the woman he loved in a terrible accident, too. He, more than most people, would know all there was to know about grief under circumstances such as these.

To her surprise, he shook his head slowly. "Don't jump to conclusions, Candace," he warned.

"I'm not. . ." she began.

"I think you are," he corrected. He put down his empty coffee cup and stood up. "Will you come back with me?" he asked.

"If you're sure Elene won't feel I'm intruding."

"She won't. What about your article, though? I know you are well into it, and getting involved in this may set you back. . . ."

Candace flung a long, level glance at him. "My article will be just fine," she said, gathering some clothes and closing the bathroom door behind her.

THEONE WAS SITTING at the table in Elene's little kitchen, and the smell of coffee filled the room. "She will be happy to see you," Theone said thickly, her accent heavy. But as she raised her cup, she managed a slight smile.

Despite these assurances, Candace hesitated on the threshold of Elene's bedroom, her eyes fixed uncertainly on the woman's slim figure prone on the bed.

There was a single dim light in the room, and she swallowed nervously because she couldn't clearly see Elene's face. Then, as she approached the bed almost silently, the other woman held out her hand and said simply, "Oh, Candace!"

Candace covered the rest of the distance between them in one swift movement and sank down next to Elene, lacing her fingers with those offered. Elene's eyes were dark pools of anguish, but they were tearless and dry. Nikolas was right. Elene was going to have to cry in order to begin washing away the grief.

"Dearest," Candace said gently. "Don't hold back."

"Oh, Candace!" Elene said. Then she was holding out both her arms and Candace was clutching her as if she were a child. And all at once Elene began to weep. Her body was racked by sobs, and Candace could feel the hot tears of anguish running down her neck, where Elene had pressed her face. All of a sudden, Candace was crying, too. Crying for herself, and for Nikolas, and for Elene. She even cried for Manos. Handsome, irresponsible, amoral Manos... who perhaps, as Nikolas had once suggested, should never have left Greece.

After what seemed a long time, George Andris's sedative began to take effect, and Elene lay back. But she said, "Please, Candace...don't leave."

"I'm not going anywhere," she promised.

She stretched out alongside Elene and could feel her starting to relax, starting to fall asleep. As if in counterpoint her own eyes closed, and it was not until quite a while later that she opened them to find Nikolas looking down at her with an expression so tender it made her catch her breath.

But when he suggested she come and join the rest of them, she shook her head.

"I promised Elene I wouldn't leave her," she said quietly, "so I'm going to stay here until she wakes up."

Nikolas didn't attempt to persuade her to do otherwise. But he did bend to touch his lips to hers, and he murmured something in Greek to her, something she'd never heard before. Candace wanted to tell him the least he could do was speak English to her. But there was no need to do this. Regardless of language, his message seemed very clear.

Daylight came, and Elene stirred. She pressed her hands to her head and moaned softly. Candace, instantly alert, offered to get her some coffee, and when Elene nodded, she got up and went out to the kitchen. Nikolas was sitting alone at the table, a half-filled cup in front of him.

"George had to get some sleep before he goes back on call," he explained, "and I sent Theone home and told her to lie down for a while herself. She will have her hands full today. She is going to call Aliki in time to catch her before she starts out for the restaurant."

"What about the restaurant? Who will run it?"

Nikolas shrugged. "It will have to be closed until things settle down," he said. "Then we'll see."

"Does Aliki own the restaurant?"

"No," he said shortly, "I do."

"And this motel?"

"I own it, too. Anything else?"

Candace was fixing Elene's coffee and she said, "I wasn't trying to pry. I only wondered, all right?"

"I'm sorry," he said slowly, and frowned. "I didn't mean to sound so...suspicious. Why don't you let me take that in to Elene while you sit down and have a cup yourself? You look exhausted.''

''I'm all right,'' Candace said. ''But that's a good idea. I think she'd like to see you about now.''

When Nikolas had left, she sat down and thought about everything Elene would have to endure. It didn't seem possible Manos was gone. Whatever else she could say about him, she had to admit there had been a vitality about him, an excitement. She imagined how tremendously he must have appealed to a quiet girl like Elene, how he must have literally swept her off her feet....

Nikolas came back into the kitchen, and in answer to her unspoken question he said, ''Elene is all right. She wants to be alone for a little while, and I think it would be a good thing just now. She needs to pull herself together before Theone comes over here with Aliki.'' He paused briefly, then added, ''Thank you, Candace.''

''You've no need to thank me, Nikolas.''

''On the contrary... your coming here has meant a great deal to Elene. I appreciate it more than I can tell you.''

He spoke so formally it was disconcerting. Had he thought things over and decided her willingness to come to Elene's side had stemmed from some ulterior motive? Even though he had been the one who had asked her for help?

Now he said more gently, ''You might as well run along.''

''What?''

Evidently he did not sense her outrage. ''You'll need to get some rest,'' he continued. ''You'll want to get back to your work, and—''

She got to her feet, seething. "How can you be like this?" she demanded. "Do you think I can just walk out on Elene and go back to writing some stupid article as if nothing's happened to her? Oh, you've made it plain enough what your opinion is of 'my sort of people,' Nikolas Mylonis. But I'm not moving an inch until Elene asks me to leave. And I don't give a damn whether you like it or not!"

Nikolas stared at her as if she'd struck him. Then, to her astonishment, he asked, "Did I hear you right? I can't believe it!" His words remained a mystery, because at that moment Theone and Aliki arrived.

Aliki clasped Candace in her arms as if she were another daughter. It didn't matter that Aliki was speaking in Greek and Candace was speaking in English. She felt the same empathy with Elene's mother she'd felt from the beginning with Elene herself. Even Theone, who had reacted so coolly to Candace at first, now warmed to her. And, Candace realized, Theone was perceptive. She surely seemed to be aware of Nikolas's vulnerability, and so naturally she was protective of him.

Nikolas's vulnerability. Candace, pouring out coffee for both Aliki and Theone, looked across the room and met a green olive gaze that seemed at this moment entirely foreign to her. *Assessing Nikolas Mylonis will always be impossible,* she thought as he looked at her in a way he never had before.

THE AFTERNOON PASSED. People came to call as the word of Manos Panagoris's death became widespread. They brought food and flowers and stayed to drink wine and coffee. Even Melina was showing a surprising new maturity. She arrived looking simple and beautiful and carrying a plate of small sweet cakes.

The callers were greeted and served in Elene's living room, although Elene herself did not emerge from the bedroom. Of course, no one expected her to. Some of the older women went in to see her and came back wiping tears from their eyes.

"So beautiful, so tragic," more than one whispered to Candace in heavily accented English.

Paul showed up looking tired and wretched and had to force a smile as he greeted Candace. "How is she doing?" he asked, drawing her aside.

"Very well, considering," Candace told him, which was the truth. Elene was pale and tight-lipped, but she was no longer closeting her grief. She had poured out the first frenzy of sorrow on Candace's shoulder during those early morning hours. And through their mutual veil of tears they had come to share something that could never be abrogated—no matter what Nikolas might think!

There were phone calls throughout the afternoon, and Nikolas handled most of them. A number of them came from Philadelphia, and even though everything was said in Greek, Candace realized the funeral arrangements were probably being made. She hardly needed a translation to get the sense of what was going on.

All this time, Paul Morrison was sitting quietly on the sidelines, and Candace's heart went out to him. There was no doubt in her mind he really loved Elene, and thus she could understand how he felt. She also truly loved someone who. . . .

She forced this someone out of her mind only to

find his magnetic gaze once again searing her. Nikolas, hanging up the phone receiver after yet another call, came across to her and took hold of her arm. Then, before she knew what he was doing, he steered her out the door of the apartment and down the steps into the motel's little reception room.

Only then did Candace recover sufficiently to say defiantly, "It's no use, Nikolas. I've told you I won't leave unless Elene tells me to, and so far—"

"No one's asking you to leave," Nikolas gritted. "But that doesn't mean you can't go for a breath of fresh air, does it?" He was leading her out through the front door and she saw his car parked just past the entrance.

"Get in," he snapped.

"Suppose I don't want to get in?"

"Candace," he said, obviously holding a rein on himself, "don't force me!"

"Brute strength never does sway me," she told him.

"No?" He looked so threatening she thought better of trying to bolt as he opened the door for her. She slid in and gnashed her teeth, preparing for verbal battle, but Nikolas was strangely silent as he drove around Spring Bayou and onto the road that led toward the gulf.

They went through a residential area, passed a school and a shopping complex and then skirted several condominiums. Finally they drove across a low, palm-bordered causeway. The road came to a dead end at a circle, beyond which were picnic tables on the sand and palm trees growing out of the beach itself. Candace could not help thinking how tropical the scene was.

Nikolas came around and opened her door, and she hardly needed his invitation to get out. She slipped off her shoes and walked across the white sand, breathing deeply. The sun, a huge molten disk, was beginning its rendezvous with the horizon, and there was a warm breeze sweeping in off the lovely, milk-jade water. It almost made Candace wish she could swim.

As it was, she walked to the edge of the sand and let the waves ripple around her toes. There was a sailboat close offshore, its sails a vivid pattern of spiraling red, black, orange and cerulean blue. Then a pelican flew overhead, swerving in an arc to plunge down into the water in quest of a fish. Evidently the fish escaped, because the pelican seemed to come to roost on the waves, bobbing with the swell of the tide. He was a big, comical bird with whom Candace fell in love at once.

The beach wasn't crowded. There were a few people picnicking, and a couple of young children were playing in the sand with bright plastic pails and shovels. An old man stood fishing along a rocky outcropping back toward the roadway over which she and Nikolas had just driven. There was enough space here, enough solitude to bring to Candace the sense of peace she so badly needed.

She felt Nikolas's hand reaching for hers and she didn't try to pull away. She stood very still, knowing this was not the moment to say anything harsh. And she wondered if Elene had ever come here with Manos and if they'd ever stood here hand in hand. The image made her shiver.

"What is it?" Nikolas asked, perceptive as ever.

"I can't believe Manos is dead."

"It will take time. It always takes time," Nikolas said, and Candace was sure he was once again thinking of Lila Pembroke. She ached for him, and it was a terrible kind of ache, beyond the reach of any sort of panacea.

But I'm going to have to live with it, she thought. *I'm going to have to live with it forever and ever.*

She asked, "Where will the funeral be?"

"In Philadelphia. Manos has family there, as you know. I thought it would be better all around. Easier for Elene."

"You won't be going back to London, then?"

"Not for at least another week," he said slowly. "I have a number of things to think out, and it would be best if I worked them out here."

"But you'll be going to Philadelphia?"

"No," Nikolas said to her surprise. "Theone and Aliki will go with Elene. I can handle some of the business with London by phone, if necessary. But . . . there is much more than that at stake."

Candace wasn't about to question him. He looked very tired, very introspective, and it was easy enough to understand why. Nikolas felt responsible for Elene, and for Aliki, Theone and Melina, as well. Such a sense of duty could prove to be a heavy burden.

They sat on the beach for a while in silence and were silent on their way back to the motel. It was not until they were at the foot of the staircase leading to Elene's apartment that Nikolas spoke to her again. Then, at the very last instant, he took hold of Candace's arm and turned her around so she had to look at him. "There is something you should know," he said quietly but with an intensity that made her heart begin to thud. The emotion was gone from his voice, though, as he said, "I think I know what you've been thinking...and you should know you're entirely wrong. I never loved Lila. I can't honestly say I ever even liked her. I admired her as an actress, yes, but I can't say I did as a person. It was no great display of romantic heroics on my part when I went in the water after her. I would have dived in after anyone who had fallen overboard, simply because I'd been brought up around the water. Swimming and diving were as natural to me as breathing. If I hadn't been drinking, I might have paused to wonder about the possibility of rocks. But of course I didn't think and...the rest is history. I would never be so foolish as to repeat such a performance."

Nikolas bent and kissed her before she could speak, and the warm pressure of his lips sent a treacherous rush of feeling cascading through her.

Then his lips curved in the faintest of smiles. "Leave your imagination to your writing, *agápi mou*," he said, his tone teasing. "Now, let's go back to Elene."

CHAPTER TWENTY-FOUR

ELENE LEFT ON A PLANE for Philadelphia the next morning, accompanied by her mother and Theone. Nikolas drove them to the airport in Tampa, and Candace knew it would be several hours before he returned. Then he'd probably be busy with his own affairs, especially the phone conferences he was setting up with his associates in London. She'd only be in the way.

She hadn't been in the way yesterday, though. She had helped serve food to the visitors until well into the night. And although she'd felt herself a "foreigner" among these people, mainly because of the language barrier, she hadn't felt like a stranger. She had even been introduced to a priest from St. Nicholas's Cathedral. He had been very friendly and was more than agreeable to the idea of having Candace sit in on some of the church classes and letting her photograph the children who attended them.

She had hoped Nikolas would ask her to drive to Tampa with him, but he didn't. So she'd gone to bed making the decision she'd sleep late the next morning, but she couldn't. Aliki's restaurant was closed, of course, and the memory of seeing another breakfast spot eluded her just now. Finally she decided to go back to the small Greek place near the docks where Nikolas had taken her for coffee and pastries.

Mike Lekakis, the proprietor, remembered her at once and came over to join her. "If you don't mind?" he said, smiling.

Candace didn't mind in the least. In fact, she was flattered.

Mike's English was very slightly accented, and she couldn't decide whether this was because he'd been born in Greece or because he'd spoken Greek as a primary language when he was growing up. Nikolas, she reminded herself, had been born in Greece yet had no trace of an accent at all. What he did have was a deplorable tendency to lapse into his native language at the moments when she most wanted to know what he was saying! She wondered if Nikolas's English might not have been thoroughly Americanized by intense voice lessons in Hollywood. Very likely so, she suspected.

Mike quickly got on the subject of Elene's loss, and one thing led to another and led to. . . Nikolas. Candace, hoping to get their conversation back on safe ground, managed to slip in what she knew about Tarpon Springs and sponge diving. And as if on cue, Mike opened right up. As it happened, he had tried sponge diving as a young man because his father had been a diver. But now he admitted with a reluctant shake of the head he hadn't been cut out for it.

"It's a rough life," he said, and shrugged. "Who knows when the red tide will come back and wipe out the business all over again? Where would a man be then, if all he knew was sponge fishing? From what the old men who remember say, it was very, very bad after the big blight. Some of the sponge boats were converted to shrimp boats, or they fixed them up for commercial fishing. But many of the boats just sank right at their moorings. There was no use for them, so they simply rotted out.

"You'll want to go to the sponge auction while you're here," he told Candace then. "It's held in the Exchange. That's that big cement building down at the end of the street."

"That's where the sponges are sold?" Candace asked.

Mike nodded. "Practically all that are brought in here. Twice a week, usually. It might interest you to know, incidentally, that Tarpon Springs is still one of the largest natural-sponge markets in the world, despite the decline in the business. There are over a hundred storage rooms in the Exchange. During the auctions the sponges are brought out and spread on the ground so they can be examined. There are several different types of sponges, and the price they bring can vary tremendously."

Candace laughed. "Before I did all my research," she admitted. "I thought a sponge was a sponge."

"Only to a point," Mike smiled. "If you plan to take any sponges home with you, pick the wool ones. They cost more, but they're worth more. They're deep-water sponges and one of them will last for years, so long as you don't put any commercial bleach on it. The yellow sponges are cheaper and not as good, but even they will last for two or three years, if they're cared for. Then we go down to other varieties that are harvested but are less desirable. Actually, there are something like five thousand different types of sponges, but only a few are considered important from the commercial point of view."

The little restaurant was beginning to fill up with late-morning coffee drinkers, most of them men.

Some carried newspapers with them and obviously had favorite tables. They settled in as if they were about to take up residence.

"An old Greek custom," Mike said. "Greek men are used to spending hours in coffee houses, reading their papers and shooting the breeze. Part of the local paper here is even printed in Greek."

Candace smiled. "One day I'm going to have to learn that alphabet," she said.

"Maybe Nick will teach you."

She sidestepped this and asked, "One thing bothers me, Mike. Where are the springs they named the town after?"

"There aren't any," he said, grinning. "The story goes that years ago there were so many tarpon leaping offshore in the gulf that one early settler said to another, 'Watch the tarpon spring!' That sounded like a good name for a town, so it stuck."

With that he left her and took over the cash register so the woman who had been watching it was free to wait on the customers.

After Candace left the restaurant, she wandered along Dodecanese Boulevard and browsed again in some of the gift shops. In one she found a tiny silver diver suspended from a shimmering chain, and she bought it as a memento. Having paid for this souvenir, she was just turning away from the counter when the gleam of gold caught her eye, and she saw a gold medallion displayed in a velvet-lined box on a lower shelf.

The proprietor was an elderly man whose English was comprehensible but even more heavily accented than Theone's. He seemed surprised by Candace's request to see the pendant, and his gnarled fingers fumbled as he handled the little box.

"It is Saint Nicholas," he said as he put the box on the glass counter top in front of her. "He is patron saint of everyone here. Saint for all who work with the sea." He grinned, displaying a large gold tooth. "You have Greek man you love," he said, making what he obviously considered a great joke. "You buy this for him. Then he always be safe."

Candace swallowed hard. The old man could not know, of course, how close to home he had come. "Thank you very much," she said, barely managing the words.

Her heart felt strangely heavy as she walked out of the shop, and glancing at her watch she saw it was nearly noon. There wouldn't be any classes at the cathedral until much later, when the regular school classes were out, so she decided to go to Paul's and pick up some more film. But before she got very far she was attracted by a display of beads outside another of the shops and paused to finger a strand of pale pink shells she especially liked.

She was looking at the price tag when she heard a familiar voice say, "So there you are!"

Nikolas. Candace would have sworn for a second or two her heart actually stopped.

He'd evidently gone by his house to change since he'd returned from Tampa. He was wearing the faded jeans again, a yellow pullover shirt and his soiled old deck sneakers. The inscrutable dark glasses were also back in place.

"I thought I might find you along here," he said. "Have you been accumulating the background color you wanted?"

"A good bit of it, yes," Candace answered. "Did Elene get off all right?"

"She did," Nikolas said easily. "Theone promised to call tonight. Theone will never get used to the idea of long-distance telephoning. She thinks it is a sinful extravagance."

Candace smiled. "Well," she said, "you can hardly blame her. When I think of it, she's had so much to adapt to...."

"Between our ways and yours?"

"Nikolas," she said, wearily shaking her head. "You know very well you are leading me on, and I will not get into an argument with you!"

"I didn't intend that you should, Candace."

"Our ways and yours, indeed! Honestly, you're so full of preconceived notions...."

He grinned, and the fact that it was a slightly twisted grin made it all the more appealing. "Now who's arguing?" he demanded, but before Candace could say a thing, he asked, "Do you like those pink beads?"

"Yes, I do. I think they're pretty. I was just looking to see how much they cost."

"It doesn't matter," he said loftily. "They are yours." With that he plucked the beads off the rack they were hanging on and disappeared into the shadowy confines of the little shop. A second later Candace heard the low murmur of Greek. Then almost as quickly he returned, thrusting a small brown paper bag into her hand. "To remember your own atrocious Greek," he said lightly. "Maybe this is a piece of jewelry you will keep!"

Candace flushed as she remembered the other piece of jewelry Nikolas had given her. If he was about to bring that up....

But he didn't. He only said, "What was next on your agenda?"

"Either getting some film at Paul's or taking the boat trip," she informed him.

"Do you need more film immediately?"

"No. I have enough to handle the diving exhibition, if that is what you mean."

"That is what I mean, Candace. I would also like to join you on the boat trip and for lunch, if I may?"

"You must have other things to do," she pointed out, beginning to feel skittish. "I mean, surely you've seen sponge-diving exhibitions dozens of times. You've even dived for sponges yourself, haven't you?"

"Come to think of it, I have," he smirked. "But that doesn't mean I would not enjoy playing tourist with you."

His presence, as it always did, was having a profoundly disturbing effect on her. It would be impossible to concentrate on work with Nikolas around, and Candace said, "I thought you had to keep in touch with London."

Nikolas paused right in the middle of the sidewalk, heedless of the tourists who had to walk around him. "Damn it!" he exploded as several people turned and watched with curious gazes. "If you don't want me to go with you why don't you just come out and say so?"

"It isn't that, Nikolas," she hedged self-consciously.

"Isn't it?"

"Oh, very well, then," she said ungraciously. "Come along."

For a moment Candace thought he was going to

refuse. But with a muttered imprecation—in Greek, naturally—Nikolas tailored his long stride to blend with her shorter steps, and the two of them started down the street together.

"How about the boat trip first?" he suggested. "It only takes half an hour. It will help us work up an appetite."

She was agreeable to this, so they crossed the street to the boarding place at the end of the dock. Nikolas bought tickets for both of them, keeping up a running dialogue of Greek with the ticket seller as he did so. The sponge boat they would be taking was just docking, and while they waited in line to board it Nikolas said, "They are interesting little boats. They have been modernized over the years, but they go back to an original Greek type of craft that was called a *sacroleve*. This was somewhat similar to a caravel type of boat."

"It doesn't seem very big for something that has to go out to sea for days at a time," Candace said.

"No, but they are sturdy," he told her. "They're about forty feet long and actually they will sleep six men, though I admit the quarters are tight ones. They are tough little boats, made originally for sail. Now, of course, they have power, as well."

The boat unloaded its cargo of brightly dressed tourists, and at once the order to board was called. Nikolas helped Candace up the three short steps and over the side. The diver, the two deckhands and the boat's captain all knew Nikolas, she discovered, and they came by every now and then to make quips with him in Greek, all of which seemed to be very funny.

Once again filled with people, the boat slipped out

into the river channel and headed toward Tarpon Bayou, in the direction of the gulf.

"We won't go very far," Nikolas told her. "They've planted a sponge bed farther out in the channel for exhibition purposes. The water is about twenty feet deep there, which is enough. I think you'll find the whole thing very interesting, and you should be able to get some good pictures as well."

Candace, watching the diver sitting in the bow of the boat, agreed. He was younger than the diver she'd met with Nikolas the other day, yet he still had to be at least sixty. It amazed her to think that he could go out on a regular basis to dive several times each day, even in an exhibition such as this. This must seem like child's play in comparison to the real task of diving out in the gulf itself.

The boat, she noted, was being steered from the stern, and the captain, who was handling the steering, was also the commentator for the trip. She judged him to be in his early forties. He was fairly tall and slim and had that seafaring look about him, even though his seafaring at present must consist entirely of these simple short trips to please the tourists.

His English was as unaccented as Nikolas's, and he was a good talker. He detailed the story of the Greeks coming to Tarpon Springs very briefly, then concentrated upon sponges and sponge diving.

Candace had been concentrating on both the action around her and the captain's comments, but she was still aware of Nikolas at her side. A moment later they were dropping anchor, and the deckhands were helping the diver don the heavy helmet and weights that would make his descent possible. Then he climbed over a ladder on the side of the boat and disappeared down beneath the water, and after a time they could no longer see even the air bubbles coming up from his hose.

Candace moved to the bow, planning to get a picture of him as soon as he resurfaced. The captain had already indicated this would be a good shot for those on board who wanted to use their cameras, since the diver would emerge holding up a sponge he had just harvested.

She wanted to get in the forefront, in order to adjust her focus, but there were a number of tourists aboard who had the same idea. Candace found herself being jostled good-naturedly for place and knew that Nikolas was watching her, and not without amusement. She gritted her teeth. This time around, she was at least going to prove her professional competence!

She saw air bubbles in the distance and knew the diver would soon be breaking to the surface and would then be towed back to the boat by a long line that would be hauled in by the deckhands. It was going to be impossible to get a clear shot from where she was, because a very large man had just wedged his way in front of her and was totally blocking her view.

Candace moved quickly, stepping up on the bow space where the diver had been perched during the trip out. She was wearing flat, rubber-soled shoes, so there was no reason to doubt her footing. Yet, something happened. Suddenly she felt herself slip, and in another instant she was flailing into space. As she fell, she heard a woman scream far above her, and then the water came to meet her with a hard slap. She plunged through it immediately and into the murky, deep-green depths.

She fought panic, even as instinct made her hold her breath. But she knew desperately that she wasn't going to be able to hold it for very long. Then she began to feel as if she were bursting, the pressure ballooning her head, and she knew she was on the verge of drowning.

In another second she was not going to be able to keep from opening her mouth, and then the water would invade her lungs. Candace now struggled violently, fighting the horror of this unknown element. Then she felt gripped in the vise of giant tentacles. Gripped and urged and pulled . . . when blackness took over.

"LET HER HAVE some air, for God's sake!"

It was Nikolas's voice. Candace knew it was Nikolas's voice.

Someone else said something in Greek and she heard Nikolas reply in Greek, and then another man said, "You don't have to work over her any longer. She's conscious. Okay, people, stand back and give her some air."

Candace opened her eyes to find Nikolas kneeling at her side. He was dripping wet. Dark hair was plastered to his head, rivulets of water were running down his face and the expression in his eyes seemed to be devouring her. He put an arm around her and helped her sit up, and she leaned against him, still gasping, still rocking.

A young man pushed through the crowd on the deck and said, "I know C.P.R., sir. If you need help—"

"She doesn't need any more of it," Nikolas said tautly. "She's okay." But his eyes were boring into her as if he doubted his own statement.

He'd been giving her C.P.R. himself, then. She had passed out under the surface, and in those last horrible seconds the water had staked its claim. Nikolas had brought her back to life. He had resuscitated her. His mouth upon her mouth, this time giving her the very breath of life.

But there was more than that. Candace tried to speak and couldn't at first, and then the few words she could manage came hoarsely. "You dived in after me!" she said.

He didn't bother to answer.

They were pulling into the docks and Nikolas said something in swift Greek to one of the deckhands. The man answered in English, "My car is closer," and Nikolas nodded.

"Get it then," he said tersely.

The ranks of people waiting for the boat were swelling, as others noticed she was being carried by a tall, dark Greek who could have been Poseidon himself. She clung to him, burying her face against his shoulder, and again he murmured something to her in Greek. She imagined for the rest of his life he would always think in Greek first during moments of intense emotion. She stole a look at him as he gently placed her in the back seat of the car that had drawn up to the curb. Then he climbed in beside her as the deckhand took the wheel. And she was frightened, because it was anger she saw on his face rather than love. She had hoped, so much, to see love.

The emergency room at the hospital was all too familiar. It was like history repeating itself, having George Andris bending over her. Only this time there was no ankle to tape up, no injury that would require a tall man to lift her up in his arms once again.

"Rest for the balance of the afternoon," Nikolas's friend said. "And get to bed early tonight. You should be all right by morning, Candace...thanks to Nick's prompt action."

Nikolas himself seemed to have disappeared. But he was there when she finally left the examination room. His clothes were still wet—as were hers—but he had combed his hair. It was sleeked back from his head so his face was set off in carved relief, and he looked completely uncompromising.

Once in the car again he asked bluntly, "Will you come to my house?"

Candace shook her head. "No," she said. "Everything I have is at the motel. I just want to get out of these wet clothes and...and go to sleep for a while."

"Melina will bring you dinner," he told her, and that was all.

He insisted on waiting until she'd got into her motel room safely, then he climbed into the front seat of the car, said something in Greek to the other man, and they drove off.

Now that it was over, Candace really began to tremble. Her fingers shook so badly she had a hard time unfastening the buttons on her blouse. She thought about taking a warm shower, then decided it could wait. And slipping into the terry robe she'd brought with her this time, she remembered the robe Elene had loaned her on her first visit to Tarpon Springs. It seemed so very long ago.

She collapsed on the bed, her mind a maze of confusion. She'd been an idiot, no doubt of that, trying to do a balancing act so she could prove to Nikolas what a good photographer she was. Was it this brand of folly he was currently holding against her? Certainly it was something.

She was still wondering about this as she started to fall asleep, but then a thought occurred to her eclipsing everything else.

Nikolas had dived in the water after her. Nikolas, who had told her that never again would he be so foolish as to let history repeat itself, had dived into the water without even pausing to think about it!

He knew the river, she conceded. But she didn't think it made much difference. In her heart she felt sure that even had there been rocks beneath the surface, Nikolas would have dived in to save her.

CHAPTER TWENTY-FIVE

MELINA BROUGHT CANDACE'S DINNER to her that night, and she had prepared it herself. There was an excellent individual tuna casserole that wasn't Greek in the least and a molded orange-gelatin salad to go with it.

She gave Candace a careful inspection as she set the tray down. "Are you sure you're all right?" she asked. "You look awfully pale to me."

"It's just a reaction," Candace admitted.

"Nikolas suggested it might be a good idea for you to move over to our house," Melina said then, not ungraciously. "There's plenty of room," she added.

"Thanks. . . but I think I'd better stay here."

"Nikolas was talking about the house a while ago," Melina volunteered. "My stepfather never did very much to the place. I guess all he was interested in was the sponge-fishing business. You saw the yard. It needs a lot of work. I told Nick it looks like a jungle and he agreed. He says he's been thinking about fixing the house up, too. If it was for me, I'd like something more modern, but I won't be living there anyway. Nick says he's going to send my mother, Aunt Aliki and Elene and me on a trip to Greece this summer. Greece and maybe a few other places in Europe, too. My mother and Aunt Aliki have relatives in other countries they haven't seen for years,

and Nick says he thinks the change of scene would do
Elene good. Also, he says somehow Aunt Aliki must
learn not to work so hard. There's no need for her to
slave as she does. Anyway, he wants to close both the
restaurant and the motel and have them renovated.''

"Oh, I see,'' Candace said, although actually she
didn't. Was Nikolas, she wondered, planning to give
up New York as his primary residence and move back
to Tarpon Springs?

"It's a good thing Nick can swim and dive the way
he can,'' Melina went on, and Candace caught her
breath. Then she realized Nikolas's actions didn't
have the same connotation to Melina as they did for
her. Melina didn't know anything about that other
dive Nikolas had taken, many years ago, off the
Mexican coast.

"John Damianos was fishing with a friend of his
on a boat up the river,'' Melina went on. "He saw
you fall overboard, and he says Nick went right in
after you. He and his friend started over to see if they
could help, but Nick already had you back to the
boat and up on the deck. I guess the only casualty
was Nick's gold medallion.''

"What?''

"He lost it,'' Melina said simply. "It was very old.
I guess the chain broke when he was underwater.
Anyway, later he realized it was gone.''

"But that's awful,'' Candace protested, shaken.

"Nick's got enough good luck of his own to get
along without it,'' Melina said cheerfully. "Anyway,
now he says the first thing he's going to do is teach
you how to swim!''

Melina actually touched her fingers to her mouth
as she said this and gave a guilty little giggle as if

she'd said too much. Then she stood up to say, "If you need anything else, Candace, just call up. Nick and I will be at the house all evening. He's expecting to hear from my mother tonight, and he's got a lot of business stuff to take care of, too."

"Thank you, Melina," Candace said. "Thank you for being so nice."

But with Melina gone, she found herself actually speaking out loud to herself. She muttered that she wouldn't call Nikolas Mylonis for help if he were the last man on earth!

She ate the tuna casserole and polished off the salad and had to admit Melina was quite a good cook. Then she wondered just what it was that was bugging her so.

She'd acted the part of a fool today and had come close to drowning herself in the process. Yet her annoyance was directed toward Nikolas. It didn't make sense. Despite the considerable trauma such a gesture must have caused him—considering his past—he had come to her rescue without hesitation.

Why was it then that she was so upset about him? Was it because he had left her here at her door so abruptly this afternoon and hadn't so much as called her since? Then he had sent Melina over with her dinner...when he could have come himself.

Melina, however, had shed some light on one thing. Even though it had seemed like an eternity, Candace must have been under the water for only a very brief space of time. This would account for her prompt recovery from an episode that could have been disastrous. Whatever else might be amiss with Nikolas, there was certainly nothing wrong with his reflexes. He had reacted so swiftly she'd never been in any real danger.

And he? He'd been heedless of his own personal safety, and this certainly had some significance. But this significance was just another piece in a puzzle she hadn't yet been able to put together.

After a time Candace brewed herself a cup of tea and sipped it slowly as she thought about Nikolas. There was a whole segment of his life he had skimmed over very lightly, and she was sure this was the area in which the greatest damage had been done. It was not the damage to his face. It was a deep, inner trauma. Just how deep, she didn't really know. She only knew he didn't trust her, and unless her article could make him believe again, she feared he would only trust her less.

The tea seemed to revitalize Candace, and all at once she went to her typewriter and began to work in earnest. It didn't matter that she felt as if Nikolas was scowling over her shoulder. She only worked harder and faster. And it was very, very late when she finished putting words on paper. Then, in the first light of dawn, she got up to make coffee and curled up in bed with her manuscript, going over it carefully.

She was satisfied when she'd finished reading. She knew what she had written was absolutely right. She had created the picture of Tarpon Springs she had wanted to. She could fill in about the Greek school at the cathedral and a few other things by using the pictures Paul Morrison was willing to lend her. The comprehensive captions she'd write for them, plus the pictures themselves, would more than suffice to round things out.

She'd had to mark up the manuscript in editing it, and now, after a second cup of coffee, she called the motel's registration desk and asked them to hold any calls that might come in for her. Then she went back to work and typed the whole thing over on fresh white paper.

It was early afternoon when the final copy was done. Candace checked with the motel desk only to find there hadn't been any calls after all. This was disappointing, for she'd hoped possibly Nikolas might have decided to check on her. Then she put through a call to Tampa International and was lucky enough to book an early-evening flight back to New York.

She knew she would need to allow a good three hours to get to the airport, otherwise she would probably end up rushing. The drive would take about an hour and a half, provided there were not too many traffic problems en route. Then she'd have to turn in her rented car and check her luggage through.

Still, that allowed her a fair margin of time in which to accomplish what she intended to do.

She packed, deciding there was no point in coming back to the motel again. Then she checked out, thinking how different it would be if this was the Grecian Gardens and the woman at the reception desk was Elene.

It took some time to make a xerox copy of the manuscript at the Tarpon Springs Public Library, but with this done, Candace put the original in a manila envelope she'd already stamped and addressed and dropped it in the nearest mailbox. She then clipped the xerox together neatly and slipped it into a pale blue folder.

There were two more errands to perform.

The elderly Greek man in the gift shop smiled

broadly when she bought the little golden medallion with Saint Nicholas's figure embossed on it. He assured her the chain that went with it was exactly the proper length and that in selecting Saint Nicholas as a patron she could not go wrong.

Candace only hoped this was true.

Finally she headed for Paul Morrison's photo shop, hoping with all her heart she could persuade Paul to really talk to her today.

And her hopes were rewarded.

THE GATE TO THE DRIVEWAY at the house on Hellenic Avenue was open, and Nikolas's car was parked under the porte cochere. Candace pulled up behind it and got out, praying her throat was going to be big enough to hold her leaping heart!

She slowly climbed the steps to the side entrance and let the heavy brass door knocker fall. She could hear the clang echo through the stillness of the house. *Nikolas has gone out,* she thought dismally.

The door opened so suddenly she was thrown off guard, and there wasn't the chance to compose her face as she'd intended to. At once Nikolas stood tall before her, looking dangerously attractive. He was wearing white cotton slacks that fitted snugly against his skin and a stylishly casual, vivid red jersey. He was barefoot, and he held a can of beer in one long, slender hand.

"Come in," he said curtly, leaning around to close the door behind her. Candace caught a whiff of the after-shave lotion that was distinctly Nikolas. It was a blend of something spicy and something faintly sweet, and this did nothing to steady her senses.

She expected him to lead her into the library or

maybe the living room, but instead he headed toward the kitchen. He paused in front of the refrigerator to point to his beer can and ask, "Want one?"

"Yes," she said, although she almost never drank beer.

He'd evidently finished his, for he took out two frosty cans and opened them with a flip of his fingernail. Then he handed one to her without asking whether or not she'd like a glass to go with it.

He sat down at the round kitchen table, leaning back negligently, but there was nothing inviting about his face. Then he asked casually, "Did I see suitcases in the back of your car?"

"Yes," she admitted.

"So, you really are leaving?" Could he be that indifferent about it?

"Yes. I managed to get a seat on a flight out of Tampa tonight."

She took a long pull of the beer and then put the can down on the table. She'd placed the blue folder next to it, and now she picked it up and handed it across to him. "I've mailed the article," she said flatly. "This is a copy."

"Oh?"

"I made the copy for you. I don't expect you to look at it now, but I hope you will read it when you have the chance."

"You actually want my opinion of it?"

"If you feel like giving it."

He fingered the folder briefly. Then, to her disappointment, he put it aside without even glancing at the contents. "Evidently you didn't feel it was worth waiting to hear the rest of the story."

"Your story?"

"Were we talking about someone else's story?" He could not suppress the rise of that expressive eyebrow.

"There's no need for you to go into it, Nikolas."

"You are quite sure of that?"

"I filled in a few of the gaps," she told him. "I talked to Paul Morrison a while ago and—"

"Yes," Nikolas said, misinterpreting this. "It seems once again you have lost a camera and all the pictures you'd taken. I'm sorry."

"It doesn't really matter very much," Candace said steadily. "Anyway, I didn't go to see Paul about photography."

"Oh?" he repeated, and she knew he was not going to do anything at all to make this easier for her.

"I hope you won't think Paul disloyal," she said. "He's a wonderful man and I . . . I just hope one day Elene will really come to appreciate him. I think she will. But today . . . well, today he answered a few of the questions I put to him."

"What questions?"

"About you, after the accident." She paused and took a deep breath. "I didn't know until today that Paul visited you a number of times through those terrible years. I knew there must have been a great many things that were very . . . wrong with you, but I didn't know how wrong until Paul told me. He told me for a long time you were really blacked out—your memory, that is. And he told me you were blind."

That had been the most dreadful thing of all to hear from Paul. She could not imagine those olive green eyes with their light extinguished.

"And then there was all the facial surgery. Years of hell for you, and I guess you didn't have support from anyone except Paul and George Andris. And, of course, Gerald Fraswell and his wife. Then the media hounded you to the point where it was almost impossible for you to get any privacy. They even invaded the ranch, despite the security system George Fraswell had installed there. Your sight had come back by then...and your memory even earlier...and it's too bad, in fact, you couldn't have stayed blacked out until the worst of it was over. But then it was decided that Nikolas Mylonis, a new man with a new face, could have a chance at beginning a new life, as well—if Nicky Mellin died.''

He had been watching her with an intentness that was painful. Now she hesitated and said, ''I don't think I need to know much more than that.''

''I see,'' he said, his voice so low she could barely hear him.

''There's one other thing, though,'' she continued, her own voice low now. ''You. .you saved my life yesterday.''

''If I hadn't gone in after you a dozen others would have,'' Nikolas said. ''There's no need to be grateful about that, Candace.''

''Melina said you lost your medallion when I tugged at you in the water.''

''When I was bringing you up,'' he nodded. ''You clutched it, and the chain was weak. But...it doesn't matter.''

''Was it very valuable to you, Nikolas?''

''It belonged to my mother,'' he said, and added quickly, ''No need to look so stricken, Candace. It's gone. Under the circumstances it certainly couldn't be helped.''

She reached for her handbag and felt for the tiny,

velvet-covered box. "I bought this," she said unsteadily. "Because I wanted you to have something that...came from me. I hope you won't take offense. I'm not of the same faith, I know, but I... well, I have come to believe in Saint Nicholas. The man in the store said if you wear this you will always be safe. And...more than anything else in the world...I want you to be...I want...."

She couldn't finish. But Nikolas didn't seem to notice she had stopped talking. He was opening the box, and as he looked down at the medallion time was suddenly suspended. Then he closed his eyes, and he shuddered.

"Please, Nikolas," Candace said, her voice very small. "If it offends you...."

"Offends me?" In an instant he was on his feet and around the table, drawing her up to him.

He broke into a torrent of murmured, impassioned Greek, and she drew back from him to say, "You've got to stop that! You've got to speak English when you're—"

"All right, I will," he said. "At least until you learn to speak Greek."

His smile was a miracle, white teeth gleaming against olive skin. "Very well, my darling," he said. "What I was saying was that in my heart I somehow needed one more sign from you, even though there have been quite a few of them lately. When you asked me about Lila, for example. It came to me that you were actually jealous. And then the other night at Elene's, when you were helping to serve all those people. You were there talking to them even though you couldn't understand half of what they were saying. *Agápi mou, agápi mou.* My love for you was such an overflowing thing that I knew I could never go on without you....no matter what you might do to me with your story."

She said shakily, "You've got to read my story, Nikolas!"

As an answer, he reached over to the table and drew the folder to him. Then he took out the manuscript, and without even glancing at its contents he tore the carefully xeroxed pages in two, and in two once again.

"That for your story!" he exclaimed. "I'll read it when it gets in print."

"But—"

"No buts, my dearest," he said gently. "You didn't write anything about me at all, did you? You never intended to. It was just as you said."

She gazed at him in wonder. "You knew that?"

"No...yes," he said. "Both ways. I knew it in my heart, but my reason kept trying to override my emotion. With you, *agapiméni mou*, logic—which is so dear to the Greeks—will always, I'm afraid, come in second."

"Agapiméni mou," Candace said carefully. "All right, Nikolas, I know it has something to do with love. But I think I really am going to have to learn Greek, if only for self-defense."

"Learn how to swim, also," he added.

"That's what Melina said." Then she looked up at him suspiciously. "You knew I was going to come here today, didn't you? You knew I'd never leave you without saying...goodbye."

"I hoped you would never leave me at all," he corrected. "But you can be sure it will be many a year before I am that confident about you, Candace!

Nevertheless, I had thought of all sorts of ways to try to convince you not to run off. Elene will be back in a few days, and I had hoped to persuade you to stay with her a while.''

"But Elene's going to Greece."

"Yes, she is. A little later."

"And so are Theone and Aliki and Melina."

"Indeed they are," he agreed. Then he added mischievously, "I would like a household with only one woman in it for our honeymoon."

"You!" Candace sputtered. "You'd already told Melina you were going to have the house redecorated and the grounds fixed up and—"

"Quite right," he interrupted. "The way you wish both, I might add. I found you here...and I will always want to return here with you from time to time. I hope you feel the same way. We shall have to vary our residences, you know, unless you can one day convince me to retire. Then again, maybe you will come to enjoy living in several different places."

"With you?"

"Definitely with me," Nikolas said succinctly. Then he held out something in his hand, and Candace saw the shimmering gold chain with the medallion at the end of it.

"Will you fasten it on?" he asked, a strangely humble note in his voice. "And tomorrow will you let me buy you not one but two rings? Not another sapphire, *agápi mou*. Just a simple gold wedding band. And to go with it, a pearl, wouldn't you agree? Because pearls are things of the sea?"

"Yes," she said, "I absolutely agree." But then she added slowly, "What did you do with the sapphire ring, Nikolas?"

He laughed. "I saved it," he told her. "I plan to give it to you on our fiftieth wedding anniversary. I think by then I should be reasonably certain you will not immediately hand it back to me."

"Honestly!"

"Candace," Nikolas said, "hurry up with the catch on that chain, will you? There is a limit to my patience."

Candace fastened the chain, and Nikolas didn't have to draw her to him once she'd finished. She moved toward him willingly and freely and drew down his beloved head so she could reach his lips. But before she took the first step on a journey that would lead them both into a realm as golden as the glories of ancient Greece, Candace laughed, a wondrously joyful laugh.

"There's a limit to my patience, too," she told him.

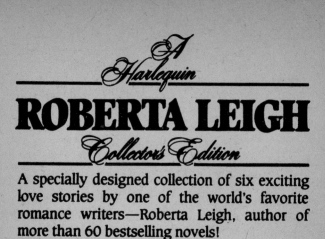

ROBERTA LEIGH

Collector's Edition

A specially designed collection of six exciting love stories by one of the world's favorite romance writers—Roberta Leigh, author of more than 60 bestselling novels!

1 **Love in Store**   4 **The Savage Aristocrat**
2 **Night of Love**   5 **The Facts of Love**
3 **Flower of the Desert** 6 **Too Young to Love**

Available in August wherever paperback books are sold, or available through Harlequin Reader Service. Simply complete and mail the coupon below.

Harlequin Reader Service

In the U.S.
P.O. Box 52040
Phoenix, AZ 85072-9988

In Canada
649 Ontario Street
Stratford, Ontario N5A 6W2

Please send me the following editions of the Harlequin Roberta Leigh Collector's Editions. I am enclosing my check or money order for $1.95 for each copy ordered, plus 75¢ to cover postage and handling.

☐ 1   ☐ 2   ☐ 3   ☐ 4   ☐ 5   ☐ 6

Number of books checked_____ @ $1.95 each = $_____

N.Y. state and Ariz. residents add appropriate sales tax $_____

Postage and handling $_____.75_____

                                      TOTAL $_____

I enclose_____

(Please send check or money order. We cannot be responsible for cash sent through the mail.) Price subject to change without notice.

NAME_____
                    (Please Print)
ADDRESS_____ APT. NO._____

CITY_____

STATE/PROV._____ ZIP/POSTAL CODE_____

Offer expires January 31, 1984   30756000000

Harlequin reaches
into the hearts and minds
of women across America
to bring you

Harlequin American Romance ™·

YOURS FREE!

Get this book FREE!

HARLEQUIN
PREMIERE AUTHOR EDITIONS

6 top Harlequin authors—6 of their best books!

1. **JANET DAILEY** Giant of Mesabi
2. **CHARLOTTE LAMB** Dark Master
3. **ROBERTA LEIGH** Heart of the Lion
4. **ANNE MATHER** Legacy of the Past
5. **ANNE WEALE** Stowaway
6. **VIOLET WINSPEAR** The Burning Sands

Harlequin is proud to offer these 6 exciting romance novels by 6 of our most popular authors. In brand-new beautifully designed covers, each Harlequin Premiere Author Edition is a bestselling love story—a contemporary, compelling and passionate read to remember!

Available in September wherever paperback books are sold, or through Harlequin Reader Service. Simply complete and mail the coupon below.

- -

1. How do you rate _____ ?

   (Please print book TITLE)

   1.6 ☐ excellent   .4 ☐ good   .2 ☐ not so good

   .5 ☐ very good   .3 ☐ fair   .1 ☐ poor

2. How likely are you to purchase another book in this series?

   2.1 ☐ definitely would purchase   .3 ☐ probably would not purchase

   .2 ☐ probably would purchase   .4 ☐ definitely would not purchase

3. How do you compare this book with similar books you usually read?

   3.1 ☐ far better than others   .4 ☐ not as good

   .2 ☐ better than others   .5 ☐ definitely not as good

   .3 ☐ about the same

4. Have you any additional comments about this book?

   _____ (4)

   _____ (6)

5. How did you *first* become aware of this book?

   8. ☐ read other books in series   11. ☐ friend's recommendation

   9. ☐ in-store display   12. ☐ ad inside other books

   10. ☐ TV, radio or magazine ad   13. ☐ other _____

   (please specify)

6. What *most* prompted you to buy this book?

   14. ☐ read other books in series   17. ☐ title   20. ☐ story outline on back

   15. ☐ friend's recommendation   18. ☐ author   21. ☐ read a few pages

   16. ☐ picture on cover   19. ☐ advertising   22. ☐ other _____

   (please specify)

7. What type(s) of paperback fiction have you purchased in the past 3 months? Approximately how many?

	No. purchased		No. purchased
☐ contemporary romance	(23) _____	☐ espionage	(37) _____
☐ historical romance	(25) _____	☐ western	(39) _____
☐ gothic romance	(27) _____	☐ contemporary novels	(41) _____
☐ romantic suspense	(29) _____	☐ historical novels	(43) _____
☐ mystery	(31) _____	☐ science fiction/fantasy	(45) _____
☐ private eye	(33) _____	☐ occult	(47) _____
☐ action/adventure	(35) _____	☐ other	(49) _____

8. Have you purchased any books from any of these series in the past 3 months? Approximately how many?

	No. purchased		No. purchased
☐ Harlequin Romance	(51) _____	☐ Harlequin American Romance	(55) _____
☐ Harlequin Presents	(53) _____	☐ Superromance	(57) _____

9. On which date was this book purchased? (59) _____

10. Please indicate your age group and sex.

    61.1 ☐ Male   62.1 ☐ under 15   .3 ☐ 25-34   .5 ☐ 50-64

    .2 ☐ Female   .2 ☐ 15-24   .4 ☐ 35-49   .6 ☐ 65 or older

Thank you for completing and returning this questionnaire.

H 1 2 3 4 5

PRINTED IN CANADA

NAME _____
     (Please Print)
ADDRESS _____
CITY _____
ZIP CODE _____

NO POSTAGE
STAMP
NECESSARY
IF MAILED
IN THE
UNITED STATES

BUSINESS REPLY MAIL
FIRST CLASS   PERMIT NO. 70   TEMPE, AZ.

POSTAGE WILL BE PAID BY ADDRESSEE

NATIONAL READER SURVEYS
1440 SOUTH PRIEST DRIVE
TEMPE, AZ 85266